CW01496834

The Survivor

J.L KERR

Copyright © 2020 by J L Kerr

All rights reserved.

All rights reserved. No part of this book may be reproduced, distributed, transmitted or stored in an information retrieval system in any form or by any means (other than for purposes of review), without the express permission of the author given in writing. The right of JL Kerr to be identified as the author of this work has been asserted by her in accordance with the Copyright, Designs and Patents Act 1988.

ISBN: 9798613039173

This is a work of fiction. Names, characters, businesses, places, events and incidents are either the products of the author's imagination or used in a fictitious manner. Any resemblance to actual persons, living or dead, or to actual events is purely coincidental.

Cover design by
Concept Creation – Zara Moncrieff.

Photography by Digitalpict photography

To contact the author, email
joannekerr2005@yahoo.co.uk

DEDICATION

For my gran who has been a tower of strength.

ACKNOWLEDGMENTS

From the first moment I started writing this book, it has been the most amazing and incredible experience. Joining Johnstone writers' group has changed my life and my writing for the better. Without them, I wouldn't be where I am today. I would like to thank each and every one of you at the group for guiding me along the way and for having faith in me.

To my family, thank you for your continued support, wise words and positivity. To my friends Margaret and Zara, thank you so much for your help and direction, for being there for me along the way and for creating my cover. I will always be grateful to you.

Margaret, Alison, Lisa, Hugh, Denise, Alan, John and everyone else at the JCU, thank you for having faith in me, for your help and support on my journey and for working beside me each week.

Megan, Heather, Louise, Jodie, Natalie, Hazel, David, Holly and all my colleagues at work, your excitement is positively thrilling, keeping me going every day – thank you!

A massive thank you to my editor, Charlie, for polishing my work and for her patience throughout all the emails.

Thank you to Tommy and Johnny for the photoshoot and Kim for being my eye model.

Your time and dedication is remarkable.

And to my readers, thank you. The fact that you purchased and read this means more to me than you will ever know.

The Survivor

CHAPTER 1

I groaned, rolling my eyes. Mum and Uncle Dave were
having another row again. This time it sounded serious.
The anger in his voice, the way his body language
showed aggression. And I wondered how long it would
be before it went too far. I didn't blame Mum though, for
getting angry at him. It was like he was taking a liberty in
using our home solely as he pleased. Felt free to roam
how he liked and he didn't care. Mum had had enough,
and to be honest, so had I.

He had been living with us for a little over a month now,
sleeping on the couch with a single duvet over him,
which he would just leave lying around in the morning,
not bothering to tidy up after himself before he flounced
around the house practically naked. No slippers, t-shirt or
trousers on, only briefs and bare feet. He never showed us
any respect. Never offered a single penny for the gas or
electric or food either. It was simply a roof over his head,
somewhere to keep warm and dry at night before waking
up and spending the whole day drinking and mouthing
off.

Mum had taken pity on him because he was Dad's
brother, letting him live with us until he had the chance to
get himself sorted out. She'd had sympathy – before he
had become aggressive. All Mum and I wanted was a bit
of peace, to get on with our lives since Dad had passed.
Dave had never acted like this when Dad was around. He
wouldn't have dared. My father seemed to be the only

one that Dave looked up to and had any sort of respect for. But now that was all gone.

Dave was a tall man and built like a tank. Standing close to six foot, with large biceps and a head of short grey hair, he was the sort of man you would never want to mess with. He scared me sometimes. The way he acted when he was drunk. He was uncontrollable, relentless, and I knew to stay out of his road as I feared he would lash out at any minute.

He hadn't always been that way. At one time in his life, he was one of my favourite people in the world. Three years ago when I was twelve, he'd had his own flat a couple of miles away from where we lived on Will Street in Elderslie. The day he was handed the keys from the council, he came around to our house (sober) and you would have thought he was the happiest man on earth. That gleam in his eye. He looked proud. Proud to have his very own home, independence and responsibility. He arrived at the door and called up to me.

'Would you like to come and see my new flat?' he asked me as I ran down the stairs.

He jangled the keys in front of me and I couldn't refuse. I loved my uncle and thought he was simply the best. We walked over to the flat, which was a couple of miles away. I skipped along beside him in the warm afternoon sun, excited to see what it looked like. When we arrived, I walked around the empty rooms with bare floorboards.

'Where's all the furniture?' I asked him with a blank face.

He looked at me and laughed. 'I've only just got the keys today, Chloe. It'll take a few weeks to furnish it.'

I sighed, pouting, feeling bored instantly. As I'd never

been in a new flat before, I had expected more. In fact, it never really did get furnished a great deal. But that was Dave for you – never made a house a home.

He used to be a nice guy and anyone could get along with him, he was just that friendly. His dark-purple pedal bike was his most valued possession and he travelled on that to work, when he had a job, and all over the place. Everyone knew him for it. I got a ride home on it once, and as I sat on the crossbar on one of his old brown cushions, he sang Queen's 'Bicycle Race' to me. He was loud and out of tune, but I didn't care; the massive grin on my face was enough. I always remembered that special moment between us.

Queen was his favourite band. He simply loved Freddie Mercury. At times I think that Dave was an inspiration to me, the way he got me listening to music I'd never heard before, movies I'd never watched. No matter how small those memories were, they would always be special to me.

It was different now with Dave. I would worry when he would burst through the door stinking of cigarette smoke and whisky. I just wanted to hide away somewhere quiet and block it all out. But poor Mum, it was her I felt for. She had to deal with it, basically because she had no other choice in the matter. She couldn't run away from it. It was her home and she had a responsibility to make sure he didn't get out of control and smash the place up. If he dared try, he would be out in a shot. She would make sure of it.

One warm Saturday afternoon, she had staggered through the front door with four large bags of shopping and attempted to make it into the kitchen. Spring had only just begun and the sun was shining in through the windows. The daffodils were blooming in the garden and the birds were tweeting in the trees. Dave was sitting in his usual spot on the couch with a can of Tennent's lager in one hand, watching a game of football. The living room smelled of stale beer and it was repulsive. Still, he didn't care. Living how he liked, he was a free man. Mum practically growled as she dropped the bags down on the kitchen floor.

'You could have at least helped me with the bags!' she shouted to him.

He smirked, a weary look in his eyes. 'You can do it on your own, hen.'

That did it. Her temper soared in that instant, and she flew into the living room with her dark-red hooded coat still on and stood in front of the television.

'You're in my road! Move. I cannae see,' he slurred, tilting his head to the side, trying to see the screen better.

She stood, arms crossed over her chest, staring at him, her face like thunder. 'That's it. I'm done, Dave. I want you out!'

He sat back in his sorry state and looked up at her. 'You want me to go?'

'I've repeatedly asked you to leave and you just ignore me constantly, like I don't matter. Well, I hate to tell you this, but this is my house and what I say goes. Now get out!'

'T'was my brother's house too.'

'Well, he's not here anymore, is he? I only let you live here because I felt sorry for you. But if this is the way you're going to carry on, then I don't want you around anymore. Pack your bags and leave.'

He stood up, swaying, his face sluggish as he faced her. 'I'm not going anywhere.'

'If you don't leave, I'll have you removed.'

'Just try it.'

I thought the argument was never going to end, that he wouldn't back down. Mum stood her ground, fighting her case, as he carried on slurping his beer until it was finished. He threw the can to the side, heading into the kitchen, and she followed him in, continuing to give him grief. I knew he would snap and I felt scared of the outcome.

He did finally lose it, and the pair stood screeching at each other. The fear of mum being injured petrified the life out of me. Dave held his fist up in the air, like he was going to hit her, his face like stone before stopping suddenly, like he was rethinking the whole thing. His fist fell to the side and he scoffed, turned and staggered into the living room and up the stairs with a bag of his clothes. He was back a few minutes later fully dressed, and I was surprised when he finally walked out the door, slamming it behind him.

An hour later though, he was back with a half-empty bottle of whisky. Mum wasn't standing for it. She was determined he was to go straight back out the door.

He held his arms out to his sides. 'I've got nowhere else to go,' he slurred.

'That's not my problem,' she shot back. 'I'm not letting you use my home as you see fit!'

'You really are a heartless bitch, aren't you?'

I stood there, eyes and mouth wide open in shock. He didn't actually just say that?

Mum gave him a look of disgust as she walked up to him and slapped him across the face.

'Get out of my house now!' she shouted, pointing to the door.

The next few moments were treacherous. Mum needed all the help she could get. But Dave was just too strong. He reached up and grabbed her by the throat as he shoved her hard. Her body slammed against the wall, her head making a cracking noise as she let out a wail. I screamed at him, trying to get him to let her go, but it was no use. I was wasting my breath and energy.

'Don't you ever do that to me again,' he growled at her, his teeth bared, his face too close to hers.

She was powerless, her eyes squeezed shut. I didn't

know if he would do something worse, maybe hurt her more. Desperate to save Mum, I ran at him, screaming and punched him in the back continuously. He stopped, letting her go. Wiping the saliva from his mouth, he gave me one look, picked up his bottle and left the house.

I walked over and wrapped my arms around Mum, trying to give her comfort as her body shook with fear. She let me hold her for a moment as she stood there, sniffing and wiping her eyes, before moving away and walking up to her room, sobbing. We desperately needed help.

The next night wasn't any better. We were living in hell and really couldn't take much more. Spending time in my room, organising my clothes for the week ahead, I always liked to keep everything tidy, my bedroom especially. The radio played on in the background and my body swayed to the rhythm as I set my school uniform out, when the front door suddenly flew opened and slammed off the wall. Coming to a halt, I listened to a drunken slur of voices and laughter. I sighed, shaking my head, and tiptoed down the stairs. Quietly, so as not to be heard, I closed the front door. Peeking my head into the living room, Dave stood with another woman, both swaying, arms around each other, trying to sing. They were loud, obnoxious and out of control. And I hated it.

'Trish hen, c'mon, let's do a duet.'

'Aye aright, what do you want to sing?'

'Eh, what about Roberta Flack, "Where Is the Love"?'

'Aye right, you start then.'

'No, you start, you can be the lead.' He laughed.

They both carried on laughing as one tried to get the other to start singing. I worried about my neighbours next door. Would they hear them? Bang through? Call the police? I felt anxious.

They started to sing, or tried to at least – they sounded like a couple of howling wolves. I decided enough was enough and walked into the living room, giving a cough to make myself heard.

They both turned simultaneously and stared at me. It suddenly felt too awkward and I seemed to freeze on the spot.

'Can you keep the noise down, please?' I asked, before turning on my heel.

'Chloe hen, c'mere a wee minute. There's someone I want to introduce you to.'

I sighed, looking at the floor and slowly walked over to the pair. They were both in such a state I was surprised they could stand up. I stood at Dave's side as he put his arm around my shoulders.

'Trish, this here is my niece, my brother's daughter. A wee beauty, isn't she eh?'

I looked over at Trish as she stared at me with beady eyes. She was about five foot two, her short black hair was greasy, her makeup looked like it had been plastered on blindfolded and her black faux-leather skirt was way too short. As much as I disliked Dave for his behaviour in recent months, I thought he could have done better. If he had only picked someone with a bit more decency who would at least have knocked some common sense into him and sorted him out, then maybe I wouldn't have judged as much. But I didn't think anyone would want him in the state he was in. I knew the girl standing in front of me was bad straight away. I knew the kind of girl she was, one who got around a lot. You wouldn't mess with her unless you wanted to be lying on the ground with black eyes. Her appearance couldn't have been any worse, and I wanted her out of my home. I felt startled as she stared at me as if I were the intruder in her house.

I turned to walk away.

Dave called out to me, 'Where you going, lassie?'

He pulled me back and I stumbled, holding out my

hands to keep me from falling.

'You want a wee drink with Uncle Davie an' Auntie Trish, eh?' he asked me, laughing as he held up a Tennent's can.

I didn't get a chance to answer him or move away. He held my arm in a firm grip and it was starting to hurt. I winced in pain, but he didn't seem to notice. He was too busy staring ahead at Trish as she scrunched her face up at him.

'Excuse me? I ain't nobody's auntie, and I certainly ain't hers!' She lifted up an arm and poked a dirty finger in my face.

I closed my eyes and shook my head, feeling disgusted and repulsed.

Dave's face darkened in an instant. I took a step back, knowing his outburst would come immediately.

'Are you trying to disrespect my family?' He raised his voice in anger. 'You think you can turn your nose up at my beautiful niece, do you? Don't you start with me, you dirty slag. You should think yourself lucky I brought you back to my house!'

If Trish had had any common sense or had known Dave at all, she would have known to back off that minute and not say another word. Either that or she didn't fear him at all. I wished she would have just stayed quiet and not say another word, but that obviously wasn't the kind of person she was.

'This isn't even your house, it's your brother's, and he's not even here. He's dead! And I'm not going to stay here another minute with you talking to me like that. I'm off – see you around, Dave!'

The relief from the pain was instant as Dave let go of my arm. I couldn't have moved away any quicker. I knew what was coming and I desperately wanted to leave but Trish stood at the living room door, hand on the handle, and I had no means of escape. I could feel my body quivering and I didn't want to watch what would happen next. Dave had a violent temper and no one ever came near him when he lost it.

He rushed over to her in an instant and grabbed her by the wrist, swinging her back into the living room. He held her in a tight grip, his knuckles white, and wouldn't let go as she twisted and pulled with all her strength, trying to get away from him. He just stood there sniggering at her as she tried her best to break free.

'Let go of me, Dave. You're hurting me.'

I watched with a sickening to my stomach as he slammed his fist into her face. With a pained scream, she staggered and fell back onto the grey couch, her hands flying up as blood came pouring out.

She looked on horrified as the blood dripped onto her hands and cried out, 'Argh! My face!'

His body towered over hers, his face like stone, his body rigid. The air was thick with tension in the room.

I slowly tiptoed towards the door without being noticed. Luckily, Dave was more focused on Trish than me. Relief flew over me as I made my way out into the hallway, standing, feeling slightly worried for Trish. She wasn't exactly a pleasant person, but nobody deserved that punishment.

She wiped her bloody face down the sleeve of her black faux-leather jacket. 'You've burst ma lip!'

He was unfazed, not moving an inch while she cried out, her voice hoarse. He needed to be stopped instantly and there was no one in this house who was capable of that. I knew what I needed to do.

Quietly making my way up the stairs and into Mum's room, I gently nudged her awake. She had gone to bed earlier complaining of a headache. She had taken some aspirin with a glass of water and gone to sleep. I was

9

surprised that she had managed to sleep through the noise downstairs.

'Mum.' I nudged her. 'You need to wake up. You need to call the police and an ambulance.'

She stirred, rubbing her eyes, and looked at me with confusion. 'What's going on?'

'Dave brought a woman back. They're both drunk and now he's beating her up.'

She let out a noise of disgust as she lifted her mobile and dialed the number.

'Yes, hello, ambulance and police, please.'

She explained to the call handler what had happened and they promised to get medics out as soon as possible. I bit my lip nervously, heading out into the hallway and peered over the bannister to listen for any noise. I winced, hearing Trish cry out distressed from blows Dave was giving her. I wouldn't wish that on anyone.

'Stop it!' she sobbed, her voice a tortured scream.

I walked into my bedroom cringing and closed the door over. Tears filled my eyes as I looked out the window. Nausea overwhelmed me. I gasped, turning around, as the door suddenly opened. Mum walked in. I let out a sigh of relief and turned back to the window.

'Something needs to be done. We can't carry on like this anymore.' My voice was hoarse.

'I know, sweetheart. I'll speak to the police when they arrive, see if I can get a restraining order on him.'

'I don't want him back here again.'

'Don't worry,' she said, rubbing my arm. 'I'm sure the police will do their utmost to keep him away. That man is a monster for what he has done.'

I couldn't have agreed more.

CHAPTER 2

Mum and I stood at the bottom of the stairs while the police carried Dave out of the house in cuffs. He had put up a fight when they arrived and they'd had to pin him down to get the cuffs on him. He'd lain on his front shouting abuse and swearing at them as his arms were tied behind his back. I had never seen anything so horrendous. It was like a scene out of a horror movie with a madman. Only it was real life.

Next to go was the stretcher. Trish looked in a bad state as they took her out and I dreaded to think of the amount of damage Dave had done to her. She was wrapped up in blankets with an oxygen mask over her face. They carried her to the ambulance, and once they closed the doors over, the blue lights flashed and the ambulance drove off.

Cold air drifted into the hallway and I shivered, my teeth chattering. I looked out at the police car by the kerb. Dave was sitting in the back next to an officer, staring at me. It was daunting. I had to look away. I couldn't face anymore.

A police officer walked up the path and up the steps. 'Mrs Stanson,' he said to Mum, 'I'm sorry to do this to you, but I really need to have a statement from both of you.'

I sighed as Mum let him in and we walked into the living room to give our statements. Hopefully, we wouldn't see Dave again.

A short while later we were in the kitchen. Mum was boiling the kettle and putting a tea bag and two sugars into each mug. The heating was on and we felt cosy and comfortable at last. After the officer had left the house, we had closed the living room door over, not wanting to look at the bloodstains all over the grey couch and the mess in the room; we would clean it up in the morning. I opened the biscuit tin, took out a KitKat and began to unwrap it.

'What do you think will happen to Dave now, Mum?' I asked as she poured hot water into the mugs.

'Well, they will take him to the station and put him in a cell for the night and let him sleep it off. Then sometime tomorrow they will question him. Don't know how long that will take, depends on how much he tells them really. Wish they would just lock him up and throw away the key.'

I nodded in agreement as she sat down at the small round table with the two mugs and picked out a KitKat for herself.

'What was Dad like when you first met him?'
She looked far away suddenly and gave a wide smile. 'Handsome, charming, a total gentleman. We were love's young dream. We met in college in nineteen seventy-six. That day had been a really cold, frosty one and I had bought a cup of soup for lunch. On my way out of the canteen, my books slipped from under my arm right beside the table where he was sitting with his friends. Feeling embarrassed, I bent down to pick them up and suddenly he was there, helping me. I lifted my head in the same second he lifted his and we seemed to gaze at each other for several seconds. I broke contact right enough, picked up my books and left. I couldn't concentrate for the rest of the day. It was like I was mesmerised.

About a week later, I was back in the canteen again and he was there, sitting in the same spot, laughing away with his friends. My heart was in my mouth. I stood in the queue, waiting to pay for my lunch, and just out of the corner of my eye I saw this figure walking up towards me. I kept my head down, and the next thing I knew he was standing beside me. I looked up, and he smiled and introduced himself and asked me if I wanted to join him at his table. I agreed, paid for my food and met three of his friends, Dan, Chris and Mike. They were all on the same course together and had jobs as well. Your father and I hit it off straight away, talking and laughing all through lunchtime. It was like destiny that we met. It was too much of a coincidence that my books just happened to slip out from under my arm at that exact spot. It was like we were meant to be together.' She laughed, looking down at the table and smiling.

We got on so well – dated for two years until we decided to move in together. We got a small one-bedroom flat just down from the college. We both had jobs. I'd worked for Sue and Win Lawyers since I left school at sixteen. I started as a trainee temp for a few weeks until they saw how qualified I was for the job, and they took me on full time after my year at college. Your dad worked for an accountancy firm, Sam Brimar. It's funny that, we were both trainee temps.

Five years after we moved in together, in nineteen eighty-three, he asked me to marry him. We were in a lovely restaurant in George Square in Glasgow and had just finished our meal. I watched him as he wiped his mouth with a napkin, looking very fidgety and uncomfortable – his fingers pulled at his white shirt collar, his eyes were anywhere else but on me. I thought there was something wrong and became paranoid, until he moved. I watched him kneel down on one knee with a beautiful ring in a box. I was stunned, completely taken aback. Never had the slightest inkling that he would ask me what he did.

"Will you marry me?" he asked. "Spend the rest of your life with me, Karen?"

'I was speechless. The man I had fallen head over heels with had asked me to marry him. How could I possibly have said no?

'I looked down at him with the biggest grin ever. "Yes," I answered. "Yes, I'll marry you. I love you, Jack."

'He took my hand and placed the engagement ring on my finger and kissed me. There was a round of applause from everyone sitting at the tables in the restaurant that night. I thought I was the luckiest girl in the world. I was over the moon. No one had ever come close to your father.'

'You and Dad never seemed to row. You both seemed so happy together.'

When she spoke again, Mum sat back against the white chair keeping her fingers round the handle of her mug. I sat, chin resting on the palm of my hand, and listened to her inspiring story with a smile on my face.

'Don't get me wrong Chloe, there were times when we disagreed with each other, but we worked it out in the end. We never had any full-blown arguments. We were never like that. We learned to get along together and live with each other. That's just how couples work.

We were married in nineteen eighty-four. Our wedding day was about celebrating the love we felt for each other with our families, close friends and work colleagues. That was what mattered most. The wedding was held at the West Shire Hotel. It was the happiest day of our lives. I wore a vintage wedding dress and Jack wore a stunning tux. I remember that day like it was yesterday. The way he looked when I walked down the aisle. He was stunning. Bette Midler sang 'The Rose' in the background as I walked along to stand beside him at the altar. We said our vows and were married quickly, before heading out into the garden to have our photos taken. I'll need to show you them. It was the wedding of our dreams.

'The reception hall was simply stunning. We walked inside, arm in arm, after the photo shoot and I can just remember how overjoyed I was. Everyone stood at the tables cheering us. Turquoise satin ribbons hung from the ceiling and more were tied in bows over the white chair covers. There were linen tablecloths and turquoise table runners. The dance floor sparkled with lights.

'We celebrated in style, enjoying our lovely meal and dancing into the night. Everything was just perfect and I wanted it to never end. But we eventually had to say goodbye. Everyone gathered around, watching, as my mum handed me an envelope. I was curious as I looked at Jack with a smile on my face. I opened the envelope and gasped in amazement as I looked at the paper document from the travel agent's. My mum and dad had only given us a surprise honeymoon in Malta for two weeks as a wedding gift! I stood there in shock and disbelief as everyone cheered and wished us the best of luck for the future.

Your dad was the best husband to me and made me so happy. Those two weeks in Malta were some of the best of my life. And our wedding day.'

As I listened to Mum talk, my eyes welled up. I knew how lucky I was to have the best parents in the world, but as she told me their story, it made their life sound like a dream come true.

'It sounds wonderful, Mum. I'm glad you both shared a great life together. And that's what you need to think about now. The good times. The great memories you both had. No matter how much it hurts. I know you miss him dreadfully; I miss him too. And he would be bitterly disappointed if he knew what his brother was doing.

This whole stuff with Dave, it needs to end now. Otherwise it'll be too late, and we will never get peace. He will just keep pestering and taunting us for weeks, months, possibly years, and it'll never end. We've still got each other and we need to stick together.

You've been off work for a long time, but I really think you should go back. Or at least phone and talk to them about it. See what they say. I'm sure they must miss you there; I mean, you've been working there ever since you left school. Moping around the house isn't going to do you any good. Once you're out and about, you'll begin to feel better again. You'll get back to your normal self.'

'Since when did you become such an expert, Chloe?' Mum sighed.

I shrugged my shoulders. 'You and Dad taught me well, brought me up great. I've learned a lot. Especially with Dave hanging around. Just…don't give up, Mum.'

She wrapped her arms around me, holding me tight. 'I'm supposed to be giving you advice.' She laughed. 'Not the other way around.'

'It's time,' I answered, looking her in the eye. 'Time to go back to work. It's been way too long.'

She looked down at the table and nodded. 'You're right, Chloe. I've been off work for such a long while. I guess it just became too easy for me, not getting up in the morning when I should, lying around in bed all day crying. It's no good. What've I become?' She shook her head.

'Hey.' I put my hand on her arm. 'It will get easier, you know,' I said with a smile.

I only wished I had confidence in my own words.

CHAPTER 3

Heartbreakingly dreadful – that's how it was to lose my father. He had been a happy working man who always had a smile on his face and was never in a mood. Always seizing the day, looking ahead. The kind of man you could count on and would never let you down. We always got on great and he made me laugh countless times. That's one thing I missed about him, the laughter. When I pictured him, his black hair combed to the side, I saw that twinkle in his eyes. He was content, and a wise man, always there for advice and the best of knowledge. Whenever there was a quiz show on the TV, he would be tuned in and answering as many questions as he could. I made a pact with Mum when he passed that we would always watch them together from then on. And we never missed an episode.

The last day I saw him, in 2004, when I was only fifteen, - It was just a normal day for us. Mum was in the kitchen making dinner and Dad was sitting on his chair watching Countdown with Carol Vorderman. I was up in my bedroom, listening to the radio and singing into my hairbrush. Everything was peaceful and content. Until that moment when everything changed.

A piercing scream could be heard throughout the house. I stopped suddenly, listening, my hairbrush still in my hand. The scream came once more, the brush was flung onto my bed as the noise seemed to echo all around. My feet pounded down the stairs to where my parents were.

Mum was crouched over Dad, gripping his shoulders and calling his name over and over. I froze on the spot, eyes wide, bewildered.

'Call an ambulance!' Mum shouted out to me.

I picked up the house phone and jabbed the numbers on the keypad. I still didn't understand what was happening, but I knew there was something seriously wrong with Dad. I spoke into the receiver, asking for an ambulance and giving our name and address, replacing the handset.

'What's going on?' I asked, confused and worried.

Dad lay on the carpet with his eyes closed as if he was sleeping. He looked peaceful.

'Is Dad dead?' I asked, shocked.

She sobbed, wiping tears away from her face. 'There's no pulse. I've tried CPR. Nothing's reviving him,' she cried.

I knelt beside Mum and my lifeless dad, trying to figure out what had happened. I couldn't get my head around it.

'I came into the living room to ask him to set the table for dinner and I found him this way. I don't know how long he's been like this. Must have only just happened,' Mum said through her tears.

'Dad?' I gently shook his arm. The tears flew down my cheeks. This wasn't happening. 'How can he just be dead? I don't understand.'

'Jack,' she gasped, putting a hand to his face. 'Come on. Wake up.'

It was at that moment we realised we had lost him. My father, Mum's husband. I would never get to see that loving smile again. Or hear him call out my name. We would never get to do any of the things that we loved to do together. Not anymore. I didn't even get to say goodbye.

I moved away and sat at his feet on the floor, arms wrapped around my legs. My eyes were blurry and I couldn't see for tears. What had been a normal, happy day had ended up being one of the worst of my life. One of the greatest people I had ever known had now gone. And I couldn't bear it.

I lost focus, just staring ahead, not taking anything in. I let myself go numb. I didn't want to take the pain of this loss. It was just too much. The paramedics arrived shortly after, one with a first-aid bag in his hand.

'Do you know how long he had been that way before you found him, Mrs Stanson?' he asked.

'No. I came in to ask him to set the table for dinner and he was lying on the floor. It couldn't have been long. I was only in the kitchen for a short while,' she looked lost.

The paramedics were given their space to see to Dad. I couldn't bear to watch. It would just send me into a frenzy. I sat on the staircase, confused and hurt and feeling a great deal of sorrow.

A few moments later Mum joined me on the stairs, sniffing and wiping her eyes.

'Oh Chloe, sweetheart,' she whispered, sitting beside me and putting an arm around my shoulders. 'How could this possibly have happened? An hour ago everything was fine. He was watching his programme.' She put her hands up to her face. 'This is bewildering.'

I sat in the safety of my spot on the hallway staircase as a paramedic went out to the ambulance and came back in a few moments later with a stretcher. I squeezed my eyes shut, holding my hands up to my face and wiping away tears. My hands were shaking. I gripped them together, trying to stop the trembling, and I felt another hand hold my own. I looked over at Mum and she gave me a sad smile. She looked like she could burst into tears at any moment.

The stretcher came out into the hallway with the body on it as the paramedics walked out to the ambulance. They spoke to Mum about going to the hospital and she said we would make our own way there. The second the ambulance moved away, Mum collapsed on the floor, sobbing.

'No! Not Jack. Why?' she wailed, holding her head up to the sky. It was unbearable.

'Mum, oh Mum,' I cried as I cradled her. We both wept by the door in unbearable heartache, just holding each other, mourning the loss of the greatest person in the world.

My perception of life seemed to change from that moment onwards. It made me realise how precious life really was. And how easy it is for life to be taken instantly. I missed my father so much and just wanted him back. To hold him in my arms again. The pain was too great to deal with. I was a wreck inside and my body trembled. I couldn't think straight.

A clicking of heels had me look up and a tall figure walked up our pathway.

'Is everything all right?' he asked. 'I just saw an ambulance pull away with flashing lights.'

Our neighbour from around the corner, Jason Barrington, had come over, concerned. I let go of Mum and stood up to speak with him as Mum tried to get herself together.

'Unfortunately not,' I answered, sniffling and wiping my eyes. 'My dad has just died. Not long ago. We don't know what happened. One minute he was sitting on his chair watching Countdown, the next minute he was gone. He's away to the hospital.'

'I'm so sorry to hear that. If there's anything I can do, then please let me know. Do you need a lift to hospital? I would be happy to drive you. Just let me bring the car around.'

Mum gave him a relieved look and I saw the slightest smile form on her mouth. 'That would be good, Jason, thank you. I'll just get my coat.'

The moment we walked out to the kerb, the silver Audi saloon was there in no time. I looked at its sleek paintwork as I climbed into the back beside Mum on the black leather seat. The interior was immaculate and looked polished to perfection with a new car scent air freshener hung up on the rear-view mirror. As he drove us to the hospital, Jason tried his best to start a conversation with Mum, but she just wasn't with us at all. From the moment we were in the car, she just stared out of the window. I put it down to shock and I let her be and spoke to Jason myself. He asked me about my own life and how I was doing at school. 'Good,' I answered, giving a weak smile. Admittedly, I wasn't in the mood to talk either, but I wasn't going to be rude to him. Especially as he had been kind enough to drive us to where we needed to be. My head turned suddenly as Mum spoke out. Her voice was quiet, but just loud enough so that we could hear her.

'I should have done something. I should have made sure he was regularly checked at the doctor's. Then maybe he would have stood a chance.'

I caught Jason looking at her in the rear-view mirror for a second, then he kept his eyes firmly on the road.

'You weren't to know, Mrs Stanson,' he answered. 'You'd be surprised at the number of people who go to their doctor suffering from chest pains. All you can ask is that they look after themselves and keep fit and healthy. As long as their cholesterol is kept down fairly low. It's normally heart disease that can trigger it. Did your husband ever show any signs of having an illness at all?'

I looked over at Mum and saw a tear roll down her face. 'No, never. He never complained at all of pain. Funny that. He was a working man; five days a week he was away at his office. We rarely had any takeaways. I always made home-cooked meals – casseroles, lasagnas – and we would go out for walks at night.'

Mum looked helpless as she sat with a tissue in her hand, her eyes red.

'Well, unfortunately, all things taken into account, I'm guessing it could have been a coronary. Scientists are working really hard these days to prevent all this heart disease. They are trying to understand and identify new drugs that will give us humans longer lifespans.'

Mum looked at him impassively 'You're a doctor?' she asked. 'Where were you when I needed you?' She turned and looked back out the window without another word. I knew to keep quiet when Mum was upset. He smiled briefly, staying as polite as possible. 'I try my best to keep both lives separate from each other. When I'm at home I try to be myself, so that people can get to know the real me, not Doctor Barrington the hematologist,' he replied with a chuckle.

'Hematology?' I answered, taken aback. 'Wow. That sounds…challenging.'

'Yes, it can be. We specialize in the blood system. We treat diseases like leukemia and anemia. It's one of the worst, yet best jobs you could ever ask for. Trying to cure a sick patient has a degree of gratification to it. There is no better feeling than when you cure a patient who has a disease like cancer, take it away from them and give them a new lease of life.'

'It's all my fault!' Mum cut in. 'I should have got him to a doctor, to at least have a check-up. Made sure he was healthy. It's a wife's job to look after her husband. I feel like I've messed up and now I've lost one of the people in the world who mattered to me the most.'

'Mrs Stanson, it's not your fault.'

'It's Karen,' she quickly chipped in.

'Karen, don't blame yourself. Look, when we get to the hospital the doctors will speak to you about what happened to him. They will be running all sorts of tests. That's us here now. You need to stay calm. Take a deep breath, and when you feel ready, we will all go in together. I'll support you and be there for you all the way.'

She looked over at him and gave him a slight smile, holding her tissue up to her cheek.

'I just feel I'm to blame, that's all. I feel hopeless.'

'Whatever happens in there, please don't blame

yourself. I'm sure that you were a good wife to your husband and you did the best job you could. I don't think your husband would have thought any less.'

CHAPTER 4

We arrived in the car park. I was surprised Jason managed to locate a space, with it being so full. Ranley Hospital, Johnstone was never quiet. A continuous flow of traffic and ambulances coming in and out on a daily basis made it constantly busy. Jason took off his seat belt and turned to Mum.

'Just take a moment and get yourself together. And when you're ready, we can go in, alright?'

She looked at him and nodded slightly, then took a deep breath, preparing herself. Moments later Jason opened the door for us both and we left the comfort of the luxurious car and headed towards A&E.

At the bus stop, a crowd of people stood looking in one direction as they waited for their bus to arrive. I coughed as we passed by, repulsed by the strong odour of smoke that lingered around the area. We approached the entrance. The automatic doors opened swiftly and we walked in. The cream-painted walls were smeared with blood at the doorway and I wondered how long it had been since the place had had a proper clean. That couldn't have been up to the proper hygiene standards.

Mum looked around quizzically as she headed towards the reception area on the right-hand side. A young man sat at the desk behind a glass partition, staring at his computer screen as he typed away. He looked up as we approached the desk.

'Hi,' he said with a smile on his face. 'Can I help you?'

Mum looked lost for a moment.

I put my hand on her shoulder. 'Mum?'

She snapped out of it and spoke to the receptionist, her voice shaky.

'My husband was brought in not long ago by ambulance. His name is Jack. Jack Stanson.'

'Okay, Mrs Stanson,' the receptionist replied, looking concerned. 'Please take a seat in the waiting area and I'll have someone come and see you.'

He lifted the receiver and talked into the phone as we found three empty seats by a door in the busy reception area. The large room was filled with all sorts of people waiting to be taken in and seen to. A young man with long, brown, messy hair sat on the seat opposite us with a large cast on his leg and two crutches beside him, and a woman who I figured was his partner sat beside him for support. A young boy sat beside his dad looking pale in the face. I didn't know what would happen or how long we would be sitting here waiting. I leaned in towards Mum and rested my head against her shoulder.

'Can I get you anything to drink, Karen? Chloe? A tea or a coffee?' Jason asked, not bothering to sit.

'A coffee would be good Jason, thank you,' Mum answered. I shook my head.

He gave a small smile and then turned and walked towards the vending machine. A few moments later he came back with two cups and handed one to Mum. She took a small sip, holding it in her hand. I was quite surprised she was remaining so stable during this hard time. I knew once she was back home she would just break down. How would we cope being back at the place that held all the memories? Everything in that house would remind us of Dad. I knew it would be hard. And for Mum, it would be a tough battle.

Jason sat beside Mum, holding his coffee, and turned to speak to her. 'Karen, I know this is a very difficult time for you and I don't begin to understand what you're going through right now. All I can say to comfort you is that I will give you as much help as I possibly can. I'll be there, no matter what.'

She put her cup down on the floor as she fumbled around with a tissue in her hand. 'Thanks Jason, that's very kind. But there's no need. Really. I'm sure we'll be fine. I have Chloe here and we will support each other. We have plenty to keep ourselves occupied. She's starting her exams soon and she needs me to be there for her. I just need to keep it together. For her sake.'

Jason looked at Mum with sadness in his eyes. 'When you lose someone so close to you, the grief can be overwhelming. Any support at all could be helpful.'

'Mrs Stanson?'

We all turned. A female doctor in a light-blue uniform stood at the door looking around. Mum and I stood up. Leaving her cup on the floor, Mum said to Jason, 'We shouldn't be too long.'

'I'll be here for you,' he replied.

We walked through the door with the doctor, along a corridor and down a narrow staircase. We arrived in a small room. I barely noticed anything apart from the one thing that mattered the most. All I could focus on as I walked inside was the mortuary trolley. It sat in the middle of the room, a plain white sheet covering the body.

My nails dug into my skin, but I barely felt the pain. I stood over the body as the doctor spoke to Mum, but I had zoned out. As the sheet was removed from his head, Mum put her hand up to her mouth in shock and tried to stop herself crying out. I took a deep breath as my stomach turned. Right now was not the time to be sick. It took everything I had not to collapse.

He lay there, his skin pale, his eyes closed. My body was tense and rigid and my breathing was ragged. I had never seen a dead body before and this one really got to me. My own flesh and blood, gone from this world. I would never get to speak to him again. Tears rolled down my cheeks and I wiped them away with the palm of my hand. My poor dad. I licked my lips and tried to speak, but all that came out was a high-pitched sob.

'Dad!' I cried out. 'Dad, I love you.' Mum moved over to me and held me in her arms, and we let it all out. Inside, I felt like screaming. I was so angry with this world. Why did he have to go? My legs gave way and I just about collapsed onto the cold floor by the table. Mum held me up for support. The doctor spoke again, and I gripped Mum and listened to what she had to say.

'We ran several tests on your husband, Mrs Stanson, and I'm afraid to say he had a disease called atherosclerosis. It means that over time plaque built up in the arteries. The fat and cholesterol in the blood eventually hardened and narrowed the arteries, causing your husband to have a coronary. We also found out that he had very high blood pressure. Do you know if he was stressed at all at any time? Did he ever talk to you about it?'

I looked on in disbelief as Mum answered, emotionless. 'I had been telling him for months to take it easy. He was always overdoing everything, and work had got to him. Jack had told me a while back that his company was in financial trouble. It broke him inside. He loved that job. And the company. He was proud to be a part of it.

'Sometimes he would work way longer hours than he should have. One night, he didn't come home until midnight. I was worried sick. I tried to phone his mobile and the office phone, but each time it just rang out. When he eventually did come home, he told me that a handful of people from the office had stayed to try to sort out the financial crisis. They went through every single document in the filing cabinets, trying to find some proof that would help them. They phoned the head office, but it was useless. Eventually, a couple of hours into their search, one of the guys found a file in their boss's office and it turned out that their boss, Thomas, had taken out a lot of finance against the company. Apparently, this guy was in a hell of a lot of debt and the company was in crisis. They had been hit badly. For months and months they had suffered.

'They got lawyers in and the boss was fired eventually. But all this took a toll on Jack. Chloe, your dad was stressed. But he never let on. No one knew. Apart from me.'

'And you never thought to tell me?' I answered, hurt. 'How could you, Mum! Dad's life was in jeopardy and you just let him carry on? You know what stress can do to people! Why didn't you get him to a doctor?'

'He didn't think it was necessary. I offered to make appointments for him, but he waved it off. Told me not to bother. He hid his stress well. Too well, in fact, but I could see what it was doing to him. Deep down, I think he was broken inside. But each day he put a smile on his face. He was courageous, your father. He had guts. He fought with everything he had, until there was nothing else to give. He never wanted people to worry about him. He wasn't that sort of man.'

There was a lump in my throat. 'I will always be proud to be his daughter,' I whispered.

'And he was proud to be your father.' She smiled. 'A couple of nights ago, he told me to tell you he loved you with all his heart. I didn't think anything of it until now. He must have sensed something was wrong. But he never let on. He didn't want anyone to know how bad he was.'

'If he'd only gone to the doctor's, he may well have still been with us today,' I cried.

We stood over the body, feeling emotional and grieving for the man we loved. Mum took my hand and held it tight as a tear slid down my cheek. Facing life without him seemed wrong somehow. Like we were leaving a part of us behind. There would always be an emptiness within us now. An emptiness that would never be filled.

'Mrs Stanson, I can give you a number to call for grief counselling, if you would be interested,' said the doctor. 'Sometimes when a family member dies, their loved ones don't know how hard it will be and they don't see the toll it's taking on them until it's too late.'

Mum sighed. 'We don't need a grief counsellor. We'll be fine on our own.'

'Very well,' the doctor replied. 'But take this card, please. Keep it in your purse, and if you feel the need at any time to call, the number is there. Twenty-four hours. Let me just go and get the death certificate. If you take a seat in the waiting room outside, I won't be too long.'

I could almost feel the shudder from Mum as the doctor handed her the card. She barely looked at it as she slipped it in her coat pocket. She turned around and we walked out the door and sat on the seats outside. Within fifteen minutes we were given the sheet of paper and advised to register the death as soon as possible. We'd had enough for one day. Tomorrow was a new beginning. We would sort something out then.

We headed back to the reception area and I felt drained at that moment with no energy at all. Jason stood up as we arrived back, looking apprehensive. I didn't think either Mum or I could face having a conversation at all. It was a quiet walk back to the car with none of us saying a word. Jason started the ignition and we headed back home to an empty house. Nothing seemed worth it anymore

CHAPTER 5

After that day, Mum and I took time off work and school. I couldn't face anyone and neither could Mum. I sobbed my heart out until there were no more tears to shed. The house was too quiet without Dad, and we couldn't even put the TV on; it was unbearable without him sitting in his chair, watching his shows. The more I thought about Dad and everything about him, the way he was, the more I would cry.

Mum had gone to the funeral director's whilst I stayed at home in bed not being able to face going with her. She was back within a couple of hours with a bag of shopping, and she filled the cupboards, keeping herself busy.

A short while later, she had just got off the phone with Dad's office to let them know what had happened. They had sent their condolences and had offered help if it was ever needed. And a few days after, Dave came by for his weekly visit. It was Tuesday, I realised; Dave always came over on a Tuesday to see us. I sat on the edge of the couch nervously as Dave sat on Dad's seat.

'Is your auld Dad at work the day, Chloe?' he joked.

Dave didn't know. He hadn't been over since the previous week, two days before Dad had died on the Thursday, there had been no way of contacting him. He never carried a mobile around with him. What were we going to say? 'Sorry, Dave, but your brother's dead.' We knew how he would take that news – not well.

I cringed inwardly as I walked into the kitchen and whispered to Mum, 'Dave's in.'

Mum looked at me suddenly with fear in her eyes and shock on her face. We were grieving. We didn't need Dave kicking off as well. She put her dish towel down and we both walked into the living room. Mum stood in front of

Dave to break the bad news to him.

'Alright, Karen. How's things, my love?' He smiled. Regrettably, this was the last time we saw Dave as a normal, happy bloke. His brother was the only reason he was as stable as he was. Without him, Dave was sure to crumble. And we were not looking forward to it in the slightest. Mum spoke out, leaving me sitting next to him, cringing at each word.

'Dave, um, there's something we need to tell you and I'm afraid it's not good news. There's been no way of contacting you – we don't know where you're living – so we couldn't tell you.'

He looked at her and gave her one of his big smiles. 'Tell me what, Karen?'

She cleared her throat before she spoke again, her voice shaking. 'I'm afraid that Jack isn't with us anymore.'

He looked at her strangely. 'What are you talking about?'

She closed her eyes and took a deep breath before giving him the news. 'Jack passed away on Thursday, Dave. I'm really sorry,' she whispered.

Dave looked confused for a moment. 'What do you mean he passed away?' Then he realised: 'You mean to tell me my brother's dead?'

She looked at him with all the sympathy she could give. 'I'm afraid so, Dave. I'm so sorry.'

He scoffed, holding up his right hand as he shook his head. 'Wait a minute. I spoke to him last week. He was fine.'

'It was two days later. He had a coronary while sitting on his chair.'

'How can my brother be dead? It's not possible.' He raised his voice.

'The funeral is to be held in the – '

'Wait a bloody minute!' he shouted, standing up and

walked towards the door. 'A bloody coronary! What...I don't understand.' He paced the floor anxiously, looking at Mum every few seconds. We watched him walk up and down. His face got angrier.

'Did he take ill before he died? Did you get him to the doctor's or the hospital?'

Mum shook her head. 'No, there were no signs.'

'So you didn't get him treated then?'

'No one knew he was going to have a coronary! We thought he was fine. He didn't show any symptoms. He was just stressed with work.'

He looked at her in disbelief and shook his head. 'Stressed? You know what stress can do to someone. I can't bloody believe this! This is on you, Karen. You're to blame for this!' he growled at her, pointing a finger in her face.

With that, he stomped out of the house, slamming the door behind him. Mum and I both jumped in fright.

I let out a loud sigh. 'This is going to take a toll on him, Mum. He's going to react badly. He'll lash out, I just know it.'

Dave never cried. He just wasn't that sort of guy. He would get angry. Real angry. And mad. We just didn't know how mad. He would come back. And then we would really know just what sort of guy he was.

Mum seemed lost and out of sorts. She kept herself busy, running all over the house, trying to get organised, but she would forget half the things she was meant to do and get angry at herself and start shouting – and then the tears would start all over again. I had to be around her a lot to keep her calm. It was hard enough for me as it was, and I was beginning to get a bit stressed.

Mum spent most of her time in her room, and when I stood by her bedroom door, I could hear her quietly crying.

I felt utterly gutted for her. She was grieving and wanted privacy, and that was to be respected, so I let her be and gave her the space she needed.

One afternoon I heard noises coming from the kitchen. I walked down the stairs quietly and stood in the doorway watching her as she moved about the room, banging cupboard doors repeatedly.

'Mum?'

She didn't answer. Didn't even look in my direction. I walked in as she continued to hunt around.

'Where are the goddamn teabags?' she said angrily. 'I just bought them last week. Where the hell are they?'

I walked over to a cupboard and picked up the unopened bag that was hidden in the corner.

'Here you go. Do you want me to make your tea?' I asked.

'No, I don't bloody well want you to make me a cup of tea. I am quite well enough to make one on my own,' she snapped.

'Okay,' I answered, taken aback and hurt that she had spoken to me in that way.

I walked out of the kitchen and left her to it, heading back up to my room, debating and feeling uncertain about going back to school. I couldn't cope with being stuck in the house. Especially the way she was. The feeling of being trapped made me anxious. I wanted to speak with her first, but I feared she would just bite my head off again. I would ask her another time. That was, if she had calmed down.

It had been seven days since dad had died and I was ready to face school the next day that was Friday. Mum had agreed the night before, saying, 'Do whatever makes you happy.' The funeral wasn't for another eight days and I desperately needed a distraction to take my mind off it. Being at school was the best option. I stood in the doorway of my living room, bag on my back and bus pass in my hand.

'Mum, that's me off now. I have my mobile on me if you need me. I'm off to catch the bus.' I walked over to give her a hug.

'Whatever,' she replied, not hugging me back. 'You just carry on and I'll sit here all day on my own. Doesn't bother me. I'll have peace and quiet now that you're all gone.'

I just looked at her, shocked.

She looked up, waiting for me to go. 'Well, go on then, get lost!'

I moved away and walked out the door, feeling hurt and upset. Mum had never spoken to me like that before. That was a first. I didn't know what was going through her mind. I was her only daughter and she was taking it out on me. Was she angry at me because she was being left on her own? Should we have been together through all of this? And the big question was, what would I come home to after school? She wouldn't harm herself, I knew that much, but now with that thought in my head, it began to worry me.

I met up with Mollie at the top of the hill outside school. I had known her all my life and I trusted her with all my heart. She was my shoulder to cry on, my companion, and we had gone through our lives beside each other every step of the way. There was never a secret kept from one another, never a harsh word spoken. We knew our boundaries and never crossed them.

She gave me a look of sympathy and wrapped her arms around me, holding me tight. 'Chloe, how are you? How's your Mum doing?' she asked, concerned.

'Not good. She was very nippy with me this morning. I don't know what's going through her head, to be honest. She won't talk to me. Dad's death is affecting her more than we both assumed it would and more than she's letting on.'

'Oh, that's awful. Well, I think the best thing for you to do is give her some space. You will be needing that right now more than ever. She will need some time to think. She's only just lost her husband.'

'I know, Mollie, but I've never seen her this bad before. The doctor who dealt with us gave Mum a card. I may have to give the counsellor a call if she doesn't get any better.'

'Chin up. Just take your mind off it for now and concentrate on school and your work. See what happens when you get home. And if things are still bad, then you can give them a call.'

I smiled at her; she was the best at giving advice – the best of friends. Mollie and I were like two peas in a pod. Utterly indestructible.

We had met on the first day of Primary One when we were out in the playground. The monitor for our class had put us together and we sort of clicked right away. We shared our snacks, our secrets and, as we grew up together, our hopes and dreams for the future. Other friendships had come and gone, but we remained tight throughout. There was one point in primary school when a boy, Seb, asked Mollie out and she said yes. At first, I was envious and felt that someone was stealing my best friend away from me. But as the days went by, I watched closely and saw the two of them begin to get bitter with each other. They eventually fell out and split up, and secretly I couldn't have been happier. Mollie came right back to me, telling me how sorry she was for ever leaving me and that she would never do it again. As it turned out, Seb and his friend Nate had planned that from the beginning. They had seen how close we were and plotted for Seb to worm his way in and break us up as a dare. Admittedly, it had worked for a while. Until she had found out what a rotten schemer he really was. She never spoke to him again after that, and he was lucky he didn't get a punch in the nose from me. Mollie and I had been the best of friends ever since.

As it was hoped, school went by slowly that day. To be honest, I dreaded going home, not sure what to expect, so had to be prepared for the worst. I walked in the door at four o'clock feeling tense and reluctant to deal with Mum's drama. What I came home to really saddened me. In the living room, Mum was found lying on the couch with a bottle of vodka.

'Mum? What's going on?' I asked, baffled. This was new.

She seemed to look up at me in slow motion, her eyelids half-shut. 'Oh, Chloe love, you're back,' she slurred, intoxicated. She sat up unsteadily, wiping her hair down with the palm of her hand, squinting at the clock on the mantelpiece. 'Is that the time?'

I sighed, shaking my head, disappointed that she had got herself into such a state. She waved me over and patted the couch. I walked over and sat next to her and she put her arm around me.

'Mum's just having a wee drink to take the pain away, alright.' She kissed my head. I could smell the alcohol on her breath.

'Don't you think you've had a bit too much to drink, Mum?' I asked, concerned.

'Me? No. Besides, I have company over, don't I?'

I looked around, puzzled, wondering who the company could be. Then I heard footsteps coming down the stairs and I turned around to see Dave walk into the room.

'Chloe, sweetheart.' He looked at me, surprised.

'What are you doing here, Dave?'

'Your Mum has agreed to put me up for a bit – you know, since your dad's not here anymore. I want to apologise to the both of you. I was out of order the other day. It was just a shock to find out what happened. I'm still dealing with it, though. You'll have to be patient with me.'

'We all are. I hope you won't be leading Mum astray with alcohol all the time,' I warned.

'Don't worry, love, this is a one-off.'

'I should hope so,' I snapped. 'Getting my Mum into this kind of state in her own home…It's not on.'

'No, you're right, Chloe. I'm sorry. It won't happen again.'

'So how long are you here for?' I quizzed him.

'Well, the guy I was staying with has moved in with his girlfriend and given up his flat. So just until I get somewhere of my own. Is that alright with you?'

'Fine,' I answered sharply. 'Just don't try any funny business, you got that?'

He held his hands up. 'Yes, boss.'

I gave him one more warning look before turning to Mum. 'You want a coffee?'

'I'm okay, darling.'

'Coffee it is then,' I answered and walked away to fill the kettle. I was in no mood to mess about and Mum would be drinking it whether she wanted to or not.

CHAPTER 6

Nothing could have possibly prepared us for the death of my father. And it was hard. The grief, the loss, not being able to see his face every day, not being able to talk to him. The morning of the funeral I was an emotional wreck – anxious, stressed, and I couldn't eat a thing. I showered and put on a black dress I'd bought from a shop in Glasgow city centre. I put a little makeup on (not the best idea for a funeral, I'll admit), straightened my hair and made myself look as presentable as I possibly could. I was feeling anything but.

Mum had put an ad about Dad in the paper the day she had prepared the funeral and word had got out. We'd received phone calls and sympathy cards, with people sending their deepest condolences and regards to both me and Mum.

I was walking down the stairs at nine forty-five, putting my earrings in, when I saw a familiar figure standing by the fireplace and talking to Uncle Dave. I stopped in my tracks as I looked at him, bewildered, wondering how this man was familiar to me. He stood just under six foot and wore a black two-piece suit and tie. I hadn't heard the door when I was upstairs, so I didn't know anyone had arrived.

He turned to me as I walked into the room and gave me a sympathetic smile. 'Chloe, honey, how are you?' He hugged me.

Feeling surprised, I returned the gesture, gently hugging him, as I tried to identify him.

He looked at me and realised I had no idea who he was. 'I'm your dad's cousin,' he said. 'Martin.'

'Ah, I'm sorry. I didn't recognise you. It's been a long time.'

'It certainly has. I think you were only about ten years old when I saw you last. I came to your birthday party. Do you remember?'

I thought back to that day. Mum had organised a get-together out in the back garden for family, relatives and close friends. The long table in the middle of the garden was filled with food, including a big cake, and there were balloons tied to the table and party banners. It was a really great day filled with celebration and laughter.

'Who would have thought the next time we met it would have been on such a sad occasion.'

I gave him a kind smile. Right now, we needed family and a lot of support around us more than anything in the world.

'Excuse me,' I said to him, and walked into the kitchen to find Mum talking to Jason. He had been there for her every day, coming around after work to make sure she was alright.

They stopped talking the moment I entered the room and focused on me.

'I just spoke to Dad's cousin, Martin. It was good of him to come.'

'Yes, it certainly was. He flew up from Lincolnshire.'

I raised my eyebrows in surprise. 'Is that where he's living now?'

'Yeah, they moved about three years ago while Georgina was pregnant with little Patrick.'

'Oh,' I replied. 'He never mentioned it.'

Mum answered the door a moment later and Dad's work colleagues stood on the path. They were invited in and everyone gathered in the living room, introducing themselves, shaking hands, talking about Dad and the great man he was. As I sat on the couch listening, I felt warmth in my heart from the kindness that was filling the room. Everyone who was there cared deeply about my father. He was well liked. That made me well up. I dabbed a tissue to my eyes, watching my makeup. I knew soon enough it would be running down my face.

At eleven o'clock, Mum, Jason, Uncle Dave, Martin and I were in a black limousine following the hearse. In the church the minister stood at the pulpit welcoming everyone. Mum had written a eulogy for the minister to read out. She couldn't do it herself and that was understandable. Hymns were sung, and by the end of the service almost everyone in the room was in tears.

I turned to Dave, who was sitting beside me. There wasn't a tear in his eyes. I knew he was never a man for crying, but we were mourning a loss here. Was he even feeling any emotion at all? He just sat with his head down, staring at the floor. I didn't know what was going through his mind, and it wasn't the time or the place to ask him how he was feeling. So I just left him to it. He could grieve in his own way and feel how he liked.

When the service was finished, Mum was the first one to walk out of the church and she sobbed her heart out. The pall-bearers lifted the coffin, walked out of the church and put the coffin into the hearse. As I looked on, tears streamed down my face. It was a beautiful but sad way to say goodbye.

At the crematorium, I walked up to the coffin and placed a single white rose on the top and wept. Saying goodbye to my father was the hardest thing I had ever done in my life. 'Keep Holding On' played in the background. I had picked this song out for Mum and me especially. It couldn't have been more significant. We mourned quietly although making one exception for Dave.

Afterwards, we headed to the eighteenth-century building that was the Stonalie Hotel. Everyone gathered to tell great stories about my father, and there was some laughter too. As we sat around a table, eating sandwiches, sausage rolls and scones with tea and coffee, we listened to one man reminisce about an Easter when my dad had dressed up in a bunny costume as a surprise. He had the whole office in a frenzy that day. There was an outburst of laughter from our table. That was the kind of man my father was: he always put a smile on people's faces.

An hour later, after everyone had departed from the hotel, we were driven home by Martin. As we walked up the path, we waved goodbye to him and he drove off. Though it was in such sad circumstances, it had been nice to see him again.

Mum opened the front door and we walked into an empty house. It was quiet. 'Where's Uncle Dave?'

'Hmm, not sure,' she replied. 'I saw him at the crematorium and he just seemed to slip off after that. Maybe he needed some time on his own to grieve. I'm sure he will be fine.'

I was doubtful. I had seen the way he was in the church and it didn't look good at all. But I thought no more of it as I changed into casual clothes and made us both a cup of tea. I sat on Dad's Kendal armchair and switched the TV on. Mum walked in and looked at me with surprise.

'What are you doing?' she asked me.

I ran my hand over the soft material on the arm of the chair. 'Thinking of the good times,' I answered with a smile on my face. 'Mum, he wouldn't want us to spend our time grieving constantly. He would tell us to move on and be happy.'

She shook her head slightly. 'I remember you fighting with Dad when we first bought that chair. You wanted to be in it all the time. You even slept in it the first night, do you remember?' She laughed.

I smiled, remembering happy memories. The old chair that had sat here before – brown with white floral patterns and bought from a friend when they first got the house – had practically burst everywhere. Dad had said it was high time he bought a new one. I was over the moon when I saw the new chair, wanting to sit in it all the time. But Dad wouldn't have it. 'I bought this especially for me,' he'd laugh, trying to lift me off it. I'd squeal and moan at him, wanting to sit in the new chair, and he'd eventually give up and join Mum on the couch. After a few days I got fed up of the new chair and took my place again on the floor, sitting in the front of the TV.

Mum went to her room with her cup of tea, complaining of a headache. It was unsurprising given the amount of crying she had done earlier. I switched on Countdown and sat enjoying my tea and chocolate digestives. Halfway through the programme, I sighed, put my mug down on the small brown table beside the chair and went to answer the door. Opening it, I was shocked to find a drunk Dave slouched to one side with a cigarette in his hand. I looked at him, repulsed by the state he was in. He simply took one more draw of his cigarette, flicked it onto the grass and pushed his way past me. I stumbled back, glaring at him, as he walked into the living room and stood looking around.

'Where's your mum?' he slurred.

Ignoring him, I closed the door over, walked past him into the living room and continued with my programme. I certainly wasn't going to encourage him. He needed to know he was in the wrong.

'Where's your mum?' he asked again with the same tone of voice.

Still ignoring him but aware of his presence, I stared at the TV, trying to make a word from the vowels that had been put up on the board. He sat down on the couch with his hands linked together.

It didn't take long before he started sniggering, and I looked across and rolled my eyes at him. I wasn't in the mood for him. Especially today. How could he? I didn't want to look at him, never mind talk to him. Next to come was the rambling, lyrics from Avril Lavigne's 'Keep Holding On'.

I turned my head and looked at him with disgust. 'That was our goodbye song to my dad, Dave – have a bit of respect, will you? And keep it down. Mum's not feeling good.'

He just looked at me and laughed. 'Ha ha, wee Chloe. Wee Coco.'

I stood up, took my cup into the kitchen and headed up the stairs. I chapped on Mum's door and waited for her to answer. Eventually, she came to the door, eyes red, with a tissue in her hand.

'Oh, Mum.'

I wrapped my arms around her and rubbed her back as she sobbed her heart out. 'I feel sick. I can't eat, I can't sleep. I've got this horrible feeling in my gut that just won't go away.'

I walked into the bedroom and heard music playing on her stereo – 'Lay Me Down'. It was one of the songs I had mixed together for her and put on a disk. We sat on the bottom of the bed.

'Do you want me to call Jason? Maybe he can get some medication for you. It may help you to get to sleep.'

She sniffed and shrugged her shoulders, looking down at the tissue in her hands. 'I don't know. I don't want to bother him.'

I sighed. 'He was the one who said to you if there was anything you needed just to let him know. I'm trying my best here, but if it's medication you're needing, it's out of my hands. Just…let me give him a call.'

'No – wait.' She grabbed my arm as I stood up to walk away. 'Just sit with me for a bit, will you, Chloe? I could really do with your company.'

I smiled at her. 'Of course.'

We sat and talked until nightfall, reminiscing some

more. We laughed and cried as Mum told stories about the things she and Dad used to get up to. There were some surprising revelations.

She turned around slowly, looking out the window. 'It's got so dark.'

I stretched, looking out. 'Yeah, it has. Are you hungry?'

She gazed away for a moment and then back to me. 'I am actually. All that talking has really given me an appetite.' She laughed.

'Chinese?' I asked with a smile.

'Why not?' She put an arm around my shoulders. 'As long as I have you by my side, Chloe, I know I'm going to be okay.' She smiled.

I suddenly felt an overwhelming burst of love run through me, and it dawned on me how much Mum really needed me to be there for her, just like she was always there for me. I wasn't just her daughter, I was her best friend too. There for support, guidance and love whenever she needed it. We had a strong bond and I didn't think anyone in this world could ever break us up.

As we headed down the stairs, I realised Dave had vanished. I was glad he was out of our sight for the night. It was just us girls. Mum phoned up the local Chinese as I got out the plates, cutlery and glasses and set them on the dining table. I was relieved I had made her feel better. I didn't like to see her sad. Now was our chance to start a new life together and this would be the perfect way to round off today.

Deep down I figured it would take a long time to recover and get ourselves back into a normal routine. I was still emotional and missed Dad like crazy. It was strange, his not being in the house anymore. But this was the way things were now.

A month after the funeral, on a Sunday evening, I was desperately trying to study. My exams were starting the next day and I was cramming hard. I needed my mind to focus; concentration was more important than ever. I had studied so much before the funeral, and since. Mum was there to go over things with me. It was her way of keeping busy as well. She encouraged me a great deal, making me feel positive and telling me I was going to do great. It wasn't just the fact that I had to pass my exams; I had to make both Mum and I proud, and not let either of us down. This term had been hard work and I was trying my best.

My sixteenth birthday was at the weekend, and before Dad died Mum had booked a surprise trip up to the north of Scotland for a couple of nights. The idea was that the three of us would go together for a family vacation. She'd surprised me with the news as I walked in the door one day after school and I'd felt a thrill of excitement go through me as she showed me the booking online. But now that Dad wasn't here, she was unsure.

'I really do still want us to go, but I don't want others to think we're just dashing off without a care in the world. I will always love your father and miss him very much every day. But then again, it's your birthday present and I know what he would say: "Make each day count. Go out there and see the world."'

In the end it was decided: my birthday only came once a year and Dad would have wanted us to go. But Mum was worried about the third place in the booking. It was non-refundable, so Mum would lose the money she'd paid for it and neither of us wanted it to go to waste.

'What about asking Jason to come along?' I suddenly called out, killing the quietness in the room and making Mum nearly jump out of her skin. 'I know he would love to go, and he would keep us both company. What do you say? You want to ask him in the morning?' I asked, sounding hopeful.

She raised her voice in anger. 'I'm not replacing your father, Chloe! That is just out of the question!'

I looked at her with hurt in my eyes, resenting her accusation. 'I didn't say you were, Mum, and he wouldn't think that either. Nobody's replacing anybody. You are just asking a friend to join you on a weekend vacation trip. Don't get angry with me. I know we would all enjoy it. Anyway, Jason's a smart guy and he'll be good with directions. He'll know where to go and we won't get lost.'

Mum sighed. 'I'm sorry, Chloe. You're right. Look, I'll ask him in the morning and see what he says.'

I smiled at her, knowing that it would turn out to be a great birthday. I really couldn't wait.

CHAPTER 7

Mum stuck to her word and called Jason the next morning before I left for school, and he said he would be delighted to join us. He was worried about Mum and wanted to know she was doing okay.

She laughed down the phone. 'I'm fine, honestly,' she replied, trying to calm him down. 'You need to stop worrying.'

They talked for a good while, discussing his work shifts and the idea of his coming over to see her for a while and bringing food with him. He'd keep her on the straight and narrow. Jason was a down-to-earth guy who would always keep his promises and never let anyone down. Mum really enjoyed being in his company, and he always made her feel at ease and put her first before anything else. He really was a lovely, caring guy. He offered to drive us to the hotel, saying he would be honoured.

I had to make sure my packing was done, as we were leaving on Friday when I got home from school. This gave me the boost I needed to get through the days until the end of the week; something to look forward to and take my mind off the exams.

I had been studying hard and knew I would get thought the exams without a struggle. I didn't expect to be worried, but as I sat on the bus on my way to school that Monday morning, I felt nervous and agitated, and I had to stop myself biting my nails. Needing a distraction, I looked out the window and watched the world go by. It was a beautiful morning, with barely a cloud in the sky. The birds flew up to their nests in the bare trees, families headed to work and school in their cars, a couple of men were in their front gardens setting up their lawnmowers. As long as I had peace and tranquillity, I knew I would be alright.

I couldn't wait to get my placement at college. Although I had somewhat enjoyed being at high school, I would be glad to move on to something new – meeting new people, making friends and doing coursework. I had my careers advisor to thank for that. She had looked into admin courses for me and helped me out with everything I needed. I knew I was on the right path and was extremely happy with that.

The week flew by flawlessly. I completed every test as well as I could, and I left school on Friday afternoon with a smile on my face and a swing in my step, just knowing that everything would be alright.

I soon arrived home, feeling excited about my travels ahead as I walked into the kitchen. Mum and Jason were sitting at the table laughing at something funny that Jason had said. The two of them were having a right giggle together; they were getting closer every day.

'What are you both laughing about?' I asked curiously.

Jason put his empty mug in the sink and turned and walked into the hallway. 'Och, Chloe, it's just some adult humour. You wouldn't want to know.'

My eyes widened and I shook my head. 'Are we ready to go?' I asked Mum.

She was sitting with a mug of tea, wearing new black jeans, a teal blouse and a pair of black boots. She nodded. 'Everything's all packed up in the car.'

I ran up the stairs and changed quickly into grey joggers, a t-shirt and trainers, and then headed down to meet Jason. He was standing at the door, wearing blue denim jeans, a white t-shirt with a Canadian maple leaf on the front and black Reebok Classic trainers. Mum made sure everything was switched off and all the windows were shut, then locked the front door.

We headed off in Jason's car, entertaining ourselves by

singing along to the radio and snapping photos of the scenery. A while later, I put my mobile away and pulled my book out of my bag and started to read The Lost Diary of Snow White.

The journey was long. After a while I started to get fidgety, and I took my trainers off and pulled my pillow up to rest my head. I yawned, closing my eyes as sleep overcame me, and I was out in minutes.

When I awoke, we were on the gravel driveway of our Scottish country hotel in Foyers. I looked out of my window with a gasp. It was beautiful. The large red-brick building stood two stories tall with a large tree at either side, and surrounding it were three acres of private grounds.

Jason parked the car and we got out. The weather was still as beautiful as when we left, and it was surprisingly mild for that time of year. As we took out our luggage we received a warm welcome from not only the owners, Kate and Michael, but also their massive Great Dane. I just about managed to get through the front door as Kate tried her best to pull an over-excited Duke away. It was my first time being so close to this breed, and I put my bag down to stroke his white and black-spotted coat and rub under his chin. He panted away happily, loving the attention from these strangers who were coming into his home.

Kate held on to Duke's black collar, hauling him back with force, as she led us into the reception. The small area had a red patterned carpet, cream walls and a large brown desk with a vase of fresh flowers to the side and a small bell. Michael signed us in and Kate led us up the stairs with our door key.

It was a surprising delight as I walked into our room. A wood-framed double bed with a red tartan throw sat just behind the door on the right, and on the other side of the room there was a window with a view of Loch Ness. It was stunning.

'Breakfast is served in the conservatory from eight until nine thirty,' Kate explained. 'The reception is opened till ten, and the front door gets locked at eleven every night. There is a phone beside your bed and the number to phone reception is zero. If there's anything you need, please don't hesitate to ask.'

Kate left us the key and closed the door behind her, and I looked around at Mum with a big grin on my face. This place was fabulous. I walked around the room, taking everything in and looking out the window.

'Are you going to unpack at all?' Mum asked.

I nodded with a sigh. After I hung my clothes up in the small white wardrobe, put my toiletries away and freshened up, we headed back down the stairs to meet Jason. He was sitting in the lounge by the fireplace talking to two other guests.

'Karen, Chloe, this is Sam and Chris. They're hikers and are heading to Inverness tomorrow.'

I smiled at the couple. Chris sat looking slightly bored, as if he would have rather been anywhere else but here with the three of us. He had an unshaved beard and long, light-brown hair that hung behind his ears. Sam seemed nice, though. She was only around five foot, with chocolate-brown, shoulder-length hair and a knockout smile. I guessed from their clothing and boots that they were just back from a hike.

'Inverness,' Mum said, Fascinated. 'That's one place I've never been. Where are you heading?'

'Culloden,' Sam replied; she had a sweet voice, I noticed. 'Yeah, my aunt has lived up there most of her life. We used to have a lot of relatives stay around us in Edinburgh, but all the family grew up and moved away. Haven't seen my aunt in about ten years, so it'll be a nice surprise.'

'I'm sure it will,' Mum replied. 'That sounds lovely. Enjoy your time anyway.'

We turned to walk away, and Sam called out to me, 'Happy birthday, Chloe. Enjoy the hike tomorrow, yeah?'

'Thanks, Sam.' I waved, happy to have met her, as we left the hotel and headed out for our walk.

We found a trail just off the path outside the grounds of the hotel which led us uphill through woodland. I laughed at Mum as she huffed and puffed her way up a load of wooden steps while holding on to the bannister. Maybe that hike would be just a bit too much for her.

We finally made it to the small village store. We browsed and I picked up a pen, a fridge magnet and a notebook with a picture of Loch Ness on it. I thought this would do nicely for taking down notes when I started college. Then we headed into the café next door and ordered minestrone soup and ham-and-cheese sandwiches.

An hour later, we came out of the café. It was pitch black as we made our way back through the woods. I used my phone torch to guide us, but still I tripped over branches and fell over small rocks a couple of times. Jason was bent double with laughter watching me stagger about the place. I was so unimpressed. My hands were dirty and so were my clothes.

'It's not funny,' I said in a joking manner, trying to get Jason to stop laughing at me.

'Oh yes it is!' he replied with a grin on his face. Clearly, I had made it too easy for him to laugh at me.

We arrived back at the hotel and I headed up to my room to get changed. That would be one walk in the dark I would never take again.

We spent the evening in the lounge by the roaring fire, Kate and Michael entertaining us with stories of their dog and the hotel. I sat with Duke beside me and rubbed his head. He was a big softy and great company. Kate and

Michael seemed genuinely nice people and they had a lovely hotel in a place where one could only dream of living.

'How long have you lived here, Kate?' Mum asked.

'Only a couple of years. We were originally down in England but decided to move up here. We found this on the market…'

'And now you're the proud owners of a beautiful hotel. Well, you're very lucky, I must say.'

I smiled at Mum as she chatted away as if they had been friends forever. Mum always got along with anyone easily.

A while after, I stretched my arms and yawned, said goodnight, and headed up to bed. Today had been a good day, but I was done. I needed to get my rest.

I woke at half seven the next morning with my phone alarm buzzing. Switching it off, I rubbed my eyes and then dragged myself out of bed, heading to the shower to wake myself up. Ten minutes later, I came out feeling fresh and ready to take on the day of adventures. As I got dressed, Mum gave me a birthday card with a gift of thirty pounds inside, and I thanked her and gave her a hug. Today was my birthday and I was determined it would be a good one.

As we walked into the conservatory for breakfast, Kate wished me a happy birthday. I picked a table right next to the window and looked at the garden outside. It was stunning. As I ordered a bacon sandwich and a cup of tea, Jason joined us from his room next door to ours and handed me a birthday card with yet more money inside. I gave him a hug, thanking him, and set my cards on the table. Our breakfasts arrived and we ate quietly.

'Mum!' I said, pointing out the window. The Great Dane was bouncing around the garden, a stick in his mouth, with Michael following along behind him. 'I really want to go out and join them in the garden.'

Mum gave me one of her looks. 'I hardly think so.'

'I want a dog.'

She scoffed. 'That's the last thing we need right now. Like, who's going to take it out for walks every day, hmm?'

'I would.'

'Yeah, right.' She laughed. 'What, before you go to school? When you come home from school? What about vet bills? Who's going to pay them? Look, Chloe, maybe one day when you leave school and get a job, then I'll think about it. But right now, it's not a priority. No more dog talk.'

I shook my head, annoyed.

Mum and I left the table and headed up to our room to gather our gear for our day trip. As we were heading out the front door with Jason, my mobile pinged. I took it out of my jeans pocket and read the text.

Happy birthday, babe! Hope you have a good day hiking and don't get lost, lol. M xxx

Mollie. It was just like her to find it funny. I seemed to get lost everywhere I went. Even on the easiest routes too. When I first started high school I got lost returning to my classroom after lunch on the first day. I didn't have a clue where I was going, every corridor I went along, was the wrong one, so when all hope had seemed lost I gave up and just started randomly walking along different corridors hoping I would find someone to help me. Not a soul was around. Everyone was in class, and there was no way I was chapping on a door and embarrassing myself asking for directions. And eventually, when I was just about to turn a corner, Mollie turned up looking for me.

'Where have you been?' she asked, bewildered.

'I was…um…I just got lost,' I replied, feeling defeated. The corridors had seemed to kill my confidence. I had walked in the opposite direction of where I was supposed to have been going and she had wondered how I had managed to wander this far. I honestly think if she hadn't found me at that moment, I would have cried.

Shaking her head, she dragged me back to class with her. It wasn't my fault. I'd just never been good with directions.

Hopefully, though, that wouldn't be a problem today. It was a beautiful morning. The sky was blue and the birds were twittering away. We left the hotel grounds with our hiking boots on, feeling content and excited. After coming off a small path and taking a right turn, we walked along a road surrounded by nothing but trees, passing other families along the way.

Within an hour, the trees began to thin, giving a slight view of the loch to our left.

'Fancy going down and seeing the water?' I asked Jason and Mum enthusiastically.

They both turned and smiled at each other at the same time 'Sure. Lead the way, birthday girl.' Jason replied

I grinned widely, skipping through the woods and down a small hill, watching my footing along the way. When we finally arrived, I looked around, embracing the beauty that was Loch Ness. The water was calm, peaceful and quiet. It was perfect.

'Have a look around, see if you can find Nessie,' Jason said.

I turned to him. 'Oh, ha ha, very funny.'

'Where do you think those tales came from then, eh?'

I shrugged my shoulders. 'I don't know, just seems a bit far-fetched to me. I mean, a giant green monster living out in the water? Someone obviously made it up.'

'Hmm. I highly doubt that, Chloe.' He turned to Mum, giving her a wink as she stood there grinning. 'How could anyone possible make up the Loch Ness Monster?'

I picked up a handful of Scottish pebbles and attempted to skim one over the water. It couldn't have gone more wrong, landing with a plonk and making gentle waves.

'For attention, I suppose,' I replied. 'Isn't that what everyone wants these days?' I gave Jason a questioning look. 'And money too. Everyone loves that.'

He laughed. 'You certainly are quite narrow-minded Chloe. See if you opened your mind up just a small bit, you may not be so naive.'

'I'm not naive!' I argued. 'I believe in things.'

'Oh yeah, like what?'

'I don't know, stuff that's out there.'

'So how can you be so sure that there is no Loch Ness Monster then?'

I turned to him. 'Okay, let's say there was. Don't you think it would have made an appearance by now? Came onto land? I mean, an animal that lives underwater twenty-four/seven is a bit far-fetched.'

He turned to Mum and the two instantly burst out laughing. It was then it occurred to me that they were having me on.

'Oh, ha ha, very funny. That's what to do, take the mickey out of Chloe on her birthday,' I grumbled.

Jason had his hand on Mum's shoulder as he laughed away. 'I'm sorry, Chloe, you're just so easy to wind up,' he said, shaking his head.

I turned away from him, continuing to throw my pebbles into the water. He gave a cough, clearing his throat, and I heard the crunching of stones as he walked towards me. I turned to him.

'Want to do it properly?' he asked me.

I held out my hand. 'Be my guest.'

He took a pebble, tilted sideways and threw it towards the water. It skimmed four times before dunking in.

'How did you do that?' I asked, surprised.

'Easy. You want me to show you?'

I nodded with a smile, and he put another pebble in my

hand and gently guided my arm. Together, we threw the pebble at the water, watching it skim three times.

'Huh. Neat.' We carried on for a while, as Jason taught Mum how to do it as well, and soon we were all skimming pebbles into the water. I turned to them both, smiling, and they looked back at me.

'Look at us three,' I beamed.

Jason smiled, but Mum put her head down and, clearing her throat, she walked away.

'I think I've just ruined the moment. We'd better go,' I whispered. I'd really enjoyed that too. It had been fun.

We walked away from the stunning view and carried on with our trek. We kept to the side for when the odd car passed, and I wondered how long the road continued on for. We came to a junction and took a right turn. A waterfall was signposted, just one mile ahead, and I knew we would get there soon.

We trekked uphill, downhill and along level paths, chatting away and joking, with Jason and his ongoing sarcasm.

'Would you know your way back if we left you here?' he said, pursing his lips, trying not to laugh.

I shook my head. 'I'll get you back for this, just wait and see.'

He nudged Mum and they both laughed, enjoying themselves. I took my bottle of water out of my bag, took a long drink and sighed.

'Thirsty?' Mum asked.

'Extremely.' I smiled, putting the bottle back in my bag. Lengthening my strides, I walked ahead of Jason and suddenly came up with an idea. I looked at Jason and scoffed.

'What?' he questioned me.

'Nothing,' I mused, smiling, eyes looking elsewhere. I had a plan. A plan that would get him back for laughing at me and mocking me, especially on my birthday. And I knew that I, Chloe Stanson, would have the last laugh.

CHAPTER 8

The more we climbed up the road, the more we could see the massive hills on the other side. The trees thinned out at times and we could see the loch again. It always amazed me. We passed a sign: North Village Primary School.

'Must be a small building. There can't be many at that school, surely?' I asked Mum.

'Not sure, love. It's a pretty quiet village, so I guess not many.'

We continued to walk up the hill until we came to a building. I laughed. 'Mum, it's the café we were in last night.'

She stopped and looked at The Long hikes Café and the store next door. 'Oh yeah.' She smiled.

The area was busy, with cars parked outside and people walking in and out of the café. We carried on the trail and found the waterfall. It reminded me of happy times.

'Mum, do you remember when my friends and I used to walk in the burn?'

'I certainly do.' She raised her eyebrows. 'You were straight in the bath when you got home.'

'And that girl we were friends with, Donna. She fell in!' I doubled over, laughing.

'I don't remember you ever telling me that.'

'Yeah.' I caught my breath. 'Beth, Donna and I were walking through the burn just next to our primary school. We had to be careful of the rocks below, so we wouldn't trip and fall. I can't remember what happened exactly, but the next thing we knew we were looking at Donna sitting in the water. It was hilarious!' I howled. 'She went straight home after that with a big wet patch on her bum. If I remember rightly, she was wearing yellow shorts that day.'

Mum chuckled. 'Yes, that friend of yours was quite something.'

I nodded. 'She certainly was one for getting herself into trouble.'

'She was quite obsessed with you, though, wasn't she?'

I raised my eyebrows. 'Was she?'

'Chloe, she tried to climb in our kitchen window using one of the garden chairs.'

I looked at her, shocked. 'That's right!' I pointed a finger towards Mum. 'I remember now. There was one time when everyone got their hair permed and she wanted to be just like everyone else, so she got hers done too, and then she would come over to ours and I would have to wash her hair and get it all curly again. She did seem to spend an awful lot of time around me for some strange reason. Wonder where she ended up?'

Mum exhaled quickly. 'As long as it's far away, I really couldn't care less.'

I couldn't have agreed more. The stories I had been hearing about Donna and what she had been up to sounded awful. I was glad she had moved on. I certainly wouldn't have wanted to be anywhere near her.

We leaned over the fence by the waterfall for a short while, enjoying the scenery. It was a mass of rocks, moss, grass and trees where the water fell below, into a gorge which then lead out to Loch Ness.

'Beautiful, isn't it,' Mum said.

'It is. The whole place is. It would be wonderful to live here. Away from everything.' I waved my hand in the air and smiled, and we shared a moment, before Jason interrupted us.

'Want to go for a swim, Chloe?' he joked.

'Oh, yeah,' I scoffed. 'And how am I supposed to get back up?'

'Just climb the rocks.' He sniggered. 'Easy.'

'You want to be careful, Jason. I may just push you in,' I warned wryly, walking back up the small hill again. He wouldn't know what had hit him. Or pushed him for that matter.

After a short while enjoying the waterfall, we hiked back up the road quietly, none of us saying much. I was still sticking to my plan, intending to get Jason back. That was until he asked me a certain question.

'Fancy going to Inverness?'

My face lit up immediately and any thoughts I had of paying him back were dismissed. Well, for now anyway. I smiled at him excitedly as we walked back up the road to the hotel to collect our belongings and money. We would be needing them.

A short while later we were back in the car again, listening to the radio as Jason made the half-hour drive to Inverness with Mum in the front seat and me in the back. I felt so lucky at that moment. I would get to see Inverness for the first time ever, and when I got back home, I would tell Mollie. I knew it would make her jealous, as she hadn't been there before. Her parents took her on holiday somewhere different every year. Last year it had been Cairo and the Pyramids. My face dropped the day she told me. I was envious.

'Seriously?' I squealed. 'I can't believe it.'

'I know, Mum just booked it today. We're off in two weeks.'

'Ugh,' I groaned. 'Please take me with you.'

She laughed. 'Maybe your mum will take you there one day. You never know.'

'I wish.' Mum was never one for places that were just too hot.

Jason parked the car across the road from a restaurant in the city and paid for a ticket. We sauntered into the premises for a quiet meal. There were only a few people sitting at the tables as we arrived. In the open kitchen at the back, chefs were cooking dishes as the customers waited patiently for their meals. This was a treat that Jason insisted he pay for to celebrate my sixteenth birthday. He point-blank refused Mum's offers to pay, and every time she placed her money on the table, he shoved it back to her.

'This is non-negotiable,' he said with a straight face. 'It's my treat. I must insist on paying.'

Mum let out one last sigh before putting her money back into her bag on the back of her chair.

'Thank you.'

'Right,' I answered, clapping and rubbing my hands together, killing any uncertain mood that hovered around us. 'Let's eat.'

We dug into the steak pie lunches the waitress brought over to us, along with our drinks.

Inverness Castle was just as I hoped it would be, if not more. With its large brown-brick walls and multiple windows, it looked a picture. A bronze statue of Flora MacDonald stood proudly on Castle Wynd facing the river. We walked inside and straight up to the top, via the winding staircase. I was surprised Mum actually made it to the top without wheezing. I gave a small laugh.

'What?' she quizzed.

I smiled. 'You made it to the top.'

'Och,' she scoffed, 'I'm not that bad.'

I turned away, laughing to myself. I didn't think a couple of weeks at the gym would be too bad.

The view at the top was breathtaking. I was simply amazed by the scenery all around me. It was magnificent. I looked over the rooftops, admiring everything, as Jason gave me what felt like a history lesson.

'…and that's Fairy Hill over there,' he said, pointing to a large hill.

A few minutes into the lecture (as I called it), I held up

my hand and butted in. 'Jason, please, can't I just admire the view?' I asked as nicely as I could.

He took a breath and gave me a slight smile. 'Sorry, Chloe, is it a bit much?'

'A bit.' I nodded, pursing my lips.

'I just thought it would be good for you to know all the facts, that's all.'

'It was. I just want to enjoy this.'

He let me be, giving me time to enjoy the view.

Shortly after, we took a walk around the city and then went to the Eden Court Theatre. We stood in the foyer looking at the cinema listings, finding little choice.

'Hmm. Do you see anything, Chlo?'

'Not really. What about Hellboy?'

'Ah!' Mum exclaimed. 'Sounds good.'

Mum bought three tickets for us and we headed in with our popcorn and drinks. I loved the cinema.

That evening, we sat around the roaring fire enjoying the blissfulness of our hotel. I'd had a great birthday, with my Mum at my side, and I really couldn't have been happier. I thought about telling Mum how Dad would have loved it here, but it wouldn't have been right, what with Jason sitting beside her. He would have, though. He loved an open fire, and the shelf full of books would have made it all the more perfect. Tonight was our last night. We were leaving in the morning and the time had gone by too soon. Every moment of my birthday had been just perfect.

The next day our luggage was packed up and back in the boot again. We were ready to go home. Well, Mum and Jason were. I, on the other hand, didn't want to leave so quickly and get back to reality.

'Do we have to leave just now?' I practically whined at Mum as she said goodbye to Kate.

'We've seen everything there is to see here, Chloe. What else is there?'

'Can't we just take one more drive around the Highlands? Please?' I gave her my best puppy eyes, hoping she would give in.

'I don't know. What do you think, Jason?'

'Well.' He sighed. 'I guess so. I mean, your birthday only comes once a year.'

I gave him the cheesiest smile I could manage. 'Thanks, man.' I patted him on the back, hopped into the car and admired our beautiful hotel once more before the car rolled off.

We took one last tour of the Highlands, oohing and ahhing at practically everything in our sights including a herd of red deer grazing throughout the hills. It suddenly felt like a once-in-a-lifetime experience; I didn't know whether I would ever get the opportunity to come back here again.

Jason parked the car at Loch Mhor and we walked over to the water. As I took continuous snaps of the view, Jason took his trainers and socks off and stepped into the water.

'Ohhh.' He shuddered. 'Chilly.'

'Watch something doesn't bite your feet in there.' I smiled.

He pointed to the water. 'You want to go in?'

'Ah no, I don't think so.'

'Come on.' He waved at me. 'It's only a bit of water.'

He ran at me suddenly and I panicked, running away from him and squealing.

'Stop!' I shouted, holding my hands up, standing next to the water. 'I'll stand here, but I'm not going in, okay?'

'Suit yourself.' He sighed. 'But you don't know what you're missing.'

We both stood by the water looking over at the hills. It couldn't have been a more peaceful time. But this was the moment. It simply had to be done. I knew I would probably regret it later. But I just had to have my one last bit of fun.

So I did it: I pushed him in.

It really couldn't have gone any better. I watched him lose his balance, his arms swinging round in a clockwise direction, and go straight down, falling into the water with a splash.

'CHLOE!' Mum screeched, mouth wide opened in disbelief. 'WHAT THE HELL?'

He came up in a moment and I stood there with a smile on my face, knowing I'd got him back for those times he'd laughed at me. He ran his hands over his face and hair as he looked at me, his face like thunder.

'That'll teach you to mock me and laugh at me on my birthday!' I called.

With his hands outstretched, he swayed out of the water and over to me. I slowly backed off, protecting myself from getting wet. He wrung out his jumper and began to sneeze.

'Has anyone got a tissue?'

'Here,' Mum said, handing him one of the packets she'd brought with her. 'Chloe, I can't believe you did that. He's going to be frozen now.'

'I'm sorry. But you were laughing at me with the whole Loch Ness Monster story and then my bad sense of direction. I don't take well to being laughed at. I hope you have a towel to sit on in the car; you're going to need it,' I mocked, and walked off to the back seat.

As it turned out, he had a couple of towels with him in the boot. He always carried some in a holdall for whenever he went to the gym. He laid one on his seat and dried himself off as best he could with the other, putting the heater on in the car.

On our way home, we stopped at a small coffee shop and ordered food for the drive, and Jason went to the toilet looking for a hand-dryer to dry his clothes off. He had gone quiet since the water incident and Mum wouldn't look at me. Once we had finished our drinks he finally appeared, looking slightly better than he had, but still with anger etched on his face. He drank his tea quickly and gave a small nod for us to leave. A bad feeling was in my gut, but I knew deep down that he would forgive me in time. I just hoped it wouldn't take too long. Loch Ness would only ever be in my memories now.

CHAPTER 9

'Oh no!'

'What?' Jason and I answered simultaneously.

We had arrived back home and parked at the kerb. Jason and I looked at Mum worriedly. I half-expected her to say she had left something at the hotel. But what came next ruined my good mood.

'Dave.' She pointed to our doorstep. He was slouched over with a can in his hand. Must have been sitting there for hours. If he thought that he was getting into our home, he had another think coming.

'He doesn't look like he's leaving any time soon. Wonder how long he's been sitting there?'

'Do we have to go and face that, Mum? It's just going to spoil the rest of the night.'

'Afraid so, love – all we can do is face it head on. And if he starts any trouble, he'll simply be lifted.'

'Good riddance,' I scoffed, repulsed by the slob of a drunk sitting outside our home.

We got out of the car, collected our belongings from the boot and took them up the path. I sighed and shook my head giving a slight glance over at Dave. He slowly looked up with drowsy eyes. Mum ignored him, walking up the steps to unlock the door. A hand suddenly reached up and grabbed Mum's leg. She squealed and Jason grabbed Dave by the shoulder.

'Get your hand off me, mate,' Dave growled at Jason.

'Well, you'd do well to keep your hands to yourself in future. Now lay off,' Jason answered back.

'How? Who the hell are you? Her lover? Not that she'd want one after my brother died. Unless she's some sort of a slag.' Dave laughed, lifted his can up and drained the last of it, then threw it into the garden. Standing up, he staggered backwards and fell down the stairs.

Jason got well out of his way, before heading into the house after me and Mum. With the door locked so Dave couldn't get in, Mum switched on the living room light and closed the curtains. We ordered from our local Chinese and watched Spider-Man on DVD. We would make sure the last night of the weekend was a good one. No way would we let anything ruin it for us.

It was three twenty in the morning when I was woken up by loud shouting coming from outside. I sat up in bed and turned my lamp on, rubbing my eyes. I walked into Mum's room to find her peeking out of the window.

'Who's out there?' I whispered, joining her.

A figure stood at the gate to the path, his back to us. I knew it could only have been one person, the one who knew how to intimidate us. We wouldn't be fooled, though. I just hoped he wouldn't wake up any neighbours. We didn't want any bitterness between us.

'Och, take a guess,' Mum said. 'I think I'll have to phone the station. He's been singing and shouting for about an hour now. It's time I had him removed. I've had enough.'

Mum turned to me, looking angry. I backed off, giving her some space. She wasn't to be messed with when she was in a mood.

She headed down the stairs and into the living room, where she lifted the phone from the small mahogany table. I stood in the bedroom doorway listening in as she reported him. Minutes later she was back upstairs again. I sat on the bed, bending my knees and curling my arms around my legs.

'Right, well, that's that dealt with.' She sighed. 'They'll be here as soon as they can.'

She walked back over to the window and peeking out around the white, flowery curtain.

'Oh, no!' she gasped. 'He's coming up the path.'

She turned around, horrified, closing the curtain quickly, and sat on the bed beside me, taking my hand. I laid my head on her shoulder for comfort and closed my eyes, cuddling into her.

'You know, Dave wasn't always like this. He didn't used to drink like he does now. Once he was a really pleasant guy who could actually sit and have a decent conversation. We had met and known each other since he was only thirteen years old, a young, fearless and bold teenager.

When it was his sixteenth birthday, September 1979, your dad had driven us over to his parents' house in Houston that evening. They'd planned a special party for Dave with all his family and friends invited.

'We arrived at around half seven in the evening to a large, white, two-storey building with a grey rooftop and a white porch lit up with lanterns. The double, black, wrought-iron gates had gold spires on the top and a painted "HAPPY SIXTEENTH BIRTHDAY, DAVID" banner on them in gold and black. A Bentley and a Porsche were parked in the driveway at the front of the house. There were two garages at the side with black doors, and a white wooden bench sat underneath the living room windows. The back garden was closed off with a large hedge and gate.

'I had always been impressed by the beautiful building that your grandparents owned. Loved the sound of my heels crunching on the gravel as I walked along the drive and up the steps as your dad rang the doorbell. How handsome and swell he was that evening. With his short black hair styled with a side parting and dressed smartly in a designer white-cotton shirt, black trousers and shoes from Burton's. I was simply enthralled by him. I was proud to be by his side, to be his lady.

'"Jack!" Anita called as she opened the door.

'He smiled, looking up at her, and gave her a quick peck on the cheek. "Mum."

'We were led into the hallway that was wide and painted white, with massive mirrors on each side of the walls. Exchanging pleasantries, she kissed both my cheeks, closing the door behind us, leading us through into the living room. A few people stood about, chatting quietly to each other with a drink in their hand. Your grandfather was sitting on the couch. I felt somewhat self-conscious, as everyone turned to me as I walked in the room.

'"Nicolas, Sam, this is Karen," Anita announced.

'I felt like an exhibit on show as they came up to me. I had never met either of them before. Nicolas and Sam were close cousins of Charlie and Anita. We chatted away, with me boasting that both parents had certainly done a spectacular job in raising such a fine young gentleman as Jack. It didn't take long before I started to feel part of the family

'See, that was the thing with your grandparents, Chloe, they were a family of honour, dignity and, above all else, admiration. They were very wealthy back then, but sensible with their money; they were smart and never squandered it. And I'll let you on in a little secret: it was them who gave us the deposit for this house. The day we viewed it, your dad went over and said to them that he wanted to buy it. And within the hour, Charlie had stumped up the money and handed it to him. Just like that. We were so grateful. Jack promised to pay him back as soon as he could, but Charlie wouldn't have it. He was stern about it.

'"No," he said firmly. "I'll not hear another word about it, Jack. That money is for you and your lovely lady to start a family. Once you both get married, that is. We can't wait to be grandparents. We've been dreaming of this day for years." He patted Jack's shoulder. "Son, your mum and I are very proud of you, and I know that when you become a father, you'll be proud of your little one too."

'Your dad went home with a tear in his eye that day. His father had been his role model all his life, and Jack was proud to be his son.

'That evening, after I had politely excused myself from Charlie, I made my way around to everyone else and say my hellos. I felt somewhat intimidated in a way after Charlie let me go. I knew never to get on the wrong side of him, that was for sure. He'd made me promise I would take care of his boy, which felt kind of strange when we had only known each other three years; I thought that was the kind of thing you left till the day of the wedding. Maybe I was wrong, I don't know. It's not like I'd done that whole thing before. We were very young. But we were in love, and nothing would stop us being together, that was for sure.

As the time went by that night, more guests arrived, and everyone was introduced. Then the room went silent but for a few hushed whispers. I heard a door close, and suddenly Dave walked into the room with his friend behind him, and everyone erupted into a cheer of: "SURPRISE!"

'He seemed somewhat taken aback for a moment, and then he sighed. I guess a party was the last thing he was expecting.

He held an arm out and smiled. '"Dad, you shouldn't have."

'"Come here, you." Charlie gave his son a hug, patting him on the back. It was clear there was a close bond between the two. It made me smile.

'"You didn't have to do this. I wasn't expecting a party."

'"Ah well, son, you know your mother. She could never let your birthday go by without celebrating." Charlie handed his son a drink and the two of them clinked glasses.

'"Cheers, Dad."

'Dave had come over to greet me. I smiled at him as his eyes met mine and held out my hand.

'"Hi, Dave. Happy birthday."

'"Karen." He grasped my hand firmly. "How are you? It's good to see you. I'm glad my brother brought you along. He never stops talking about you. He's a lucky guy, I'll tell you that much."

'I felt myself blush as I tried my best to hold it together. Dave was a really nice guy. Relaxed, friendly and very outgoing. He was the same height as Jack, with brown hair and perfect smooth skin, and he was wearing blue Levi's jeans and a blue-and-white-checked shirt. He actually used to be somewhat of a looker, your old uncle. That ran in the family, though. They were all good-looking.

'He introduced me to his mate, Cal, who had been working beside him for a couple of years at a carpet firm – I didn't quite catch the name of it, but he seemed to enjoy it. Trying to make conversation with Cal was like trying to get blood out of a stone. All he had to offer was one-syllable words. I was here to get to know people, but it was futile with the birthday boy's friend. I gave up trying in the end and stood around, giving a smile here and there, before Cal finally left to chat to some others and Dave went to get us a drink.

'That gave me a chance to look around the room. I had never really appreciated it before. It had flowery Eldora Ivory wallpaper and a floral carpet, and a large chandelier hung from the ceiling. A small, square TV sat in the corner on a stand. Art filled every wall. It seemed like a very classy and elegant room.

'An arm slid around my waist, and while usually that would have made me jump, I sensed who was behind me immediately. I leaned towards Jack as he kissed my head.

'"Alright, my love?"

'I would always be alright whenever he was with me. He'd made me the strong young lady I had become.

'"Dad's just about to make a speech." He took my hand and led me to the front of the crowd, towards his parents.

'Everyone waited for Dave to come back into the room. The second he set foot inside, he froze, staring over at his father with the two glasses in his hand.

'"David, come over here, will you." Charlie held out his arm.

'Dave walked over to his dad. He kept his eyes on the floor as Charlie patted him on the back.

'"Son, we just want to say a massive congratulations on your sixteenth birthday. I know that, like Jack here, you will make us proud and be a great man and find yourself a lovely young lady. Your mother and I are so proud of you both. I know we've had our ups and downs and our disagreements, but as long as you stay on the right track, I know you'll do just fine." He smiled, took one of the champagne glasses from Dave and clinked them together. "Cheers."

'That had surprised me. Jack had never mentioned anything about any disagreements in the family. I would quiz him about it later. But right now, we were raising a toast. A toast to someone who would soon be my brother-in-law, and to be honest I couldn't wait to be a part of their family.

'Everyone raised their glass, wishing Dave a happy birthday. But Dave's face was a picture, and not a happy one at that. He glowered at Jack. I kept my head down, peeking up through the gap in my hair, as I watched him stare Jack out. Something within Dave seemed to change that night. I think it dawned on him that Jack was and always had been Charlie's favourite son.

'After we got home, with me feeling slightly lightheaded from all the champagne, I changed into my nightwear and slipped into bed. Jack pottered around the room sorting some things out.

'"I noticed your dad's speech didn't go down too well with Dave then?" I quizzed.

'"Hmm. Oh, I never noticed," he replied, going through some paperwork, not seeming interested.

'"That was something else, though. But I thought your family always got on great together?"

'"Hmm."

'"I mean, I didn't honestly think you had any disagreements at all with –"

'"Leave it, please, would you?" he practically shouted.

'His voice made me jump slightly. I sensed there was something wrong, but instead of arguing with him about it, I left it.

'"Well, night then," I replied, pulling the covers over me and closing my eyes. Jack was slightly distracted and I wasn't going to cause any trouble.

'After a few minutes, I felt the mattress move and his arm went around my waist.

'"I'm sorry. I'm just worried, that's all."

'I turned my head to him. "About what?"

'"Dave." He sighed. "He got himself into a bit of trouble."

'And that was the night I found out everything about your uncle, Dave Stanson,' Mum told me.

CHAPTER 10

I gazed speechless at her, eyes wide, impatiently waiting to hear more of her story about my uncle. There was no way I was going to my bed anytime soon. I was wide awake and wouldn't sleep at all now.

With her lips pursed, she looked away, deep in thought. I gave her time to resume the story, which I knew would be filled with a lot of emotions. I hoped she wouldn't cry.

She had so many fond memories of my father and the wonderful time they'd spent together. It had been cut too short, though. I had only wished Dad were here to share the memories with us.

'I just realised your uncle will be forty-one this September. Every year he received a birthday card from us with some money in it. We always sent him a card for every occasion – birthdays, Christmas, Easter. But not anymore.

'After that night, Jack gently advised me to keep my distance from Dave. He mentioned something about his not being too healthy for our relationship, whatever that meant.

'Anyway, Dave's sixteenth party was a great night. The music, the drinks, the banter. Dave pulled me onto the dance floor. I was surprised. He was really skilled. He took my arm and swayed me round and round, all the while keeping his eyes on me. Everyone clapped and cheered us both on. I felt happy and excited; I was having so much fun.

'When the music ended, everyone went to sit down and I turned around to go, but Dave gripped my hand and held it tight, pulling me into him. He gazed at me and I couldn't help but stare back. It was like I was dazzled by him. I felt myself being pulled into a rhythm as "Born Free" played in the background and he wrapped his arms around my waist. I couldn't pull myself back.

'"May I have this dance?"

'I turned to my right and saw Jack standing there with a smile on his face, holding his hand out to me.

'Dave lifted my hand and just before he placed it into Jack's he kissed my knuckles. "Thank you for the dance," he whispered, and left us both to it.'

I scoffed, laughing, imagining my mum and Dave dancing together. I tried to picture a version of Dave as a young lad, such a ladies' man. I shook my head, dismissing the image. Maybe I was better not thinking that way at all. I knew what Dave was like now, but he couldn't have been that bad before. It simply wasn't possible.

'Mum, did Dave ever, you know…try it on with you?'

'NO! God, no. I would never have let him do that to either me or your father. I loved Jack too much. It was just that after that night I found out from your father that Dave was more than a one girl kind of guy.'

'What! You mean two on the go at once?'

Mum cleared her throat. 'There was actually one time when he had more than two,' she replied honestly.

'Wow. I can't believe it. Dave!' I said, shocked. That wasn't nice. Actually, it was pretty damn horrible. Dave having his way with three girls at the one time. I wanted to find out more. So much more.

'How long did that go on for?' I asked.

'Oh, I'd say a few weeks. Jack and his parents had a word with Dave about it. It was Jack who'd found out and told them. He didn't want anyone thinking that his family had some sort of reputation. He wasn't best pleased with his brother. Dave's parents warned him it would all blow up in his face. But he wouldn't listen. He would take the girls out on separate nights…until one girl met another outside the cinema. With Dave.'

I gasped. This story had just got way more exciting.

'The girl was standing at the front of the cinema with her friends, chatting, laughing and having a good time. They turned around and saw Dave walking up with another girl on his arm. He never even noticed the group of girls until it was too late.

'Well, from what I heard he didn't get away lightly. Scratches all down his face. The girls he was dating who was already there actually flew at him. She was mad. She felt hurt and betrayed. Of course, she had every right to be. He was her boyfriend too and he was stringing her along. Apparently, she kneed him so hard in the groin he actually had to go to hospital. One of the staff from the cinema noticed the commotion and ran out to find him lying in the foetal position on the ground screaming out in pain. It didn't take long for the girls to scatter. The guy from the cinema phoned an ambulance and Dave was taken away quickly. Well, they did warn him. He never saw or heard from any of those girls again.'

'Oh my goodness, Mum,' I said, shocked. 'Was he okay?'

'Well, his face was badly cut and he was a bit shaken up after all of it. He was sent home from the hospital with painkillers for the swelling and he didn't speak to anyone for days. Spent a lot of time in his room. He must have been embarrassed and ashamed that they all knew what had happened. To this day he's never spoken of it.'

'Wow. Bad boy, Uncle Dave.'

'Yep, sure is. I didn't ever get the chance to get close to him, right enough. Your father made sure of that. He was determined that I had to stay clear of Dave. Even at special occasions where we had to spend the day together at the family home. And if he ever came near me, Jack would pull me away. He was protective like that, you see. That was the difference between him and Dave. Jack was loyal.

'One Sunday, we were all sitting round the massive antique

table in the dining room. The room was overly large, with vintage glass units filled with photos of family and certificates from school. Their house was like a showroom – floral wallpaper and carpets throughout and never a thing out of place. Jack was sitting on my right and Anita was on my left, with Dave sitting opposite and Charlie next to him. You could tell there was some tension in the air between the two boys, but Anita and Charlie tried their best not to let it get in the way of their afternoon. Jack had spoken to me about it one time and said he'd never been able to trust Dave again after what had happened.

'We were all finishing off a lovely roast when Anita said, "Well, that was a lovely meal. Who's for helping me do the dishes?"

'Dave stood up, lifting his plate. "I'll do them. If Karen helps me dry them." He raised his eyebrows at me.

'I stared in shock, feeling too intimidated to answer. A chair moved away at my side.

'"Over my dead body," Jack growled at him, standing up, and his fists thudded against the table.

'"Stop this now!" Charlie called, standing up and looking between both sons. "You are both grown men, one not as mature as I would have hoped…" Dave shook his head and looked away as his father glanced at him with disappointment. "David, Jack, dishes now. Karen, I'm sure Anita would like to take you for a walk round the garden before you head off home, yes?"

'I looked up at him nervously. "Of course," I said, my voice small, lifting the cardigan I had brought with me. I handed my plate to Jack, giving him a weak smile, and headed out into the garden after Anita.

'"Don't let them get to you, dear." She smiled as we walked around a large birch tree in the middle of the garden. "They're just having one of their rifts. It'll pass."

'"But Jack will never trust Dave again after what he's

done. He's sabotaged their relationship."

"'They're brothers. That's what they do. Siblings fight all the time." She laid her hand over mine. "Don't worry about it."

'I didn't want to argue with my soon-to-be mother-in-law, but I knew that this would affect them for a long time to come. I could see it with Jack, the way he was. He never, ever spoke about his brother the way he used to. There used to be a fondness between the two, but now, after what Dave had done, I knew things would never be the same.

'I watched Anita as she spoke fondly of her two sons. I knew how much she loved them both and that she would never want to take sides. Even after what had gone on, I could see the denial on her face. It was like she couldn't come to terms with it. She just thought one day they would be back to how they were before. But I knew that would never really happen.

"'What were the boys like growing up?" I asked.

'She laughed. "Oh, they were a wonder all right. Always running around the garden chasing each other. Sometimes they would fight over toys, but they always made up. That's how I know, dear. They will be okay."

'Anita had spent over twenty years caring for her two sons, but this time, it wasn't toys they were fighting over. It was the fact that Dave had cheated on these young ladies. Jack and Dave were adults now and maybe Anita had to wake up to this fact. Was there something in her past that she had hidden, perhaps, and that was why she wouldn't come to terms with this? It was the total imbalance of what was once a lovely, normal, caring family, and it had taken something as big as this to destroy the closeness that they had.

'The weeks eventually turned into months, and things began to go back to normality. Dave had become relatively quiet and reserved whenever I saw him. He would simply give me a polite nod and a "hello". I really didn't want to be as gullible as Anita and believe that he had changed, but then again, I just wanted to have a little faith. If anything, I think that incident taught him a valuable lesson.'

'Don't date three girls at the same time?' I chipped in with a smile.

'Right.' Mum laughed. 'You know, there are photos of those days back then. I have them in the cupboard. You sit there. I'll be back in a minute.' Smiling, she walked into the hallway.

I couldn't resist. With a big grin on my face, I followed Mum out into the blue-painted hallway. She switched on the light, opened the door to the white cupboard, pulled out a small ladder and climbed up to the top shelf to lift down one of the many boxes. The rest of the shelves were filled with bathroom things, bottles of perfume and laundered towels. Holding the box under her left arm and holding on to the ladder with her right hand, she slowly climbed down the steps and turned to me.

'Chloe, take this into the room for me.'

I carried the large, heavy, white box into her room, placed it on the bed and opened it. Smaller boxes lay inside with names and dates on them. Everything was organised neatly. I looked up at Mum.

'Well, go on then,' she smiled.

I felt quite excited as I pulled out a box. The label read 'CHRISTMAS 1984'. Inside were stacks of photos of the two families together on the special day.

'We would always have Christmas dinner at Anita and Charlie's house. Anita wouldn't have it any other way. She insisted.'

There were black-and-white photos of kids opening presents, playing with their presents, standing and sitting together. A small boy, who looked only about four, stood with a remote control. I had to look closely until I realised the remote was for a toy car he had got as a present.

'Mum, who's that?' I pointed to a couple standing beside Mum and Dad.

She looked over. 'Oh, that's my parents, your gran and grandpa, spending the day with all of us at Charlie and Anita's house.'

I was surprised to see old photos of my parents and their parents when they were younger. Mum looked so much like my gran. It was really great to see the pictures, especially the ones of my dad when he was so young.

'Why have I never seen these before, Mum?'

'I don't know, sweetheart. They've been lying in that cupboard for years. I guess I just forgot all about them. Still, I'm glad you have them now to look at. These will be your photos to keep.'

'Thanks, Mum.'

We sat on the double bed browsing through so many photos, talking and laughing, for a short while until we came to the last one. And when we finished, I organised them in order and packed them into the boxes that they'd come in. Mum placed them back in their spot on the shelf as I yawned and stretched my arms, cosying under Mum's duvet.

'It's very quiet outside. Do you think he's gone?' I asked.

'Oh, I don't know. I wish he would just leave us alone.' Mum peeked out of the curtain – just as he started shouting.

'Karen, Chloe, let me in. Come on!'

We jumped in fright as we heard a massive bang come from the front door and he thumped it over and over with his fists.

'Damn,' Mum called out, agitated. 'He must have seen the curtain move. He's never going to give up.'

He called to Mum again and again, swearing and shouting. I clenched the duvet cover tightly in my hands as

I quivered in fear. It was beginning to get too much to handle and the noise was unbearable. Cringing, I threw my hands up to my ears, trying to block out the sound, and I squeezed my eyes shut. The banging wasn't stopping and he wasn't giving up. How much more of this trauma could we possibly endure?

I listened for a moment and realised he was chanting 'Let me in' over and over, never stopping. Mum was pacing the floor, back and forth, running her hands through her hair. This was affecting her in a terrible way.

I was too busy keeping my hands over my ears to notice she'd left. When I realised I was alone, I was worried she'd gone downstairs. I ran out into the hall, but she wasn't there.

'Mum?'

'Never going to go.'

I opened the door to my room and found her in the middle of my bed, with her knees under her chin, her arms wrapped around her legs, rocking back and forth and staring at the wall. She looked as if she was going crazy. My body seemed to be frozen on the spot with shock at that moment she needed me to help her and I didn't know what to do. Not being able to think properly, I just stood, watching her move backward and forwards. Going into a panic, I ran my fingers through my hair, feeling overwhelmed. In that moment it felt as if we were trapped and never getting out. There was only one thing that could be done, that I needed to do to save us both.

Leaving Mum sitting there on her own with no one to help her, I walked out the room, locking myself in the bathroom where there was nothing around me but tranquillity and peace, I took a deep breath and tried to think straight, looking at the little blue word plaques on the corner shelf above the tub: 'relax' and 'calm'. Something about them seemed to take the rigidness out of my shoulders and I felt myself relax slightly.

I walked over to the sink and looked in the mirror. A thin, pale, white face stared back at me. The girl in the mirror showed little emotion. Her blue eyes looked weary and there was a messy bun tied on the top of her head. I looked away and turned on the tap, splashing cold water over my face and dried it with a towel. Mum needed me to be out there with her I walked back into the room with my mobile in hand and sat in front of her as she continued to rock back and forth. With my left hand, I dialled the number and held the phone to my ear, listening to it ring, waiting for an answer. Within about seven seconds the ringing stopped.

'Hello?'

'Jason, it's Chloe. I need your help. Something has happened to Mum and I think she's raving. She is mumbling and won't close her eyes.'

I heard rustling on the other end and footsteps.

'Has she hurt herself?'

'No. I think it's the strain of what he's doing to us.'

'Is he still outside?' Jason gasped.

'Unfortunately.'

I heard a muffled curse and wondered how long it would take to help Mum. She needed to come out of this trance. Fast.

'Okay, Chloe, here's what you need to do. I need you to listen carefully. Place your face in front of hers, but not too close, and speak to her in a calm and gentle manner. She needs to be able to listen to your voice.'

With my mobile lying on the bed, I cupped Mum's face in my hands and gazed into her eyes.

'Mum,' I said gently. 'Mum, can you hear me?'

'Everything, everywhere, taking over, torment.'

I stayed focused on her, willing her to emerge.

'Mum. It's Chloe. Can you hear me? Listen to my

voice. Focus on me. Can you hear me, Mum? Focus on my voice.'

I began to repeat this, staying calm and trying to help her, feeling positive that I could bring her back to me. I took her hands and held them and in that instant she looked straight at me. Unsure what would happen next, I waited patiently. Her body stopped moving and she looked around. She had come back to me. Tears welled in her eyes.

'Chloe?' She looked scared and lost.

'It's okay, Mum, I'm here. You're alright.'

I rubbed her arm, giving her comfort as she looked around the room.

'How did I end up in here?'

'You don't remember?' I asked, surprised.

She shook her head and a tear rolled down her cheek. I wrapped my arms around her for reassurance as she began to sob quietly.

'It's too much. I can't cope…'

Holding her in my arms as she let it all out, I picked up the phone and spoke to Jason.

'She's come out of it now – just upset, that's all. It's the stress.'

'Okay, Chloe, good job. I'm going to leave my phone on for the rest of the night in case you need me. If anything else happens, give me a call.'

I hung up, focusing on Mum. I needed to get her back into bed.

She looked up at me, exhausted. 'Where is he? Is he still here?'

'I don't know, Mum. You need to get some sleep.'

I walked her back to her bed and pulled the duvet over her as she closed her eyes. It was doubtful she would sleep – or that I would, for that matter. But we would give it a shot anyhow.

I left the room, turning out the light as I went, feeling drained. Damn Dave. He was making me mad now. I cursed quietly, truly despising my uncle, wishing he would disappear off this earth and never be seen again. 'Go to hell, Dave,' I whispered, climbing into bed and closing my eyes. It had been a pretty awful night, with his stupid carry-on and his drunkenness. He came and went as he pleased. I hadn't a clue where he was coming from, and I really didn't care. Mum and I just wanted peace.

CHAPTER 11

I could remember a time when I really used to admire Dave for his strength and courage and the way he would just go through life doing whatever he pleased with little responsibility and not a care in the world. I knew better now, though. At his age, he had amassed very little. He had no home of his own and was a freeloader. And without a family to call his own, he had nothing to keep himself grounded. My father was his world, and without him there was really nothing to keep him going anymore. He was simply unmanageable.

When I was ten, Dad and Dave would take me up to the woods for a trek every Sunday and we'd have loads of fun, running in between the trees and playing hide and seek. I was always the seeker, spending a large amount of time searching for them peeking around every tree. Finding them was always easy. One day on my hike up a small hill, not watching the ground below, I stood on a large pile of what I thought were leaves. Carrying on innocently until there was something stinging me all over, and I jumped with the pain from whatever was following me. To anyone who could see me I must have looked unhinged, with my arms flailing, running around the woods and screaming at the top of my lungs. At that point I had never felt so terrified in my life. The adrenalin ran through me as I dodged any tree or branch that was in my way, unable to escape the small swarm of wasps that continued to sting me all over.

Dad eventually caught up with me, managing to calm me down as he lifted me into his arms and carried me home. I had no jacket on as it was a warm day and I cannot begin to describe the pain I was in, having been stung seven times. It was unbearable to a ten year old.

When I eventually got home, Mum shouted at them at the top of her voice: 'I told you to keep an eye on her!' She gave Dad and Dave a right telling-off. She dabbed the stung areas with vinegar, soothing me and telling me I would be okay. I sat up on the kitchen table rubbing my eyes; my cheeks were stained with tears.

Time ticked by and eventually the pain ended, but ever since that day I have been terrified of wasps. That's another awful memory that will never, ever leave me.

Mum ran a bath for me to make me feel better, and when I came downstairs later on, Dad fussed over me, constantly asking how I was feeling. He smothered me with kisses, telling me how sorry he was and that he would never let anything happen to me ever again. It didn't take much to forgive him, as he spoiled me with treats and toys the next week.

But everything was forgotten by Wednesday, when I was given the best gift that any child could receive in the world. It was after school and I was sitting on the floor in front of the TV watching my cartoons when Dave walked in the door with a small dog. The TV was dismissed instantly and I jumped up excitedly, feeling over the moon. The little dog – a mongrel with long fawn-coloured fur – panted happily as I bent down on my knees and stroked his back.

'Is the dog for me?' I asked hopefully.

'He certainly is, my darling. Although I'll have to keep him at my flat for now – is that alright?'

I nodded, happy that I had a new best friend in my life, rubbing his chin.

'What's his name?'

'Well, I was hoping you would be able to give him a name. What do you think he should be called?'

I sat in front of the dog giving it some serious thought

(as serious as you could get for a ten year old). As I ran my hands through his thick fur, a name came to me suddenly.

'I think we should name him Max.'

'Hmmm,' Dave answered, rubbing his hands along his chin. 'Max. I think that sounds perfect. What do you think of that then, eh, Max?' he asked the dog. The dog looked up at Dave and wagged his tail.

'I think he likes it.' I smiled. 'Oh, thank you, Uncle Dave.' I jumped at him, giving him a bear hug. 'Can we go for a walk now, please?'

He looked over at me, smiling. 'Of course we can, sweetheart. Anything for my wee Chloe.'

From then on Max and I were rarely apart. In the days and weeks that followed, we went everywhere together. One day Uncle Dave took me to a large shop and I waited outside with Max. Dave came out sometime later carrying a large bag of dog mince. I couldn't wait to get home to feed him. That afternoon Dave cooked the meat and I dished it out into Max's bowl. Dave put it outside on top of the bin to let it cool for a while, and we went into the living room to play with Max and his toys. A few minutes later Dave went back out to get the mince, only to find the bowl was empty. It turned out the birds were hungry too and had decided to eat Max's food. Dave laughed at that, finding it funny that the birds had eaten his dog's dinner. He wasn't angry at all. Just had to be more observant next time. I ran outside, looked up to the blue sky and pointed at the birds flying way up high.

'You naughty birds, you stay away from my dog's dinner!' I called.

That evening we played for hours out in the garden together. I threw Max his new ball and he ran quickly to catch it and bring it back. He was taught to sit, give a paw, stay and roll over. Dave, Max and me – it was one of my favourite childhood memories that would stay with me forever. We were unbreakable.

My uncle was never one for settling down. I guess he just wasn't the commitment kind of guy. As the years went by, I thought of him more like a lone ranger really. He never depended on anyone, and rarely spent long in a job either.

One weekend, I heard the ice cream van playing its tune as it turned the corner into our street. Mum gave me money for a cone and I excitedly went out to get my treat. I received a big surprise as the glass window opened and out popped Dave.

'What are you doing in that van?'

'This is my new job, Chlo. I'm the driver's assistant. What do you think?'

'Does this mean I can get my sweets for free now?'

He tilted his head back, laughing. 'I'll say something, you're a trier alright.'

He handed my cone over and I gave him the money, making a sour face. Weren't family supposed to get discounts? I thought so. The job didn't last long, though. He came over the next week complaining that he'd had a fight with his boss that morning and been sacked on the spot. I felt gutted that I would never see him again in the van. But a week later he'd landed another job, as a dish-washer at the local Indian restaurant down the road.

It kind of annoyed me that he moved around so much and could never stick at anything. If he'd only put his soul into something and given it a good try, maybe, just maybe, he would have actually enjoyed it. He was too much of an impatient guy at times, and he never got to know anyone either.

The only person in life he genuinely had a soft spot for was his niece; that was what kept him around for so long. If anything ever happened to me, he was there in an instant. It was then I knew he really cared. Had love in his heart.

For me anyway. I could see it in his eyes, and I just knew that there was one person in his life that he would do anything for. I don't suppose there was anything Dave wouldn't have done for me. I think back then it was possible that he would have walked to the ends of the earth to make me happy.

I appreciated him for his kindness and generosity, and sometimes, when we were in his flat having a heart-to-heart, I saw the sincerity in his face. I knew if Dave had made the effort, he could have made himself a better man. I spent a long time hoping for that – until my dad died. Dave changed after he found out, and every single thing that I loved and respected about him simply disappeared. It was like I didn't know him at all. Not really.

CHAPTER 12

Back to the night that Dave was causing grief, pounding at the door for us to let him in and after I had helped put mum to bed. I stood at the top of the stairs, feeling hesitant. Part of me thought about going down to confront Dave to see if I could get him to move away from the front door. But another part of me thought better of it. That was the more rational part. Still, I felt that he needed one last chance to prove he was the loving uncle I'd once had and not this new, drunk, horrible man that I didn't want to be anywhere near. It really saddened me that I felt like I'd lost him, but there was one small bit of hope left. After everything we had been through over the years, he deserved this one last chance. It just had to be done.

I was prepared to do this. I needed to find out.

Mum had contacted the police earlier and they'd said they would be over to remove him. So I needed to be quick. I walked quietly down the soft, carpeted stairs and stood behind the front door. He sat on the other side, mumbling to himself.

'Dave?' I called quietly.

'Who's that?' he slurred.

'It's Chloe. Look, you can't stay here tonight. You really need to move away before you get yourself into a whole lot of trouble.'

'Let me in. Please.'

'Dave, do you remember when I was younger?' I asked, trying a distraction.

'Eh? What do you mean?'

'When I was just a child and you bought that wee dog – do you remember?'

'Hmm, aye, I remember, wee Max. Och, I loved that

dog.'

'Do you remember when you took me up the woods, you, me and Max?'

'Aye, hen, I do. Why? What's all this about anyway?'

'Well, I miss the old times, when we used to have loads of fun. You're not the same anymore. You've changed. You – you scare me now. I want the old Uncle Dave back. I don't want this drunken slob anymore.'

'HA!' He laughed. 'Drunken slob, eh?'

There was silence for a minute. I sat at the door, quietly listening for any movement.

Eventually, he sighed and said, 'Times have changed, ma lass.'

'Yeah, but you don't have to. Deep down, I still love you, Dave.'

I heard a light thud against the door. I wished I could have changed him and made him a better man.

'I love you too, pet. Don't you ever forget that. Okay?'

I leaned my head against the door, closing my eyes. 'Okay.'

I sat on the floor, not moving. All I wanted to do was open the door, let him in and throw my arms around him. I hoped the chat we'd had would have opened his eyes and made him realise he'd made a blunder. I wanted him to be sorry for his mistakes. But was he?

I kneeled and reached for the door lock, then hesitated. Was this a good idea? What if it was all an act and he was just trying to soften me up? Was he really that devious? I was his only niece, and the thought of him doing that to me was barbaric. I lifted my hand and quietly put the chain on the catch. If he really was that deceitful then at least I'd have this to protect me.

I stood up and turned the lock, pulled the handle down gently and opened the door slightly so that just part of my face was showing. I looked down as he sat forward and turned around.

'Chloe?'

'Please...don't move. Just stay where you are, okay?'

'But I'm not going to hurt you, darlin'.'

'Just stay on that step and we can talk this way, okay?' I said, trying to convince him.

'Please, Chloe. Just let me in.'

He stood up and reached out to me, slipping his hand and wrist through the door. His black leather jacket got caught in the gap, and his hairy hand waved around, trying to take hold of my own.

'Hold my hand, please. I miss you, my wee angel. You were right. About the times back then. I miss them too. We really bonded great, me and you. But since your dad died, well, I've just got a bit lost, you see. Look, it's too cold out here to stand and talk. Why don't you just open the door and you can make us tea, yeah?'

I was hesitant. Doubtful. But above all I needed to find out. Giving him the last bit of trust I had, I placed my hand in his, silently praying it would be okay.

'See? That was easy, wasn't it?' he said softly as if talking to a child, placing his other hand over mine.

I stared at him, looking for any change in his face at all. It was there. I saw it in his eyes. The softness vanished as his face turned vile.

'Now open the bloody goddamn door, Chloe!' he shouted, pulling my hand towards him tightly.

I gasped out with the pain as my face smashed against the edge of the door. I cried out, squeezing my eyes shut, and then squinted to see his face was inches from my own. I was in danger. His teeth were gritted as he growled at me.

'I swear if you don't open this door right now...'

He had been treacherous the whole time and I'd been gullible to believe he could ever be the man I wanted him to be. For a moment all I felt was hurt. Hurt and betrayal.

His own niece. How could he do that to me? Pretend that everything was fine, when in fact it really wasn't.

Still gripping my hand, he pushed the door handle frantically, trying to force the chain off the wall. I managed to move my face back from the door. With my arm caught, the sharp shoves he was making were excruciating, and I squealed out in pain, calling for help. He was too strong for me and I didn't have the strength to break away from him. Tears escaped my eyes as the frame was jammed into my arm. He wasn't stopping anytime soon.

Then he moved, sliding up at the door, forcing his whole weight against it. His grip on my hand loosened and I pulled it in quickly. Fear ran through me. Would he eventually get in? I knew the chain wouldn't budge, but the screws that held it in could have loosened. Panicking, I pushed my weight against the door, trying to close it over, giving it everything I had. Right now, it was a contest of who was the strongest. Only time would tell who would win.

'Stop!' I cried out, begging with him, pleading. 'Just leave me alone!'

He would terrorise us until the very end and we would exhaust every possible outcome until there was nothing left. We would never give up.

My feet slipped over the carpet as I pushed as hard as I could, shutting my eyes tight as I cried out in pain. His strength was immense. I gave a large scream, begging for someone to help me. I had never seen him so mad before. Not like this. He wasn't the man I knew and loved. And he probably never would be again. He wasn't 'lost', as he'd said; the caring part of him had died along with my father. I would never get it back again.

'Chloe? What the hell's going on?!'

I looked up the stairs and saw Mum standing there in her housecoat, utter disbelief on her face.

'Mum!' I shouted. 'Help me! Dave's trying to force his way in!'

She ran down the stairs in her slippers as fast as she could and came to the door. Peeking through the gap, she gasped.

'My God!'

All she could do to help me was to try to force the door shut. Together, we stood with our backs to the door, pushing as hard as we could. Within a few moments the door finally gave way and slammed shut. Mum turned around quickly and locked it as fast as she could.

'What the hell were you thinking?!' she yelled.

I threw my hands up to my face, sobbing my heart out with shock and fear. 'I'm sorry!'

I heard her sigh as she gave in to my tears. 'Oh, Chloe love. What have you gone and done?'

Out of everything that had happened in my life, I'd never felt so hurt, betrayed and angry as I did in this moment. I just couldn't get over the fact that this man whom I'd known all my life could do this to me. That was it. I was done with him. I didn't want anything to do with him ever again. The trust was now gone.

I sniffed, wiping my nose on my hand. I didn't care about anything right now. I felt utterly exhausted and done. My eyes nipped with the tears.

'I just wanted to give him one more chance. He's my uncle, and I thought I could change him for the better. But apparently not. After this, I'll never trust him again. Oh Mum, it's just not fair!' I sobbed, throwing my arms around her. I was utterly heartbroken.

'I know, sweetheart. But you must realise that Dave has changed a lot. And he'll never be the same man he used to be. I know it must be hard because he's your uncle and you loved him a lot. But you need to believe me when I say you can't go near him ever again. Do you understand me?'

'But how could that part of him just disappear? I don't understand. It's just like he's becoming a monster. Tormenting us. It's just grief and hassle with him all the time now.'

We sat on the bottom step of the stairs and she rubbed my back, trying to calm me down. I missed him and hated him at the same time. It was confusing and my head hurt. I turned to Mum.

'I think I'm going to go back up to bed now.'

'That's a good idea. Try to get some rest. But Chloe, you have to promise me something. If he ever comes near this door again, you stay well away, do you understand me?'

I gave a sad nod and turned and headed up to my room without saying another word.

There were so many questions running around inside my head and I had no answers to right now. But I knew this much: I needed sleep. I laid my head down on my pillow and closed my eyes, taking deep, soothing breaths. Finally, I fell asleep, hoping tomorrow would be a fresh start for me and Mum. There was nothing we wanted more.

The next morning, I let out a sigh as I sat down at the kitchen table while Mum dished out cereal, tea, toast and Nutella for us both. I'd only managed to get around three hours' sleep, and I felt absolutely knackered. With no energy, I had no idea how to make it through the day without falling asleep.

Mum tried to make me feel better by putting on the radio. 'Somewhere Only We Know' was playing. Keane had recently become one of my favourite artists and I had to make sure I got his album. This song couldn't have come on at a more perfect time for Mum and me really. What we needed to do was stick together as a family and make sure nothing came between us. The bond we had was just too great; we simply couldn't break it.

As we finished our breakfast, the house phone rang and Mum couldn't have run any faster to pick it up. I turned down the volume on the radio to listen in on the conversation, hoping it was the police to say they had arrested Dave. I heard an 'Oh no' and walked into the living room to stand by Mum's side. From what I could tell it was a man's voice on the line and he sounded serious. I looked at Mum worriedly as she put her hand up to her mouth, looking like she had just received the worst news ever.

I waited until the call ended and she moved, practically collapsing on the couch.

'Well? What's going on?'

'Bad news, I'm afraid. Dave's on the loose.'

'WHAT!' I shouted, making her jump slightly. 'How? I thought the police were coming to lift him?'

'Yeah, they were on their way when they got a call about a burglary and they had to deal with that first. Dave must have left just after all that carry-on, fearing he might be arrested. He's wandering around God-knows-where and they haven't a clue where he is.'

Mum looked dazed and lost. The headache I'd had hours ago was suddenly coming back. I pinched the bridge of my nose. This was a catastrophe. Dave wouldn't give himself up to anyone and he would never stop until he got what he wanted. And what he wanted was to hurt us. And to have this house.

The thought of him randomly lurking around somewhere, anywhere, made my skin crawl and I shivered just thinking about it. What if he was lurking around some bushes just outside, keeping an eye on us? Could we go outside now? Was that possible? It seemed very unlikely given the fact that he could approach us at any time and, given his strength, we would have no chance. So we had no choice but to stay indoors. I suddenly felt trapped.

'What about school? Have I to take the day off? What about every other day? What if they never find him? I can't just stay off altogether –'

Mum cut me off. 'Chloe, please, just give me time to think. Now, the police said as he's a danger to us and the public, we have to stay indoors, just in case he follows us. I mean, for all we know he could be lurking around outside this house, and if you went outside to a taxi, he could grab you, so it's really not the best idea to be wandering out. Not even up the path. Any option is dangerous. We need to stay safe.'

I sat on the couch feeling angry and scared. The fact that Dave was so persistent in intimidating us was unnerving – and wearing. More than anything we both just wanted to be left well alone. Would the police even catch him? There were so many places he could be and they couldn't search everywhere for him. We would have to leave the house at some point. There was no way we could spend days on end in here. It was out of the question.

Unless he was caught and put behind bars, we would constantly worry, be on the lookout all the time. Thinking about this made me angry to the pit of my stomach. I paced the floor, trying to come up with a solution to our problem, while Mum called Jason. After leaving a brief message, she hung up and sat down on the couch.

'He's at work just now and can't get away till he clocks out around five. I'll text him and let him know what's happened.'

While she retrieved her mobile from her bedside cabinet and texted him, I stood at the window, looking around. The street was empty, as were the driveways. All I could hear was the sparrows chirping outside in the conifer tree Dad and I had planted when I was younger.

I quickly called the school, letting them know I

wouldn't be in today, saying there was a family incident. The receptionist was totally understanding. Her tone of voice seemed calm and soothing, putting my mind at ease slightly.

It didn't take long before a police car turned up in front of the house. Two officers walked up the path and Mum answered the door and let them in while I sat on the couch. My mood was low and talking was the last thing I felt like doing. I knew my face was tripping me and I had to fix it. They would be expecting a statement about the night before and that thought made me want to be sick. I would rather have been at school than sit here and repeat the whole harrowing experience. The more I thought about it, the more it broke me, piece by piece. Having to go through it again was horrific. But it needed to be done, and the sooner it was over, the better. I just wanted to put it all out of my mind for good.

I felt slightly self-conscious as they walked into the room with their hands holding on to their vests and their walkie-talkies strapped to their shoulders.

'Hello, I'm Officer Kinsley and this is Officer Dibsley. We understand there was an incident last night involving a family member of yours?'

To us, Dave would never be a member of our family again. After what he done, he had been disowned by us and we wanted nothing else to do with him.

Officer Kinsley took out his notepad and pen, waiting for one of us to speak. Mum stood at the window with her arms crossed and a sour look on her face.

'Well, tell them then.' She looked at me.

'I – I, um…I made a mistake last night. A pretty huge mistake, and I wish I'd never done it all. Because I just feel it's made things so much worse.' I fumbled with my fingers nervously.

'What mistake did you make?' Kinsley asked.

I looked at Mum for support, but she wouldn't look at me. I picked at my nail.

'Um, he – Dave – was sitting on the front step and I went down to speak to him. I opened the door, and that was when he tried to force his way in. Luckily, the chain was on the latch. I don't know what I would have done without Mum to help me.'

'What did you want to speak to him about?'

'When we were younger, he used to take me out with a dog he had. I thought if he could relive those memories, it could have made him a better person. But now I know that could never happen.'

'So, what was he doing here in the first place then?'

Mum filled them in, once more giving every detail of the harassment and torment, while they looked on, nodding, taking notes and generally looking somewhat concerned.

'And have you done anything to antagonise him or make him angry?' Officer Dibsley asked, looking at me.

I raised my eyebrows in disbelief. Was he serious? Our lives were in danger and he was asking about Dave's angry temper?

'No!' I said defensively,

'You're bound to be feeling scared and angry right now, but there is a man out there with a temper, and if he meets anyone else it's possible they could come to some harm too. Everything is taken into consideration. Your safety comes first, of course. Can you think of anything that may have made him angry?'

I felt my face go red. I'd been thoughtless and the officer was right. What if I did antagonise Dave and make him angry? It wouldn't have been difficult, considering the way he was feeling. I was only thinking of how to make him happy, but he was probably feeling too messed up with everything that was going through his head. He would be out there wanting revenge for this morning.

'I may have got him angry. But that wasn't my intention,' I said quietly.

The officer looked at me with a straight face. 'What did you do to make him angry?'

'I wasn't thinking properly. I'm not defending him in the slightest, but it's possible that I did antagonise him. I didn't mean to. I tried to reach out to him. It was stupid and inconsiderate, given what he's going through. I just wanted to talk. But now, after what he's done to me, I never want to see that man ever again. He's a monster and needs locked up.'

Mum sat on the couch, an arm around me for comfort as the tears welled up. She gave the officers the rest of the information, and a photo of Dave from two years ago that had sat on the unit in the living room. She looked at it once more with a sad face and I could tell she was trying to hold back the tears. The photo was of Dad and Dave at one of their friends' wedding dos. Those were happier times.

Officers Kinsley and Dibsley left with the photo, closing the door behind them. I threw myself back on the couch and let it all out. Nothing could have possibly made me feel any worse.

Half an hour later, I had calmed down. I lay with a blanket over me on the couch, staring at the TV. Being here wasn't doing me any good. In fact, if anything I felt worse. It was like I was in a deep black hole and nothing could get me out. I needed a change.

Spending the rest of the day in the house certainly wasn't going to help matters at all. I got my phone out of my bag to text Mollie. Hey, Mol, won't be at school today. Something has come up. Will see you soon. x

I set my phone down on the arm of the couch and almost immediately got a response back.

Are you okay? x

Yeah, I'm okay, just personal stuff. Don't want to say in a text. x

Ah, okay. You want me to pop over after school? x

There was an image in my head of Dave hiding out in a bush and watching her as she walked up my pathway. I didn't want her to be in any kind of danger. She had to be kept safe as well.

I don't know if that's such a good idea, considering what's happened. I'll tell you everything later when I see you. x

Okay, sounds worrying. But as long as you're alright. Cheer up, babes. Not long to go till we graduate high school. Party time! Woop woop! x

She always made me smile, no matter how I was feeling. It lifted my spirits.

I'll be alright. As long as I've got you there. x

I sat my phone back on the arm of the couch. That man was making my life a misery and I was feeling fed up, unhappy and emotional, wishing he was behind bars and they could throw away the key. I wasn't in the mood for anything, so I just sat there, not moving. This was a new low for me.

CHAPTER 13

'Come on, Chloe, get up off the couch!'

Mum had been moaning at me for the last two hours to do something around the house. I could tell she was getting annoyed by her facial expressions and her tone of voice. My mood hadn't shifted at all. In fact, if anything it had got worse. I looked at her and rolled my eyes.

'Did you just roll your eyes at me? I've told you never to do that and you know better. Now, if you're going to be spending all day like this, you can just stay in your room!'

She was giving me a strict warning, but I simply couldn't be bothered anymore. I looked away, giving another eye roll.

'Shut up.'

I could feel her presence lingering beside me and I knew I had overstepped my boundaries. But at that moment, I really didn't care. The anger in her voice should have scared me and there would have been an apology from me if my self-esteem had been thoroughly crushed.

'Chloe, don't speak to me like that! Apologise right now!'

I sighed. Mum just wouldn't give me peace.

'Chloe, apology!' she shouted.

I gave her another eye roll and a sigh.

'You'd better change your mood, lady! Because I am not putting up with this. Go to your room!' she bellowed, her face, screwed up with anger.

'Mum just bugger off! Really can't be bothered with this. Will you just leave me alone!' I shouted at her and stood up, grabbed my jacket and stormed out the room.

'Chloe, you get back here right now, lady! I'm warning you. Chloe!' she shouted.

I walked out, slamming the door shut behind me, flouncing down the path. I swung the gate open as hard as I could, not caring if it came off the hook. I turned left and walked briskly down the steep road.

This was the worst mood ever. I had never felt this way before and didn't know how to control it. There was a temper on me and a fierce anger roared from deep inside. I had never felt so much hatred before. There was so much negativity circling around in me, and I didn't have time for anyone or anything. I needed to get away from it all. From everything.

Out of the hatred came tears. And I scoffed at myself, feeling stupid. Why was I crying? Was it the anger? Or the falling-out with Mum? I couldn't let anyone see me like this. Wiping away a tear, I took a deep breath and put on a brave face, walking away from what used to be my happy, peaceful home. I needed some space.

I heard cars and buses passing by on the main road down below. That was one of the things I loved about this area. You could have heard a pin drop it was that quiet.

I spent the morning walking around the streets, until I finally headed for the town centre. My watch showed it had just gone three minutes past twelve. People were out for lunch and the roads were busier than ever.

I spent some time going in and out of the shops, browsing. When I'd finally had enough, I headed into Greggs and picked up a chicken-salad sandwich and a bottle of Coke. I ordered a chocolate doughnut from the counter, paid for my food and sat on a bench across the road.

As I relaxed under the warm sun, savouring my favourite sandwich, I made a friend. A plump blue bar pigeon flew down in front of me, eyeing up my food. I tore off a small piece of brown bread and threw it to the bird, and it ran to peck at it. I leaned back and relaxed, watching the pigeon, thinking this was the first time I had felt peaceful in days. All the anger and frustration that had built up inside me earlier was now gone. I tore off another small piece of bread as more birds came flying down, and within five minutes a whole flock of pigeons were beside me, pecking away at the ground, looking for food. My sandwich was now finished, and I tore into my doughnut happily, washing it down with my drink.

The sun shone down on me and I closed my eyes. It felt good to sit here, content.

I turned to my left to see a little old lady and her husband sitting on a nearby bench and feeding the birds that had just been in front of me eating my food. They laughed happily as they watched the pigeons running around, picking up the crumbs. The woman looked over at me and we gave each other a friendly smile. I hoped as I got older that I would be as blissfully happy as the couple seemed to be. There was something about that moment that was rather special.

After finishing off my lunch, I put my rubbish in the bin and left, ready to face my mum. It was to be hoped she had calmed down by now.

Walking up the road, not looking forward to what lay ahead, I switched on my iPod and turned the music up. Listening to Westlife, I imagined what a perfect life my friends and I could have in the summer. We would take a road trip together after graduating. After all, we had talked about nothing else at school and it sounded like a once-in-a-lifetime opportunity. Nothing had been set in stone, but it made me a lot happier just thinking about it. The freedom of the open road, the excitement of the drive as we all sang along to the radio, laughing and having a great time. That was what life was all about really. Just having fun. The reality of my life right now didn't actually bear thinking about.

Deciding to take a different route, I cut through the village, taking a detour towards the woods where Mollie and I used to play together as kids. The woods surrounded a massive golf course, which we would always run through, ducking and laughing every time we passed a golfer.

I made a right turn and headed into a narrow, quiet street where there was an entrance to the woods. Passing a large metal fence along the way, I walked along the trail, viewing the course on both sides. There were no golfers around today. I guessed everyone was at work. Which made me feel a little lonely.

My walk had certainly given me time to think about what had happened this morning. And I was beginning to feel bad about my flying off the handle and walking out. I had left Mum on her own and she would be worried sick about me, scared something may happen. I was fine, but she wasn't to know that. The area was quiet, and no one ever hung around here. Not that I knew, anyway. I would be back home soon and would apologize for the upset that I had caused her. Mum and I never fought. It had taken something serious for me to get that angry.

A thought came to me suddenly. What if Mum went out looking for me and ended up getting into danger instead? I started to worry and picked up my pace, my breathing speeding up. What if Mum was the one to get into danger just because I had run out? What if she had put herself in jeopardy for me and something had happened to her? I was too afraid to phone her in case she was mad at me. I had to get myself home as quickly as I could. Anything could have happened in the time I had been away, and I would never forgive myself if it had.

What the hell had I done?

I walked through the trees as fast as my legs could carry me, passing small blackbirds chirping away. I'd come to my senses, realising it had been the worst idea to walk out of the house and leave Mum on her own and defenceless. After what we had been through the night before, I should have known better. Much better.

I was nearing the top of the hill that looked over my street, feeling anxious. That was never a good thing. Feeling that way would only lead to getting panicky, and therefore emotional. And I certainly didn't want that. I had to keep calm and keep my wits about me.

I passed a rope swing that my friends and I had made one summer. We played on it all the time, spending endless hours here. We would be out early in the morning and back home just in time for dinner. It was our favourite place to play as kids. Now it was there for others to play on and enjoy. I was surprised it had lasted this long without being destroyed. Still, it was good that kids had something fun to play with at the weekends and on holidays.

The last time I had passed this area I had come across a small deer. Never being so close to one before, I got over excited and walked towards it, astonished, taking a chance at an amazing opportunity that I would probably never get again. As I took a step forward though, it backed off and ran off through the trees, leaving me feeling thoroughly disappointed. What was I thinking? Did I actually expect the beautiful animal to wait for me to approach it, take its picture and stroke it? As silly as the idea sounded, it would have been simply wonderful.

I carried on homewards, shaking my head at the funny memory of my meeting a deer.

CHAPTER 14

I didn't hear the footsteps. I didn't know there was anyone behind me until it was too late. There was no sense of fear to make me run as fast as I could to a safe place, a place I was protected. And after that moment I knew I would never be safe again.

A hand suddenly reached out and grabbed hold of my right shoulder, making me jump and scream with fear. My heart pounded in my chest as I turned, with a gasp of utter shock, to find a messy-looking Dave behind me. His head was shaved and he wore a stained navy-blue jumper and combats with filthy steel-toe-capped boots.

Being here was one of the worst mistakes I could have made. I had found myself in a very dangerous position. He looked dodgy, like he was being hunted. His hands were tucked into his jacket pockets, his collar pulled up high and his eyes darting around.

'What the hell are you doing here?' I cried out.

'I'm trying to hide,' he said. 'I saw a police car come around, so I made a run for it. What are you doing here? Are you tracking me down?'

I gave a snort of disgust. 'As if I'd want to be anywhere near you after what you've put us through.'

There was no way I was going to tell him that Mum and I had had a fight. It would have been like he'd won.

'So, what are you doing out here then?'

'That's none of your business!' I yelled, frustrated. 'Why are you terrorising us, constantly banging on the door? Why can't you just leave us in peace and get on with your own life? You know if they catch you, you've had it. Just do us both a favour and hand yourself in and leave us alone! You wouldn't be wanted in the first place if you hadn't started all that carry-on. You've given me no choice here.'

I slipped my right hand into my pocket to retrieve my mobile, but he caught on quickly and I didn't stand a chance. With a firm grip around my arm, he pulled me towards him.

'Listen, lassie,' he growled. 'If you think I'm going to give up and hand myself in, you can think again. I'm not spending a minute in jail, so you'll just have to keep your big mouth shut.'

He poked me in the shoulder, and pain stabbed through my arm. I flinched, closing my eyes, rubbing the sore patch. His breath was vile against my face. A sob escaped my throat as his grip tightened around my arm.

'Dave, you're hurting me!' I cried.

He stood, oblivious, his eyes fixed on his grip. I didn't think it was possible for his hand to get any tighter. Every time I tried to get away, he would pull me back. I clearly wasn't going anywhere.

'Stop pulling away. I'm not letting you go, Chloe. Now you will just have to do as you're told and be a good girl, do you understand me?'

His head moved from side to side as he tried to figure me out. I felt like the prey caught by the predator. By now the pain was immense and I couldn't take anymore. I cried and pleaded with him to release me. He was a vicious monster, his face inches from mine.

'LET ME GO!' I screamed.

He stood back and laughed, taunting me, making me fight even more. I was trapped and couldn't move. I didn't understand why he was doing this or how he could be enjoying it. Why did he have my arm gripped so tightly and what did he plan to do with me?

I fought until I had no energy left. Giving up with a loud

sob, I threw myself down to the ground, making him move forward slightly, his hand still round my arm.

'Get up, Chloe. I'm not finished with you yet.'

I closed my eyes, feeling tired, and shook my head. I had nothing else to give. I was done.

He tugged at my arm. 'Chloe, get up!'

My eyes opened wide suddenly as he started to drag me away.

'Dave, where are we going?'

I tried to grab at the ground underneath me and I dug my nails into his skin, but that didn't faze him in the slightest. I used all my force and watched as the blood came dripping from his hand. He suddenly turned, his face vicious, and gripped a fistful of my hair. I screamed out in pain as he grasped my face and wrenched it towards his.

'You, lady, are getting on my nerves now. Why the hell can't you just do as you're told? You are coming with me and that's final!' he growled, shoving my head away.

I fell to the side slightly and he grabbed the back of my coat and dragged me from behind. He really had lost it now. There was no doubt that he would hurt me. Having no other solution to a way out, I gave in to his demands.

'Okay, okay, stop.'

The moment I said it, I regretted my decision. But it was either walk or be dragged along the ground, for however long he would lead me. My clothes would be ruined and my body would ache. The pain was something I couldn't endure.

He came to a halt and I stood up slowly, keeping my head down, for I couldn't look him in the eye. Then I followed him to wherever he was taking me.

As I watched the ground below my feet, I realised he was leading me away from the golf course. Like a little timid mouse, I looked up at the area around me. We were headed towards a field. I had never been out this far before and it scared me that I may not come back at all. What was his plan? I had questions, but I knew he would only get angry with me if I asked.

With his fist gripping my hood, I knew my chances of escaping were poor. I was just glad he hadn't taken my mobile from me yet, or I would really be screwed. I kept my hand around it in my pocket. There was no way I could take the chance and make a call. He would destroy it immediately and I would have nothing. I had to bide my time with him.

'Dave, where are we going? Please let me go.'

His silence was deafening as we continued out of the golf course and up through field after field, getting further away. Fear took over me and I had never felt so lost in my life. My heart pounded. My body trembled with fear. It was pointless trying to break free.

Anxiety over took me and I began to whimper. I wiped my hands over my eyes. My confidence had now left me.

'Dave, please, just stop. Talk to me. Tell me where we're going. Give me something at least.'

He stopped dead for a few seconds before turning around. Staring at me with a poker face, he spoke, his tone hollow and emotionless.

'I don't have a house of my own, Chloe, do you know that?'

Sarcasm ripped through my voice. 'Yeah, I know that. You're just determined to make our lives a misery. We just want peace.' I rolled my eyes at him and turned my head away.

'All I asked for was a roof over my head. Couldn't even give me that.'

He walked away, dragging me behind him. The grass started to thin and get really muddy. My shoes were sinking. It would have been pointless complaining. He wouldn't have cared.

A few moments later we arrived at another area of woodland. The atmosphere seemed to change, and I felt his hold on my hood loosen slightly. I knew we had arrived at something, but I didn't know what.

As he pulled me in deeper, I noticed something ahead that looked like a small den. Chunks of trees had been put together like a tepee, sturdy and well built. At the front of it there was the remains of a fire, burnt pieces of wood. This must have been where he had been sleeping all this time. In the woods. I'd thought he was with someone else. I was wrong.

'This is where you're living now?' I asked, shocked.

'Well, you didn't give me much choice, did you?'

He let me go, crouched down and disappeared inside the shelter. Seconds later, he reappeared, waving his hand. 'Come in.'

I was hesitant. I could have run, but he would probably have caught me and I didn't want to get hurt. The ground was too muddy and I wouldn't have got very far.

I crouched down and joined him inside. It was very small. Room for only one, really. I looked at the old, blue, tattered mattress that lay, unmade, on the grass, empty cans and wrappers beside it. He sat down on the end of the mattress, lifted a can, opened it and guzzled down a mouthful.

'This is where you live?' I asked again.

'Aye.'

'How long have you lived here?'

'Few months.'

I was gobsmacked. How could anyone live out here and survive?

'You've only brought this on yourself, Dave.'

He scoffed, shaking his head and rolling his eyes, and slurped his can of Tennent's. I hesitated, feeling awkward and unwelcome, my hands nestled in my pockets. Then I crouched down and got out of the shelter.

'Chloe, where're you going? Get back here.'
He staggered out of his den, shouting fiercely, and chased after me. My adrenaline kicked in as I looked behind and saw just how close he was. Looking ahead, trying to find the way out of the woods, I stumbled over a large tree trunk and slammed down onto my left shoulder. I screamed as the pain shot through my body. I lay, unable to move, for a moment.

When the pain eased enough, I pushed myself up from the ground and ran again, not wasting a second to turn back. I gripped my shoulder with the opposite hand and gritted my teeth. My heels dug into the mud around me, slowing me down. I knew there was no chance of escaping as I heard him grunting, catching up behind me.

He grabbed the hood of my jacket and pulled me back with full force. I took a sharp breath and stumbled, losing my balance. Everything around me blurred – the clear blue sky, the tall trees. I fell over, and my head cracked off something hard and cold. My eyelids closed and the darkness took over.

I didn't know for how long I'd been unconscious. I woke up in Dave's small wooden tepee den, and the stench of alcohol was sickening. The back of my head throbbed. I opened my eyes, trying to adjust my hazy vision, only to realise I was on my front, the side of my head almost plastered to the sticky, muddy ground. I couldn't see properly. I couldn't move my arms and legs to stand up. Lifting my head slightly and tilting it to the side, it dawned on me: I had been bound and gagged. Dave had tied me up.

Panicking, I let out a muffled scream for help. It was useless. I was face down on the ground and my wrists were tied tightly behind my back. Sharp pains soared up and down my arms. The ground was cold, hard and uncomfortable. My breathing hitched and I feared for my life.

I looked around, trying to move and loosen my arms. My hair was a matted mess and had become plastered all over my face. Rubbing my head against the ground to move my hair was useless. Nothing would get me out of here. I was working myself into a frenzied state, wondering how the hell I was going to escape, when I looked up and saw him. I froze.

He was slumped on the filthy mattress with a can in his hand, looking like something out of The Evil Dead. Was it possible that he looked even worse now than when I'd first seen him today? My stomach heaved from the smell of his rank bare feet beside my face. I tried to move my head away.

This is it, I thought. He's going to kill me.

'I wouldn't bother trying to break free. You're not going anywhere, lass.'

He stared at me, not moving an inch. His face was saggy and his eyelids drooped. He looked like he hadn't slept for days. Beneath the dirt, his pale face looked thinner. It wasn't surprising, given the way he was living now. No decent meal to cook. Surviving on cheap snacks and alcohol wouldn't get him very far. Dave had set the bar lower for himself than ever before and he had no one to blame but himself. He continued to stare at me as I tried to wriggle free.

I lay still, having used up the last of my energy, and listened carefully to his rough, shallow breathing. He looked like he was in a trance. He looked like an ogre, I thought. A mean, malicious, nasty monster who would do anything to get what he wanted anyway he could.

I moaned and waited for a reaction from him, but nothing. I continued until he finally gave me a swift kick in the face. I squealed out, crying from the agonising pain.

That was a warning for me. Giving up – for now – I laid my head down on the ground and sobbed quietly.

Then he made a move that startled me, making me jump with fear: he leaned forward suddenly, then back again. I frowned, unsure of his intentions, and I clenched my hands into fists, terrified. He continued on, rocking back and forth constantly. Then he opened his mouth, mumbling words I didn't recognise. He became louder and louder, until it dawned on me what he was saying. He was raving and calling out my mum.

'It's all her fault. It's all her fault. Karen. She took him away. She took him away from me. He was supposed to stay wi' me. He's gone. All her fault…'

My eyes widened in shock at what he had just said. He blamed Mum for Dad's death. He'd said it was her fault. This was his revenge. He had me bound and gagged and he sure wasn't going to let me go anytime soon.

I closed my eyes and began to sob as loudly as I could with the gag in my mouth, wriggling around. I let the tears flow, scrunching my face up, praying that someone would come and find me before it was too late.

'Shut it,' he mumbled.

My loud sobbing had brought him out of his daze. I couldn't just turn off the waterworks; it wasn't possible. This was my life on the line. I had really messed up, and there was no one to blame but myself. I was surprised he hadn't lost it with me, the amount of crying I'd done. My eyes nipped and the tears stung my cheeks. There wasn't much else I could do except pray quietly for help.

Once the tears had finally stopped, I listened for any noises outside, giving myself a distraction. Calm was the one thing I needed right now. That and my freedom. Some birds tweeted nearby and that relaxed me a little. But that was it. No other noises came from these woods. It was too quiet. We were so far from home that no one could possibly hear anything.

As time passed by, I slipped in and out of consciousness. I was worried that the blow to my head earlier had given me a concussion. If I had no memory loss, I would need to keep a mental note of my actions.

At one point when I woke up again, I looked up to see Dave with some sort of shiny metal thing in his hand. Watching him intently, curious about his actions, it dawned on me that the shiny metal thing he was holding was a large kitchen knife. Turning it slowly around in his hand, he gently grazed his fingers up and down the teeth of the blade with a daring look in his eyes. The fact that this man wasn't in his right state of mind and could possibly kill me in an instant was traumatising.

I begged and pleaded, hoping to somehow get him to rethink his actions. But the more I did, the more he seemed to enjoy watching me suffer. It was exhausting.

Hours passed by. My throat was raw from crying and I was slowly giving up the fight. I made many attempts to slacken the rope around my wrists, until it became too achingly tiring. From that moment I didn't think I would ever get away from the monster in front of me.

It was obvious he was taking pleasure in watching me plead for my life, like the monster in a horror movie who watches his victim scream in terror right before he chops them up. There was a self-satisfied smirk on his face as he twirled the blade in his hands.

Then, finally, he'd had enough. He stood up, leaned over me quickly and placed the sharp blade right under my throat. I froze, petrified, not moving a muscle as I feared the edge would cut through my skin.

'Are you going to shut the hell up or am I going to have to slit your throat?' he snarled.

I whined, a timid and terrified plea of agreement that I would do as I was told. After this there would be no sound out of me again. I knew just how far he would go to get the result he was looking for, and Dave never, ever failed.

Satisfied he had the answer he wanted, Dave leaned back and I felt the sharp blade leave my skin. I let out a deep sigh of relief. I was free to breathe again. Backing off, he took the knife away, and I planted my face down on the ground, feeling totally and utterly defeated.

Lying on the ground for so long gave me time to think. This was the most irresponsible thing I had ever done. I hadn't really been in the greatest frame of mind when I walked out, but still, it had been a completely foolish and idiotic thing to do, and now I was full of nothing but regret and sorrow because I was paying the price. I had been tied up and threatened by an unbalanced and disturbed man, and I really didn't know whether I was going to make it out of this alive. The fact that I hadn't arrived home yet must have been seriously worrying Mum. If I knew her, she would contact the police, and hopefully they would have someone out looking for me. Dave needed serious help.

The incoherent mumbling and raving began again. He swayed back and forth, repeating the same thing over and over. I was desperate for someone to arrive and save me. I just wanted to be set free. It was difficult to handle being trapped and unable to protect myself. I needed to escape.

I wriggled towards the entrance, but he just stood up and dragged me back to the spot where I had been. I tried again and again, but he would just pull me back. I gave it everything I had, not giving up. I would keep going and going until I had no more strength left. Someone was bound to turn up eventually to rescue me. Surely. This was utter torture.

It required a lot of energy to keep moving, pushing my body to the limit. As if I wasn't in enough pain as it was – putting even more pressure on myself was torture. I somehow managed to find the strength to carry on, until all the energy left my body. I closed my eyes and drifted in and out of consciousness, not knowing what time it was or what was happening to me anymore, while Dave sat watching over me, keeping me trapped in the hell that was his den.

CHAPTER 15

I woke later on in the dark to dull sounds outside. Feeling hazy, I blinked my eyes continuously, trying to see properly. I saw several white flashes around the front of the den and heard distant voices outside. I opened my eyes in an instant, realising the voices and flashes were real. I was being rescued. I began to moan loudly, trying to wriggle my body free, pleading for help.

Suddenly, a man popped his head into the den and looked around. He locked his eyes on Dave just as Dave lifted his head and jumped with a start, his eyes widening with shock as he realised he had been caught.

'I've got her. She's in here!' the man shouted. I was startled moments later when a loud ripping noise came from above. Mum must have got a search party out looking for me. I sighed with relief as I realised people were tearing the den apart.

Voices called from outside and the lights shifted. I turned my head away and scrunched up my face as it all became intolerable. Piece by piece, they tore away the branches, and I slowly started making out bodies.

'I'll get you out now, love,' an officer called to me. I looked over at Dave in fear as he stood up and growled, clenching his fists, and then screamed and made a run for it. He didn't last a second before officers grabbed him and he fell over with a thud. He had been caught.

I moaned constantly, pleading for someone to come and release me. The gag had irritated my skin and made my face ache, and I was in an incredible amount of pain. I wondered how much longer I would be left to suffer in complete agony. It didn't take long before a female paramedic arrived, kneeling down beside me.

'Hi, my name is Jennifer,' she said softly. 'I'm with the ambulance crew that's here to help you. I'm just going to take the gag out of your mouth, okay?'

I nodded and she gently loosened the material and cut it away with the small blade she carried with her. I panted, licking my chapped lips.

'Water,' I whispered. 'I need water.'

'Can I get some water here, please?' she called to the others.

Someone handed her a bottle and she gently put it up to my mouth. I took a small sip, relishing the cool liquid running down my dry, achy throat. After taking another few drinks, I expressed my gratitude and she began to untie my arms and legs.

I took to Jennifer immediately. She was kind and friendly and made me feel secure and comfortable. I had suffered nothing but utter misery in the several hours with Dave, and it gave me satisfaction to know that he had been taken away and was hopefully gone for good now.

My whole body seemed to sag as the rope was loosened and placed into a forensics bag for evidence. I stood up slowly, rubbing my arms, relieved to feel a sense of freedom at last. For the hours that I had been tortured and held captive I'd feared it would never end.

Jennifer carefully guided me out of what was left of the den, and I held on to her for support. I walked slowly, taking it one step at a time, until we were at a clear and safe distance and she could examine me. Thick, dark clouds were moving in; the air suddenly took a turn for the worst, and a shiver went through my body. I stood, wrapping my arms around myself, feeling cold. There were police officers everywhere.

As Jennifer did her checks, I could hear the racket the officers were making as they destroyed the home that Dave had built. I turned around slightly to watch them do their work, feeling impassive. I had come out alive and would hopefully find solace after this difficult and disturbing time of torture.

As exhausted as I was, Jennifer assured me that I had no concussion after my fall, just a cut on the head, but she said they would take me to the hospital to keep an eye on me. As we walked out of the woods in the darkness, she encouraged me to keep talking, and I explained what had happened, the events leading up to the kidnapping and how we'd both ended up here. She was sympathetic, nodding along, and kept me calm the whole while, ensuring me that I would be safe now and that he was gone. As grateful as I was, there was an overwhelming tiredness that I couldn't seem to shake off. My eyelids drooped and I squeezed my eyes shut, trying to keep awake, but really all I wanted to do was sleep.

We went across fields and out through the woods by the golf course, and I suddenly felt the road under my feet. I sighed, grateful to be walking on the asphalt once again. As much as I used to love those woods, it would be a really long time before I set foot in them again. Maybe never.

The ambulance was waiting at the kerb for us. Jennifer held my arm as I climbed into it steadily and sat up on the stretcher ready to be taken to hospital.

'Thank you,' I whispered, before sobbing my heart out. I felt liberated.

My rescue would be life-altering in many ways. I couldn't have been more grateful to my saviours for turning up that night and saving my life the way they did. But the trauma that I had been put through would have a tremendous effect on me, so much so that in the coming days I wouldn't be able to face seeing or speaking to anyone. My self-esteem had been broken and, feeling low, I would be unsure how to go on each day. Dave had won in that sense. Yeah, sure he could have killed me, but he didn't. He just held me captive for hours, making me believe I would never see another day. Deep down somehow, I think he knew that he was going to get caught and I would be rescued.

I played it over and over in my head, reliving the worst hours of my life, trying to figure out what his plan was and why he'd made me a prisoner. I vividly remember he was raving. That the kidnapping was simply to punish Mum. As if she was to blame really. In his eyes, it was all her fault, and it looked like he would do anything in his power to make her suffer. Even if that meant kidnapping her daughter.

My head pounded. Every bone in my body ached for a warm, soft mattress to sink into; I was desperate for a peaceful night's sleep. The trolley I sat on was barely comfortable, but the paramedics made me feel safe and protected from the stresses and strains that I had been put though.

The drive to the hospital was steady. This late at night the town was quiet, the street lights reflecting off dark roads. I was grateful the day was coming to an end. I would simply deal with everything in the morning once I'd got a decent night's sleep. Unless I tossed and turned in the small hours feeling restless; then I would be exhausted the next day. There was nothing worse than a sleepless night.

At the hospital I was helped into a wheelchair and taken to the third floor. Mum was already waiting for me in a corridor, sitting on a chair to the left outside an empty room, her head bowed and a tissue in her hand. The expression on her face was pained. Guilt overcame me and tears threatened to flow. I had caused her to feel the way she was now. It was all my fault. I realised that I had put her through misery and suffering. I had been a fool.

Wherever Mum went, she was always smartly dressed. Even for a trip to the hospital, she'd made herself look presentable: she wore black trousers, heeled shoes and a buttoned-up overcoat, and her auburn hair was brushed tidily around her shoulders. But her eyes were all blotchy and red. That, right there, made me feel absolutely dreadful.

My heart went out to her. I had let her down when she needed me the most and I felt truly ashamed. She looked up in my direction and let out a gasp, her eyes wide.

'Chloe! Oh, thank goodness!' she cried. 'I've been worried sick about you. I didn't know where you'd gone. I have been out of my mind!'

I stood up from the wheelchair and traipsed over to her. My arms suddenly feeling like ton-weights, too heavy to move. Holding me at arm's length for a moment, she gazed at me, confused.

'Your face is all bruised.'

I gave a gentle nod, looking away. She took me in her arms and I clenched my teeth, moaning, as pain shot through my upper body. She jumped back, looking worried.

'What's wrong?'

I unzipped my jacket and took my arms out the sleeves to show her the rope injuries on my wrists and the multiple bruises all over. The red marks cut deep and were too painful to touch.

'What did he do to you?!' she gasped in shock. 'My poor girl.'

I felt anything but a poor victim. If I hadn't left the house then none of this would have happened. She tilted my chin up slightly, enquiring about the cut under there too.

'Oh, he threatened to slit my throat.'

Her face was a picture as she slowly took in the damage that had been done to me. I looked at my black parka and registered that it was all ripped. I loved that jacket. Mum had got it for me Christmas just last year. Wouldn't be wearing it any longer, though.

I shuffled into the room – painted a pale pink – and lay on the hospital bed. The doctors and nurses fussed over me and gave Mum a thorough summary of my injuries. They said they would keep her up to date on my progress and make sure I got back to complete health as soon as possible.

A nurse came in and greeted us both. She spoke to Mum as she put a clipboard at the foot of the bed. I noticed it only briefly and turned my head away without giving her a smile. I felt drained, empty, and had no confidence left in myself at all. My whole world had been turned upside down and the security I had was shattered, leaving me absolutely gutted and detached from everything and everyone.

My body felt numb. I sat on the edge of the bed while the nurse spoke to me, but I wasn't listening. She walked over and reached down to a buzzer, which I realised was an alarm for the patients in case of emergencies. Mum took my hand and looked at the nurse, then at me curiously, watching to see if I was taking anything in. I blinked, glancing up at her briefly, before turning away and looking out the window into the darkness outside.

Leaving a gown down at the bottom of the bed for me, the nurse then left and closed the door behind her. I slid over to the middle of the mattress and crossed my legs.

'So, I take it you phoned the police when I left then?'

Mum gave a small nod, running her hand down my hair. 'Yes, I did. I knew you would be in danger and I told them it was an emergency. I watched from the living room window as the police cars came speeding along the road. It didn't take long for them to start their hunt.'

'I'm sorry, Mum. Sorry I've put us both through this.'

She let out a sigh. 'All I care about now is that you're here with me, safe. I'm never letting you out of my sight again.'

I closed my eyes, letting a tear roll down my cheek. I would never forgive myself for what I'd done.

CHAPTER 16

When I woke up the next morning my head was fuzzy from the night before. Blinking, I turned and looked around the room. It was empty, no Mum here to wake up to. Loneliness crept in and I pulled the covers right up over my head, not sure if I would be able to cope with today. I knew what it would bring: nothing but doctors doing their check-ups and police in to question me. I would have to make myself presentable in order to deal with whatever came my way. There was simply no other option.

Mum waltzed into the room a minute later with a plastic cup in her hand – tea, I assumed. Blowing on the top, she looked over and saw I was awake.

'Morning, sweetheart. How did you sleep?'

'Eugh,' I grunted. Honestly, it hadn't been too bad. I had managed to get my eight hours, despite being in a busy hospital. It was the thought of waking up somewhere that wasn't my own room that got to me.

'That bad, huh?'

'No,' I moaned. 'I just want to go home.'

She sat on the edge of the bed beside me, putting her hand on the side of my face and giving me a slight smile.

'I know you do, honey, but you had a bad day yesterday and the doctors just want to keep an eye on you to make sure you're alright. Listen, I went home and picked you up a change of clothes and other things you'll need. I know it'll make you feel better.'

I smiled at her as my spirits lifted slightly. My mum really was the best, and I didn't know what I would have done without her. And I knew that sometimes I didn't deserve her, but she stuck with me throughout.

I forced myself out of the bed, picked up my bag of

personal belongings and walked into the bathroom for a wash. Fifteen minutes later, I was feeling fresh. Mum had brought me my own soap and towel, which she knew would make me feel a lot better, and I'd changed my clothes. After brushing my hair, I tied it back into a ponytail and I sat on a chair with my book, waiting for the inevitable.

It had been so quiet in the room that I jumped at a knock at the door later that morning. Mum answered it. A tall, slim man with a briefcase entered, looking ever so intimidating, followed by a woman with bobbed black hair and a black suit. I looked at them both, feeling slightly startled, wondering what they were doing coming to see me. Then I realised they must be doctors.

'Hello there. I'm guessing you must be Chloe, yes?' Mr Brown Suit asked with a smile on his face.

I looked up at him nervously and nodded.

He came to stand at the foot of the bed. 'I'm Doctor Charles Demuir and this is Emily Bateson.' He waved his hand in the air. 'I'm a psychologist, and Emily is a counsellor. We're going to be looking into your incident for the next few weeks and trying to help you recover. Can I ask how you are feeling this morning?'

I felt my throat suddenly close up and my face go red as everyone looked in my direction for an answer. I let out a low, mumbled, 'Okay.'

Dr Demuir pulled two chairs over and he and the counsellor sat across from us as he opened his briefcase. I didn't want them in my room. Not while Mum was here with me anyway. I wanted it to be just the two of us.

The doctor took out a pen and booklet to write down notes and began asking me questions – about my feelings, whether I understood why I was here, whether I scared or feeling helpless. I sat there thinking as they waited patiently for answers, watching me intently. How did I feel? The answer was simple: empty and unhappy. Honestly, I just wanted to hide away from the world. I had been hurt really badly. Nobody could possibly understand how I felt at this moment in time. Nobody could heal my soul. It was shattered. I needed a miracle.

The doctor explained a lot to me, telling me it was normal to feel this way after what I'd been through and that if I worked on getting better, I would feel happy again. We spoke about different kinds of strategies that could work, simple things like breathing and relaxation. He told me that my adrenal glands had set off my adrenaline and that had changed the way I was feeling. I sat on the edge of my seat, intrigued to learn more.

Sitting forward with his elbows on his knees, Dr Demuir told me I didn't have to rush into anything straight away, that I could be patient and take as much time as I needed. They would be there, he said, if I ever wanted to talk. He promised that the offer of counselling sessions was the best thing for me, and it would really help me to find a way out.

For a moment I thought this was a losing battle and I would never get to see the light at the end of the tunnel. But then I thought, what if I could? What if this feeling inside me went away, with the help of these doctors, and I was actually able to feel happy again? Was that even possible? The thought alone lifted my spirits just the slightest bit. There was only one way to find out if this would work like they promised it would. As low as I felt, I knew something had to be done.

He opened his briefcase again and gave me a leaflet containing information about the session that was on offer which I read thoroughly. This would be a really hard fight. But I had to prepare myself to take on anything and find the light at the end of the tunnel. I truly hated what had happened. It was like my soul had been ripped out and Dave had taken the best of me. I would have to give it everything I had just to get myself back and feel normal again, so I could move on with my life.

After I had agreed, he wrote some notes in his booklet, before letting Emily take over. Emily was nice, warm and caring. Every word she said I took in, and she made me think I could put my trust in her and overcome the demons that had begun to haunt me. She promised me I would get through this with her help, and that they would both be along every week until I had made a full recovery. I could only nod, still feeling a bit too fragile to start having any kind of conversation. As nice as they both seemed, I knew it would take a while for me to fully open up and let them in. It would happen at some point, though.

Mum stood up and thanked them for their time and help. She saw them out and closed the door, and then sat beside me on the bed and put her arm around me for comfort.

'Why did he have to do this to me, Mum?' I cried out in despair. 'Why?!'

It was all she could do not to burst into tears as well.

I had been sitting on the same spot in the chair for hours, unable to move, with my arms wrapped around my legs. The horrors of the day before flashed back to haunt me. The knife at my throat, his vile breath in my face. I shut my eyes and winced, turning my head and gritting my teeth. It would take a long time for me to heal from my ordeal.

Looking out the window, I watched cars coming in and out of the car park down below and the people walking in and out of the building, parents with their newborns in car seats leaving the maternity ward. I could watch them all day and just block everything out of my mind.

Shortly after lunchtime, a doctor led two male officers in to question me about the kidnapping. Mum walked to my side and took my hand for support. I was badly shaken, upset, and I certainly didn't want to keep talking about it. But I had no choice in the matter when it came to the police. They were only here to help me and to do their job. I took a deep breath and answered every question as best I could. I told them everything before breaking down again.

They left, after thanking me for my time and the information, and I lay on the bed, closed my eyes and wept. Mum was beginning to feel distressed as well, and she paced the floor anxiously, running her hands through her hair and over her face again and again. It was then that I knew this had taken a big toll on her too. How could I possibly work on getting myself better and moving forwards? Only Dr Demuir and Emily could help me with this. The sooner I recovered and got back to my normal self, the better. This was awful.

Mum tried her best to make me feel happier by bringing me my favourite drinks and snacks from the cafe that day. She knew how much I loved my food. But even a chicken-salad sandwich wouldn't suffice. She must have known then just how low I really was, because nothing had ever put me off my food before. I turned my head away from the food, knowing I wouldn't be able to keep it down.

I knew that I'd been selfish when I'd left the house. I hadn't been there for Mum and we were supposed to be a team and stick together. Had I blown my chances with her this time? Would she ever forgive me? Only time would tell.

I dozed off in the late afternoon. What with not being able to eat and my energy levels being at an all-time low, I slept for a good three hours. It probably had a lot to do with the medication that they had given me too. I was glad to get the rest. Knowing I was in a safe building took the stress away, and the person I needed the most was by my side.

I received a surprise when Jason popped in to see us both. Mum had texted him all the details while she was with me and he had said he was worried about me.

'What trouble have you been getting yourself into now, Chloe?' he joked, taking a seat beside Mum.

I rolled my eyes, shaking my head, knowing he was only having a laugh. Jason always liked to keep the atmosphere happy whenever he was around. The man was a serious smooth-talker and could make my mum do anything using just the smooth tone of his voice. That was how much of an influence he had on her. He was a great guy, though. As much as I hated to say it or even think it, he was good for my mum in a way that no one else could be. He was protective, loyal, faithful and above all honest. And he seemed to really care about me as well. Mum and I were a package deal, and you could hardly take one without the other.

She had once told me I was the only child she had ever wanted; she was content to have only one daughter. The day I was born she was absolutely thrilled. The love was unconditional. So, the thought of losing me at any point in her life was too much to cope with. Holding my hand in hers, she promised me we would be alright, and Dave would never come near us again.

There would always be fear and paranoia caused by the trauma that I had gone through. But hopefully, with the help of the psychologist and the counsellor, I would get past it and learn how to move on. I was adamant that I would be happy again, no matter what it took.

Every so often, though, the visions would come back to haunt me. His horrible face inches from mine, the knife to my throat, being kept prisoner. They made me clam up and cringe. Even though he was behind bars, he would always be in my head, tormenting me.

Just after dinnertime one of the doctors came in to see me and announced that I was good to go home. I was both relieved and anxious at the same time to be going back to the place where Dave had kicked off and terrorised us.

'Don't look so worried!' Mum declared. 'You'll be safe at home. He's behind bars and won't hurt you again.'

I guessed it was easy for her to say that. She hadn't been through what I had. Or maybe she was merely trying to make me feel a little calmer. I let it go, keeping quiet and trusting her judgement.

The drive home in Jason's Audi was quiet but pleasant. I leaned against the leather headrest, enjoying the cool air that circulated throughout. The weather had taken a turn for the worst: dark grey clouds formed up above and the rain poured down, splatting off the roof and dripping down the glass. I was grateful that I didn't have to be out in that.

We arrived home and I headed for my room. I got into my unmade bed, throwing the duvet over my head to block the whole world out, wishing the ground would just swallow me whole. I lay there until I couldn't face it anymore. There was nothing but loneliness, and I couldn't lie still, constantly tossing and turning.

Giving up, I went down to sit in the living room with Mum for company, hoping it would make me feel better. But there was barely any difference. My agitation – constant twitchiness and darting my head towards the window – caused a loud sigh from Mum.

'Chloe honey, you need to try to relax. There's no one outside. We're safe here. All the windows and doors are locked.'

Deep down I knew it was just my paranoia eating away at me. But that didn't stop me feeling apprehensive. Mum switched on the TV and turned it to an African wildlife programme, thinking it would fascinate me. I was a huge wildlife fan.

'Oh Chloe, look!' Mum called, sounding excited, as she watched an antelope trying to escape from the cheetah chasing it.

Normally, this sort of scene would amaze me and I'd be glued to the screen without moving. But today I wasn't interested. It felt like I had hit rock bottom and it would be a long way to reach the top.

CHAPTER 17

As the days rolled by, I could feel the medication starting to take effect. The tension that had taken hold of me slowly faded away as the beta blockers did their work. They had been prescribed for what the doctor had diagnosed as anxiety due to the suffering that had been caused by Dave. I felt calmer, more relaxed and able to think more clearly. I felt like the weight was lifting off my shoulders. It was a relief.

The police had been in contact to give us an update on the investigation into Dave. We had no interest in him in the slightest, but as we were his only next of kin, we were to be informed of the proceedings. When they caught him at the den as he tried to escape, he was searched and arrested by the police, then jailed without bail and held in custody for forty-eight hours. We needed to be at the court to give evidence against him. They would be keeping him in remand until he appeared there for all the charges against him. Dave in prison was the best thing we had heard in a long time. We were both relieved to hear such good news. Maybe, just maybe, we would be able to relax.

'One thing I do want,' Mum fired down the phone at the officer who had called her, 'is a restraining order against him, so when he eventually gets out, he'll never be allowed to come near our home again.'

She looked beat when she ended the call. She sat on the couch and I brought her in a cup of tea. I sat with her and she explained the action that would be carried out.

'Oh Chloe, I thought he would never finish. The officer gave me a long, drawn-out speech about how it would have to go through the courts first. But if they did agree on it, it would be a Section 5 Protection from Harassment Act.'

She waved her hand around in the air as she gave me every detail. 'Because this offence he's committed is so bad, he said that it would be highly likely they could make it happen.' She rubbed her hand over her face. 'I guess that will be another weight off our shoulders.'

'I just want to put him out of my mind and life for good,' I replied. 'Maybe this will be the closure I really need so I can move on again.'

'Yeah, hopefully that will be the case and we can finally get back to normal.'

More than anything we needed calm and peace at home. Happiness was what I truly wanted; without that, life looked pretty bleak.

The days went by slowly. I felt trapped in the house, as I couldn't leave. I didn't like the idea of being stuck in the one place without having my freedom to do whatever I wanted, but my medication kept me calm.

As I sat on the couch one afternoon watching TV, I called Mollie from my mobile.

'So, I'm on the mend. It's a slow recovery, but I'll get there, hopefully.'

She gave a small laugh. 'What are you talking about?'

I gasped, realising she had no idea what I was referring to. She didn't know what had happened to me. I'd never had the chance to tell her. What was I going to say? That I had been kidnapped, attacked and almost killed by my uncle, but I was on the mend and making a good recovery? I sat there racking my brain for something to say.

'I, uh, I've been in a slight accident and I won't be coming to school for another few days.' I pursed my lips.

'What kind of accident? Are you okay?'

'Yeah, kind of. I don't really want to talk about it over the phone. Could you just come around and see for yourself?'

'Yeah, anything you want. I've really missed you,

Chlo. I've been dead lonely here without you.'

'I know.' I smiled. 'Me too.'

'I'll be there in half an hour, okay?'

I freshened up and made myself presentable. But when she arrived and I opened the door, she looked like she had just seen a ghost.

'WHAT HAPPENED TO YOU?' Mollie stood on my doorstep and took my face in her hands.

I'd had just under half an hour before she arrived to think up a story to tell her about my 'accident'.

1. Falling down the stairs = No. That wouldn't work. That would leave me dead, with a brain injury or crippled for life.

2. Beaten up out in the streets = Definitely not. She would want to know who the culprits were, and she would be out hunting night and day until she found them. That was how much she loved me; she would do anything for me.

This was proving difficult. I couldn't begin to think of anything else to explain what had caused these injuries, and I really didn't want to lie to her either. I'd never told a lie in my life. Which left me with:

3. She had to know what had really happened. Would she think any less of my family anyway? I didn't think she'd be my best friend if she did.

I sat her on the couch and, with total honesty, and told her the truth. She was in tears as she took in everything I said, and she hugged me tightly. I flung my arms around her and closed my eyes, feeling relief. There's an old saying: Honesty's the best policy. No matter what happens in life, no matter what you do, people will always appreciate an honest answer. Even if they don't like the answer you're giving them.

We sat and talked for a good while, and she told me about our teachers, the work and our classmates. Everyone seemed to be missing me and wondering where I had got to. I told Mollie to catch everyone up and say that I would be back soon.

She also told me about a dream she'd had the night before that made my skin crawl. She was attacked by a load of killer albino spiders with red eyes and massive teeth. They came in through her open bedroom window and they chased her out of the house and down the road.

'Honestly, Chlo, it seemed so real! It was terrifying. They were about four feet tall and horrible.'

'You'll be glad that was just a dream then, eh?'

'What do you mean? Are those things actually real?' she asked, eyes wide in shock.

'Of course they are. I mean, they're not four foot tall with teeth, but they are very real. Have you never seen an albino spider before?'

'Ew, no! Gross.'

I laughed at her, lifting my Irn-Bru from the coffee table. Honestly, she was so funny sometimes.

Mum insisted that Mollie stay for her speciality, homemade mac and cheese. It was my favourite dish, and my best friend was there to enjoy it with me. We had a good catch-up. Mollie put me at ease a bit more and I began to feel happier. I loved listening to her stories, and when she got excited about something her voice would go up really high and she would let out a tiny high-pitched squeal. It was pretty amusing. It was a special night of bonding between us. Our friendship was tight.

As we sat around the table and ate, Mum asked Mollie about school, exams and her career choice. She gave Mollie a lecture about going to college, and Mollie responded that she would give it a try.

'You'll love it. That's where Jack and I met,' Mum smiled away, looking proud.

I put my head down as I relived some sad memories.

What I would have given to have Dad back sitting at this table. I still missed him loads.

Shortly after dinner, Mollie headed out down the path and waved goodbye as she shut the gate over. I closed the door, wiping away a tear, feeling slightly emotional. After putting one of my favourite CDs into the stereo, I lay down on the couch, closed my eyes and let Faith Hill take me away.

CHAPTER 18

The next morning I had a visit from Dr Demuir and Emily. They spent nearly an hour with me, going over my strategies and how to overcome things. As time passed, I began to open up to them. The fact that I'd plucked up the courage to speak to people was recognised and rewarded, as the last time they'd seen me I had been withdrawn. Talking to them about my feelings and opening up was a step in the right direction.

Learning how to get my confidence back was an issue we discussed as well. There was a fear of going outside that I had to overcome. I knew it was out of my comfort zone, but I had to try. At that moment I was afraid of the battle. But it was just a case of taking small steps and trying my best.

I knew Dave was safely behind bars where he couldn't get anywhere near us, but I still had the fear and I didn't like it. This had been a life lesson, and I made a promise to myself that I would never do anything like it again. It had been the most terrifying ordeal of my life, and I was glad to be alive, safe and well. The plan was to move on and keep my mind busy with other things, like graduating with my best friend. Honestly, I couldn't wait.

After nearly two weeks spent at home recuperating, I finally got the courage to go back to school. Mum assured me it would be fine, but I was nervous. There were plans to make regarding my future and what direction I was heading in. A lot of important choices were to be made.

When I finally arrived at school, relief flooded through me. Everyone I knew was as friendly as ever. I received a lot of smiles and hellos from certain classmates and even a couple of high-fives too. That really put a smile on my face. There were a lot of great people at this school who were so friendly and nice. It just made the world a better place.

Although everyone tried to talk to me that morning, and there were giggles and whispers at the back of the class, I kept my head down and got as much work completed as possible. I had worked really hard this past year to the best of my ability, as I knew how important getting a job was.

The time that the doctors had spent with me and the work they had done was amazing. I was beginning to see the change in myself. It was a great transformation.

Throughout the classes, there were discussions regarding future plans, college and employment. It was an exciting time, but I was glad to be leaving and going on to something new all the same.

Those five years at school had been pretty enjoyable and we'd had so much fun going on different class outings and bus trips. I had been lucky to make such good friends and we would certainly keep in touch. One of the girls even mentioned hiring out a campervan for us.

'It would be, like, so awesome,' she boasted, flicking her hair through the air and fluttering her eyelashes at one of the boys who sat next to her. 'My dad said there's a place called Clachtoll, and it's supposed to be unreal. White sandy beaches. We could light a fire and have a good laugh. You all just need to give me your numbers!'

Mollie and I secretly glanced at each other, and I pursed my lips. Honestly. As innocent as Shelly was, she was a bit of a drama queen. Still, it sounded fun.

Leaving school was like the end of an era. Everything was finishing up and people were moving onwards. Even Mum was going back to work again. She had contacted her boss, Sue, who had agreed that she could start back as soon as she was ready and said that her desk had always been waiting for her. Mum was relieved.

The idea of working in a new place was exciting and learning something new that I could possibly teach others one day sounded like a great opportunity. But what I really wanted to do was work in an office. I would need to speak to Mum and see if her boss could possibly give me a job; they could train me up as an office junior. That thought made me smile.

'These bills aren't going to pay themselves, Chloe.'
I had just walked in the front door on my final day of school. After flinging my bag over the bannister, I joined Mum, who was on the couch reading the Daily Express. She had been dropping hints here and there over the past couple of days, making sure I was picking up on them. She wanted to have a chat with me about my future.

This was where I was to be extremely responsible. As Mum was going back to her full-time job the following week, I had to make sure she wasn't the only one getting the shopping in and helping with the bills and chores. It would be a new experience for me. As long as I was out earning money, that was all that mattered really.

The peace and quiet that surrounded us was wonderful. Jason had been over a few times, making sure we were okay. Mum had given up arguing with him about it. The closeness they had was growing, and I was beginning to get suspicious. I hoped nothing would come from this so soon. She had a right to be happy, but there was a time and a place.

When the weekend arrived, Mum booked a table for them at the local Chinese, after which they planned to go to a bar in town for a drink. She gave me a list of numbers, and if anything was wrong or something happened, I was to ring immediately. But this was their Friday night together. A Chinese and my DVDs would keep me happy and entertained all night. I loved my movies.

With my legs tucked under me on the couch and my thumb on the play button, I couldn't have been more annoyed as the phone rang. I closed my eyes, giving a loud sigh. It really couldn't have come at a worst time. Thinking it could be Mum calling to tell me something, I picked up the receiver and answered with a less-than-happy tone.

'Chloe, is that you, hen?'

I froze on the spot, recognising the voice that spoke to me on the other end. My body shook and the fear that had slowly disappeared came back to me all over again. The fact that he had the cheek and the nerve to phone this house after all he had put this family through! If I hung up, though, he could call back again.

'What do you want, Dave?'

'Is your mum there?'

He couldn't know she was out with Jason. He would go ballistic and think she had betrayed my dad and moved on. It wasn't like that, though. Jason was a friend and had been since the day my dad died. He was there for my mum and had got her through the worst part of her life. She was grateful to him.

'No,' I answered, my voice as steady as I could keep it. Inside, I wanted to scream at him and tell him to stay out of our lives for good. But I wouldn't give him the satisfaction. I wondered just how he had the nerve to call here and think everything was okay.

'I really need to speak to her the now. It's urgent.'

I took a deep breath, staying as calm as possible, and spoke gently, trying to get him off the line quickly.

'Like I said, Mum's not in, and she won't be back till later.'

'Well, where she is then?'

'She's out with a friend for the night.'

'What friend? I didn't think your mum had any

friends.' He laughed sarcastically. 'Well, does she have her mobile on her then so I could call her on that?'

I could see Dave wasn't going to give up so easily. He just wasn't the type to let go.

'I don't think you should have her number, given the current situation. You have no right to phone this house. Shame on you for even doing so. Go crawl back under the rock you came from.'

I slammed the phone down, extremely angry, gritting my teeth. How dare he? How dare they let him phone here? There was no shame in him whatsoever. I didn't ever want to hear his voice again, let alone see him.

My fear began to turn into anger. I would never shed a tear over him ever again. There was an overwhelming rage building up inside me and I didn't know what to do. I paced the carpet, the anger pouring out of me was uncontrollable. A loud growl escaped my throat and I threw my fist, punching at the air in front of me, and then punching the couch, letting out my fury.

Taking a deep breath, I tried to calm down, hoping this wasn't the start of harassing phone calls. We would have to change numbers or go ex-directory. I sat on the couch and played my Van Helsing DVD, wiring into my Chinese delivery so chow chicken meal and forgetting all about that phone call. I would get on with the rest of my life. Without him.

Later that night, just as I was about to doze off, a rattling at the front door caused me to jump awake. With my head on the pillow, I listened out for noises. I heard a key slipping into the lock, and I relaxed my tense shoulders as Mum and Jason fell through the door, laughing.

I dragged myself out of bed with a yawn and walked down the stairs, giving them both a look of annoyance. It was obvious they'd had a bit to drink; they were giggling a lot. Mum turned to me and seemed to sober up instantly, standing up straight and brushing the hair out of her face like someone who had just been caught doing something naughty.

'Oh, Chloe sweetheart, I thought you would be sleeping. It's after twelve,' she said, darting her eyes to her watch and then up at me, embarrassed.

'Yeah, well, I was nearly sleeping when you woke me up with the noise and giggling.'

Mum gave Jason a guilty look and Jason just put his head down in shame.

'Well, um, I, uh…I'd better go. I'll come around tomorrow for dinner?'

'Yeah, sure, Jason, that sounds good.'

I scowled at Mum, not happy with the way she was acting. It definitely wasn't like her. She never used to act like that with Dad. The idea of Mum being with someone that way made me physically nauseous. It wasn't that I didn't like Jason. I just didn't like the idea of Mum and Jason together and the way they were behaving. And there was me thinking they weren't like that. I guessed I couldn't always be right.

Leaving my mum and Jason whispering in the hall, I traipsed back up the stairs to bed.

CHAPTER 19

Monday morning arrived, and Mum looked bright and chirpy as she hummed to herself and walked around the house, getting ready before leaving for her job back at Sue and Win Lawyers. Susanne and Winifred were a great team to work for, Mum had said. She had missed being there every day and was excited to get back into it. The work that she did involved road accidents. Sue and Win Lawyers would be there to help the victim with their claim. Mum had loved helping a client to win their lawsuit.

I briefly remember going to her office once, a long time ago when I was in primary school. Due to a sickness bug I hadn't been well for a couple of days. Dad had driven me in the car to see Mum off to work. We arrived outside and Dad parked at the front entrance. I held my face to the window as I gazed up. It looked astounding: a large glass building three storeys high. Ever since then I had wanted to travel up there and see what it looked like inside; see the rest of the world from up there. I thought Mum was so lucky to work in an attractive big building. She said that's why she spent so many years at college, because she had dreamed of getting that perfect job. She had worked hard for it and it had finally paid off.

Mum was back at work. I had finished my final year at high school and graduated. Dave was gone. We had our freedom back, and it felt great.

When she got home from work at six o'clock that day, Mum seemed like her old happy and relaxed self again. It was good to see her that way. It made me feel good too. I was on the couch watching Home and Away and eating my favourite mac and cheese. We greeted each other as she walked in with a smile on her face. It looked like the weight had been lifted from her shoulders as she sat at the computer, shaking the mouse, bringing the monitor to life.

'Mum, what are you up to?' I asked curiously.

Without giving me an answer, she typed away at the keyboard, going onto the First Choice website and looking up holiday destinations. She turned around to face me as I raised my eyebrows in surprise, my eyes darting between her and the screen. Was she serious? This was a turn-up for the books. A good one, but the one I was least expecting.

'Well?' she asked, grinning like a Cheshire cat. 'What do you think?'

I put my unfinished bowl down on the table, wiping my mouth with a napkin, and joined her at the desk. There on the screen was a package deal for a week in Salou. A large hotel with a pool at the back, only a short walk from the beach.

'A holiday? For us two? Really? Are you sure?' As surprising as it was, I had my doubts.

She laughed, shaking her head. 'Of course. We can lie on a beach, get a tan, perhaps even go on a jet ski!'

I put my arm around her shoulders. 'Are you sure you're feeling alright, Mum?'

'Yes, of course. Why wouldn't I be? We have our freedom back. We can do whatever we want. Well, for the meantime anyway. So, a week away isn't going to hurt, is it?'

She smiled, leaving the room. I looked at the screen, still slightly hesitant. The purchase wasn't complete yet. She had to pay and confirm everything. Not that I wasn't happy about going on holiday to Spain. It sounded brilliant. But it was all happening so soon.

She waltzed into the room minutes later with her purse and sat down at the computer. I put my hand on her arm and she looked up at me.

'Are you sure about this?' I asked again. 'Not that long ago you were slightly depressed and fed up. Maybe you should speak to someone and get advice.'

'Chloe, what are you talking about?' she answered, rolling her eyes at me. 'I'm absolutely fine! Don't doubt your own mother, for goodness' sake. Now, if you don't mind, I'd like to finish my booking.'

I turned, lifted my unfinished mac and cheese and took it with me to my room, leaving her to it. I seemed to overthink everything these days. I worried too much when there was actually nothing to worry about.

She explained to me later that evening that her friends at work had given her a lot of advice about what to do for the best, suggesting a holiday would be a great break away. That seemed to put my mind at ease. We hugged it out as she told me I was silly for worrying. Mum would be just fine.

The days flew by after that, as my time was spent sending out the CV I had made at school, hoping someone would accept me for an interview. It was time to start earning a decent wage and take a step in the right direction. The chats were well and truly over as Mum received a copy of my CV. I couldn't wait to get an office job.

The weekend arrived, warm and sunny, and I spent it shopping for clothes in Glasgow's busy Buchanan Street. Mollie and I had a great laugh trying on lots of summer clothes in each shop we browsed through. As busy as this place was, it was therapeutic for both of us. In between shopping, we stopped for a Twinings English breakfast tea in House of Fraser, before heading for lunch at the fancy Princess Square shopping centre.

As I sat in Il Pavone with a mouth full of spaghetti, Mollie thought then would be the best time to ask me how Mum was doing. As much as I loved Mollie, there really was nothing more off-putting than talking through a mouthful of food. I sat there chewing slowly and then washing it down with a glass of Pepsi, making her wait until I had finished before giving her my answer.

'Yeah, I'd been worried about her. Thought she was going through some stuff. Turned out it was just me overthinking it after all. My brain always runs ahead of me. Mum is perfectly fine.'

'Oh, well, as long as you're both doing alright, that's all that matters really. You excited about Spain?'

I made a sour face that she didn't believe for a second. She laughed, drinking the remains of her Pepsi while trying to get the attention of the waiter for another refill.

'Yeah, my suitcase is waiting to be packed. Just can't wait to get on that plane and up in the air. We're going on jet skis apparently.'

'Oh, lovely. I'm sure I don't need to tell you to have a great time.'

She really didn't. I knew it would be a blast.

Giving a loud sigh, I clicked my seatbelt together and looked out of the small window to my right. From the inside of the plane, Glasgow Airport looked dull and drizzly compared to where we would be in two and a half hours. It was the week after Mum had started back at work, and her boss had given her a couple of weeks off. We both really needed this holiday. It was good to get away from everything.

It was five forty in the morning and I'd been up since three, after having only four hours' sleep due to a careless mistake I'd managed to make yet again...

We had cooked an early roast-chicken dinner the afternoon before and then relaxed on the couch for an hour, watching Mum's favourite episodes of My Family on

147

DVD. Then I got organised with my packing. I took the clothes out of the dryer, folded them and put them in my suitcase. I didn't want to overload, as Mum said there was a limit to what they'd accept on the plane.

When I had finally finished and zipped up the lid, it dawned on me that I couldn't remember where I had put our euros. Mum had got six hundred pounds changed and she had given me the responsibility of counting it, dividing it up between the two of us and putting it into two envelopes with our names on them. I distinctly remembered counting them and putting them into the envelopes on the kitchen worktop. Then I'd walked into the living room with the two envelopes in my hand and let Mum know I was going to put them in the suitcase so I wouldn't lose them.

We ended up staying up much later than we had planned that night. Mum asked where her money was, and I gave in and told her I didn't know.

The suitcase was searched. Everything was pulled out. I began to worry frantically. All I remembered was that the last place I'd seen them was in the suitcase. But they weren't there. I started to get anxious and panicky, worrying what we were going to do for spending money. I could have cried, stamped my feet and yelled out. Why did this happen to me? Every time I was going somewhere, something always disappeared and I had to search for it for ages. I truly was fed up of this happening to me.

I knew the money wasn't in any other room, but I decided to give it a shot anyway. The chest of drawers and the wardrobe in my room had been checked. I hunted high and low, never giving up, no matter how tired I was. Mum was disappointed in me, and it showed. She went quiet and had a sad expression on her face. I had let her down. How could I have been so careless and forgetful, losing something so important? We really would be stuck without the euros.

The time had now reached ten forty and I still hadn't got any closer to finding the named envelopes. I was in my room. Everything had been pulled out and checked thoroughly, but there was no trace. I had about just given up when I heard my name being called from downstairs. I ran down, worried. Why she had called me? Was I in more trouble?

Mum stood in the middle of the living room by my red suitcase holding up the two white envelopes with our money inside. I felt my shoulders slump in relief and instantly began to relax. She wasn't angry or disappointed anymore. Instead, she had a smirk on her face as she stood watching me, shaking her head.

'Where did you find them?' I called out in a high-pitched tone.

'In your suitcase, Chloe, where they were all along. You put them in the zipped part at the front.'

Deep down I had known all along they were definitely in the suitcase. I had just been looking in the wrong place. Mum took charge of the euros from then on and put them in her own bag – and she would remember where she'd put them.

I had never been more relieved that night to be in my own bed. Although we would only be getting a few hours' sleep – the anticipation for the next day was great. Everything was ready to go and organised.

When the alarm clock beeped at three, we anxiously jumped out of bed, had a wash and dressed quickly, before sitting down at the kitchen table with a cup of tea and waiting for the pre-booked taxi to arrive. I wasn't really looking forward to going outside into the cold and wet Scottish weather, even if it was only for a few seconds. But it was good that we were going somewhere warm.

The airport was quiet as we headed to the gate to put

the luggage in and get our flight tickets. The large building was astounding, and I stayed by Mum's side for fear of getting lost. Browsing around, we found a restaurant, and I sat at a table while Mum ordered our food. This place was fascinating. There were so many shops, and it took all the self-control I had not to buy anything before we took off.

'Hungry?' Mum asked, making a noise of derision.

To anyone else, it would have looked like I had been starved, the way I was ploughing through my bacon roll and washing it down with a glass of orange juice. In my defence, I was really hungry. The last meal I had eaten was the day before, and I could really put away my food. Mum often wondered where it all went, considering I was so thin.

The terminal had got surprisingly busy by the time we handed in our tickets. After standing in a small queue, we finally boarded our First Choice plane, settled in and got our books out for a quiet read.

Now, looking at the view outside, I watched as the ground beneath us flew past – and then we were up in the air. I turned to Mum with a large grin on my face. The take-off was my favourite part. It was such a thrill. Switching on the air-con, I closed my eyes and revelled in the cool air blowing down on me.

'Good morning, this is your captain, Vic, speaking with flight information. We have now departed from Glasgow Airport and are flying at an altitude of thirty-seven thousand feet. We will be arriving at Reus Airport in around two and half hours. There is no expected turbulence, so we should have a pleasant flight all in. Spain has some lovely blue skies and a top temperature of twenty-eight degrees, so it's nice and hot over there. On board we have a duty-free trolley, which will be coming around shortly. Please keep your seatbelt fastened until the seatbelt sign turns off. Have a pleasant flight. Thank you.'

'Can I have a tea, a butter croissant and a Versace perfume?' I asked the hostess a short while later as she came around with the snacks and drinks trolley. Mum sat in the aisle seat browsing through her magazine, none the wiser.

After the hostess and I exchanged items and cash, I placed the products on Mum's table. She looked clueless.

'Just a wee thank you, Mum.'

She put her hand on my arm. 'Thank you, sweetheart! That's too kind. Just don't spend all your money on me, though.'

I chuckled, knowing she was going to be in for more treats when we arrived. There was nothing she didn't deserve.

I couldn't get off the coach any faster as it dropped us off outside the Brigetta Hotel at around nine that morning. I was just too excited. Stepping out into twenty-eight-degree heat was nearly too much for me to take. The coach driver pulled out the cases and we made our way into the cool, quiet reception, which featured shiny marble flooring throughout.

We were greeted warmly by a tall, dark-haired man as we parked our cases at the front desk to check in. Mum handed over our passports and was given our room key.

'Come on!' I called excitedly to Mum, practically bouncing on the spot, as she slouched over, trying to get the key-card into the slot. The second I heard the click of the lock, I was in like a shot with my case. The room was cool and dark. I dashed over and pulled the curtains apart and unlocked the balcony door.

'Chloe, would you calm down, love!'

'I can't help it!' I exclaimed. 'I'm just so excited to be

here!'

I leaned over the balcony, watching the people down below, some lying on loungers, some in the pool. I wanted to be where they were.

'Can we go out to the pool, please?' I practically begged.

'We've only just arrived.'

'I know, but I just really want to be in that water right now.'

She gave me a smile, shaking her head. 'Alright, go change into your swimsuit and we can go downstairs.'

'Yes!' I punched the air with my fist happily. After quickly changing in the bathroom, I joined Mum with my swimsuit on and a towel over my arm.

'Aren't you going to unpack?' she asked.

'Na. I'll do it later. I promise.'

She opened the door and we dashed downstairs. I simply couldn't contain my excitement about being in the water. The moment I made it to the poolside, I dived in with a massive splash, leaving onlookers gasping and moaning in annoyance as the water poured out over the edge, narrowly missing them.

That was the moment I'd been waiting for.

As I happily swam my lengths, Mum sat on the poolside eating a toastie and drinking iced water she had ordered from the bar outside. She looked happy and relaxed, enjoying the view.

I bobbed my head out the water, holding on to the side. 'You coming in?'

She smiled. 'You have fun just now. I may join you later.'

I turned away and carried on with my swim, feeling love and admiration for her. My mum was one in a million, and I knew how lucky we were to have each other and to be here in this lovely hotel. We had a whole two weeks to relax, have our meals cooked for us, take in the culture and even possibly learn to speak some Spanish. It would be something I would remember for a really long time.

Just before midday, I walked out of the bathroom, freshly showered with a towel wrapped around my head, and sauntered through the room. I opened up my suitcase, finding shorts, a t-shirt and a hairbrush, and made myself presentable. Mum was browsing online on a computer downstairs while she waited for me.

Every moment spent here was utterly thrilling. I hadn't taken anything in before, but now was my chance to look around. This was my first time in a Spanish hotel, and it felt really exciting to be here in this moment. There were two single beds, and a desk with a small flat-screen TV on top and a fridge underneath. The balcony, with a white plastic table and chairs, looked out onto the pool at the back. I picked up my digital camera and started snapping away, getting everything in the frame. Feeling happy with the pictures I'd taken, I sat my camera on the desk, grabbed my bag and door key and went down to meet Mum.

CHAPTER 20

The sun burned down on us as we made our way through the narrow streets towards the centre. I glanced around, amazed, taking everything in. This city fascinated me. Rows and rows of palm trees lined the streets. We passed by chemists' and small supermarkets and I whizzed in and out, excitedly hunting for gifts. Shopping before lunch sounded like a treat, but we had to decide where to eat first. There were so many options.

In one small shop, I picked up a light-blue picture frame and Spanish bull ornament. I would print the best photo of Mum and me here when we got home, frame it and put it on the mantelpiece. That would always remind us of the great time we'd had together.

After I finished up shopping, we headed into a small restaurant. The waiter came over to take our order.

'Hola. Puedo tener pizza de queso?'

'Si. beber?'

'Dos Cocas.'

'Gracias.'

Mum smiled proudly as the waiter walked away with our order. I looked at her, curious and surprised.

'When did you learn to speak Spanish?'

'Oh, when I was waiting for you at the computers. I had that memorised, and a few other words too. It's quite easy to pick up their language'

'What did you order?'

'A pizza for us to share. And two Cokes.'

'Ah. Cheese?'

'Of course. I know you won't eat anything else.'

'Go on then, teach me a few Spanish words.'

So she did. As we waited for our food to arrive, she

pulled out a small notebook and went through a list she'd prepared, with phrases like Buenos días (Good morning), Gracias (Thank you) and Que tengas un buendia (Have a nice day).

'Am I boring you?' she asked a little later.

'Hmm?' I answered, looking up at my unimpressed mum as I sat picking at my nail. 'Oh, sorry, what were you saying?'

'You weren't even listening, were you?'

I sighed. 'You were going on and on about the language and the history. I just want to enjoy my holiday and have fun.'

She gave a small snigger. 'Was that a bit much?'

I wrinkled my nose. 'Just a bit. Let's keep this holiday light-hearted, yeah?'

'Of course.'

She smiled, looking up at the waiter as he placed the bill on the table. We both took out our purses and put ten euros each on the table. After waiting for our change, we left, walking towards the hotel, to put my bag in the room before taking an evening stroll.

The clean, sandy beach was pleasant and surprisingly quiet as we strolled along, sandals in our hands, beside the small waves lapping at our bare feet. We picked the perfect spot to put our towels down, nearly forgetting about the sun cream we'd packed. I couldn't remember feeling this content and relaxed before. This holiday was simply the best thing we had ever done.

The moment was soon disrupted by a large woman kicking sand in my face as she sauntered a little too close to me, heading in the direction of the sea. She was stripped bare, revealing a large pair of tattooed wings on her back. I coughed and wiped my face clean as I sat up in annoyance.

'Bloody hell!' I called a little too loudly, not caring if she heard or not.

'What's wrong?'

'I just got sand kicked in my face by that bloody woman,' I grumbled.

Mum shook her head. 'Just rise above it. Be the better person.'

'Nope,' I replied, watching the woman as she attempted to sit on her inflatable lilo. It was then that I made my move. I stood up, wiping the sand from my legs as I got myself prepared.

'Chloe, what are you doing? Sit down.'

I ignored her and made a run for it.

'Woo-hoo!' I shouted, running from the sand into the sea with my arms flailing about over my head. I kicked the water hard, not giving a damn as it splashed the large, tattooed woman. She turned to me, her face like thunder.

'Oi!' she called angrily. 'What do you think you're doing?'

I simply lifted my arms up in a non-caring motion with a smile on my face. Then I walked away happily and joined Mum on the sand, lying down and closing my eyes. I had loved every second of that.

Over an hour later, we had managed to walk the full distance of the beach, watched the waves, talked and laughed until the sun set. Arriving back at the hotel at half past seven, we sat down and enjoyed a lovely three-course meal in the restaurant. The couple sitting at the table next to us caught my eye. They were both gazing at each other, all the while holding hands. Mum and I smiled simultaneously.

'Happy anniversary, my darling,' the husband said to his wife in a Scots accent.

That, right there, made me take to them straight away.

The woman turned to face me.

'Hello.'

I beamed. 'Hi there. You're Scottish too, right?'

'That's right. Over on holiday for our fortieth wedding anniversary.'

'Oh, congratulations. When did you arrive?' I asked.

'This morning at nine.'

'Oh, so did we.' I looked at Mum, surprised we hadn't noticed them earlier. 'How long are you here for?'
'Seven days. Dougie here surprised me with this a week before we left. Needless to say, I was over the moon. He's always been romantic that way, though.'

I gave them a large grin, delighted for them both. They looked like a couple who were still very much in love. And after forty years too.

As the time ticked by, we pushed our tables together and chatted for the rest of the night, ordering more drinks from the waiter, who was collecting empty dishes and putting clean tablecloths on.

The next morning, Mum and I sat down to our croissant and orange juice breakfast, before taking another walk around the Spanish town. We looked in more tourist shops, and I picked up some postcards and keyrings. Then we walked along the beach again, taking in the beautiful scenery while I snapped away with my camera. I found this place wonderful and everything about it impressed me. We made way for the tourists who drove past us on their beach buggies, while others simply lay on their loungers, lapping up the hot sun. I felt lucky that this was my first holiday abroad. There were people at my school who were too poor to go nice places like this. Mum had done well saving up to get us here. I was grateful.

As we made our way back through the hotel and out to the pool area, I looked around for a couple of empty loungers, wanting to find just the right spot that would keep us out of the shade. I suddenly felt a hand pushing my shoulder swiftly, and before I knew it, my feet left the ground. A high-pitched scream escaped my mouth as my body hit the freezing-cold pool and the pristine water nipped my eyes. Using the full force of my arms, I pulled myself back up to the surface and let out a massive gasp, getting the air back into my lungs. I pushed my hair out of my face and rubbed my sore eyes.

'You pushed me?' I squeaked.

Mum smirked at me as I grabbed the railing and climbed out of the pool. My shorts and t-shirt were a dripping wet mess. I stood in front of her, shaking my head, as others laughed at my expense. I was surprised; I honestly wouldn't have thought Mum had it in her. But we were on holiday and she was entitled to have a bit of fun. I would get her back. It was just a matter of biding my time. Her smirk turned into laughter and she covered her mouth with her hand.

'Oh Chloe.' She chuckled.

Perhaps it was the fact that the water was too cold, but I didn't find it funny at all. I would get my revenge.

As the hours and days passed by, I began to be sneaky around her. Her suspicions rose, and she watched me at every turn, not trusting my motives. I would make her pay; I just had to get her back. Revenge day was yet to come.

The hotel lounge was quiet when we sat down after another lovely meal in the restaurant. Watching the DJ as he began to set up his equipment, I sipped the glass of fresh orange I'd got from the bar beside us and checked my phone for any new messages. There were none. Giving a sigh, I placed the phone down on the table and turned to Mum.

'Have you spoken to Jason yet?'

'No. Why would I have?'

I shrugged my shoulders. 'I don't know, maybe he's missing you and wants to hear your voice.'

She scoffed. 'Come on, Chloe. Don't be daft.'

I watched her eyes as she looked ahead. I had my suspicions about them both. I let it go just enjoying my night as the room and bar filled up with guests, the DJ played his set and couples went up for a dance. The music carried everyone away and it suddenly became a very entertaining night. The pensioners up the front were dancing, linked arm in arm, twirling around happily. It was one of the funniest things I had ever seen. These were people who knew how to dance and were giving it style. The music was upbeat and everyone was on their feet.

As the hours passed by, the crowd started to thin out. Couples gave in, going back to their rooms.

'Come on, Alfred, it's time to go.'

My attention was drawn to a senior lady who was trying to persuade her husband to leave the dance floor. The gentleman looked happy enough dancing away, moving his arms and hips in a rhythm as he amused people sitting in the front row, clapping, laughing and cheering him on. To me it looked like he'd had a bit too much to drink as he carried on entertaining the few guests who were evidently keeping him going. His poor wife had a hard time of it as she tried to coax him away. The extrovert danced on in circles up the aisle and I for one couldn't tear my eyes away from the enjoyable and talented entertainment.

Mum yawned loudly and she lifted her arm and looked at her watch.

'Well, I think we should call it a night, don't you, Chloe?'

'Na,' I answered, enjoying myself too much. It wasn't often I got to see this kind of live entertainment.

'We should head up,' she tried to coax me. 'We have

an early start in the morning.'

'Why, what's happening tomorrow?'

She shook her head in that 'not saying a word' way, and I knew I wouldn't ask again because she'd get annoyed. Lifting her bag, she stood up, waiting for me to join her.

'I'm not going up just yet,' I answered, watching the crowd up front. 'I'll be up later.'

Sighing, she turned and left me to it. I smirked, watching her walk away. I knew it wouldn't be long before she was back down again.

I checked my watch. It was only ten thirty. I let myself forget about her for a while as I watched the crowd in front of me. I just hoped she wouldn't be too mad.

I strolled to the bar and got myself a Pepsi. Time slowly ticked by. I was enjoying my night and having a good time. I sat at an empty table near the front to get a better view. The '80s music boomed loudly from the speakers in the room and the air began to get stuffy. Mum didn't come back down, but I didn't let it bother me. I relaxed and laughed at the show, and I stayed until the end. Then I headed out of the noisy atmosphere and up to our quiet room, preparing myself for what was to come.

Mum didn't speak to me that night. She wasn't happy with me as she stomped off to reception to collect fresh bedding. Her sheets were soaked.

I told her I would get my revenge. Nobody played a prank on Miss Chloe Stanson and got away with it.

'Hurry up, Chloe!' Mum coaxed me the next morning, standing over the side of my bed and pulling the blanket away, trying to persuade me to get up.

I rubbed my eyes, squinting at her. 'What's the urgency?' I moaned.

'I'll tell you when you're up and dressed.'

Grumbling, I forced myself out of bed and into the

bathroom, where I made myself presentable. When I came out, Mum was holding up a printed-off scuba-diving gift certificate that she had booked through a website.

I gasped in amazement. 'When did you do this?' I squeaked happily, taking hold of the piece of paper.

'When I booked the holiday for us. I thought you needed an extra surprise. And I knew it would make you happy.'

'Happy? You have no idea! Oh Mum, I just don't know what to say!'

I was close to tears. This gift was honestly just too much and I didn't even know where to begin thanking her. For everything. It was a sheer delight. I took hold of her in a mighty bear hug and squeezed my eyes shut. My mum had always gone to extra lengths to make me so happy and keep a smile on my face. I guessed she just thought I needed it after everything I had been through.

I browsed through the booking, reading the fine print, feeling all the more excited that it was actually happening. It felt like a once-in-a-lifetime opportunity. And I would enjoy every moment.

As I sat at the entrance of the hotel enjoying the warm breeze and looking out for whoever was coming to collect me, I heard a voice call out to my left:

'Are you waiting for the coach?'

I looked over at the young English woman, who was struggling to fold her toddler's buggy. She had shoulder-length, wavy, brown hair and her freckled face seemed to glow in the sunlight. Her son simply stood by her side with a forefinger in his mouth, looking around.

'No.' I shook my head. 'I'm waiting on someone coming to collect me. I'm off scuba-diving today.' 'Oh, that's brilliant.' She smiled. 'Our holiday has been cut short, unfortunately. My son has developed pneumonia

161

and we have to get home immediately. My husband Tom, and the other kids are staying on, though. Why cut their holiday short?'

'Oh no! That's awful. Have you not seen any doctors around here?'

She shook her head briskly. 'Can't afford it.'

'Oh.' I bit my lip, feeling sorry for her. 'How are you getting back to the airport?'

'Taxi,' she replied, holding her kid close to her side.

For the next few minutes we waited in silence, until at ten on the dot a white van pulled up with La Tour de Salou on the side of it.

'Well, I hope your son gets better soon.' I smiled.

'Oh thanks. Enjoy your dive.'

We waved goodbye to each other and I walked over to the van, to be greeted by a tall Spanish man wearing flip-flops, khaki knee-length trousers and a white t-shirt.

'Hi. I'm Chloe.'

'Chloe, hi. I'm Carlos.'

He shook my hand and opened the passenger door for me, and I climbed in. Something about this moment felt really natural and calm. Normally, sitting beside a stranger in a van would leave me rattled with nerves. Not today. I felt really relaxed, comfortable and happy. He sat confidently with both hands on the wheel as he drove, telling me about the diving challenge I would be taking on shortly, the mask and the oxygen tank I would be wearing. I felt so excited as I listened to his every word.

After picking up another two passengers, he told us about his adventures with an octopus and showed us a few photos on his phone. It looked amazing. I couldn't wait.

We arrived at a quiet beach, where he parked outside a hotel. We changed into our wetsuits and got our flippers and eye masks. I sat on the wall beside the others as Carlos clipped the large tank to my back and helped me to stand up. I thought I had carried heavy things in my life, but this was something else. The weight was extraordinary. Bending forward to carry it made it slightly easier on my shoulders.

Relief spread through me as we walked the short distance to the water and I stepped in slowly until we were waist deep. Even though the ocean was cold on my bare feet, I felt warm from having the wetsuit on. Holding on to each other for support, we got on our knees, steadily maintaining our balance, as we put on our flippers and masks. Carlos then talked us through the procedures and spoke clearly about what to do.

With our heads under the water for five minutes, we learned how to breathe in the mask, until we felt confident enough to start swimming. With the eye mask completely covering my nose, it was a slight struggle at first, but I quickly learned to adjust.

Being able to swim under the clear and calm water was an exhilarating experience. As we made our way through the ocean I paddled slowly and steadily, staying level with the tank, making sure it stayed on my back. Carlos swam beside me, making sure I was okay. My nerves heightened slightly as the water deepened. I turned to my right as a swarm of little fishes swam past me. The view in that moment was spectacular. To be here underwater with these little vertebrate animals was such a thrill. I was so grateful to have this opportunity. The fish passed by nonchalantly, and we continued on into the depths on the ocean.

I tried to paddle faster to keep up with the others, who were well ahead of me now. The saltwater seeped into my mouth and I began to choke. Panicking, I waved my arms around, desperate to attract Carlos's attention. Feeling scared, I badly needed oxygen then and there. He swam to my rescue and was at my side in seconds, pushing me up to the surface.

'Okay, now remember, Chloe, if you ever need to resurface again, you have to use the button on the cable right here. It will whoosh you back up to the top. Alright?'

I nodded at him and then got down on my knees and popped the regulator back into my mouth, trying my best to breathe once more. Swimming past a large rock, I began to feel at ease, enjoying my underwater swim – but only briefly before I began to choke once again. Forgetting Carlos's instructions, I panicked, desperate to resurface for air.

My arms sloshed around as I tried to signal for help. The fact that I couldn't inhale at all was simply terrifying and I hated that this was happening to me. Surely there was something wrong with the regulator that meant the oxygen wasn't flowing through properly. What annoyed me in addition to this was the fact that I was holding the other divers back as well. I hated to think that they were annoyed at me. All they wanted to do was go down for a dive, and here I was getting myself into a fluster. There must have been a simple solution.

As I floated around helplessly in the water, Carlos came back to me once again and helped me up to the surface. The second I reached the top I took the mask off, taking a large gulp of fresh air, glad to have it back in my lungs. I just knew I wouldn't be able to make it any further, and that crushed me.

'Chloe, I don't think it's safe for you to go back down again. Can you manage to swim to those rocks over there while I join the others? I'll be back shortly.'

I nodded in agreement. We were on the same track there. I watched him swim away under the water and then he was gone. I was left floating around in the ocean by myself, and I had never felt so alone, scared and vulnerable.

I tried to make my way to the rocks for safety. Emotions

ran high. I prayed that I would make it back. Not being able to breathe underwater was a terrifying thing. There was a massive fear in me and this was a big risk. But it was one I had to take. There was no choice. I had to try to swim. It was either stay here and wait until help came or give it a shot myself.

I could see the beach from where I was. It wasn't that far away. I put the mask over my mouth and tried to swim under the water and back to the shallows. It didn't happen. I didn't get the chance to swim. The tank fell over and I went with it. I was on my back, helpless. I took the mask out of my mouth and it bobbed around on the water. I tried to turn myself around, but it was no use. Things really couldn't have got any worse. The tank was just too heavy and I was running out of energy. I felt doomed.

I gave it shot after shot, all the while getting weaker and weaker. The realisation dawned that I wasn't going anywhere. All I wanted was the chance to swim underwater. But that wasn't going to happen. I gave up trying eventually. The tank was just too heavy and I had no energy left. To anyone watching, it would have looked like a lifeless body was floating on the top of the water. There was nothing else to do but look up at the sky and watch the clouds and birds pass by.

I didn't want this. To be stuck here. Trapped. I thought about trying a backstroke to see if it would take me to the rocks, but it was useless. I wasn't going anywhere. My neck and head began to ache from being in an upright position. Nothing worked the way I wanted it to. I gave up.

Dizziness and sickness took over shortly after. I turned my head to the side and heaved again and again. I felt so ill. I didn't care whether anyone on the beach was watching me. I didn't care how I looked. The only thing I wanted was to be back at the hotel and feeling well again.

Needing to move I turned my head to the right, looking

over to the rocks. The chance just had to be taken. I swam the backstroke, feeling relief when I moved in the right direction. At last I was getting somewhere.

Arriving at the rocks, I managed to turn my body around to face them. I held on and waited. Waited for this heavy tank to be taken off my back, to go to the beach and be driven back to my hotel. All I wanted was to be rescued.

I looked at the rocks. It seemed like an easy climb to the top, but that was energy I just didn't have. I had given everything I had and now I was floating around in the ocean with nothing else in me. I was done.

I lifted my right foot onto a rock under the water but it wouldn't stay, slipping off at every chance. There was no hope, only desperation. I looked towards the beach. There were parents standing around in the water playing Frisbee with their children. They didn't notice me. Only one guy stood looking out and watching. I didn't care, though.

The water began to hit the rocks and I worried that it may start to get higher. I watched with caution.

Time moved on. I began to get emotional and cried out, pleading for Carlos to come back with the other divers and help take this tank off my back. It was too much of a weight for me. I was anxious and had just about given up when I turned around to my left and he was there. They had come back. I could have cried with relief.

'Were you sick?' he asked as we arrived at the shore.

'Yeah, I was. I felt ill in the water.'

'Sometimes the saltwater can do that to you.' He looked at me with concern. 'Here, let me take that.'

I leant over slightly, and he took the heavy tank off me, putting it over his shoulder with ease. I wondered just how strong he was as he could lift two at the same time.

'Give me your flippers.' He held out his hand.

I gripped his arm, lifting one flipper off and then the

next. He took them from me without the slightest bit of annoyance on his face.

We all walked back to the van with me feeling low, emotional and empty. I wasn't in the mood to speak. There wasn't any happiness in me anymore.

CHAPTER 21

We arrived back at the street, changed and headed to my hotel. Today had been absolutely ruined. I had been really looking forward to scuba-diving, but I hadn't understood how challenging it was. I'd really wanted to enjoy my time under the water. What I would have given to swim with the marine life and have had the privilege and the pleasure of sharing it with everyone else.

I had mentioned scuba-diving to Mum one day a while back after I saw an advert on TV that made it look amazing. That must have played on her mind. She had given me the opportunity and I had been eager to do it. When I had seen videos of divers underwater, it had seemed really easy and simple. But to me it wasn't as easy as it looked.

I felt utterly miserable on the drive back. I could have wept. In that moment, I never wanted to set foot in the ocean again.

Carlos pulled up at the front of my hotel and I handed him the payment.

'So you have my email address and phone number?' he asked.

'Yes. Thanks for today,' I replied.

'Okay, I will send you an email in about an hour,' he said, shaking my hand.

I climbed out of his van and sluggishly dragged myself over to the bench at the front. I turned around and the van was gone.

I didn't waste time waiting on the lift. I rushed past the reception, not caring if anyone saw me, to the toilets, where I locked the door behind me. I hung up my bags, knelt on the floor and wretched over and over, bringing up everything I had left. My body shuddered and my stomach heaved in pain. Nothing could have possibly made me feel any worse. I just wanted to hide away.

I flushed the toilet and sat on the cold, tiled floor. I hated this feeling. The only thing that would help right now was to go up and lie in some hot water and close my eyes. Baths always seemed to make me feel better in any situation.

After waiting until I had my strength back, I stood up, walked out the cubicle, washed my hands and rinsed my mouth. Outside, I passed by reception and climbed the three flights of stairs to our room. I gave three quiet knocks before Mum answered with a big smile on her face.

'Well?' she asked. 'How did it g—' Her grin turned to shock in an instant. 'Chloe, what's wrong?!' she gasped.

'I need a bath,' I whispered.

Looking worried, she guided me into the bathroom, her hands gentle on my shoulders, and I sat on the side of the tub, leaving my bags at my feet. Turning the taps on, she put the stopper in and left the room. She rummaged about before coming back in with a bottle of cold water. I drank it slowly. The cold liquid going down my throat felt good. She took the bottle from me and put it on the surface next to the sink.

'What happened, Chloe?' she asked, hands resting on her hips.

'I don't want to talk about it. Not now. Maybe when I'm feeling better,' I answered hoarsely.

'I'm guessing from the mess you're in that you got into the ocean alright?'

I stared into the running bath water, refraining from answering her. I felt low.

'Okay,' she answered, lifting her hands up in defeat. 'You know where I am if you need me.'

She walked out of the bathroom, closing the door quietly behind her. I stripped, stepped into the clean, warm water and lay down. It felt good. There was nowhere else I needed to be that day but in that tub. I could have lain there for hours and not moved a muscle.

I hated what had happened out there. But I was glad to be soaking in the hot bath. My thoughts returned to earlier, when I'd swum beside the small fish. What a moment that was. More than anything I wanted this ill feeling to go away. The saltwater remained repulsive in my mouth and made me want to heave some more. There was nothing else to give.

Lying in the tub was therapeutic and eventually it seemed to wash everything away. After soaking for over an hour, I pulled out the plug, came out the bathroom with a towel around me and made myself presentable. Feeling hungry, I poured myself a can of Pepsi out of the small fridge and devoured a bag of cookies I had purchased while out shopping. That made me feel better instantly.

I looked in the large, rectangular mirror that hung on the wall. The girl in the reflection stared at me with no emotion in her face. Just a blank expression. Her cheeks were a pale pink. Her blue eyes stared back at me, asking, Well, are you happy now?

I thought about that for a minute. Was I happy? I'd tried a new challenge and come back having failed. No, I wasn't happy in the slightest. But at least I'd given it a shot.

I spent a short time in the cool, air-conditioned room before joining Mum down at the poolside. The weather was warm, the sky was a clear blue, and guests were sitting on their loungers, some with their sunglasses on, getting a tan. I joined Mum at her table. She was wearing light-blue shorts, a t-shirt and a straw sunhat. Her eyes were closed and her head was back as she took in the heat. A bottle of suntan lotion and a half-empty glass of clear liquid sat on the table. I pulled a chair out and sat next to her. She didn't move.

'You're drinking?' I asked.

'I'm on holiday, Chloe, I'm allowed to enjoy myself,' she answered sarcastically, not looking at me.

I gave a short laugh and shook my head. Leaning back, I closed my eyes.

'You ready to talk yet?'

I sighed. 'What do you want to know?'

She pushed herself upright on the seat, arms on the rests, and looked straight at me. 'Well, for starters, why you came back and nearly collapsed at my feet. What happened out in the water?'

I sat up and stared at the ground. 'I couldn't do it. It was the mask. There was no oxygen coming out of the regulator. I couldn't breathe under the water and I had to swim to the shore. The tank fell over and I was left floating on my back. Which left me dizzy and sick. And that's why I was ill.' I cringed, feeling disappointed in myself.

'I'm sorry, Chloe.' She rubbed my arm. 'At least you gave it a try. That takes guts, in my opinion. Going out there and doing something like that is brave. I don't think everyone could do that, but you did. And that's what you've got to think of. Not the fact that you were ill or that you couldn't complete your task, but that you tried your hand at something new and exciting. That's one thing about you – you go out there and give it a shot. You have the power within yourself to give it a go. And so what if you didn't succeed? At least you came back having given it everything you had, and you can tell people, "Well, you know what? At least I tried."'

I looked at her for a second, realising she was right. I gave her a smile.

'Yeah, I did, didn't I? I never thought about it that way. Thanks, Mum.' I gave her a hug.

Ham baguettes and Cokes were ordered by the poolside as we sat reminiscing. Mum told funny stories, and I laughed and began to enjoy myself once again. Today was the last day here and I had been having the time of my life. Apart from the recent hiccup, this holiday had been wonderful. I didn't want to go home.

Our last dinner in the hotel restaurant was as good as it had been every other night, and just as busy as well. I took as many photos and videos as possible of the restaurant, pool area and the front of the hotel, before we headed back up to our room to pack everything into our suitcases. We made sure we were organised for the journey home. I double-checked that nothing was missing for our early start.

We took our luggage down the stairs the next morning and handed in our room key. Breakfast was supplied to us thanks to the staff who were kind enough to open early. We had only just finished eating our croissants when our coach arrived and we headed off to the airport.

We rushed through the airport terminal, handed in our luggage and got our boarding passes, then browsed around the tax-free shop, looking at all sorts of goodies. Nearly salivating, I picked up a large pyramid of Ferrero Rocher.

'Oh, you're not seriously going to buy that, are you?' Mum laughed.

'I don't see why not.'

'You'll never get through it!'

'Watch me!' I replied, handing the cashier my euros.

I walked out, bag in hand, and Mum followed. We sat on seats near the exit and waited. The area slowly filled up with families and I began to get anxious. Two young blond-haired girls sat beside me debating about their dolls. Their argument was getting severely heated.

'But my dolly's name's Moira because that's what my grannie is called, and I love my Grannie Moira.'

'But I want my dolly to be called Moira too. That's not fair. Mum!' the second girl shouted.

I glanced over at the parent, who seemed less than interested in her daughter's complaint. I gave a loud sigh as I felt a headache starting. This would be an unpleasant morning.

Half past ten rolled by and I looked up from my book to the departure board.

'Oh no!' I groaned.

Mum mirrored my actions and she closed her eyes, sighing, and shook her head. Our flight had been delayed. Waiting around in this airport was causing me serious anxiety. I stood up to leave.

'Where are you going?'

'I need to go for a walk. I'll be back soon.'

I sauntered around the departure lounge, feeling relieved to be away from the wailing I'd had to listen to. I checked the board constantly, watching for any updates. By the time I got back around to Mum she was speaking to a lady who was just leaving.

'Good news.' She smiled. 'Someone made a mistake, and the plane is infact outside and will be boarding shortly. We're going home, Chloe!'

I grinned happily, relieved we wouldn't have to spend much longer here. I didn't think I could have taken much more.

With my seatbelt fastened, I sat back and relaxed, unwrapping a chocolate and nibbling away as I looked out from my window seat. Reus Airport would only ever be a memory now. We would be back home in two and a half hours. The pilot made his announcement over the tannoy as the plane began its departure. The take-off was my utmost favourite thing. To me, it was a little piece of excitement. I smiled gleefully. With my drink and snacks on the table

in front of me and my legs stretched out, I was sated and relaxed. There was simply nothing better.

The mountains and fields down below amazed me as we passed them by. This week simply had been something else. Spain was an exciting adventure and if truth be told, we had had the best time. I was missing it already. My heart grew heavy. We were going back to normality. To colder weather and rain. I leaned my head against the back of the seat and sighed, looking out the window and contemplating life and the world. The home that I had lived in for the past sixteen years was suddenly unappealing now. But I knew that I had to go back and face it. Face the responsibility of finding a job and going to college. Paying bills.

I shook my head, dismissing everything, and smiled as we passed over a large ocean. I knew that sometime in the near future I would be doing this all over again.

CHAPTER 22

We arrived back home after two in the afternoon. Mum handed me the house keys and I unlocked the door and pushed it open. Everything was quiet and peaceful. There was no 'welcome home' from our lovely holiday in Salou. There was no one to tell us to sit down, put our feet up and relax, while they made us a cup of tea and we told them our wonderful holiday stories. It was just us.

I sensed something was off straight away with the hallway I had just walked into. It didn't feel right. I stopped to look around, accidentally standing on the post that had been delivered through the letterbox. Mum called my name, annoyed that I had just halted in my tracks for no apparent reason and that she'd nearly bumped into me. She stopped too, and barely had enough room to close the front door behind her.

I lifted the mail from the floor, gazing around slowly, looking from left to right as I took in every inch, trying to suss out what was wrong with the current situation. My eyes stopped dead on Mum's vase. She'd picked it up a few years a goat a car boot sale at Barrowlands. It was small and white with lilac flowers on it. It wasn't on the table on top of the white crocheted coaster anymore. It was lying on the green tartan carpet on its side.

I tried to remember the morning we'd left the house to head to the airport. We hadn't bumped into anything on our way out the door. We'd made sure everything was in place as we left. So why was the vase lying on the floor? There had been no one else in the house to look after things while we were gone. We hadn't thought we needed to leave our keys with anyone.

But maybe that was a bad idea. Maybe we should have left our keys with Jason and let him check on the house from time to time while we were gone for the week.

I walked over to the small mahogany table, picked up the vase and placed it back where it had been when we left. Oddly enough, the picture frames on the walls were out of place aswell. I walked over and straightened them up.

I turned around to head into the livingroom – and gasped. The floor was covered in papers and broken ornaments scattered all over the place.

'Uh, Mum, you're going to want to see this.'

With a puzzled look, she walked to my side. Putting the suitcases up against the other wall, she gently gave the glazed white door a push. It creaked opened, the top hinge hanging loosely from the door frame. As we walked into the livingroom, I couldn't believe what I was seeing. Mum let out a gasp as she lifted her hands to her face.

'Oh my God!'

We stood beside each other looking around the room. Everything was a mess. The couch cushions had been pulled out and scattered on the floor. The dining room table and chairs had been thrown to the side. The TV screen had been smashed. Our living room was a complete disaster. My heart pounded in my chest as tears filled my eyes.

'Mum, what's happening?' I cried out, clinging on to her jacket, scared to move anywhere. We weren't safe anymore.

She walked forward and my arm fell to my side. For the moment I was paralysed. The thought that someone may be in our house with us this very minute terrified the life out of me. My whole body cringed. My eyes watered and my lip trembled. I could barely make out her footsteps as she walked slowly from one side of the room and back again, her eyes wide with shock and terror, her hands curled up into tight fists by her side.

I slowly walked back into the hallway. The fear of someone being behind a door and jumping out at me replayed in my head. I turned to the kitchen. It was just as messy. Dodging smashed dishes and broken cups, I tiptoed cautiously, careful not to stand on anything.

Cupboards had been flung open. There were barely any dishes left inside. A slight draught in the air caught my attention. I looked over to see jagged shards of glass sticking out of the window frame and realised this was how they'd got in. Broken pieces of glass lay over the kitchen worktops. I ran my hands through my hair as I tried to keep it together. I was scared, hurt –full of emotion.

'Why would anyone want to do this to us? What have we ever done to anyone to deserve this?' I asked. A tear rolled down my cheek.

Mum walked over and held me tight to her, kissing my head. 'I don't know, sweetheart. Don't you worry, they'll get whoever did this. You'll see.'

Mum seemed so strong right now, but I had no idea how she was feeling on the inside. Her face was impassive, and she gave nothing away. I was her only daughter and I would respond in kind. We would be there for each other, no matter what.

We needed to find out who had broken into our home and done this to us, who had been watching us, known we were out and decided to ransack our home. Mum and I were a quiet family, never one to broadcast our news, especially to let people know we were on holiday. Jason had been the only one who knew and we both trusted him implicitly.

Mum called the police on her mobile in the livingroom. I could hear the worry in her voice. She sounded shaky and stressed, like she would burst into tears at any moment. I guessed she wasn't so strong after all. It upset me to hear her sound so broken on the phone.

As I walked up the stairs, every inch of my body cringed. I was careful not to touch anything as I turned into my room. My heart sank as I saw the tip in front of me; it was like a knife to my gut. They had invaded my personal space. And messed it up badly. Really badly. My computer screen, tower and CDs had been thrown off the desk and smashed to the floor. The floor itself was covered with broken ornaments and more papers. My mattress had been tipped over.

We had only been back home a few minutes and we had to endure this nightmare. The fact that someone had been in our home was bad enough; it was scary that they'd broken in and smashed up stuff. But damaging all of our personal belongings, that was just too much to bear. They hadn't left a trace of anything behind. That was clear without a doubt.

With my shoulders slouched and my body feeling exhausted already, I turned, wiping my nose and eyes on the sleeve of my jacket, not caring about the mess. I wasn't finished yet.

I stopped dead at Mum's bedroom door and froze. My eyes opened wide in shock and terror. A high-pitched scream escaped me and my body trembled; I couldn't seem to stop it. It felt like we had been watched from the moment we had left the house a week ago. I didn't want to move. There was too much of a fear of turning around or closing my eyes.

KAREN. CHLOE. I'LL COME FOR YOU.

The red spray-paint, the colour of blood, dripped down the back wall above mums bed– a warning to us. Someone had come here to tell us they were watching us. They knew where we lived. I couldn't breathe. Those words niggled away at me, eating at my very being.

Nausea crept in and it took everything I had not to kneel

and be sick on the spot. I rushed to the bathroom and threw up, sharp pains stabbing in my stomach. Who had been in our home? What did they want? Were our lives in danger? I felt like I was living in a horror film in my own house. I had to get out of there.

After flushing the toilet with the sleeve of my jacket, I rinsed my mouth and washed my face with cold water at the sink. I looked in the mirror and away again, the fear of someone standing behind me too traumatising.

Adrenaline kept me going. My limp legs got me down the stairs, out the front door and over to the small garden wall, where I let out a high-pitched wail before collapsing to the ground, crying out in pain. The grass was cold as I sat with my hands over my head, petrified. Whoever had done this to us had made sure we would suffer. They wanted us to be scared. It was working.

I sobbed my heart out sitting in my own garden, not caring if anyone saw or heard me. If they were that concerned about me, surely they would have come out to see what was wrong. I closed my eyes for a moment, taking a deep breath. Getting myself so worked up wasn't doing me any good. It was only making things worse. I had to try to calm down and think rationally.

Mum walked out and stood in front of me. 'Chloe, what's going on?'

'Your room. There's spray-paint on the wall.'

'What?'

She reluctantly traipsed up to her room, and it wasn't long before she came back down, her face pale as if she had just seen a ghost. She joined me on the soft grass, and we waited.

I stared at the house in front of me. All memories from my life seemed trivial now. As a young child I'd played out in the garden here, on the swing with Mum pushing me. I would shout 'Higher, Mum, higher!' and Mum would laugh. We'd had picnics sitting on our tartan blanket – sandwiches, carrot sticks and crisps. Thinking about everything was only making it worse.

Someone knew us. Someone had planned this. We had been watched. The thought of a strange character lurking around our home made my skin crawl. This had always been, for as long as we had lived here, a good neighbourhood with neighbours we could rely on. No one around here would have done this. The only person we knew who could have done such a thing was Dave, but that was impossible. He was in prison. He couldn't get out. Unless he'd escaped. And that thought was absolutely terrifying.

The police didn't take long to arrive. As the car pulled up, Mum reluctantly stood. She greeted the two officers who came up the path and led them into the house. I recognised the officers almost immediately. They were the same two who had been here before to arrest Dave. At least they knew our situation.

Mum came to the door, calling me in. She hadn't been the only one reluctant to join the officers. I was hesitant too. But unfortunately, I had to give a statement.

The officers stood in the living room in front of the fireplace. They were tall and intimidating, with their hands inside their vests, looking slightly impassive. I felt somewhat unnerved. Mum described the sequence of events from the moment we arrived at the door until I came down the stairs in a state of turmoil. It had been a real catastrophe. Both officers scribbled in their notebooks, all the while asking for details.

The officer who was dealing with me must have noticed how tense I looked as he started some small talk while the other officer continued to chat to Mum. It put me at ease. The tension seemed to slip from my shoulders slightly as I engaged in the conversation, relaxing in the officer's company.

When Mum had finished making her statement, they marched up to the rooms to view the damage, speaking into their walkie-talkies.

I thought about Dave in prison. He had become conniving and manipulative towards us, and he'd probably be the same with anyone in the prison aswell. It saddened me greatly to know that someone I had known all my life had turned out this way. If it really was him behind this, then he had given people on the outside the job of ransacking our house as revenge for his being stuck inside. That was my thought anyway. The intruders would have had to have been smart and hide out of sight so no one knew who they were.

When the forensics team finally arrived, they searched the whole house, taking samples of everything they found. We could only sit on the stairs in the hall and wait it out as they did their work. Mum wrapped a blanket around me. I felt gut-wrenchingly empty. My home had been destroyed, and all the Feng Shui that had harmonised it had now gone. It was just a broken house.

The police waited until a joiner came to put a new pane of glass in the kitchen window frame. I leaned my head against the wall as I sat, bone tired. We had planned a quiet arrival home, and instead it had turned out to be a total and utter disaster. Just anarchy. I simply couldn't have wished for anything worse.

The joiner finished his work and left with the officers. The house was quiet again. I stood up, holding on to the bannister for support, my legs like jelly. My eyes nipped, and I felt low. The plan for the time ahead was to get the courage to move forward from this and get back to normality again. The only thing I wanted right now was my bed. To feel content and fall into a deep, peaceful, relaxing sleep. But there was no way I was setting foot anywhere near my bedroom, and on that note, I didn't want to be near this house anymore. I wanted out. Simply disgusted by the low life scum that had done this to us. They were vile.

Mum paced the green tartan carpet slowly, concern etched on her face. It had looked as if she had aged ten years. I could see this was taking a toll on her. She had a heart of gold and would have done anything for anyone. She didn't deserve this. Neither of us did. I tried to comfort her, but I didn't know if it was working or not.

It felt too depressing doing absolutely nothing, so I headed into the livingroom and fixed the couch up, putting the cushions back in order. I covered Mum with a blanket as she lay down, her arms wrapped around a small cushion. She smiled up at me and took my hand.

'You're a good girl, Chloe, you know that? I know your father would have been so proud of you.'

I forced a smile on my face, holding back tears of emotion. Honestly, I didn't know how I was doing it. Strong, me? No chance. Right now, it was just a battle.

'You get some rest, Mum. You will feel better.'

She let my hand go as she shifted to lie on her side, and pulling the blanket up over her shoulders, she closed her eyes. Backing off slowly, I walked out the room. Now was my chance. I grabbed my jacket from the bannister and headed out the front door, just as the cold rain began to pour down.

I didn't care about the weather. I didn't care about the fact that my Nike Air Max were getting soaked in the deep puddles as I walked. I felt the water seep in through the air holes and drench my socks. My feet were now damp and cold.

I turned into a gravel driveway, passed a Ford Focus hatchback and reached a red door I knew well. The large Georgian house was red-brick. The venetian blinds were closed over in the attractive rectangular windows of the livingroom. I took a moment to reflect on memories from years ago. Like Easter when we were just kids. I would sit outside on the red-tiled steps on a sunny day, eating my Cadbury's Easter egg. I remember the inside of the house back then. It seemed huge. With their flowery wallpaper, brown and cream carpets and family pictures hanging on the walls, the place was immaculate. It looked like a show home to me. Like it was never lived in. I was a happy kid back then with no worries, in my own little world.

Coming out of my daze, I rang the doorbell, shivering where I stood. Through the blinds I could see a slight glow of light and I imagined the cosy, warm livingroom inside. Seconds later the porch light came on and the hall blinds twitched. I heard the jangle of keys as the door was unlocked and a face appeared in the gap.

'Chloe?'

I was frozen to the spot in the torrential rain. My hair clung to my face. The door opened and Mollie grabbed my jacket and pulled me inside and closed the door behind me. She looked warm in her cream jumper and Levi's jeans and her shoulder-length, curly, black hair was neat around her face.

She guided me over to the staircase and helped me take off my soaked jacket, shoes and socks.

'Chloe, you're shivering. What were you doing out in that rain?'

I sat on the step, feeling dazed and stunned. 'House was broken into. Trashed.'

'What? Didn't you just get home today?'

'We only just arrived home. Place was a total disaster. We weren't even burgled. Burglars take things. These ones didn't. They just trashed the house.'

She sat down on the stair beside me, looking shocked. A moment passed before she spoke again.

'Are you sure they didn't take anything? Jewellery? Money? Valuables?'

I shook my head. 'No. I don't know what this was, but it certainly wasn't a burglary.'

I laid my head against her shoulder and closed my eyes. Without a doubt this had been the worst year of my entire life. And I hated it.

Mollie let me take a bath while my clothes dried over the radiator. I took my time soaking in the Ashton bathtub, trying to take my mind off the trauma of today. I could hear music coming from her room and I smiled, knowing that she was just as much a fan of Britney Spears as I was.

Later, Mollie asked questions about the house and the holiday, of which just a small part was another ordeal in itself. I couldn't take my mind away from Dave, though. It simply must have been him who organised it. I hated that man to the core. I needed answers. The forensics team would get back to us one day soon, hopefully.

Suddenly, something came into my head. What if we had been at home when the intruders broke in? What if we had been up in our rooms, sleeping, while they were ransacking the place downstairs? The thought made my skin crawl.

Mollie was chatting away to me, but I was too distracted to listen. I walked to the window in the front bedroom and peered out of the blinds. The thick clouds that covered the sky had turned dark grey and the pouring rain bounced off the streets. I watched a man run quickly with his small pug wrapped up in a waterproof coat, one hand grasping his black umbrella and the other holding the leash. I looked from one side of the street to the other, taking in the houses, cars and trees. My eyes suddenly stopped on the corner. I squinted to see better and moved slightly closer to the window.

A black figure was sheltering from the rain under a tree.

For just a moment I thought I could see a face. A face so chilling it made my skin crawl. The figure suddenly stared up at me.

Gasping, I took a step backwards, away from the window. Mollie let out a cry behind me. She had been too close; I had stood on her foot. Saying a quick sorry, I rushed out of the room and down the stairs. I flung the door open and ran out down the garden path.

I looked over to where the figure had stood just moments before. There was no one there anymore. I stood, getting soaked all over again, looking around, desperate to find out who it was. I was being watched alright, I knew that for sure. I wanted to scream, 'What do you want from me?!' I felt angry and upset at the same time, and I wondered if I wasn't the only one being watched.

Mollie came running out and brought me back into the house. I was determined to find out who these intruders were. But that was one mistake that I simply shouldn't have made.

CHAPTER 23

I called Mum in a panic to make sure she was alright. Her voice was quiet and she sounded off. Whether I had woken her up or not, I wasn't sure. She never let on. Her voice began to tremble as I described the man watching me from outside under the tree. I could hear the fear in her voice and I tried to reassure her that I was alright, but I wasn't even convincing myself. I took a deep breath and forced myself to be courageous. We had to get through this horrific ordeal. This was our life and we wouldn't let whoever it was get away with the damage they had caused.

Mollie's parents questioned me, feeling concerned for our safety. Her dad, Stan, even suggested we go to a bed and breakfast, just to lie low, but I wasn't convinced. Stan drove me home, even though it was only around the corner, and he waited until I was inside and the door was locked. He drove off with a wave as I watched from the living room window. That was one time I was envious of his family. They had a happy home.

'You walked out?' Mum said accusingly. She was on the couch, where I'd left her earlier. It was a slight relief to see she had got some rest at least.

'Yeah,' I sighed. 'I had to get a bit of fresh air.'

'After what's happened?' she practically squealed at me. 'You shouldn't have left. You don't know who could be out there. Don't leave again until I know we're safe.'

I sat down bedside her on the couch, putting my arms on my knees. 'I had to get out the house. I just feel so violated.'

She sighed. 'I know how you feel. I feel the exact same way.' She entwined our fingers, locking our hands together. 'But we need to stay together at home. Safe. You can't just go running out any time you feel like it. We have to be honest with each other and stick together.'

I shook my head, squeezing my eyes shut. 'I just couldn't cope anymore. I panicked. I felt trapped. But I won't leave again. Not until we know that the intruders who were in our home have been caught and arrested and we're safe. Have the police spoken to the neighbours? Did they hear anything?'

'Yeah, a few doors were chapped. I haven't been informed of anything, though. We'll just need to wait and see.'

'I'm honestly not sure if I can take anymore. With what's happened already, I don't know how I'm getting through every day.'

'Oh sweetheart.' She held me tight, trying to comfort me.

With how I was feeling already, I didn't think anything would make me feel better. My stomach growled loudly. At least I still had my appetite.

'I'm going to order in food. You want your usual?'

'No.' She waved a hand dismissively. 'I won't eat.'

'Yeah, you feel like that just now, but what about later on? You may get hungry.'

'You do whatever, Chlo,' she replied, rubbing her hand over her face.

I turned to the phone, ordered our Chinese meals and got the money out of my purse. During our wait, I fixed the table and chairs and gave the livingroom a quick hoover. I desperately needed things to get back to normal.

We ate our Chinese meals quietly that night, and Mum picked at her food. With no television to watch, the room was silent. Every slight noise made Mum jump. She was a nervous wreck and it showed clearly.

I put my arms around her for comfort as she dabbed her

eyes with a tissue and wiped her nose. We were there for each other. That was all that mattered really.

The doorbell rang. I walked out, silent and wary, into the hallway. After gazing into the peephole, I opened the door. Jason stood at the bottom of the steps, looking casual, with his hands in the pockets of his black parka and his hood over his head. The rain had eased slightly and the sun was trying to break through the clouds.

I welcomed him in and he walked straight up to Mum and wrapped his arms around her. She let out a gasp of surprise, happy to see him and to be back in his arms.

'I'm so glad to see you, Jason.'

He took her hands in his. 'Me too. I really missed you, Karen. I was lonely while you were away. Did you have a good time?'

'Well, I did…'

He turned to me. 'What happened?'

I rolled my eyes. 'I went out scuba-diving. And it went horribly wrong.'

'Oh Chloe, I'm sorry. Did you get to see anything at all?'

'Yeah, I saw a few fish. And that was it. It's a lot harder than it looks.'

'Yeah, I'll bet.' He turned to Mum. 'It's so good you're back, but next time I'm coming with you.' He smirked, turning his head. 'Hey, what happened to your TV? Did you have a falling out?' he joked.

'Um, no. That's another story,' she answered sadly.

Mum sat him down and explained everything to him. He looked shocked and worried as he tried to comfort her. She awkwardly fidgeted with her hands, trying to keep herself together, taking a deep breath every now and again. I worried that one day she would have some sort of breakdown. Right now, it seemed very likely.

'I don't even know what to say, Karen! I'm so sorry.'

Jason's face was a picture alright. He looked totally shocked and bewildered. Like he couldn't believe this had happened to us. I think having him here with us gave Mum the extra bit of support that she really needed.

'It's okay, Jason, you weren't to know. It gave me such a scare when I came home to a trashed house. I don't think I can cope, with this…with any of it anymore.'

He moved closer together, so his knee touched hers, and rubbed her arm. 'You can't get yourself into a state like that. It won't do you any good. And anyway, I'm here. I'll look after you, Karen. I'll always be here for you.' He wrapped his arms around her and the two of them sat holding each other.

It felt somewhat awkward for my mum to be so intimate with him as I stood there in the doorway. I left them to it and walked into the kitchen to start cleaning up, giving them time together. I had really warmed to Jason now and he felt like part of the family. He made Mum happy and that was what she really needed – someone to be there for her, care for and support her. It left me feeling a little bit lonely. But Mum was happy with him. That was all that mattered.

Jason helped me clean up the mess in the kitchen. I was careful of the glass that lay on the worktop and used the small dustpan and brush that we kept under the sink to put the mess in the bin. It seemed to take forever to get the kitchen back to a decent standard again. The worktops were scrubbed down, and the floor was brushed and mopped. I wiped the sweat from my forehead as I finished up.

'Right,' Jason said, standing in the livingroom with his hands on his hips, his black t-shirt soaked in sweat. 'I insist that you both stay with me over the next few days. It will give you both the reassurance that you need and you'll get a decent night's sleep. You'll be safe there.'

Mum opened her mouth like she was about to argue with him, but then closed it again. She knew he was right. I was more than happy to leave. To sleep in this house in the state that it was in would have been simply insane. We packed our holdalls full of clean clothes and our personal items, and left the house in its sorry state, not looking back.

At Jason's house, we set our luggage down in the hallway for the time being.

'Make yourself at home,' he said as we entered his spacious, brightly decorated living room, and went to put the kettle on to make us a cup of tea.

Mum and I sat on the black-leather two-seater couch. Everything was simply stunning. The walls were painted white, and there was real dark-wood flooring throughout. I looked around the room, feeling really quite impressed and inspired by the beauty that surrounded me. With the finest art on his walls, he was a man of exquisite taste alright. I stood up and walked towards one of the smaller canvases to get a closer look. It was a painting of a beach, with brown sand, white waves crashing and a tiny lighthouse far off. It looked pretty expensive and must have been painted by someone extremely talented and professional.

Jason came in with our cups of tea and set them on the glass coffee table.

'I like your paintings, Jason. Where did you get them?'

'I painted them myself, Chloe.'

'You painted these?!' I was speechless. Over the few months that we had known this gentleman, he had never said a word about being an artist. He had been more than modest.

'A doctor and an artist. Huh!' Mum said, looking up at the art, impressed. 'This is very fine work you have here, Jason. Have you ever thought about selling them one day?'

He gave her a kind smile. 'No, I've never been in it for the money. I'm really quite comfortable.'

She turned away, giving a small laugh and shaking her head.

These paintings had been a really nice surprise and I knew they would be a great distraction for me while we were here.

'If you like, Chloe, I can take you out to my shed one day and you can try your hand at something new. It's really up to you.'

I raised my eyebrows in surprise. Was there anything this man wouldn't do for us?

'Thanks, Jason,' I replied, giving him a large grin. He was making me happier by the minute and I had almost forgotten why we were here in the first place.

Jason was at ease lounging around his home, trying to make us feel more relaxed and comfortable. He had a collection of great DVDs in a large display cabinet in the dining room, but as much as I wanted to watch one of the great classics, like Only Fools and Horses or Fawlty Towers, my heart just wasn't in it.

Lying in bed, tossing and turning unable to settle thinking about the person hidden under the tree. The more I thought about it, the more I questioned it. This had to be connected. I finally crashed an hour or so later into a peaceful night's sleep.

The next day Mum and Jason were at work, so I had the house to myself. I divided up my day between emailing CV's to employers and making homemade lentil soup. Then I sat on the couch, loaded Google and typed 'prisoners' into the address bar. I shouldn't have been as shocked by what I saw. It was my own fault really. Or maybe I would have found out anyhow.

A prisoner had been released on parole from HMP Nostow while Mum and I were away on holiday for the week. Pictures showed him standing before a judge, while the public sat behind him, looking on. The man was wearing a navy-blue two-piece outfit with his hands in cuffs. The caption under the picture indicated that he had been released due to good behaviour.

It was so clear that this was not a coincidence. Around the same time this man was released, our home got broken into. What would Mum think of this new information?

Day turned into night. Mum was cooking dinner, Jason was on his way home from work and I had just been for a cycle on his exercise bike. I was determined to do a cardio workout for at least half an hour to burn a few calories. The distraction was badly needed.

The weather outside hadn't changed much. It had been drizzling on and off all day, but I was in a warm, cosy house and it didn't bother me in the slightest. There was no need for me to be out in that at all. The cycle had made me feel good and taken my mind off things for a while.

After dinner, I went for a shower and later on joined Mum and Jason on the couch to watch Emmerdale. I lifted the laptop from the coffee table in front of us and opened it up to the page I had been browsing earlier.

'Mum, do you think it's a coincidence that this has happened?'

She looked over at the screen and gasped with surprised, then gave the article a thorough read.

'I hope not. I guess it could be possible, but did Dave and this man out on parole know each other? That would explain why we were targeted then. Maybe I should phone the station just incase. The officers might know something after all.'

She walked into the hallway, out of earshot, to make the phone call. Just as I was beginning to feel slightly better, it all seemed to be crashing down on us again. Were we never allowed to feel happiness?

'So how are you feeling, Chloe?' Jason asked, looking

concerned.

I looked away from the TV for a minute, lifted my mug of tea from the table and wrapped my hands around it. Looking over at him, I shrugged. 'You know. We're both pretty devastated that this has happened. I hate going outside now. It's put Mum and I both on edge. And now this?' I pointed to the laptop screen. 'What are the chances? I'm scared, Jason. I'm really scared.' Even I could hear the emotion in my voice.

'You'll get through this. You've just got to give it time. I'm sure everything will work out for the best. And if this is the man who broke into your house... well, there's really no doubt about it: he will get caught.'

Mum walked back into the livingroom, her mobile still in her hand. The police had told her there was a lead in the case and they needed us to go down to the station. We rushed to the car, Jason looking just as worried as Mum and I were. I felt nervous and had an unsettling feeling in my gut.

Jason parked outside, and we walked into the small, white building. I felt nauseous standing around with all these uniforms coming and going. The walls of the reception were covered with small pamphlets about drug abuse, rape and murder, giving numbers and helplines. The world seemed like a more terrifying place from in here; like that was all that happened. I sat down beside Mum and Jason, hoping this visit wouldn't take too long. I would rather have been anywhere else but here.

A young female officer guided Mum and me into an empty room, while Jason waited outside. The rectangular room was painted dark blue with a grey carpet and contained only a black wooden table and chairs. What little light there was came from a small rectangular window above. She flipped the switch on the wall and the room suddenly lit up brightly, which made it seem more inviting.

Two officers arrived with folders in their hands. There was brief eye contact as they sat down opposite us. The light-haired man that faced Mum opened his file.

'Good evening. I'm Inspector Dunlop. This is Officer Adams.'

Adams nodded while scribbling notes on his pad of paper. The inspector glanced at the information in front of him while speaking.

'You were called in here today because there has been a break-in at your home. You left for a holiday, on the sixteenth of July, I believe, for a week, during which time your home was broken into through the kitchen window. There were no witnesses and no one saw anything suspicious. So we have come to the conclusion that this was done during the night.

'Now, the forensics team spent a lot of time on their findings. It's not good news, I'm afraid.'

Mum and I looked at each other worriedly.

'The team found fingerprints from two men at your home. We have a positive match. One of the men is highly dangerous, not long out of prison. His name is Bert Rifnick. He was in for actual bodily harm, burglary and assault. He is now wanted for questioning over the break-in and damage to your home. Have you ever heard from or seen this man at all?'

I sat there horrified. Actual bodily harm? Assault? This man had been in our home. A man we had never met or heard of. I tried my hardest to keep my emotions at bay, but it was impossible. I put one hand over my mouth to stop myself crying and Mum took the other. I was scared. I didn't have any answers. I didn't know what to do.

'No, we have never heard of that man. Never had a connection with him. But I know someone who just may have. What prison was this man in?' Mum asked.

The inspector gave a loud sigh before answering, a look

of pity on his face. 'Nostow Prison. Like I said, he's not long been out, only a couple of weeks, but that would have given him enough time to get the job done. But why he chose your house to carry out his first offence is another story.'

Mum spoke in a low voice, linking her fingers together and placing them on the table as she sat forward. 'I think I may be able to help you out with your investigation. You said he had come out of Nostow Prison? Well, as it turns out, my brother-in-law is in there aswell.'

There was an awkward silence in the room. My nerves felt rattled.

'Could this possibly be connected? Could they have both known each other inside?' Mum asked.

'It's possible. We will find this man. Don't worry. Now, Mr David Stanson…that is your brother-in-law, correct?'

'Yes,' she replied.

'And have you been in touch with him at all? Any phone calls?'

'We haven't heard from him since he was arrested. He put us through a lot and we don't ever want to see or hear from him again.'

I put my head down as a memory came flooding back to me.

'That's not entirely true,' I cut in, feeling guilty.

Mum turned to me. 'What do you mean?'

I bit my lip nervously. 'Um, he kind of phoned the house one night, when you and Jason were out. I was so upset about it, I just put it out of my head.'

Mum looked at me, shocked. 'You mean to tell me that he was in touch with you, that he phoned our home, and you "forgot" to tell me about it? When was this exactly?'

'It was the night you went out for a meal and then you came back drunk. Mum, I'm sorry.'

Mum scoffed. 'I was not drunk, Chloe, I only had a couple of glasses of wine.'

'Well, it seemed like it at the time,' I said defensively.

She went to say something, but stopped, glancing at the two men sitting in front of us. She didn't say another word as Inspector Dunlop scribbled some notes down. Then we gave him other details regarding Dave that he asked for.

'Now, I must advise you to stay well away from the prison at this time. No matter how angry or upset both of you are feeling, you must not contact David at all. Phone calls included.'

Mum let out a snort. 'Oh, don't you worry about that, Inspector. That won't be a problem.'

He thanked us both and finished up the meeting. I breathed a sigh of relief as I walked out of the room with Mum behind me. It was over. I came out of the building feeling light-headed and sick. This planned attack on our house would be enough to drive anyone over the edge.

We got back to Jason's feeling deflated. Now that we knew there was an ex-convict out there who had been in the same prison as Dave, we guessed that this couldn't have been just a random break-in. We lived in a good area. With our neighbourhood watch, there was never any trouble. Up until now. Everyone looked after everyone here.

I said goodnight to Jason and Mum and headed up the stairs to the spare bedroom. As it was only my second night in this room, it still fascinated me. Jason took pride in his home and it was obvious to see. With the dark-brick-effect wallpaper and Mirabel wardrobe with sliding glass doors, it was exquisite. I climbed into the double Leona ottoman bed and sank into the memory-foam mattress. Taking my iPod from the bedside cabinet, I switched it on. With my earphones in, I closed my eyes and drifted off to Savage Garden.

CHAPTER 24

The next morning the sun shone brightly, trying to break through the closed venetian blinds. Stretching with a smile, I awoke from the best sleep I'd had in a long time. The bed was so comfortable.

What made it even better, I discovered, was the hidden remote control in a little pocket on the left-hand side. I pressed the middle button at the top of the remote and the bed frame opened up to reveal a TV rising from the hidden compartment at the foot of the bed. I switched on the TV and flicked through the channels, before switching it back off and hiding the TV back in its compartment again. Jason had a bedroom that one could only dream of. It was incredible.

I replaced the remote control, stood up and walked to the window. I opened the blinds slightly and looked up. The sky was blue and there wasn't a cloud in sight. The birds were twittering away in the hedges down below. Today was a new day and a fresh start.

I gathered my clothes from my holdall and laid them out on the bed, then walked into the large bathroom. I took my time lathering in the large Saturn walk-in shower, feeling pampered with the luxury, before getting dressed in my Hollister jeans, t-shirt and hoodie.

I skipped down the stairs for breakfast and entered the large kitchen. It was simply beautiful, with black marble worktops and gloss white cabinets and white brick-effect tiles on every wall. Mum and Jason were sitting on barstools with mugs of coffee, reading the Daily Record. Greeting them warmly, I passed by to make myself a cup of tea and put two pancakes in the toaster.

Having taken my breakfast into the living room, I

switched the TV on to BBC News. A woman presenter sat behind her desk chatting to the camera while the breaking news scrolled by at the bottom of the screen. They were talking about stocks and shares, the economy of the UK and climate change. I was just getting into it when Mum walked into the livingroom, lifted her phone from the frosted-glass coffee table, glared at it for a moment and looked down at me.

'We've decided to go back to the house today, Chloe. What do you think? Are you up for it?'

My heart sank. That was the last thing I wanted. I dreaded going home.

'Really? Do we have to?' I whined, gutted that I wouldn't be staying at Jason's anymore. Living here had become really enjoyable. It had been a home away from home.

'Well, we can't stay here forever and forget what's happened. That's the reason we're here in the first place. We just have to deal with this head on.'

That was the worst thing I had ever heard.

Within the hour we were standing outside our front door. I set my holdall on the path as I gazed up at the two-storey house, which featured sandstone walls, a grey rooftop and chimney, all the while waiting for Mum to take out her keys from her crowded bag and unlock the door.

My body was tense and rigid as we walked in, reliving our return from Spain. Leaving our bags in the hallway, we got to work clearing away the mess.

It took hours. Jason repainted Mum's bedroom wall and got rid of the smashed TV. The furniture in my room was in desperate need of some TLC. Everything had to be rearranged and cleaned. My desktop computer was placed back on my black Lawson desk with all the wires reconnected. I switched it on and crossed my fingers, then jumped for joy a little as the machine whirred to life and the screen lit up. My paperwork was organised, my bed was made and my room received an extreme hoovering and polish. I placed my jewellery box with its contents back on the shelf above my computer.

Shania Twain was on repeat and it brightened up the day a little. The windows were washed, and by dinnertime things were a whole lot different. There was only one thing missing: we needed a new TV for the livingroom. Mum made us all tea while I searched online with the laptop.

The next day, we headed out for the short drive to Argos. Mum locked the front door as Jason and I walked up the pathway. We were so busy chatting that we didn't see the man until it was almost too late. The guy walking by us just missed bumping smack into Jason, before turning back with his hands up and saying, 'Sorry, mate,' and then walking on. Regaining my composure, I stared at him as he turned the corner. Something about that was most definitely off.

Jason called me to get into the car. I shook my head, annoyed, as I climbed into the back seat and we drove off. It was such an odd thing to have happened, but I thought no more of it as we headed to Braehead shopping centre.

We picked up a thirty-inch, widescreen Philips television and new Yale CCTV cameras for the back and front doors. The cameras had night vision and contained a preinstalled hard drive that would record hours of footage. Mum and Jason put the items in the boot of the car and we drove to a carvery just a mile away from home. Mollie's parents had taken me here for dinner a couple of years ago, and since then it had been one of my favourite places to eat.

The restaurant was bright and spacious. Parents cooed over their children while enjoying their meals, couples sat together eating quietly and New Radicals played in the background. We sat at a four-seater table with our drinks (Coke for me and Jason, white wine for Mum) and our meals. As my dish was served to me, Mum and Jason chuckled at the food on my plate – gammon steak with a slice of pineapple and a portion of chips; it looked mouth-watering. Digging in, I savoured my meal, greatly enjoying every mouthful.

As we climbed out the car outside the house a couple of hours later, Jason opened the boot ready to carry the TV out. Giving him a helping hand, I picked up the cameras and turned to walk up the pathway. I stopped dead in my tracks to let a man pass by, and as he did, I got a good look at his face.

I realised right then and there who this person was. It was the same man who had bumped into Jason earlier on and apologised for nearly knocking him over, and it was the same man I'd seen under the tree outside Mollie's. I was positive of it.

My whole body cringed. Every single detail of the stranger was memorised now as he walked off and around the corner. I tried to compose myself as fear ran through my body. I turned to face Mum.

She was helping Jason with the TV. When she saw me looking, she gave me the loving smile she always had for me.

I whispered to her, pointing, 'That's him!'

She looked at me, wondering what I was talking about. It took a moment before she clicked. Then she let go of her side of the box as her hands went to her face.

The TV fell to the ground with a thud. Jason murmured something to himself in annoyance before asking Mum to help him again. She took no notice; she looked as if she was going to collapse. Putting the cameras on the wall quickly to free my hands, I took her arm and gently guided her up the garden path to the house. I took her keys out of her bag, opening the door, and walked her into the livingroom, where she sat on the couch, staring into space.

I ran outside, closed the boot and collected the cameras, then followed Jason as he struggled with the awkwardly large box up the garden path and back into the house.

It felt like we were constantly contacting the police, but we had to: this man was a big threat to Mum and me. She had gone back to her old state, so Jason had no choice but to call the station yet again and ask for Inspector Dunlop. He gave a clear description of what the man looked like, what height he was and what kind of clothes he was wearing.

The police arrived at the house within the hour and walked around the area to do their search. It was another afternoon of disruption. I was starting to think that we would never get a peaceful life, that we would always be pestered one way or another.

Time ticked by. I curled up on the end of the couch and wrapped my arms around a cushion as tears flowed down my cheeks. I sobbed my heart out for the rest of the afternoon and well into the night. Our life would always be tormented, no matter what.

Daylight left the sky and darkness took over. The blinds on the windows were still open and lights flickered by. I knew the police were still out there hunting for him. I prayed this torment would come to an end. Jason had covered me up with a blanket and taken Mum up to her bedroom to try to calm her down.

A sudden knock at the door had me jumping to my feet in shock, my heart pounding with fright in my chest. Slowly managing to pull myself together, I opened the door to a police officer. He stood at the bottom of the steps with a serious look on his face.

'Hi. Is your mum or dad in?' he asked.

I called Jason. He came down the stairs and invited in

the uniformed man, and they both introduced themselves. The officer informed us that they had found the man who had been stalking us. He had been at his home by the time the police had caught up with him and had put up a fight, unwilling to be arrested and taken in. The officer advised us that there would be a court hearing for all who had been involved and we would be getting a letter letting us know the time and date that it would take place. It turned out that two men had been involved, brothers living in the same house.

'Is there any possible chance that Karen, I mean Mrs Stanson, could get an injunction against these people? I mean, she and Chloe have been hassled enough,' Jason said.

'Well, it is possible,' the officer answered. 'She needs to apply for a non-molestation order. You download and fill in an application form and make two copies. The form needs to be taken into court and handed in as a witness statement, telling the court what has happened. You should receive a letter within two weeks for a hearing.'

'Okay, thank you for your help, Officer. I'll see you out.'

Jason let him out and the officer walked down the path and closed the gate behind him. I looked at the police car and saw another officer sitting beside the perpetrator who had been stalking us. He watched me from inside the parked vehicle, lifting up his cuffed hands as he pointed at me with a malicious grin on his face. He continued to stare at me until the car moved away.

At that moment negative emotions overcame me. I closed the door over, threw my back against it and squeezed my eyes shut. It would simply be a matter of not letting him get to me.

I walked into the kitchen to find Jason making a mug of tea.

'Did you not make one for me?' I joked sarcastically.

'I didn't know you wanted one, Chloe. The kettle's just boiled. Help yourself,' he answered curtly.

Jason was in a mood. And who could blame him? I took a mug out of the cupboard and made my tea in peace, giving him a chance to calm down.

'I'm sorry you've been brought into this mess, Jason.' I turned to him with a guilty look on my face, my back against the counter. He stood opposite me, eyes down, blowing into his hot mug of tea. His silence was deafening.

'We didn't want any of this to happen. To be honest, I think Dave has just lost it altogether. He's out for revenge because of what happened to his brother. But he's not the only one feeling empty and heartbroken. We both miss Dad. Mum the most. She was his wife, after all.

'When Dad died, I think it did something to Dave. It changed him. He lashed out. He was hurt and had no one else to turn to. If he'd communicated with us about how he was feeling, then maybe Mum could have helped him. She would have got him doctor appointments and treatments. And maybe if he'd done the right thing, he wouldn't have ended up in prison.'

Setting his mug on the worktop, Jason ran his hand over his face and sighed. He looked tired and run down, with dark shadows under his eyes. 'Well, you're right about one thing. That man needs help. I think he has a serious condition that needs to be looked into. The way he was around you and your mum…it was horrible. I can see how it's affected you both. Emotionally and physically. I'm not the sort of guy to go bad-mouthing people, and I won't.

Not even your uncle. I just hope he gets the treatment that he needs. I know you might not want to hear this, but he is still your family.'

I scoffed. 'Not after what he's done to us he's not. That man will never get another chance as far as I'm concerned.

He could drop off the end of the earth for all I care.'

Jason looked at me in surprise. 'You don't really mean that.'

I raised my voice. 'I do!'

He sighed. 'You're a much better person than that. You're a strong-willed young lady. And just out of school. You shouldn't have to put up with this, you have too many things to think about. Which reminds me, what's happening with college? Your mum told me you applied.'

'Yeah, I'm still waiting for them to get back to me. I just hope I get in.'

'You will. Have more confidence in yourself. You'll do well.'

'Thanks, Jason,' I said with a smile.

I finished my tea, washed my cup and put it on the drainer, then walked up the stairs to the airing cupboard. I took down blankets and left them on the couch. After saying goodnight to Jason, I left him to it and headed up to bed.

It was after ten when I woke the next morning. Strolling downstairs to find Jason already left for work, I picked up the mail that had just come through the letterbox. There were two letters for Mum and one for me. Saying good morning, I handed Mum her two envelopes. She was sitting at the dining room table taking her tea and toast. She looked a lot better than she had yesterday. Her cheeks were a light shade of pink. She was dressed in casual gear – black bootcut jeans and a cream knitted cardigan. Her auburn hair was brushed to perfection and sat tidily around her shoulders.

'How are you feeling, Mum?' I asked.

'I'm alright, sweetheart. I'm sorry if I upset you yesterday. I think my body just went into shock and it got a bit too much for me.'

I walked over to her and gave her a hug.

'I'm glad you're okay.' I smiled.

Sitting on the foot stool, I opened my letter. There was a stamp on the outside that read 'Grey Acre College', the college outside the town that I had applied to. I had planned on taking a tour during the holidays just incase I got in, but with so much going on around the house, I hadn't had the chance. Maybe Mollie would go with me if she had the time. I read it aloud.

Dear Miss Stanson,

Following your recent application to our college I am pleased to tell you that you have secured a place on the NC Computing course. You are required to meet with the course leader, Sam McKinnon, on the 1st August, and your induction day will be on the 27th of August. Please bring with you this letter, your CV and photo ID.

I look forward to seeing you then.

Kind regards,

Roy Harvey

I looked up at Mum with a massive smile on my face. I had landed myself on a course that I had been looking forward to for months now. Happiness overwhelmed me and I was on a complete and utter high. I threw a fist punch in the air. Things were finally moving forward.

Mum stood up, wishing me all the best, and gave me a hug. All in all, I think this was a good distraction for her. It was what she needed to take her mind off everything else and make her feel happy again.

I ran up the stairs, took my mobile from my bedside table and speed-dialled my best friend. She squealed down the receiver the moment she heard the news. This girl had been in my life since primary school and I was glad she was my best friend. She told me she was proud of me and was genuinely happy that I was going in the right direction.

But this opportunity was just the start of a long and hard journey ahead. We arranged to take a tour of the college that day, so I would be prepared. I got myself ready in almost no time, grabbed a quick scone on the way out to eat for my breakfast and rushed round to Mollie's house. We got the bus to the town centre, then another one straight to the college.

We arrived outside the building. Walking through the glass revolving doors, we entered the quiet reception area. On the rear wall was the large logo in blue. A young brunette was speaking on the phone, and a few people sat around the small, round tables to the left. This looked like a great place for students starting out or in their first, second or third year of college. I was just glad I had been lucky enough to get in.

We walked around the whole building, including the conference centre, finding a library before finishing our tour in a large canteen. We sat at a small table for two with two teas and a couple of muffins. Mollie didn't stop asking me questions the whole time. Her eyes lit up as she spoke; she was overcome with excitement. We had both spent a lot of time together through the years and a lot of changes were beginning to happen. I knew we wouldn't get the chance to see each other a lot anymore. It didn't exactly sink in that well for either of us how much we would actually miss each other.

'So, are you going to move out and get a flat then? Be an independent student?' she asked with a posh accent.

'Um, I don't know,' I replied, wrinkling my nose. 'If I left, Mum would be on her own. I'm not sure if she could cope well.'

'Yeah, but she has Jason now. She won't be lonely. She

will miss you, though.'

'Yeah, but it seems a bit early. I'll see what happens in the future.' It wasn't something that was on my bucket list.

'Seems like someone's procrastinating,' she joked, lifting her head and looking up at the ceiling.

I tutted, rolling my eyes, and shook my head.

'Are you going to get yourself a boyfriend out here then?' She smirked.

I laughed. 'I don't think so. I know that's how it worked out for Mum and Dad, but I don't know if I'll be going down the same route. I just want to study, do my exams, pass this course and then get a job. I'll worry about that kind of stuff when the time comes.'

She nodded at me like she didn't believe me. It was the truth. I just laughed at her.

We left the college and made a short walk down to the town's shopping centre, where we browsed around before finding all the stationery accessories we could possibly need in Poundland. With a full carrier bag in my hand, The Great Café seemed just the right spot for lunch as it was only a brief distance away. We ordered two bowls of soup and cheese toasties, sharing a can of Irn Bru.

After the meal we took the bus over to the Showcase cinema to watch the comedy-horror Sean of the Dead. We came out of the theatre feeling happy and full of laughter. The movie was certainly one that could be watched again and again without ever tiring of it.

After the quick bus ride home, Mollie walked me to my front door and said goodnight and good luck to me on my new adventure in college. I gave her a hug, thanking her for today. She had been there for me when I needed her, and I hoped that one day I would be there to return the favour. As she held me tight for an extra few moments, I had a feeling she was trying to tell me something. She didn't need to say it with words, though. I knew what she was thinking. We were both on the same page. Today had been awesome.

CHAPTER 25

I closed the front door and peeked into the living room to find Mum and Jason sitting over a homemade spaghetti bolognaise. The livingroom was slightly dark; the only light came from the two candles on the dining table. This relationship was moving forward much more quickly than I had anticipated. They continued to eat and giggle over their meal, but Mum called out to let me know there was some leftover food in the kitchen.

'I'm not hungry,' I answered. 'I had food at The Great Café.'

'What's that?' she asked curiously.

I stood at the edge of the livingroom, desperate to disappear from the area that was filled with the smell of Italian food and romantic music coming from the small stereo in the corner by the phone.

I looked over and gave her a smile. 'It's a large café in the town that does all sorts of food. We had soup and a toastie. It was delicious.'

'Oh, sounds lovely,' she answered. 'Did you have a nice time out? Did you get a tour of the college?'

'Yeah. Mum, the campus was awesome.' I walked over to the table. 'The inside was stunning; they have so many facilities and a large canteen. I'm so excited to get started. It's unreal!' I squealed.

Her smile glowed in the lighting in the room. Her chin rested on her hands, clasped together; her elbows rested on the table. 'I'm glad you're happy, Chloe. Good luck with everything.'

'Thanks, Mum.'

'Oh, Chloe, Jason set up the new TV for us, and I've

got someone coming to install the cameras for the back and front doors.'

Sighing with relief, I felt my shoulders slump. 'Really? That will give us some peace of mind then. When will they be here?'

'Tomorrow morning.'

'Not soon enough, in my book,' I murmured, walking up the stairs and leaving them both to their romantic dinner and soulful music.

I had set my alarm that night for eight a.m, as I knew the handyman was coming over early. As it bleeped, waking me up from a peaceful sleep the next morning, I turned over, throwing my arm at the noisy clock, clicking the button and shutting it off. For a moment I lay still. The only sound was my shallow breathing. A minute passed before my eyes blinked open, taking in the new morning.

Throwing back the covers, I dragged myself out of bed with a groan, wiped my eyes and took a quick shower to make myself presentable for the day ahead. Walking down the stairs humming quietly, I wasn't paying attention to the rooms in front of me; my focus was putting the kettle on to make a cup of tea. I should have been more aware. I heard him before I saw him.

'Morning, Chloe.'

A high-pitched squeal escaped my mouth as I quickly turned and headed back the way I'd come, taking in Jason out of the corner of my eye before running up the stairs and closing the door to my bedroom. I threw my back against the door and put my head in my hands. My mum's boyfriend had just seen me in nothing but two towels around me. Embarrassment took over.

I got dressed quickly, leaving the towel on my head, and headed back down the narrow staircase for the second time, running my hand down the white-painted bannister. Jason was still standing where he had been before, leaning against the kitchen worktop. He wore a white shirt, blue tie, black trousers and expensive-looking black shoes. His jet-black hair was combed neatly against his head and his pale skin brought out his sky-blue eyes. I realised I had been staring for just a second too long and looked away quickly. Another awkward moment.

I heard a snigger, and when I looked up, he was laughing at me. I decided to play along for the fun of it.

'Find me funny, do you?'

He smiled at me. It was quite breathtaking. 'Well, as a matter of fact I do, as it happens, Chloe. You don't know it but you're a very funny character.' He laughed into his mug.

I felt my face heat up and a grin appeared. I looked up at him under my lashes.

'Very funny, Jason, ha-ha,' I answered jokingly.

We carried on playing along together until Mum came down the stairs. I suddenly felt very self-conscious and headed up to my room to find my hairdryer and my straighteners. Moment over.

As it turned out, Mum had given Jason her spare key so he could let himself in. And by 'spare' I mean Dad's key. Yes, you could imagine how I felt. I was livid. Livid at the fact that my mum seemed to be missing my dad just that little bit less every day and had apparently now decided to start giving his belongings away. I mean, don't get me wrong, I had taken to Jason – he had become more and more like family. But it was like he had slowly begun to take over. I hoped he wouldn't expect me to call him Dad anytime soon.

I waited to confront Mum until Jason left for work at eight forty He gave her a long, tight hug, saying goodbye, and patted me on the head with a smile, saying, 'See ya.' Then he left with his briefcase in his right hand and his jacket over his left arm. He looked very presentable. The moment the front door closed I turned to her. My face was like thunder.

All jokes aside, this was another small step forward that they had both taken and it had surprised me. I had a feeling in my gut that just wouldn't go away. Was it hurt? Was it upset? That I had been kept out of such an important secret? Even though it may not have been a big deal to anyone else, it was to me. Mum could have spoken to me about it in the first place and asked my thoughts on it.

I had it out with her, confronted her and asked her what the meaning of it was and why she couldn't have taken it upon herself to ask me first before jumping in.

'Why didn't you tell me you were going to give Jason a key to our home?' I asked, feeling hurt. I looked at her angrily, wanting a quick response.

She looked blank as she shrugged. 'I really don't see what I've done to upset you, Chloe. It's only a key that I gave him. Nothing major.'

'Mum, it's the fact that you didn't even ask my opinion about it or how I was feeling. You just went ahead like I didn't deserve a say in it. That hurt, Mum.'

She gave a laugh of derision. 'Chloe, even if I wanted to, I couldn't – you were asleep. You had an early night last night and it was simply a spur-of-the-moment kind of thing. We were just sitting in the livingroom chatting away and he took my hand all of a sudden and –'

'La-la-la!' I quickly threw my hands up, covering my ears, blocking out her voice and anything that would horrify me. I didn't need to know intimate details of my mum's love life.

'So that's it then?' I asked, dropping my hands. 'No secrets? That's all there is to it? No moving in? Nada?'

She laughed quietly. 'Honestly, That's it, Chlo. I didn't think it was that big a deal. I trust Jason and I think we're going places. He's an incredibly decent guy and he's there for me –well, both of us actually. And he cares about me. A lot. I just wanted to show him how much I care for him. Simple,' she said, shrugging her shoulders.

I thought about that for a moment, my expression questioning. I looked her in the eye. 'And has he gave you a key to his house yet?'

For a split second I saw panic on her face. She realised I was watching and quickly changed her expression and came up with an excuse. 'He's still to get his key cut, Chloe. He'll do it when he gets some time off work. He's working a lot of late shifts at the moment.'

'So if he's working a lot, when will he get the key cut then?' I didn't believe a word she was saying.

'Well, I don't know, Chloe. I'm not in a desperate rush!'

'Yeah, right!' I scoffed, walking into the kitchen. She was putty in his hands.

Mum set about organising the washing and making sure the house was presentable for the guy coming over that morning.

It was a quiet one. We got on with the tasks at hand, mine being texting back school friends who were wishing me all the best in my next adventure in life. My reply to the first was simple: Going to college in August. I waited for a response. Thirty seconds later my phone pinged.

Fantastic! Congrats and good luck! xx

Shelly had always been a girl with high spirits. That was one thing I really liked about her. She never put anyone down.

At nine thirty on the dot, the handyman arrived at our house. He was wearing a navy-blue jacket, a grey t-shirt with the logo '**MIKE the handyman**' and a pair of navy-blue combat trousers. He was around five foot three, with a scruffy beard and long, thick, straggly, wavy hair tied back in a ponytail. There was something about him that made me take to him instantly. He shook hands with Mum and me as he introduced himself, and then, placing his large tool bag down in the hallway, he got to work right away, setting the cameras up with ease before installing their software on the laptop.

A while later, I made us all a pot of tea as Mike finished up his work and began putting his tools away. He chatted away about local events.

'Did you hear about the arrest around here?' he asked, kneeling down to arrange his tools.

'Hear about it?' Mum scoffed. 'We lived it.'

He turned to her suddenly, eyes questioning, his hands on his knees. 'How do you mean, Mrs Stanson?'

'The guys who were arrested were the ones who broke into this house,' she answered.

I heard a clunk as one of his tools fell into the bag. He stood up slowly, not taking his eyes off Mum. He walked over to her, looking concerned.

'Those men were in your house, Mrs Stanson?' he asked quietly.

With a mournful expression, she looked him in the eye. 'That's why the cameras have gone up. To prevent things like that happening again. We need safety around here.'

He looked like he was lost for words. 'That's awful. I'm so sorry. I really hope nothing was stolen.'

'Nothing at all. That's just the thing. It was a warning to us, but I hope it doesn't happen again.' Her face changed in an instant as she smiled at him, handing him his payment. 'You've done a great job for us today. It will give me peace of mind, knowing the cameras are there.'

He looked lost suddenly. 'You hear about this kind of thing happening and you don't think it will happen to you, but then it does and...' He trailed off.

Mum and I glanced at each other before looking at him. He seemed to come out of his daze in a moment and shook it off.

'Okay, Mrs Stanson, I've left my card on the table for you with my number on it. Feel free to call me any time if there's a problem.'

He picked up his tool bag, walked out of the house quickly to his white transit van and drove away, leaving me feeling bewildered. And with that, he was gone.

Mum walked out to the front path and looked up at the live camera. She lifted her finger, pointing up at it as if she were talking directly to them.

'There's no hiding from us now, 'she said, a warning in her voice and her face fierce.

I looked at her, my eyes wide, as she disappeared back into the house again to start hanging out the washing. Mum was desperate that we would be safe, no matter what it took. She wasn't about to let anyone else mess with us and ruin our lives, that was for sure.

It was plain to see that Dave had had some kind of nervous breakdown. He had lost all control. And he needed to get a lot of help. I wondered whether as his next of kin it was our job to make sure that he got back to normal health. He desperately needed to see some sort of psychiatrist. Maybe they would be able to understand him and work out what was wrong.

As long as he was behind bars for a really long time, we would be safe and happier. But as the days and weeks passed, neither Mum nor I would forget what he'd done to us. The fact that he'd nearly destroyed us would always be there to haunt us. Forever.

I knew I was being foolish to even think of him. Even though he wasn't here, he was still messing with my head and I desperately wanted to wash my hands of him. Mum and I both needed closure. I put my head in my hands and tried to calm myself down. I needed some fresh air and a walk.

Taking my jacket off the banister in the hallway, I let Mum know where I was going and walked out of the house. I headed over to Mollie's place. No matter what she was doing with her day she always seemed to have time for me.

We took a walk around the village, staying well away from the street near the woods. It was too soon to go anywhere near there. I put my hands in the pockets of my purple waterproof jacket as we walked along together. The birds were singing in the trees. It was a peaceful atmosphere.

'I don't know, Mol,' I sighed. 'Dave's face continues to haunt me every single day. But a small part of me is hoping that he gets proper treatment. Not that I care, because I don't. I'm saying this because he needs it. He obviously has a mental issue and –'

'Listen,' she urged, 'I'm not one to judge, you know I'm not. I'm not going to tell you what to do and how to live your life. But can I just give you a piece of advice? Stay clear. Move on with your life and forget about him. You don't need that.'

I turned on my heel as she suddenly stopped.

'He nearly killed you, Chloe! Do you remember when you got back from these woods, how traumatised you were? Can you remember that feeling?'

I nodded, not saying anything.

'You hold onto that feeling whenever you think of him. That was what he did to you and how he made you feel. You really don't want to be giving him any other chances in the future. You don't want that messing with your head every day.'

'I guess not.' I smiled, hugging her gently. Mollie was always right.

I never imagined this was how my life would pan out – living in fear of my own relative. I imagined a peaceful life full of happiness and laughter. Mum, Dad, Dave and I spending time together as one great family, taking a drive out to Loch Lomond on a Saturday and heading out onto the water on a boat. Coming home and watching the Alfred Hitchcock movie The Birds with a tub of popcorn. I had always thought we were so close and happy, us four. Those times just seemed like a faded memory now.

All I wanted was to move on and away from everything. A holiday with blue skies and white sandy beaches. Heading along the road to the Isle of Harris with my friends in a campervan, taking in the spectacular view, singing along to Nickelback and having a laugh, just enjoying life. We would walk around the island during the day and sit out on the beach at night in front of a roaring fire and tell stories and jokes while the wood crackled away. That, right there, was my little piece of happiness. That was bliss. And I had to make sure that my dream would turn into a reality.

CHAPTER 26

We kept ourselves busy during the rest of the holidays. When Mum got a day off work, we packed a bag and took day trips on the train – to Balloch, Stirling and Edinburgh. I had never been more fascinated by these Scottish cities and towns. The landscapes were simply magnificent. We walked for endless hours, marvelling at the culture and beauty, stopping at tourist shops to pick up a few souvenirs. I brought Jason back a Nessie pen from my travels, which I thought would help him with his paperwork. He found it surprisingly delightful, putting it in his briefcase for safe-keeping. I knew he would look after it.

I began counting down the days until I started college. There were nerves of anticipation and excitement. More than ready to start, I was raring to go. Mum had high hopes for me. She seemed just as excited I was.

'Don't you worry, you'll do just fine,' Jason tried to assure me. Knowing I would be okay, I nodded in agreement, wishing I was there already.

If only that was all there was to think about. We were waiting patiently on word coming about going to court regarding my capture. Nerves were rattled every day as we waited to receive a letter, and we jumped every time our mail clattered through the letterbox. As much as we were reluctant to go, it was a requirement that was compulsory.

The day we went to the hearing was an awful day for me and Mum and it was one I never wanted to think about again. As exhausting as it was, we felt a weight lift from our shoulders. The defendants both pleaded guilty to the break-in and they were sentenced to a minimum of three years without parole. We felt justice had been served.

One day, we lay in the back garden on sun loungers. My hand-held fan cooled me substantially from the burning-hot sun. The weather had been really hot the last couple of weeks and we had taken advantage of it, spending every moment out in the garden while we could, lapping up the heat. We lay side by side with a small garden table in between us and a glass jug of iced water. I wore my new bikini and sunglasses, trying to get a great tan. We simply didn't get enough of this.

After a good hour or so –during which time we both fell asleep – Mum left to go and fetch the mail. Moments later, she arrived back at the kitchen door with a white envelope in her hand and a fearful look on her face. She carefully opened the seal and pulled the letter out, and her hand went to her face. I gazed up at her as she stood there, looking nauseous. Without saying a word, she passed me the single sheet of paper and walked inside quietly. The letter read:

Dear Mrs Stanson,
I am writing to let you know that, following discussion, a date has been set to hear the case against your brother-in-law, Mr David Stanson. The court hearing will commence on Monday16thAugust 2004 at 10a.m. Please make sure that you arrive fifteen minutes prior to the court hearing.
    Yours sincerely,
    Mary Sacroy

They had finally written to us, giving us a week's notice. We had to prepare ourselves for that date and be strong. Not let Dave see any weakness or how he had traumatised us.

I walked into the livingroom, where Mum was sitting. The blinding sun cast a bright light through the front windows and heat radiated throughout the room. Tiny specks of dust glittered all around, slowly falling onto the thick, soft carpet. The bright light made Mum's hair glisten as she sat at the dining table. She had her head in her hands and her shoulders were slumped; she looked sad and defeated. I didn't have to say anything. She knew how I felt too.

This letter had been anticipated, but it was still a shock to the system. I had never been near a court before, so I didn't know what to expect. I didn't know if Mum had either. To be perfectly honest, the thought of going to court scared me. Standing in a large building surrounded by lawyers and special officers who were trained to deal with the people who came in and out of the building all the time…it was sure to make me feel nervous and edgy.

I walked across to the table and put my arms around Mum, and with that she burst into tears. I held her in my arms until she was all cried out. She kept apologising.

'It's the thought of seeing him all over again,' she said. Her body shuddered and I held her tight and rubbed her back, trying my best to soothe her.

Seeing her sitting there so broken made my heart ache. My poor mother. This had really got to her. We had both been badly traumatised by Dave. It dawned on me then that I really didn't care whether or not he had an illness. My uncle could go rot in jail for the rest of his life.

Time seemed to fly by that week, and the day of the court hearing arrived. Trying to drink the tea Mum had poured for me that morning, I sat nervously beside her on the couch. My stomach was in knots. I couldn't eat a thing. The air was thick with tension and we both waited anxiously in silence. A small part of me felt like we were being sentenced ourselves. There was a shadow of gloom over us. Not a smile on either face. Jason was taking time off to give us a lift there and support us. Mum felt bad for having brought him into the mess, but he was there for support nonetheless.

I began to feel ill as the time to leave got closer. Staring at the clock, I watched as the seconds and minutes went by. Tick-tock, tick-tock. The room around me felt hazy and my vision blurred. Bile rose up in my throat and I forced it back down again. Dizziness took over. Giving up, I ran to the bathroom and flung my head over the toilet, heaving. I didn't want this day to happen.

'Chloe, are you okay, honey?' Mum shouted from downstairs.

Managing to take a breath, I answered in a hoarse voice: 'Yeah. I'll be down in a minute.'

I sat back on my heels, taking deep breaths, trying to find the energy to keep moving. There was a dreaded fear that came with this day, and the sooner it was over, the better.

Jason appeared right on time and we gathered our coats and headed out to the car. I opened the back door and the cool air conditioning hit me right away. The interior of the car had just been valeted. A sat nav was mounted on the windscreen and the leather seats were immaculate. Jason took pride in his vehicle. This was his baby.

He took it upon himself to make the journey a pleasant one, making us laugh often. The drive was bearable until we arrived at the car park. I climbed out from the back seat, staring up in amazement. The building was huge with high pillars. I suddenly felt very queasy and it took all the strength I had not to run in the other direction. As the three of us walked toward the Court, I prayed that the jury would be on our side. They just had to be.

We entered the security lobby, where we passed through airport-type screening. Our bags and pockets were checked, and our keys and mobiles placed on a table. It was a very formal and harrowing procedure, and so far, every minute of being in that building I wanted out of it.

After reclaiming our belongings, we were directed to the reception desk. We gave the receptionist our names and reason for our visit, and she made a quick phone call. A uniformed man appeared and directed us to the witness room.

We took a seat in the small room and waited to be called in. Every moment we sat there was nerve-racking. Mum had to stop me biting my nails and constantly fidgeting. My body trembled. The last thing I wanted was to walk through that door and come face to face with the man who had endangered my life. The whole run of events had been connected, from Dave kidnapping me to the break-in. In my eyes, it was too daunting to bear.

Within a short while, the door opened and a man came in, calling for Mum to go through. Knowing just how freaked out she could get, I grabbed her hand, willing her to stay brave. She stood up and walked out with him in silence.

I waited patiently until it was my time to go. I didn't know where I had found the strength. My knees trembled under me and I grabbed the doorframe to stop myself collapsing.

When the man came back, I followed him out into the hallway. He opened a door and held it for me. I stopped in my tracks, preparing myself. This was it, the moment of truth. Adrenaline rushed through my body as I stood there, mentally preparing myself for what was to come. The urge to be sick overwhelmed me and I took a deep breath. Dave was in the room, the other side of the door. I wished Mum was by my side for support. Be brave, Chloe, I thought, and I walked into the room.

Rows of faces stared over at me...

CHAPTER 27

'Well, that went better than I expected!' I sighed, sitting on the ottoman in our livingroom.

We were back home at last. Mum and Jason were sitting together on the couch, just a little too close. I really didn't mind anymore. We had all been through enough pain and heartache to last us a lifetime. What we needed now was happiness in a home that we loved. I sat there watching them as they held hands, looking pretty pleased with themselves. Mum was happy again. We would get on with our peaceful lives and have no interruptions at all from anyone. No hassle, no stress, just contentment.

'It certainly did, Chloe,' Mum said. 'I really didn't think it would go the way it did. It just goes to show...'

'I want to make a wee toast.' I smiled, raising my glass of Appletiser. Mum had bought beverages at the Tesco in town on the drive back. 'We've been through a lot recently. We've loved, lost and had unbearable heartache. If there's anything I've learned, it's to make each day count. To health, happiness and a prosperous, bright future.'

Mum looked at me, fascinated. 'You've taken the world on your shoulders and it's changed you for the better, it seems. I'm very proud of you and the young lady you have turned out to be. To a bright future ahead.' Mum held up her glass and we all clinked. 'Cheers.'

I smiled gleefully at Mum feeling proud of me. It really had turned out to be a great afternoon after all!

The night crawled upon us as we sat in our livingroom, happily chatting away, reliving memories of years ago. Jason told us about his childhood, and we all laughed at the story of his Auntie Rose buying him Barbie and Ken dolls for his birthday when he was seven. When he opened his presents to reveal the dolls, he threw them to the floor in a bad mood. He was not a happy kid. I got the giggles, laughing at Jason's Barbie doll tale, thinking that would be a story to be told for a long time yet.

As I'd got to know Jason a little better every day, I'd begun to have a great deal of respect for him. He told us another story, about when he knew within himself that he wanted to be a doctor and save people. He was only a young lad at the time when a terrible thing happened, leaving three of his neighbours dead.

His mum and dad had ended up living in squalor due to his dad being made redundant. The plumbing company that he worked for had gone bankrupt, leaving all employees out of a job. Jason's parents hadn't had enough money for a decent place to live, so they'd taken the cheapest place they could afford – a rough old building in the southwest of Glasgow that by now had been bulldozed and rebuilt.

They kept to themselves, staying out of trouble. Doors and windows were locked constantly due to thefts in the area. They didn't dare open their door to anyone, for it would have been a drunk asking for money. Jason remembered the last night he spent in that awful place and the terrible memories that haunted him.

He was curled up on the couch with his parents watching a comedy show on the TV when it all happened. They heard screaming coming from the close. Wondering what was going on, his dad moved from the couch and opened the front door, only to be met by screaming tenants.

'There's a fire! Fire! Get out of the building. Quick!'

Everyone was running riot with fear, trying to get themselves and their children out of the burning building. Jason's dad grabbed everything he could and got his family out to safety. As they emerged from the front of the tenement, they looked up to see smoke coming out of top-storey windows. The fire brigade had arrived quickly and they were trying their best to put the fire out, but unfortunately not everyone made it out in time.

Jason found out later on that it was a drunk who lived in the close who'd started the fire. He had come home from the pub late that night, staggering all over the place, reeking of whisky. Apparently, according to the firemen and the police, the drunk had been cooking in the kitchen and had fallen asleep, leaving the cooker on. When the fire was finally extinguished, the firemen went up to the flat and found him lying dead on the couch.

Jason vividly remembered sitting on the kerb in the dark with his spaceman pyjamas on, watching the firemen rush into the burning building with their hoses. That image must have haunted him forever. To have witnessed that at such a young, vulnerable age – what a catastrophe.

Jason's dad managed to get in contact with his sister, Jason's Auntie Nancy, who lived over in Ireland. Nancy was a wealthy woman who had a four-bedroom house built from scratch, and she invited them to stay for a few weeks. They were desperate to get their lives back on track and to seek work over there and make a good life for their only child. Jason smiled as he spoke, saying it worked like a charm because they never came back. It was only Jason who came back to Scotland for university. His parents were happy to live over there, sending birthday and Christmas cards every year. He was in touch with them nearly every day, hearing how happy they were. He missed them very much, of course.

One day, after university and in the third month of his new job, Jason received a phone call from Nancy, and he just knew something was wrong immediately by the sound of her voice. From the minute she began speaking to him she was talking in riddles. In the end, he had to force the news out of her: that his parents had died in a car accident.

On the day before the funeral, he got the ferry over to Ireland to see his aunt and to say a final goodbye to his mum and dad. Devastated by the tragic loss, Jason took such a long time to recover from the grief.

As he finished telling us his story, he sat there close to tears. My heart went out to him. Mum wrapped her arms around him in comfort. I knew how painful it was to lose a parent. But to lose both? That sounded like too much to bear.

Taking a deep breath, I relaxed in the warm sun, thinking about how happy we had been since leaving the courthouse. It was like a huge weight had been lifted from our shoulders. There was a difference in us. We were a lot happier now.

It was the last day of the holidays. The sun warmed my skin as I rubbed my Nivea suntan lotion onto my front and shoulders. Lying with my eyes closed and my sunglasses on, I listened to a blackbird chirping away in the bush up the back of the garden. It had made a nest for itself. That made me smile.

I jumped with a start as the side gate opened suddenly and Mollie walked in.

'Mollie, hey!' I called, standing up from my lounger and gave her a quick hug.

'Hiya, Chloe.' She squeezed me tight. 'Hi, Mrs Stanson.' She waved over at Mum, who looked up and smiled and said a quiet hello, before getting back to her book. 'Listen, Chlo, I can't stay long. I just came over to tell you some great news. I've got a new job!' she gushed.

'Really? Oh, that's fantastic! Where is it?'

'So, you know Dad's the manager of Eastern Glasgow Hotels? Well, the reception were looking for staff and I had given Dad my CV, so they called asking me for an interview, and I went, and they've only gone and hired me!'

'Oh my goodness, that's fantastic news! Congrats. Oh, Mol, I'm so happy for you.' I hugged her once again, feeling thrilled for her.

Eastern Glasgow Hotels was a fancy building which hosted big events like weddings, business parties and various functions. Mollie's family seemed to be very lucky in life. As happy as I was for her, I couldn't help but feel a little envious too.

We promised to keep in touch, as we would both be busy with college and work in the upcoming months. I suddenly felt like a part of me was leaving and I felt a huge aura of warmth and love. I grabbed her just as she was talking to Mum and wrapped my arms around her.

'I'm really gonna miss you.' My voice was muffled in her long, soft, thick, black hair.

A tear rolled down my cheek onto her t-shirt. I squeezed my eyes shut. This was a new adventure in life that would make us a little more distant. She wrapped her arms around me and squeezed me tight, laughing and saying she only lived around the corner. I rubbed at my face, wiping away my tears. We would plan a night out to the cinema once the next holidays arrived.

I walked her to the front gate and waved her off as she climbed into her dad's Mercedes and the car zoomed away. I closed the gate and re-joined Mum out the back. I would really miss Mollie. I wished that she was going to college with me. But I had to accept that our lives were going along two different paths.

I heard the door close behind me as I walked over to the witness box. Every inch of my body quivered nervously. The room fell silent and the only breathing I heard was my own. I stared at the floor, too scared to look around. The jury had to know how this had truly affected me, how it had nearly destroyed my whole life. I would never from this moment on, let another human being control me the way Dave had, and let them think I was naive.

All I could picture in my mind was my uncle when I was only around eight or nine, laughing as he threw me up in the air and caught me in his arms. That man was gone for good. I missed those days and my uncle, the way he used to be.

The judge spoke to me first, asking me to take an oath and raise my right hand. I stood looking at her as I repeated the words.

'I swear by Almighty God that I will tell the truth, the whole truth and nothing but the truth.'

I waited to be questioned.

Dave's solicitor, Mr Chavis McAvee, approached me. My palms began to sweat. He looked me in the eye. He was so close.

'Could you tell me your full name, please?'

'Chloe Abigail Stanson.'

'And what is your age?'

'I'm sixteen.'

'And what are you in relation to the defendant?'

'I'm his niece.'

'And are you in school?'

'No, I graduated school in July and I'm starting college soon.'

The questions continued and I struggled to hold it together. My body shook with nerves and there was a feeling of intimidation. When it was finished, exhaustion took over. I struggled to get back to the witness room; my legs felt weak and limp. I sat back down on a chair and could have cried. This day was really getting too much to bear and I just wanted it to be over and for Dave to be put away.

Mum was brought back into the room with me. I ran to her and we both hugged. She rubbed my back, telling me everything would be alright and that she thought he would go down. I hoped she was right. She handed me a tissue and I wiped my eyes and tried to calm myself down, taking deep breaths.

The door finally opened a while later and we were taken back to the courtroom to be seated in the public gallery. I managed to get a look at him. Dave was sitting in the dock, facing the judge. He was wearing a suit and he looked very different to the last time I had seen him. His hair was shaved off. The weight had fallen from his face and his eyes had a darkness around them. There were bruises. Prison didn't suit him at all. The pages had certainly turned in his book. He sat quietly, keeping his head down. Dave had changed. And not for the better. He seemed beaten in a way that made him look unconfident and done-in.

The court clerk walked over to the jury and asked for the spokesperson to stand. Clasping my hands together, hoping they would say the right thing, I closed my eyes and waited.

'What is your verdict in respect of the accused?'

'Guilty by majority,' the man replied.

I opened my eyes. Relief overwhelmed me.

The clerk recorded the verdict and read it out to the jury, and as they nodded to him, people in the gallery whispered among themselves.

Dave's lawyer spoke shortly after. 'This is a very serious charge that my client is facing. Now, Mr Stanson has no serious record or bad medical history, your honour, and it seems that we may well be looking into getting some treatment for him.'

The judge looked on as she took notes, getting ready to serve Dave his sentence.

'Please rise, Mr Stanson,' Judge Adams called out.

I watched Dave stand up with the officers beside him.

The judge spoke. 'David Stanson, you are hereby sentenced to five years 'imprisonment. You abducted your only niece and nearly killed her. Your conduct is appalling and disgraceful. Do you understand what's been said to you?' she asked.

'Yes,' he answered simply.

'Very well. That is all. Thankyou. Good day.'

We had won. Victory was on our side. After everything he had put us through, this was what he deserved. He would start serving his time immediately. We wouldn't be seeing him again.

They took him along the aisle by the dock to the cells underneath. As he walked along, he lifted his head swiftly and stared in our direction. His face was like thunder, and in that moment I knew what was going to happen. We wouldn't be so lucky that he'd go without saying a proper goodbye. We watched with caution.

He stood between the two officers and he roared: 'I'll get you for this, Karen Stanson, you hear me? You fucking bitch. I'll kill you! I'll kill you, Karen Stanson!'
Dave went on to threaten me as well. He promised he would come back to get me. He pushed, pulled and grunted, trying to break free. The officers used all their force to restrain him, and they got him out the room. The door closed behind them and the room went silent.

'All rise,' the clerk of the court called.

Everyone stood and the judge and everyone else packed up their belongings and left.

I sat frozen to the spot. I was in a cold sweat. Feeling shivery, I wrapped my coat tightly around myself. I wanted to get out of here.

'Well,' Mum sighed, standing up. 'That's that done with. He's gone now. We're free, Chloe. Let's go home, shall we?'

I looked up at her and couldn't have agreed more. He was out of our lives for good.

Jason was sitting on a bench waiting for us as we walked out the doors. He stood up and we left the courthouse in silence. That day had delivered what I hoped: a fresh start for me and Mum. And there was something I knew for certain: I never wanted to set foot inside that building again.

CHAPTER 28

I blinked, coming back to reality. The court case was still going around in my head. Somehow, I just couldn't shake it off, though I knew I had to let it go. It was over and done with. I looked over, hearing a voice talking to me.

'…you want to? Chloe? Are you even listening to me?' Mum asked, sounding irritated that I wasn't paying attention.

'Hmm?' I replied. I hadn't heard a word she'd said.

'I wonder where your head is sometimes, lady, I really do. I was saying you need to go and get ready; we're going out.'

'Oh. Where?' I asked curiously.

'Oh, just…somewhere.' She smirked, winking at me.

I followed her into the house and we both headed up the stairs to get ready. I put on my good Hollister jeans and flannel shirt. I figured she would be taking me somewhere nice. I knew she would. She was my mum.

We took a walk downtown to a little Italian restaurant that I had never been to before. We sat at a small table at the back. As we were served our drinks, Mum told me this was a celebration for me the day before college started. I smiled at her, shaking my head. She was always full of surprises. We clinked glasses and she wished me all the best for the following day.

Our meals arrived and I savoured my pollo Milanese. I smiled at the waiters as they spoke to us with their Italian accents, and I wondered whether they were authentic; I was sure I'd heard a little Scottish in there too.

Standing in the reception area of Grey Acre College, I bit my lip nervously, feeling slightly paranoid. Not knowing which direction to take, I asked the young girl behind the desk for help. She happily showed me the way, and I entered a quiet room. Another couple of students were sitting at the far side, waiting around. The brightly lit room was painted dark blue with posters on the walls and had a midnight-blue carpet. I choose the seat nearest to the door and waited, taking my notepad and pen out. As it was my first day, I had made the extra effort to get here a little early, as I didn't need the stress of rushing. Not today.

The rest of the students finally turned up and we waited quietly. It was an awkward silence. Then a man walked into the room and welcomed everyone to the word processing class. Steve, as he introduced himself, was six foot, with wavy light-brown hair and a chiselled face. He was nice – easy-going and friendly. It gave me the reassurance that I needed to carry on with my day.

He spoke about our course, what we would be working on for the next few months and what kind of job we would get when we passed the course. The prospect of passing at Grey Acre College sounded amazing and a dream come true. I would give everything to achieve my goals.

I must have looked lonely when everyone walked back into the room after first break and took their seats to get started. I noticed someone watching me out of the corner of my eye. She walked over and sat on the chair beside me.

'Want some company?' she asked.

'Gladly.' I smiled. The prospect of spending any amount of time on my own when I had only just started my first day sounded lonely and daunting.

She introduced herself as Katrina. I learned that she was also sixteen and just out of school. We faced the front of the room, watching Steve as he wrote on the whiteboard our instructions for the day's tasks. Katrina was nice. She was the same height as me, with short blond hair tied back in a ponytail and oval glasses. She was funny and made me laugh alot. I think that was why I took to her really easily.

The more time I spent at college, the more friends I seemed to make. Not wanting to be unsociable, I finally plucked up the courage to talk to the guy sitting next to me. The tense feeling left me somewhat as he spoke, introducing himself as Eric. He chatted away, telling me he lived in Fisley Drive with his girlfriend. She had been in the army and now she was a helicopter pilot, and they were due to get married next year and go on honeymoon to Rome, Italy. I smiled, congratulating him. He was only twenty-five.

The weeks flew by and turned into months. I worked hard at college with the help of Eric and studied hard at home, passing every test that came and went.

A new girl called Nadine started her course later in the year and made friends with me and Katrina. We got on alright, but as time went by, I began to feel the friendship between Katrina and me getting a little distant; she wasn't as friendly to me as she had once been. Meanwhile, Nadine was beginning to get closer to Katrina, and I could see their friendship blooming. On the days I sat beside them at my computer, I listened to them chatting away about their likes, dislikes, hobbies and Nadine's new favourite game, Tetris. I really couldn't get over the way she was so excited about it. I took a sneaky peak as she gushed over the game

'Look how cool this is! I swear, Kat, I'm on this constantly. I just love it!'

I got back on with my work, typing away as they continued to show their enthusiasm over the tile matching puzzle game

After Nadine's show-and-tell, they started chatting about the cinema and the new releases that were coming out. Now this got me going. I couldn't exactly keep quiet when they were talking about movies. There was nothing I liked more than the cinema. Sitting in a nice, comfy chair in a large auditorium with a box of popcorn on my lap and a drink by my side, watching a great movie with either Tom Cruise, Jim Carrey, Sandra Bullock or Jennifer Aniston. What? Was I too boring? Not good enough for the rest of the crowd?

I figured if I waited for my turn to talk, it would never happen.

'...and did you see that bit when they were on their bikes and one fell off the cliff and...'

'Have you saw the trailer for the new I, Robot movie?' I butted in. At that moment I didn't care what they were talking about. I wanted my say.

They both turned and looked at me. Nadine frowned and shook her head.

'Well, apparently, all these new robots are created to keep humans safe, but then strange things start happening, and the robots end up going out of control. Isn't that cool?' I asked.

Nadine just nodded her head and made a sad attempt to say, 'Right.' Then she went back to Katrina and started chatting again.

All I wanted was a conversation between the three of us and they couldn't even do that. My self-esteem was at an all-time low as I got back to my work. I really missed my girlie chats. I had been trying my very best to make friends with Nadine. She wasn't exactly ignoring me, but she wasn't becoming a great friend either. I just had to accept the fact that we were nothing more than acquaintances.

Then, one day out of the blue, Nadine invited both me and Katrina to her birthday do. She bragged to Katrina about how rich her parents were and how she was getting a fancy limo for her birthday. I feigned surprise. The after party was to be at her house, while her parents were out for the evening. They were giving her the house to herself for the night, as it was her seventeenth. Anyone who was listening in would have thought she lived in a castle, the way she was talking about her house.

I happily agreed to go, pretty much because she wouldn't let me say no. To be honest, I needed the night out and a night off from studying. That was all I seemed to be doing recently. It was something to look forward to aswell. An evening in a limousine sounded absolutely fab.

It was only when the next day came that Katrina told us that she couldn't make it. She had other plans. I was extremely disappointed.

Friday evening arrived, and I found myself in front of Grey Acre College. I stood waiting in the cool air for a short time until Nadine finally arrived with a couple of her friends. She looked lovely in a dark-purple dress, her hair done up in a braided bun, and a ton of makeup on, as if she was going to a prom. After she had stopped squealing excitedly, she introduced her other friends, and I barely managed to make out their names: Sammi and Mitch. Sammi was slightly smaller than her, with long black hair, and she was wearing a black leather jacket, a frilly dark-purple top, black bootleg jeans and stilettos. Mitch, who stood at around five foot six, was wearing a long black trench coat with black trousers and black shoes. I stood there wary at first, trying to figure them out, but then I realised we were going to get along just fine.

We stood chatting excitedly about the limo; none of us had been in one before. We discussed who would be singing first on the karaoke, with Nadine claiming, 'It's my birthday, so I get to sing first; it's my day.' I laughed inwardly to myself. That just didn't sound childish at all.

The long, pink car arrived and barely a second went by before Nadine climbed in first, squealing about how marvellous it looked inside. Mitch glanced, wide eyed, at me and we both sniggered. It was clear we were sarcastically thinking the same thing. This was going to be a fun night.

The driver opened his door and came around to greet us all. A man with thinning grey hair, he introduced himself as Angus and gave us the rules of the limo. Angus seemed a friendly man and quite the joker.

'How long have you been driving this limo?' asked Nadine.

'I've been driving limousines for over ten years,' he replied, his voice sounding rather distorted.

We got into the limo and Angus started up the karaoke machine. After informing us that the mini bar was full of snacks and drinks which we were welcome to help ourselves to, he left, closing the door behind him.

Nadine opened a bag she had brought with her and, giggling, she pulled out not one but two two-litre Coca-Cola bottles which contained a clear liquid. The penny dropped instantly. The rest of the night was going to be ruined, I thought.

As it turned out, we had a lot of fun in the limo with the karaoke, and even although none of us could sing, we gave it a shot. Mitch passed the mic to me as 'Ice Ice Baby' came on and he swayed, clapping his hands, encouraging me. I was having the time of my life right there.

Nadine got out plastic cups to fill with the clear liquid from the bottles that she had inside her bag. She quickly filled her own cup, downed her drink and then handed one to me. I lifted it up to my nose and gagged. She had clearly been mixing drinks together. I simply refused, and she just looked at me like I had slapped her in the face. She tried to force me to drink the stuff, but I had no intention of doing so. Finally giving up, she swore under her breath and rolled her eyes at me, like I was the one in the wrong.

We were dropped off at Nadine's house after the hour-long drive. After pushing the car door opened, she clambered out onto the pavement with Mitch grabbing her arm to help her, laughing all the while. She gripped a bottle in her hand, refusing point blank to let anyone take it from her as she staggered along. The car moved away and she took Mitch's hand, twirling herself up her pathway and singing 'The Rhythm of the Night'. We could do nothing but stand back and laugh. It was the one day of the year she could do what she wanted, and it was amusing.

When she finally got to the door, it seemed to take forever for her to find her house keys. Every time she tried to look, she got the giggles and would hiccup, leaving the other two bent double laughing. I stood back watching, feeling amused at these teenagers and their carry-on. After a bit of moaning and sighing, she finally found them, unlocked the door and let us in to the dark hallway.

I walked in and immediately smelled an odour like stale smoke and urine, which made my stomach turn. Nadine switched on the lights to the rooms as she staggered around the hallway, bumping into walls on the way. The white flowery wallpaper in the downstairs hall was turning yellow and the corners were starting to peel away, and the brown carpet was filthy, covered in dog hair. Bits of food were stuck to one wall. Holes had been punched in the living room door and the handle was falling off. I wondered worriedly what I was letting myself in for as I avoided standing on the kids' toys that were scattered around the living room. Nadine had been bragging to Katrina in college about how nice her home was, but in reality this house was rough. It was like an obstacle course trying to get a seat on the couch. The place was a midden.

Nadine put one of her CDs on, turning the volume up way too loud. She lifted one hand in the air, holding her near-empty bottle in the other as she drank out of it.

Staggering in and out of the livingroom, she attempted to dance as 'It's My Life' blasted out of the speakers. Sammi walked over to me and took my hands, and then the four of us were up on the floor dancing around. I closed my eyes, lifted my arms in the air and let my body flow to the rhythm. I didn't care that anyone could see me.

Sammi placed her hands upon Nadine's hips and the two of them danced out into the hallway and out the front door, singing away. Taking a seat on the cream leather couch, I smiled to myself, feeling on a complete and utter high.

'Are you having a nice time?' Mitch asked me as he walked over and turned the volume down on the stereo.

'Yeah, I am.' I smiled. 'It's been a really good night.'

'I'm glad Nadine has a friend at college. It's good you came out to celebrate with her,' he replied, walking over.

He sat down – too close to me. If I wasn't feeling nervous before, I certainly was right then. His aftershave was intoxicating and the energy that I'd had seemed to vanish suddenly. His eyes slowly darted around my face; his hands were in my hair. His breath was hot on my skin. He closed his eyes and inhaled.

'You're very beautiful, do you know that?' he whispered.

I looked down, feeling self-conscious and timid.

'We have a couple of minutes to ourselves.' He leaned over and kissed the side of my face slowly and gently.

I moved his hands away. 'I'm not that kind of a girl,' I said.

He opened his eyes. 'Relax and enjoy the moment,' he whispered as he bent to put his lips on mine.

'Mitch, what the fuck?' Sammi yelled. She was standing in the doorway watching us, her mouth wide open.

I jumped up in shock, feeling guilty as I instantly

239

realised I'd been caught out. I didn't know where to look. I rubbed the back of my neck, feeling nervous.

'I think Gemma will have a word or two to say about this, mate!' Sammi warned angrily, walking out the room.

'Who's Gemma?' I asked Mitch defensively.

'My girlfriend,' he answered nonchalantly.

I was shocked and disgusted. Widening the gap between us so he couldn't touch me, I took my phone out of my pocket and looked at the screen.

One missed called and two texts.

I read the first text.

Hey, girl. It's been too long. We need a catch-up. Missing you loads. x

With all that had been going on at college, Mollie had slipped my mind. No doubt she had been busy too, hence the reason she was only contacting me now.

I smiled and looked at the second text.

How's college treating you? Made any new friends yet? Don't forget about me. xx

I replied:

Hey, babe. Yeah, college is good. Too much work. 🙁 Studying well. Keeping busy. Yeah, defo need a catch-up. I'm free tomorrow if you want to go shopping? Xx

Then I texted Jason, asking him to come and pick me up. I sent him the address and put a smiley face emoji at the end. As I waited for a reply, I looked over at Mitch. He was staring at me.

'What?' I asked.

'Texting your mum?' he teased.

'No,' I scoffed.

He sighed. 'Look, it's complicated with me and Gemma. We're in a bit of a sticky situation right now and I just needed to let my hair down. Can you understand that?'

'Sure. But did you need to let your hair down with me?'

I asked, disgruntled.

He rolled his eyes and smiled. 'I wasn't doing any harm. It was just a bit of fun really.'

'You're two-timing your girlfriend, Mitch!' I raised my voice.

He turned his head away. I gave him time to think things through while I went to find the girls. They were in the kitchen. No doubt talking about me. I chapped on the door frame.

'Can I come in?' I asked.

'Sure, just as long as you're not up to any nonsense,' Sammi replied with a don't-mess-with-me attitude.

'Sammi, it wasn't like that. I wasn't teasing him or anything. It was him who came onto me. And that was all that happened. How was I to know he had a girlfriend?'

'You shouldn't have let him touch you like that. It looked too…intimate.'

'Yeah, well, I'm not that kind of girl.'

My phone bleeped twice as I received two texts. The first was from Jason, telling me he would meet me outside in twenty minutes, followed by a yawning face emoji and a smiley face. I knew I could always rely on him. The second text was from Mollie to let me know she was free and couldn't wait to spend the day with me tomorrow. A thrill went through me. I couldn't wait.

Sammi turned back to Nadine and filled up their drinks again. I walked into the living room and picked up my bag to leave. I'd had enough.

Mitch lingered awkwardly. 'Chloe.'

'Yeah?' I turned to him.

'I'm sorry about that. We're going through a rough patch right now. I only hope me and Gemma can work things out. My head's pretty messed up at the moment.'

'I understand that, but you can't go around cheating. It'll give you a bad rep. I hope you can work things out with your girlfriend. I'm going home, Mitch. It was nice to meet you. I'll see you around.'

I turned to walk out. I heard a sigh.

'Chloe, wait. I'll walk you out.'

I said nothing but walked out the room into the kitchen with Mitch behind me. The girls were sitting on the worktop. Sammi was smoking a cigarette.

'Right, well, I'd better be off then, Nadine. Thanks for the night out. I had a nice time.'

She staggered over to me, intoxicated. 'Cheers, doll, for coming. I'll see you Monday,' she slurred, giving me a hug. 'How are you getting home?'

'Someone's coming to pick me up,' I replied.

'Right. See you then.'

I opened the door and walked out into the cool night air, feeling relieved. I heard Sammi call out to Mitch, asking where he was going. 'Home' was all he said as he followed me out the door and closed it behind him. As fun as that night had been, I was glad to be going home.

Mitch and I stood outside Nadine's house waiting for Jason to pick me up. I simply had to get out of there and away from Sammi's scornful looks. I didn't fancy feeling awkward the whole time, and Nadine was just too drunk. I'd had all the drama I could handle for the year.

The peace and quiet outside didn't last long. I could hear the music blasting in the living room. Nadine had turned her stereo up full blast again. I was glad I wasn't her neighbour.

'So, Nadine says you're studying computing then?' Mitch said, killing the awkward silence.

'Yeah, we are. We've got IT, central services, front of office… What about yourself?'

'I've got into Glasgow Uni to study digital design and web development. It's an HNC course. Then I'll be doing my HND next year. I'm really interested in JavaScript code and it would be cool to see how it's all written out. Then hopefully I'll get a job as a web developer.'

I looked at him, impressed. 'Seriously? That's amazing!'

'Yeah. I just hope I can get through it all. And the exams. I heard they're a lot harder than they seem.'

I suddenly felt inspired right then. Mitch had guts. I wished him all the best for the future. I was so passionate about my dream job; I hoped Mitch would get his too.

'Well, good luck with everything.'

'Thanks, Chloe.' He smiled.

We stood in silence for the remainder of the time until Jason's car pulled up at the kerb. I opened the passenger door and climbed in as Mitch introduced himself.

'Hi, mate, I'm Mitch.' He reached his hand over and they both shook hands.

'Alright, I'm Jason. You want a lift home, bud?' Jason asked.

'Do you know where Ponley Street is?'

'Yeah, I think so. You can keep me right, though. Jump in.'

Mitch climbed into the back seat and we headed towards his home. It wasn't long before we pulled up outside his flat. Mitch climbed out, saying goodnight to us both and thanking Jason for the lift. I looked out my window at him standing by the kerb. He blew me a kiss goodnight and I rolled my eyes at him as we drove away.

'Ah, see, a wee bit o' romance in the air tonight,' Jason joked, trying out his best Scots brogue accent.

'Don't be daft,' I laughed as he drove us back on the motorway.

Laying my head against the window, I looked up at the beautiful clear blue sky covered in stars as we drove home in silence. The full moon shone brightly down on us. I felt content, a rare moment of peace. The car travelled smoothly along the motorway, passing trees, buildings and a great view to my left. This was something that I wanted to do more often.

CHAPTER 29

The next morning, Mollie and I took a trip to Braehead shopping centre. We browsed around the shops until lunchtime, when we had our favourite popcorn chicken meal at KFC. It was good to see my best friend again. I told her about my time at college and my evening out with the girls and Mitch. She told me about her new experiences working in the hotel, gushing over a wedding they'd catered for yesterday. After spending too much time in the restaurant, we walked over to the Odeon to see the new movie, Without a Paddle, ordering popcorn and drinks.

After we took two buses back home, I walked Mollie to her front door. Today had left me positively glowing and it had really cheered me up. She was the boost that I needed to get me through these next few months. I hoped to sail through my tests. I just had to pass this course.

On Monday morning, as I sat beside Eric in class, he became ever so inquisitive.

'So how was your weekend?' he asked me, staring at the screen as he typed away.

'Fine,' I answered casually. 'Actually...' I turned to him, feeling enthusiastic. 'It was pretty awesome. I went to a party in a limo, nearly kissed a guy, went to Braehead, had a KFC and –'

'Whoa, whoa, whoa,' he said, holding a hand up in the air. 'What do you mean you nearly kissed a guy? What guy?'

'Shh!' I whispered to him, not wanting Nadine overhearing.

'Right,' he whispered, glancing over at her. 'Details.

Now.'

I rolled my eyes. He stared at me, waiting for a reply.

'It was one of Nadine's friends from the limo party. We kind of got close and he nearly kissed me. Well, he did. But it was on the cheek.'

'Oh my God, Chloe! You go, girl. What was he like?'

'He was tall, thin and a little too friendly,' I said with wide eyes. 'He tried to come on to me when he already has a girlfriend. So, you can imagine my disgust.'

'You should have just gone for it,' Eric joked, sniggering.

'Shut up!' I laughed. We totally weren't having this discussion. I got back to work, ignoring his funny remarks and jibes.

Four o'clock rolled on and we headed out of the building. Eric and I hugged goodbye and went our separate ways. I stepped outside just as a torrent of rain came pouring down. I power-walked to the train Station. Relieved that I was no longer getting soaked, I weaved through the crowd of passengers watching the board up above as they waited to get to their destination. Pulling my ticket out of my purse, I made a dash for my Largs train home.

The carriage that I climbed aboard was full. The rain had made me a soaking-wet mess and I just wanted to be home, warm and dry.

I walked in the door half an hour later just as Mum was sorting out dinner. I called to her that I was going for a shower as I made my way to the bathroom.

Twenty minutes later, I was in my nightwear with a towel wrapped around my head. Mum had dished out the dinner, and as I sat rolling spaghetti around my fork, she asked me about my day.

'It was good,' I answered through a mouthful of mince. My walk home had made me hungry enough to scoff down my food like I hadn't eaten all day. I pushed my plate away as I finished up. Mum was quiet. This wasn't her normal behaviour. I wondered whether something was wrong.

'What's up?' I asked.

'Nothing,' she answered, looking anywhere else but at me.

I said, 'Don't give me that. Something's off. Just tell me what it is. If it's bad, I can handle it. I'm not going to break down. I promise.'

She finally looked at me. 'I have something for you.'

'Okay.' I could tell from her tone that it was bad. There was no smile on her face. No enthusiasm. I prepared myself for the news to hit me.

She passed me a white envelope addressed to me. I opened it carefully and quickly read the letter out loud.

Dear Miss Stanson,
Further to your application for the role of Admin Assistant at our firm Sue and Win Lawyers, it is with great pleasure that I offer you an interview on Wednesday 27th September. Please arrive fifteen minutes prior to the interview. I look forward to seeing you then.
Yours sincerely,
Winifred Kirlyson
Sue and Win Lawyers

Happiness went through me as I read the letter. It wasn't bad news after all. It was great.

I looked up at Mum. Her body language changed in an instant as she replaced the poker face with a massive grin and laughed. 'Sue and Win Lawyers!' she said, looking proud.

I couldn't believe it. I had my first interview.

'Congrats, Chloe. You've done very well for yourself.'

I smiled happily. In about a week's time, I would be sitting in the office of Sue and Win Lawyers. It sounded thrilling. I thanked Mum once again and headed up to my room to prepare for my interview.

Later that evening, I set my written notes down on my bed as I rubbed my face and, yawning, looked over to my clock. The digital face read eleven twenty-five. Preparing for my first interview had taken me all evening. I lay down, feeling overtired.

I closed my eyes, trying to relax and get a decent night's sleep for college. I had Zac the next day for central services. That was one class I simply could not fail. I needed top marks to pass the course.

'We need to go study,' Eric said nonchalantly. We were in the college cafeteria the next afternoon. I had just finished eating my cheese toastie. A half-empty bottle of Irn Bru and an untouched chocolate muffin sat in front of me. The thought of studying any more sounded exhausting.

I looked at Eric. He had been there for me every step of the way and I really appreciated it. I honestly didn't know what I would have done without him. His brown eyes gazed into mine and his jet-black hair fell over his face slightly. He was wearing the red checked shirt that I loved with his black jogger jeans. His porcelain skin was flawless. I tried my best not to stare. Too much.

I shook my head, giving a loud sigh. No studying today. I didn't have the energy. Maybe because I was up half the night preparing for my interview. At which I was really hoping to impress.

He slowly nodded at me, looking serious.

'Really?' I moaned. 'Do we have to?'

I just wanted to give up everything right then and there because I was too tired; I wanted to go home. This was a first. I would have normally jumped at the chance to go and study with my new college buddy. I really loved spending time with Eric. He was someone I had been able to confide in and trust. We had become closer every day.

'Come on,' he stood up and pushed the wooden chair away from his legs and lifted his bag. He took my hand as I looked up at him with pleading eyes. He was holding his own and knew that I was easy to budge. I gave up, basically because I would have gone anywhere he asked me to. I grabbed my bag and slung it over my shoulder. Okay, so we were going to study.

We left the canteen and strolled through a walkway and into another building and up a set of stairs. We arrived in the busy library a few minutes later and took a table at the back of the room. I needed to focus with no disruptions; this work needed my full concentration. That was why Mum had made a pact with me at home, so that whenever I was studying, the TV was off, as was the Wi-Fi. That was the only way I could get things done.

So, we got out our paperwork and pens and he began helping me through it. I can do this, I thought. With a test coming up the week after and top marks needed, I hoped I could.

We were halfway up the stairs after leaving the library when I turned to Eric, giving him a smile. I felt happy and lucky to have such a great friend. He smiled right back at me as we continued to walk.

An idea suddenly came to me. Turning around, I lifted my arms up like Rocky Balboa. Eric began laughing at me as he put a hand up to his face, embarrassed. The students who had walked up behind us looked at me, wondering what on earth I was doing. Deciding to make a go of it, I dropped my bag and began jumping up and down, calling out, but not too loudly, 'Yey!'

I could hear other students in the corridor shouting over to me. It fell on deaf ears as I stopped to pick up my bag and joined Eric again. We continued on, passing the students, ignoring their wolf whistles and calls of, 'How you doin, gorgeous?'

Eric shook his head at me. 'You're nuts,' he said.

I didn't care. With the number of steps we had just climbed, it needed to be done.

We were back in the last class of the day, IT. College and studying were all I seemed to be doing and I barely had my phone on me these days. It was just too distracting.

The lecturer was at her desk. Eric and I were sitting together, typing away like the rest of the class. He leaned back and began tapping his pen against the desk, humming to himself, and quickly got shushed by the lecturer. I turned my head, raising my eyebrows at him. Seriously? I thought. He whispered something that sounded funny and I began laughing quietly, and that was it, he'd put me off and I'd lost my concentration. Some of the other students started whispering and laughing. Great, we had distracted the class. Nice going, Eric.

Four o'clock rolled by again and we were heading out of the building. The weather hadn't got any better. I really didn't want to go out in it, but I had no choice.

'You know, you should really get yourself a car. Save you from getting soaked,' he said to me.

'Yeah, that actually sounds like a great idea. Maybe once I have some money saved up, I'll think about it.'

'You look tired, Chloe. Make sure you get an early night tonight.'

'I will,' I told him while yawning. I hadn't felt this tired in a while. It just wasn't a good feeling at all.

He walked over and wrapped his muscly arms around me. I closed my eyes and wrapped him in a bear hug. We unlocked after a moment and walked out the doors into the rain. Waving goodbye, we went our separate ways. I was glad tomorrow was only a half-day. I needed to catch up on sleep.

I arrived home soaked once again and with a pounding head. My body ached and my energy was gone. Hopping into the shower, it felt good as the spray hit me. I let all the tension and worry wash away as I closed my eyes, savouring the hot water heating up my cold skin.

After my luxurious shower, I dressed in my nightwear and Mum and I sat at the table for dinner as we talked about our day. I emptied my plate, took the dishes to the kitchen to wash them and headed up to my room for an early night, doing a little light reading before falling asleep.

My half-day at college always rolled by quickly. It was one of my favourite days and I honestly couldn't get out of the building quickly enough. I left college and headed through the busy town centre at lunchtime, focused on getting to the station in one piece without bumping into people. I got my train, managing to get a seat near the doors, and pulled my iPod out of my bag, selecting Ocean Drive by Lighthouse Family.

I was home within the hour, opening the door to a silent house. I threw my bag to the floor as I headed into the living room. I had the house to myself and it was peaceful. My trainers were kicked off as I put my feet up on the couch and lay back, continuing to listen to my music, before falling asleep with my tartan blanket over me.

I woke hours later to the noise of the front door closing over. Mum was home from work. She walked into the living room and looked down at me lying on the couch.

'Hello, love.'

'Hey, Mum.' I sat up and yawned. 'How was work?'

'Och, what a day,' she replied, sitting beside me and leaning her head on the back of the couch. 'We had divorcees in the office. It was not pleasant.'

'Oh dear,' I replied. 'Did it get sorted out eventually?'

'Well, let's just say the husband has a bit of a chip on his shoulder. Anyway, enough about work. Do you fancy joining Jason and me at the carvery for dinner?'

'Sounds lovely.' I grinned happily.

CHAPTER 30

It was a really lovely evening at the restaurant. The staff were attentive and the food was delicious. I tried the chicken tikka masala, which turned out to be my favourite dish. We chatted and joked until it was time to leave, and then we walked out the door into another torrent of rain and had to run to Jason's car. He drove slowly out of the car park as the rain battered the windscreen. The window wipers were on full and I was actually surprised Jason was able to see where he was going. After a few minutes the rain eased off and Jason turned the wipers down. He sped up slightly as he drove us towards home, but if I thought it would be a quick drive back, I was very wrong.

I caught Jason looking in his rear-view mirror constantly. He looked on edge as he tried to get us all home safely.

'What's wrong?' Mum asked worriedly.

'Nothing.' He shrugged it off. 'Don't worry about it.'

'It's not nothing, Jason. You're fidgety and it's making me edgy. Is there something wrong with the car?'

'Not exactly.'

'Then what is it?' Mum raised her voice, frustrated.

He looked over at her for a split second before answering quietly. I strained to hear what he said, only to feel regret instantly once I heard it. I closed my eyes, trying to block the horrible feeling out of my system. If Jason was right, then I had every right to fear for my life right then. And I knew instantly who was behind it.

'How do you know for sure, though?'

'Karen, every turn in the road I have made, every road I have taken, that car has been right behind me.'

'Are you positive? I mean, it's getting dark. You could be mistaken.'

'Trust me, Karen. I'm not mistaken. We're being followed.'

He looked at her as he tried to make her believe him. She looked unsure. He sighed, looking ahead.

'Okay. Watch this then,' he said.

He signalled right as he came up to a roundabout and began to turn, but went all the way around and back onto Botna Avenue again. As we drove along, he checked his mirror.

'See? The same car has just followed us right round and back onto the same road. I'll make a few turns and see what happens.'

Sure enough he did. He took a right turn on to Tirriway Road and another right onto Rutver place, going around another roundabout. The car behind stayed at our back.

'Well, who the hell is this guy and what is his problem?' Mum cried out.

'I have no idea, Karen. I'm going to pull over. See what happens.'

He signalled left and pulled into a parking space on Rutver place. The car behind drove past us very slowly, almost stopping. Jason looked out his window, trying to see who was in the other vehicle. I'd say I had never been so scared in my life, but that wasn't true.

At this point, the weather had cleared up and it was only just beginning to get dark. The car that had followed us picked up speed and moved away, and Jason managed to make out the registration number. He called it out to me and I typed it into my mobile quickly. I let out a sigh of relief. That had been too close.

'I was worried it was going to stop,' Mum said. 'Did you see who it was?'

'No,' Jason replied. 'The car had tinted windows. Do

you have any idea who that could've been?'

'This has got to be him,' Mum replied, frustrated. 'I mean, why would anyone else want to terrorise us like this?' She turned around to me. 'Chloe, have you noticed anyone following you around recently?'

'I don't know. I haven't seen anything.'

'Are you alright?' she asked. She must have sensed how I was feeling.

'Yeah,' I lied. 'I just want to go home.'

'Well, that was pretty intense. Home sounds like a good idea.' She smiled.

Jason did a U-turn in the road and drove back the way we had come, keeping an eye out as we headed home. I felt like a nervous wreck and really just wanted this nightmare to end.

Back at home, I watched Jason pace from one side of the living room to the other as he left a message on Inspector Dunlop's mobile. Eventually sitting down on the couch, he shoved his hands through his hair, looking stressed. Dave was behind bars but still taunting us. It couldn't have been anyone else. We would have to come up with a plan that would keep us safe so no one would come near us.

I stood in the living room feeling anxious and agitated, biting my nails as I peeked out the window. A few lights were on in the houses across the road. Although the street was quiet, I just couldn't shake the feeling that we were being watched.

Windows and doors were checked all around the house as we made sure everything was locked and secure. I checked the surveillance footage on the laptop, rewinding it back as far as it would go to check for anything unusual. I stopped the video and froze, my thumb on the pause button. I couldn't believe what I was seeing.

There was a black car parked outside our house. It

looked like the same black car that had been following us earlier. The windows were tinted. I gasped. The driver got out the car and closed the door behind him. He wore a baseball cap and kept his face out of view. I looked at the clock. Two thirty-eight in the afternoon, Monday 15th September. Mum and I were both out.

The driver looked from one side of the street to the other, making sure there was no one around, before he made his move. Opening the front gate, he walked onto our path and up to our windows. Putting his face and hands up, he peeked into our living room. He then walked over to the front door and tried the handle, before walking around the back. He was visible again within a few seconds, as the gate to the back garden was locked from the inside. Leaving our grounds, he headed back to his car and drove off.

I played the recording again for Mum, and she let out a gasp as she watched the intruder walk around our grounds and then close the front gate behind him. She put her hand to her face, looking horrified, her eyes wide.

At that moment we jumped as the front door rattled. Jason looked out the peephole.

'It's alright, it's just the inspector,' he said.

I felt my shoulders slump as Mum and I walked over to the door and Jason let him in.

Dunlop stood on the top step, wearing a navy-blue jacket and black trousers. His eyes appeared swollen and heavy from lack of sleep and he looked like he wanted to be anywhere else but here.

'Hi, you left a voice message for me? I'm here to take a statement,' he said, not looking at all happy.

Jason let him into the livingroom and we filled him in, giving him the registration number of the car and the camera footage. He wrote everything down on his notepad. I sat with my hands over my face, agitated. This would cause anyone stress and upset.

'Okay, I'll get this down to the station and have a look over it. I'll be in touch,' Dunlop said, and he walked out of the house and to his car.

We were all fed up and wanted this to be over and done with. It was getting a bit too much.

The next morning, Mum and Jason were at work and I stayed at home feeling like a nervous wreck. Loitering around by the window, I watched for any cars that passed by. Being alone at a time like this really seemed to make me more fearful than I already had been. Every noise in the house made me jump, every creak made me think someone was around. I was constantly looking over at the living room door, expecting someone to walk through it any minute. Something had to be done to take my mind off it.

Boredom had set in by two o'clock. I sent a message to Mollie and waited for a reply, but it never arrived. She would have been too busy with work. I decided to do some exercise, thinking it would motivate me. Two minutes each of planks, sit-ups, star jumps and rope skips seemed to do the trick, and by the time I had finished the sweat was pouring off me. I drank a full glass of iced water to quench my thirst, put my exercise things away and threw myself down on the couch, satisfied with my workout. It had definitely made a difference to me as I seemed a bit happier.

Mum came home to find me on the couch binge-watching Season 2 of Smallville on DVD. She sighed as she dumped her bag in the living room and headed straight for the kitchen to make a start on dinner. The lasagne that she made from scratch was as good as it always was, and I put my finished plate in the kitchen and slumped back down on the couch again. After Mum had washed the dishes, she joined me and we watched the programme together. I smiled, knowing she was genuinely interested in what I was watching.

It was ten forty-five before Mum finally switched off the TV, forcing me off the couch and up the stairs.

When Friday morning arrived, I decided to try my best to get through the day, even though I felt somewhat groggy. I simply had to make a plan to do something different that weekend. Maybe hiking. Who knew?

'Morning, love,' Mum called as I walked into the kitchen. She was sitting on a barstool with the Daily Record and a bowl of All Bran.

I poured myself a bowl and joined her at the small table, my stomach rumbling. Whizzing around the kitchen, I made my toast and marmalade, and ate quickly before preparing to leave for the station. Mum argued about my choice of transport, phoning a taxi for me before I could even get a word in. It came quickly and I was heading to the station in no time.

I got to college in one piece, and with a sour face at that, but glad not to have to look over my shoulder every minute. As much as I was scared, I simply had to carry on as normal and try not to let this get to me.

I met up with Eric at the entrance and he began chatting away about Andrea, saying that she had picked out a Saskia wedding dress from Joyce Young in Glasgow. He wasn't allowed to see it until the big day and, according to Eric, she had warned him about browsing online.

'I had to promise her I wouldn't go sneaking around.' He laughed.

His wedding was getting closer and he looked genuinely excited at the prospect. I forced a smile on my face for him, although I was feeling anything but my usual chirpy self that day. He must have sensed my feelings, as he asked me repeatedly what was wrong. I feigned not feeling great as I got on with my work. He didn't say a word after that.

Lunchtime came, and as we sat in our usual spot in the canteen I picked at my baked potato. My mood still hadn't changed. Eric left shortly after, saying he had something he needed to do, but I had a feeling he was avoiding me. I felt bad for not opening up to him about it. With the mood I was in, it wasn't surprising he had gone.

I left college at four on the dot and practically ran for the train home. I'd only been back in the house for five seconds when the phone rang. Mum answered it as I joined her in the living room, sitting down to read the Weekly Gazette. The front page read:

LOCAL WOMAN WINS BIG ON THE LOTTO!

A woman who was sacked just a day before she won the lottery says she is ecstatic with her big win and is changing her life completely. Fran Tabcasy, 38, says she is tired of scraping by and is planning on dreaming big.

'I have always paid my way. But unfortunately, due to tough times, I had to take out loans,' she said to the Weekly Gazette. 'I work 48 hours a week and I have found myself struggling sometimes. I pay my rent and my council tax, like every other good working citizen. But the one time I couldn't come into work, I was sacked. I woke that morning in sheer agony with my back and I couldn't move. I wasn't able to get out of my bed to call my work. And just because they were short-staffed and I wasn't there, they let me go. I've been suffering back problems for months now and I'm currently on the list for physiotherapy. I've been waiting a long time.'

She was asked how she is planning on spending her big win.

'A large house,' she replied. 'With a swimming pool. I've been told that swimming is good for back pain. I live in a damp two-bedroom flat with my son on a small estate. It's about time we were out of there anyway. Who knows, maybe I'll even buy a house in Spain,' she laughed.

I smiled, finishing the article, and shook my head. Some people just got really lucky.

'Chloe, that was the inspector on the phone,' Mum called, dashing around. 'He wants us to go down to the station immediately.'

She came in from the hallway with her jacket and bag, mobile up at her ear as she left a message on Jason's voicemail to let him know where we were going. I sighed, looking up at the ceiling. Here we go again, I thought.

CHAPTER 31

'It's not good news, I'm afraid, Mrs Stanson.'

Dunlop pulled a chair out and sat in front of us. We were in the same room we had been in previously. He had paperwork and photographs of the driver in front of him, and no smile on his face. Mum sat with her arms on the table, waiting for information.

'We've checked the CCTV and the registration number. The driver of both the car that followed you and the car that was parked outside your house is connected to one of the prisoners who committed the break in.'

For a moment I couldn't breathe. My mind felt numb and my stomach turned as I squeezed my eyes shut. This wasn't happening. It couldn't be. We were being hounded constantly. Mum was nearly in tears. It didn't look like Dave was going to stop anytime soon. It made me sick to the pit of my stomach thinking about it all.

'But we got an injunction against him,' she said, her voice shaky.

'True, you did that. It seemed he has breached it and now he'll be looking at doing more time inside. Well, that's for the courts to decide really. Right now, he's been taken in for questioning. I can't give you any more information than that. Just be extra careful when you're outside. You don't know if there's anyone else lurking around. There could be others that we're not aware of.'

'This is impossible. I mean… how? Just how?' Tears streamed down her face.

Dunlop passed her a box of tissues and she took one and wiped her eyes, sniffing and sobbing quietly.

'I thought that having the CCTV up on the wall would

keep them away. Doesn't look like anything's working anymore. Not even the system. These men won't stop until they've completely ruined our lives,' she cried, shaking her head. I put my arm around her. What a mess we were in.

We left the building, once again seeming no further forward. This was exhausting. I felt like all we were doing was going back and forth and not really coming up with a result.

I was just about to head up to my room that night when Mum finally spoke to me. Neither of us had said much earlier. I guess we both felt a little broken.

'If it comes to it, we may have to move. I know it would be a lot for you with college. I'm sure the lecturers would understand if you took a week off.'

'They would just follow us. That would be completely pointless,' I answered in a strained voice.

Mum let out a long sigh. 'You're right. They would.' She put a hand over her face. 'I don't know. I really don't know,' she said, shaking her head.

It looked like we had hit a wall.

We decided to take our mind off it for a bit and try our best to enjoy the weekend. Staying at home was one thing neither of us wanted to do, and I was worried Mum may have anxiety issues. The stress and worry of watching over our shoulders and keeping an eye out constantly was taking a toll. We needed a break.

Jason, Mum and I left that Saturday morning to spend some time in the Lake District. We finally arrived after the two-hour drive and I could have squealed, I was so delighted with the view. It was strikingly beautiful. I couldn't believe how lucky I had suddenly become.

After checking into the Dipinlake Hotel, we headed outside for a hike, equipped with hiking boots. We spent endless hours walking around and taking pictures while hiking up a hill in Buttermere, with Mum panting all the way. I laughed, telling her how unfit she was.

'I'll need to join a gym when I get back home,' she said. We just laughed. That was never going to happen.

This place was just the thing for us both. It was simply wonderful. As we walked along with the water by our feet, I stopped suddenly, holding my breath and staring out at the hills on the other side. Mum stopped ahead of me, followed by Jason in front of her.

'What's wrong?' Mum asked.

I looked at her and smiled. 'Listen. There is absolutely no noise at all. It's just so quiet and calm.'

They both stared out at the water, quietly listening. There was simply nothing else quite like it.

Jason broke the silence. 'Come on. Let's finish our walk.'

I followed behind them both as we walked on for hours, mostly in utter silence. It was a surreal experience, a place of perfection with a view that could be enjoyed for a very long time.

When we arrived back at the hotel, I joined them in the bar as Mum and Jason had a drink to unwind and relax before our dinner arrived. I devoured the roast beef I'd ordered, savouring every mouthful. It was a well-earned meal after the long walk around the hills.

After dinner, I left Mum with her sauvignon blanc and Jason with his small scotch while they chatted about work and ordinary things.

My night was spent soaking in the bathtub and reading Harry Potter and the Philosopher's Stone. I had been swept up in this book; finding it a fascinating read and couldn't tear my eyes away from it. Finally finding the strength to put the book down, I climbed into my luxurious bed and drifted towards sleep. The room was quiet, peaceful and relaxing, with a great sense of calm. I thought back on all the good times I'd had recently, which made me smile. When it seemed like our world was crumbling down upon us, just how much strength, I wondered, did we really have to get through it?

Mum and I sat down to our continental breakfast the next morning while Jason dug into his full English. If it were up to me and we had the money, we'd have stayed for a whole week in this exquisite hotel. But I had college the next morning and Mum and Jason had work. This break away had been so perfect that we didn't want to leave. But as it was, we dragged our luggage out of the rooms on the Sunday morning and into Jason's car. I sat in the back seat with a sour face. Home was the last place I wanted to be.

I sighed, looking at the house in front of me as Jason parked the car. It wasn't a place I felt happy and safe anymore. My childhood home just felt like a shell of a house, simply waiting for something that would eventually destroy everything we had worked for.

I unpacked, had a shower and put on a wash before Mum phoned in dinner for us. Tomorrow is another day, I thought. I had a test to sit and an interview to go to on Wednesday. And quite frankly I would be a lot happier when both were out of the way. I had an early night, finishing up Harry Potter before falling asleep.

Monday morning arrived and my heart pounded with nerves. When I came down into the kitchen for breakfast, I couldn't eat a thing, only managing to drink two cups of tea before heading out into the cool morning air. The walk to the station did me good and I felt a lot better by the time I arrived for my train. It seemed to be a peaceful morning so far and I hoped the day ahead would go smoothly for me.

The students were messing around as I walked into the room to sit my test for IT. The boys were laughing while playing games on the college computers, and the girls were all mysteriously buzzing around someone, sounding worried. I couldn't help but overhear what they were talking about as I took my seat. The girl they had crowded around, Dina, had got a new tattoo a couple of days ago, her boyfriend's name written across the top of her arm. It had got infected. I looked over and could just make out the writing. It was red and blistering. My eyes widened in shock. It looked bad.

Dina was prone to showing off in front of everyone else. She bragged about getting the tattoo at a place called Art from Ink.

'I haven't even told my mum about it yet,' she laughed.

'Doesn't it hurt?' one girl asked her.

'Not much. It stings a little, but it's not as bad as it was when I first got it. Nicky had to hold my hand when I was getting it done. But he's totally worth it.' She sighed, looking up and smiling at the girls.

'You're crazy,' another girl replied, sounding serious. I nodded to myself, thinking, Yeah, you're right there. You couldn't pay me enough to print someone else's name on my skin.

One girl suggested going to the doctor's to see about getting treatment to heal the infection before it became any worse. 'I'll go with you,' she suggested, trying to be there for her friend.

Dina agreed that they would make the appointment at break time. No matter what happened, I didn't want to see that arm get any worse.

The lecturer, Sally, walked into the room shortly after, and settled everyone down and handed out the test papers. I took a deep breath, looking over them as the test started and the room grew silent. I bit my nails, racking my brain on some questions, but eventually I saw it through and got it finished in plenty of time. I felt positive at the end as I was the first person to leave the room after answering all but two questions I was unsure of. I handed the paper to Sally as I walked out the room and headed to the canteen.

I joined Eric for lunch and we sat down to a slice of pepperoni pizza, discussing our tests. I had been relieved in class when I had realised the questions weren't as bad as I feared they would be.

'We've both been studying really hard and should pass easily. Have a little faith.' Eric smiled, giving me a wink.

I couldn't help but giggle, feeling relaxed again after a tense morning in my I.T class.

'You were very quiet the other day, Chloe,' said Eric. 'Is something bothering you?'

'Oh.' I looked around the canteen, making sure we were out of earshot before I whispered, 'We've had more trouble with some dodgy characters. You know, the one who broke into our house. He had someone else follow us the other evening when we headed home from the carvery. It really creeped me out and I just wasn't in the mood at all that day. Couldn't face anyone. I'm really sorry if I made you feel like we had fallen out or something. It just got to me, that's all.'

He looked crushed at that moment. 'I'm sorry, Chlo.' He took my hand in his. 'I really care about you and I honestly thought I'd done something wrong.'

'No, never.' I sat up quickly, grabbing his hand tightly, and then recoiled instantly, feeling awkward and looking away. He leaned over the table, smiling at me. I gave him a shy smile, feeling silly.

'Chloe, don't ever feel awkward around me. We're pretty much best friends. I couldn't have asked for anyone nicer. I'll always be here for you. I've told you this already.'

'I think I may have trust issues,' I confessed, staring at the table.

He placed his forefinger under my chin, tilting my head up. 'I understand that. But you'll need to have a little faith. I'm not going anywhere.'

'Promise?'

He placed his hand over mine on the table, staring into my eyes. 'I promise.' He smiled.

My heart nearly burst out of my chest. He was the sweetest.

CHAPTER 32

Wednesday flew by and I sailed through the interview for the receptionist job. I walked into the room feeling insignificant and came out with a big grin on my face, delighted. Sue asked when I could start, and I told her I could do the Wednesday, Thursday and Saturday if they needed me in and she was quite happy with that. I went home full of excitement and told Mum the good news. She was extremely happy for me and told me to phone Mollie when I had the chance. I decided that I would phone her at the weekend; that way we would get more time to talk and catch up. I somehow felt like we were slowly becoming distant from each other.

College was…well, it was college really. I sat test after test, studied so much my brain hurt, and exhausted things to every possible limit. It was a good distraction, though.

Eric had been shocked when I confided in him regarding my uncle and the dreadful things he had been doing.

'You've got guts,' he told me, writing something down on a piece of paper and handing it to me. 'Here's my number,' he said. 'If there's ever a time you need someone to talk to, I'm here, Chloe. Just call me.'

We became inseparable from that day on and hid nothing from each other. He even arrived one morning with an elegant silver envelope addressed to me. As I sat at my desk, feeling ever so suspicious, he looked at me, grinning.

'What's this?' I asked him.

'Open it.' He smiled.

I couldn't resist. I opened the seal of the pretty envelope, careful not to tear it, and gently pulled out the crisp, silver-laced card. It was their wedding invitation. The card read:

Michael & Emily Thomson

Request the pleasure in inviting

Miss Chloe Stanson and guest

to join Andrea Thomson & Eric Morgan on their special
day

to celebrate with them on

Saturday 17th February at 1pm at:

The Beak and Wing Hotel

11 Inklee Lane

Glasgow

Please respond by 20th December to:

Michael & Emily Thomson

109 Ellington Drive

Newton town

Glasgow

I looked up from the invitation. 'You invited me to your wedding?' I gushed.

'Not only you, Chloe, a guest as well.' He smiled.

I sat up, leaned over to him and gave him a very long hug as happy tears escaped my eyes. He was a keeper.

He began to talk about the wedding and Andrea, who had been planning their big day since… well, the day he asked her to marry him. She had made a wedding book containing everything she wanted for their special day, and he told me how happy she had been organising it and that he felt like their relationship had become stronger.

'I'm honestly head over heels with her, Chloe. Right now, it just feels like a dream come true. Andrea knows we're best friends, of course, and she's happy for me that I'm doing well at college and she's dying to meet you.'

I looked at him warily. 'Really?'

'Of course. Unfortunately, with her working crazy shifts and organising the wedding, we haven't had much time together. She's been out a lot at her mum's trying to plan everything, while I've been at home studying. But she knows we have a special bond.'

'And she's fine with that?' I asked, unsure.

'Yes.' He laughed. 'You worry too much. You'll get to meet her at the wedding. I know you'll get along great. You're a nice person and a real character. I feel lucky to be spending time with you. I hope you never have to go through anything like that again with your uncle. I can't imagine how traumatised you were and how awful it must have been. I'm here for you. Anytime.'

I just looked at him with love in my heart. He was one in a million.

CHAPTER 33

As I waited at reception to start my first day at Sue and Win Lawyers, a small thrill of excitement went through me. The brightly lit room I sat in had white-painted walls with a black-patterned feature wall at the back. There was a long charcoal-coloured couch and two large areca palm plants either side of the glass entranceway. It was pristine and welcoming.

The girl at the desk had made a quick phone call to say that I had arrived. I had only been sitting a couple of minutes when Sue came through to the reception. She quickly greeted me, and with her warm, caring aura, I took to her immediately. With her cropped blond-streaked hair, she managed to blend in with the decor, and she was wearing a knee-length charcoal-coloured skirt and crisp white blouse.

She introduced me to the receptionist, Willow, who would be working on the days I was at college. Willow was lovely, positive and bubbly. Her long, straight, red hair flowed halfway down her back and her face was freckled. It turned out Willow was at Glasgow University studying to become a lawyer. I wished her all the best, and then Sue took me for a tour of the building.

We walked down a short corridor. I could immediately smell the fresh pine furniture polish as I was led into Sue's office. The room was immaculate. The walls had been painted a bright white with a dado rail halfway down. A mahogany desk sat in the middle of the room with a computer screen and keyboard to one side, paper files and a folder. A stacked bookcase filled the wall on the left side and a collage of framed photos took pride of place behind the work area. You could tell Sue had strong family bonds.

Sue was a firm-handed woman who, although very friendly, didn't mess around. Her nature was subtle. She spoke very caringly about her family, their business and how it had been handed down to them by their mum, dad and aunt. It had gone from Stan, Fran & George lawyers to Sue and Win, and had been through the generations. It came as quite a surprise to find out that Sue and Winifred were sisters, although I had kind of guessed that when I first met them. They were very alike.

As Sue walked around her office, she told me a story about her family from a long time ago. Back in the 1940s, her great-great-uncle Pillard, began the business with a supplier. She pointed to a wall behind me. I stood up, turned and walked over to see the black-and-white photo on the wall. Standing leaning on a stick beside an inscribed name plate at the side of a small, quaint shop was a tall, thin man with a top hat. He reminded me of Stan Laurel. I shook my head, feeling overwhelmed that over the generations Sue's family had managed to make something that was once a tiny little shop into a large, glass-fronted, three-storey building. And it certainly had a lot of stories to tell. It was very inspiring.

I had a look at the rest of the photos as Sue continued to chat away, telling stories about her family's past and the work they'd done. I imagined what their lives were like back then, without all the technology that we had today, and how different it must have been. There were photos from every generation of the family to which the business had been handed down.

Today, the business was prodigious and had an immense look to it. Sue and Winifred had made a great reputation for themselves with their business, and I knew it would make me proud to be a part of their team and stand with them. It was an opportunity I had to work hard for.

Sue was an inspiring woman who could create ideas and make them become reality. It was amazing. I couldn't wait to start.

She took me out of her office and gave me a tour of the storage room, kitchen, other offices and the stationery store, which were upstairs. Other colleagues introduced themselves and I was given a special welcome into the family business. A pleasant, fuzzy feeling went through me. I hoped I would fit right in.

My day was spent learning to answer the phone, write in the logbook and issue badges to guests who came in. As I stood behind the reception desk, typing away at the computer and welcoming guests who had arrived, I glanced outside at people passing by on the street, workers in their uniforms and shoppers with their bags full. A man stood at the front of the building with his back to me. I thought nothing of it and got on with replying to emails.

Time passed by, and the longer he stood there, the more I began to worry. An hour and a half quickly passed and he still hadn't moved; he just stood there with his hands in his pockets. He was around six foot, wearing a navy-blue two-piece suit with his dark hair combed back. Gradually, the street emptied as it was well past lunchtime, and I figured I would say something to one of the staff in case they knew him. It was over an hour later when I finally chapped on Sue's office door.

'Hi, Sue. Sorry to bother you, but a man has been standing outside the building for two and a half hours. I'm just wondering who he is.'

She looked at me quizzically while sorting out her files and paperwork. 'Have there been any appointments missed today? Have you checked the diary?'

'Yeah, it's been checked. Everyone turned up today.'

'I'm sure it's nothing, Chloe. Maybe go outside and speak with him, see what he's waiting for.'

'I'd rather not, if it's all the same to you.'

'What's wrong? Don't be scared. Just go out and speak to him. It'll be fine.'

I shook my head fearfully. 'I can't.'

'Sure you can. Just ask him if he's waiting for someone.'

'Sue, it's too hard to explain right now, but I can't go out there.'

'Nonsense. On you go now.' She waved her hand at me as if shooing me along, and she sat at her computer, continuing with her work.

It was up to me now. I had to go out and confront this man. Whoever he was. The thought of it was sickening.

I walked out of Sue's room with my head down. It was now or never. Approaching the reception area, I gasped suddenly with fright as I caught the man outside staring at me through the window. Tense with fear, I stood frozen on the spot. What was happening? Who was this man staring through the window at me and what did he want? We couldn't simply stand here gawking at each other. I decided to make the first move and confront him.

I took a step towards the door, wanting to find out what was going on, but the man outside suddenly turned and walked away. I halted in my tracks, feeling shocked and confused, wondering what the hell had just happened. Trying my best to shake the horrible feeling off, I put a smile on my face ready for the next associates to arrive.

The day seemed to drag after that. As hard as it was, I put that incident out of my head, forced a smile on my face and got on with the job I was paid to do.

Sue came out of her office, asking for a couple of printouts, and as I handed them to her, she questioned me about the man outside.

'Oh, I don't know. By the time I came back out here he'd gone.'

I couldn't tell her what had really happened. It didn't even bear thinking about. It had left me totally shaken up.

'Are you alright, Chloe?' she asked, concerned. 'You're looking a bit pale. Are you feeling okay?'

'Yeah, I'm fine,' I answered, trying to keep my voice steady.

'How has your first day been so far? Are you enjoying it?'

'Yes. It's been good, thanks,' I answered honestly, smiling. I really was enjoying the first day in my new job.

'Well, let me know if you feel unwell. Don't want my staff getting sick now, do I?'

She smiled at me and walked back to her office. I shook my head, knowing how oblivious she was as I stood working away at the computer, silently longing for my shift to be over.

As five thirty rolled by and the first day finished up, I thanked Sue and said goodbye to the rest of the team and I left the building, concentrating on getting home for my dinner after a full day's shift in Glasgow.

I sat down in the last carriage of the train, taking the weight off my feet. My new shoes made my heels ache more and more with every hour that passed. Figuring that was the least of my problems, I leaned against the glass and closed my eyes, blocking out the sounds of the rowdy carriage.

Just over ten minutes later, after a short nap, I stood up and was groggily pushing my way through the mass of bodies clogging up the aisle when I suddenly came to a grinding halt.

He had been standing watching me, not even bothering to hide away. The man who had been outside my work for over two hours was now on my train.

I felt a shudder as I was shoved slightly forward by the passenger at my back. I heard a quiet tut and a mumble, and I managed to regain my composure and quickly walk off the train. I turned back as the doors began to close and looked inside. He was watching me out of the single window in the door, showing no emotion. The train rolled off and I was left standing on my own in the cold, pouring rain.

I could have collapsed the moment the train left the platform. Alone and scared, with nobody to come and collect me, I pulled my mobile out of my bag and called a taxi to take me home. I wasn't in the mood to walk anywhere.

When I arrived home, I made another call to the police station, telling the officer everything that had happened and giving him the best description that I could. As hard as I tried, I couldn't hold back the tears as they flowed down my cheeks. My emotions had got to me once again. It wasn't surprising given the fear that I had been through.

Was this another man Dave had hired to watch me? I didn't know how long this would go on for. Would he keep it up for months on end? Carry on torturing the life out of us until we finally snapped?

I was done. Done with Dave and his men following my mum and me around all over the place. Done with fearing for my own safety and whether or not we had a bright future in front of us. Right now it didn't look that way. There was only one thing I wanted in life at this moment. I wanted liberation.

CHAPTER 34

Autumn flew by and slowly, winter began to descend on us. The nights drew in, the leaves fell from the trees and it was very cold. As much as I disliked the wind and the rain, I couldn't wait for the snow to fall. I loved having my waterproofs and boots on and walking through the woods seeing the trees all white.

When I was little, every time it snowed Dad used to go out the back with me to build a snowman. I can distinctly remember tugging at his jumper impatiently one winter's afternoon as he sat on the bottom steps in the hallway trying to get his boots on while outside the snow grew thicker on the ground. I was extremely excited, as most children are at a young age – the thrill of running out into the garden and gathering up a great big lump of snow, only to throw it up in the air, laughing. I made Dad join in as well, and we both messed around in the snow making snow angels. We really did have the best time and it was great fun. Another time, he came home with a sledge, and I jumped on and he pulled me all around the garden until it got dark. I had the best memories, and the best dad in the world. He was my hero.

Life began to get pretty hectic. When I wasn't at college, I was working, and when I wasn't working, I was studying. With eating less every day, I could feel the effect on me. It had worn me down.

Coming home from college one afternoon feeling too tired to do any cooking, I hung my bag and coat up on the bannister and headed up to bed, exhausted. Mum wasn't happy when she came home to a dark house and no meal on the table after doing overtime.

'I make the effort for you, so you should do the same for me, Chloe. It's just not acceptable,' she practically growled at me as she looked at a takeaway menu. 'What are you going to do when you move out into your own place? Starve yourself?'

She didn't understand how tired I'd been and I wasn't in the mood to argue with her. So I let her be. She went on at me for a full fifteen minutes. I zoned out halfway through, reading my TV magazine. She wasn't impressed.

Eric and I seemed to be bonding more than ever, which I didn't think was even remotely possible. He understood me in a way no one else did, and I appreciated him for the kind, caring guy he was. He would make me laugh a lot with his jokes and he always made me feel good about myself. I thought part of the reason he was so close to me was because of what I had been put through with Dave; it made him rather protective in a way. I wasn't going to fight that, though. Eric was special. He was the reason I smiled when I came to college every day; he seemed to make the day brighter somehow, and I loved the way he looked when his eyes glistened.

It had occurred to me that I had feelings for him. These weren't just best friend feelings either. I felt affection for him that I had never felt before. For anyone. Up to this point, I had tried my best never to let on. I would never have him catch me gazing into his eyes and smiling. But I worried that one day I may slip up and he would find out. This was simply getting out of hand.

College was going really well. I passed every test and was thrilled with the outcome. The endless studying really had paid off. I was extremely proud when, in my last class one day, I read my latest pass mark and saw it was a ninety-eight per cent. Sitting with the test paper in my hands, I looked at it, astounded.

'I can't believe that every test so far has been a pass. I

wasn't too sure I would do it. But I did. And I really couldn't have got through it without you.'

I leaned over, wrapping my arms around Eric, and held him tight, running my fingers through his hair. 'Thank you,' I whispered.

Then it suddenly dawned on me what I had just done. I pulled back quickly, feeling mortified. Shit! I thought. I had let my feelings get in the way.

'You okay?' he asked, looking bewildered.

'Yeah,' I replied, looking away.

Shame filled me and I felt like a complete idiot. I had been trying so hard not to let my feelings get in the way, and the one time I had forgotten about things, I'd slipped up. The one great friend I had, whom I could confide in, who was sitting right in front of me, engaged to be married, and here I was crushing on him. I knew better than that. This was most definitely wrong.

'I'm sorry, I don't know what's come over me all of a sudden,' I said, shaking my head and moving my chair back. I just knew I shouldn't have done that.

'Chlo, what's wrong?'

'Hmm?' I began, reading an article on Yahoo News for a minute. Finishing up, I looked over at him. 'What's up?' I asked with a smile, acting as if nothing had just happened.

He sat there with a questioning look on his face. 'Something bothering you?'

'Not at all.' I smiled, leaning over the desk. There was a sudden awkwardness in the air. I turned my head away just as Zoe, the central services lecturer, started talking.

'Okay, class, now you all have your test papers in front of you and most of them are good results.' She looked over at Katrina and Nadine and they looked away awkwardly, facing anywhere else but the rest of the class. Something told me they hadn't quite passed. I wasn't surprised, to be honest, given the amount of time they spent messing around on the internet. They obviously hadn't been studying a lot. More fool them.

'We have a lecturer coming in today from Edinburgh for a bit of a chat with you about your future and finding jobs. Now I know that one or two of you already have a job, so this needn't apply to you, but for the rest of you, please take the time to listen. Her name is Lucy and she will be here in half an hour with a PowerPoint presentation from her work. Any questions that you may want to ask can be answered at the end.'

Zoe handed out feedback forms rating the course, the classes, the lecturers and so on, which I filled in and handed back, rating it great with no complaints. From day one I had thoroughly enjoyed my time here, making a friend and completing all my work. I passed it back to Zoe and sat down in my seat and turned to Eric. I felt bad. He didn't deserve this. He was a decent guy.

'Eric.'

He turned to me with a poker face, waiting for me to talk.

'I'm sorry,' I said. 'I'm just being an idiot. Forgive me?'

'What exactly are you sorry for, Chloe? You've been acting strangely for weeks and I haven't a clue what's going on inside your head. Is it college? Work? Too much getting to you? Have I done something wrong? I can't forgive you if I don't know what I'm forgiving.'

I felt under pressure in the moment and simply wanted to burst. Open up and just tell him how I felt. Get it off my shoulders and hope for the best. But I knew it wouldn't go the way I hoped it would. It would end badly. Always did.

'Please don't,' I whispered quietly.

'Please don't what?' he answered, looking slightly frustrated.

I couldn't deal with this right now. I couldn't deal with

him being annoyed with me. So I left the class and took a walk around the college.

I arrived back just as Lucy walked in the door carrying a little more than she could cope with, it seemed, as she struggled with a box on one arm and a laptop bag on the other. I sat in my seat, avoiding looking at Eric. Lucy set up the PowerPoint presentation on the laptop she'd brought with her, and several minutes later everyone had turned to watch the screen. She had a look around the classroom, smiled and introduced herself, telling us that she lived in Edinburgh and worked full time as an institute admin secretary at Edinburgh University, which required an HNC. She clicked the mouse on her laptop, explaining a lot about each slide in fine detail.

Around fifteen minutes into the slideshow I was feeling drowsy. My eyelids began to droop and I struggled to keep them open. It didn't take long before I gave in to sleep, missing out on Lucy's admin slides. It was only after Eric shook my arm that I jumped up, wide awake, hearing laughing coming from the other side of the room.

'Not getting any sleep?' one of the girls laughed.

I ignored her and gave my eyes a rub, sitting up and looking back at the screen as Lucy clicked from one slide to the next.

'If I'm boring you, feel free to leave anytime,' Lucy said, staring at me before turning back. I knew never to get on the wrong side of her.

An hour and several questions later, Lucy was gone and all her stuff with her. I was glad. Nothing she had to offer interested me in the slightest. I stretched, trying to wake myself up, and I put my paperwork in my bag, collected my stuff and headed for the door, glad to leave my last class of the day. As I reached the door, I felt someone grab my arm and I turned to find a slightly annoyed-looking Eric glaring at me.

'Chloe, we need to talk.' He stood tall, his jacket in his hand and his bag slung over his left shoulder.

Other students came out of their classes, passing us by, their heads turned towards us. I didn't like the feeling of being gawked at. It made me feel self-conscious.

'Eric, I don't want to talk here, not now. There're too many people. We'll talk soon, yeah? I have to go home.'

'Okay, when then?' he asked impatiently.

'I'll call you tonight when I have time, I promise.'

He shook his head, obviously not happy with the way I was dealing with things, but he accepted what I had to offer. 'Okay, tonight. We'll talk. Don't forget now.'

'I won't. I just need to catch up on sleep. Then I'll have a clear head. I'm just shattered.'

'Looks like you need it. You look exhausted.'

I'm not going to lie, I felt it. Every bone in my body ached, but I ploughed through nonetheless. As much as I had been enjoying my first full year at college, I would be glad when I had completed the course. I needed some me time.

'I'll speak to you tonight, Eric,' I said, and quickly rushed away from him to get my train home. I wasn't ready to talk yet.

I got home after falling asleep on the train and nearly missing my stop. Needing a slight change in my routine, I ran up the stairs, changed into my workout clothes and came down feeling ready for action. Leaving my phone on the couch, I grabbed my iPod and headed outside.

With my earphones in, I set my stopwatch for an hour and did a few stretches to get me started before my jog around the football pitch. Coldplay blasted away in my ears and I blocked out everything else, focusing on getting around the track at least three times. I paced myself, taking a quick swig of water with each lap I ran, before finishing up and heading home for a shower.

A while later, I was standing in front of the fridge with my hair wrapped up in a towel, deciding what to eat for dinner. I couldn't face a proper meal, so I made something simple, quick and easy –toast and sliced ham with a hot chocolate. I took my plate into the living room, sat on the couch and picked up my mobile. Two missed calls and a text, from the one and only.

You haven't called like you promised. I'm still waiting. Won't give up. Slightly worried. Call me. Eric. X

He certainly wasn't the kind of guy who would give up. Eric was very persuasive when he wanted to be. Maybe that was one of the reasons I had developed feelings for him. Who knew? The longer the whole situation went on, the worse I began to feel. I thought about calling him. But a chat on the phone about feelings was hardly appropriate.

Throwing the phone back down, I tried to catch up on the missed episodes of Corrie that I never got to watch because I was too busy studying with Eric. Within half an hour the phone rang once more and I contemplated answering it. There was never going to be a good time to have this conversation. I pressed the button to answer.

'Hey, where have you been? I've left you messages and tried to call you. Why didn't you reply?'

I had to lie. There was no other option on the phone. 'Hi, Eric. I fell asleep when I came home. That's me just awake now, though. Told you I was tired.'

'Well, I've been worried sick over here. Look, I don't know what's going on with you and I don't pretend to know, but you need to tell me what's going on.'

I ran my hand over my face, worrying about how much deep water I was getting myself into. The very thought of telling him made me cringe to my inner core. Maybe there was a way we could work at this and be friends all the same.

I told him it wasn't something I was happy to talk about over the phone, and he finally agreed we would speak the next day after college in the library. I really didn't want to do this to my closest friend whom I had only known barely three months. But this had to come out into the open. I hated secrecy. I had to tell my friend that I had a crush on him. Just what could be more mortifying?

The next day, my classes passed quickly and I found myself sitting opposite Eric at the back of the library, unwillingly about to pour my heart out to him and declare my feelings.

It wasn't going to be easy. For either of us. For I knew deep down that within five minutes he would be gone out of the building and never want to speak to me again. How heart-breaking would that be?

'Well, out with it then,' he said as he leaned back against the chair watching me, his arms crossed against his chest.

I felt like I was back in high school, getting into trouble with the head teacher. I sat closer to him at the table, trying to be as comfortable as possible.

'You've been really off with me. I'm trying to be as patient as I can, but you're not helping much. So, here we are. There's nothing stopping you from telling me now. What's going on, Chloe? Is it Dave? Are you still being hassled? Do you –'

'Please stop,' I cut him off, putting my hand up to halt him from rambling on. I needed a second to process my thoughts. How would I begin? I decided I was just going to put it out there.

'Eric, you are one of the nicest guys I have ever met. And I'm lucky to have you as my friend. You make me laugh all the time, even on days I'm not feeling great…'

'Chloe, where is this going?' He sighed, looking

slightly fed up.

'The thing is, Eric, um… I – I kind of have feelings for you,' I said, staring at the table, hands gripped together so tightly that my fingers were red. I couldn't bear to look up. I knew he would be horrified at what he'd just heard. Inside I was cringing, hating myself for feeling the way I did. I wanted to run out of the room and pretend this hadn't just happened.

I listened for any movement, but it was quiet. I slowly looked up and he was watching me. No emotions showing. What was he thinking? My nervousness was growing by the second.

'Eric, please say something.'

'What can I say? Shit, Chloe. How? Why? I – you're my closest friend. I'm bloody engaged, for crying out loud. I don't…'

He began fidgeting around in his chair, unable to stay still. This was really messed up and I knew he wouldn't want to talk to me. I made a snap decision and stood up to walk away, staring out the window as I spoke.

'I'm sorry. I should never have let this happen. If you don't want to talk to me again, I'll totally understand. I think it would be in both of our best interests if I didn't attend your wedding, Eric. When it comes to it, just tell Andrea I have the flu or something. I'm sure she'll understand.'

I took a breath as I looked down. He sat staring at the table, not moving.

'Eric?'

He looked up at me with eyes like a seal pup's and I wanted to sob my heart out. I gritted my teeth and held my breath. This was torture. What was he thinking? How much I'd hurt him? How much he hated me right now? I didn't blame him; I would have hated me too. I had been such an idiot.

'How long have you felt like this?' he asked.

'A while.' I could really have kicked myself. Poor Eric. 'If it's any consolation, I feel like shit right now. I don't want to keep saying sorry. That's not going to fix anything. I wish I didn't have these feelings, but I do. I'm only human.'

He rubbed his head, looking like he was trying to come to terms with what I'd just told him. There was another awkward moment as we both tried to work out what to say to each other.

'What do you want from me, Chloe?'

I gave him a surprised look. 'Nothing! That's just it, I'm not telling you this to act on it at all. Look, I'm really sorry this has happened and I'm going to try my best to forget about it. I just don't want to lose my friendship with you, that's all.'

'It's a bit late for that, don't you think?' he said.

'Eric, please. Don't fall out with me just because of this. I can work on it. I can forget it ever happened and move on and –'

'Just expect everything to be normal?' he finished.

I looked at him. 'Don't fall out with me, please.'

'I don't know how to be around you anymore.' His voice was hoarse.

I felt like part of my world was crumbling and there was no sure way of fixing it. I didn't know if there was any way back from this. I was losing a great friend. This just wasn't happening.

'I need some time, Chloe. Just please give me some space.'

He stood up and walked out of the library without saying another word. I stood there feeling emotional as tears flowed down my cheeks. And just like that, friendship over.

CHAPTER 35

The next few weeks passed in a blur. College was dreary now without Eric to talk to. I felt like part of my soul had been ripped out and I couldn't seem to find happiness without him. He was still at college, though, sitting across with the guys on the other side of the room, the only true friend I had here and without him it was too lonely. Sometimes when I was working on something, I'd turn to speak to him about it, but he wasn't there. He was out of my life now, and I didn't know if I would ever get him back. It was heart-breaking.

Work was busy. Due to it being near the Christmas rush, the diary was full. I guessed that was a good thing really, because I was rushed off my feet and the time flew by, giving me no chance to think about anything. It was good to get home at the end of the day. With no more studying to do until next year, I finally had some time to myself.

I was on the train home one drizzly, bitterly cold afternoon when I remembered Mollie. We hadn't spoken for weeks. I contemplated calling her, and then decided against it. A crowded train really wasn't the best setting for a private conversation; I didn't want anyone overhearing talk of my non-existent love life. That chat would have to keep until I saw her again. We would catch up at some point soon.

That evening was another quiet one, spent at my computer ordering Christmas presents online. Mum and Jason had gone out on their weekly date for dinner and drinks at the Italian restaurant, and that gave me time to get something really special for them. I decided to purchase gifts that they would actually use, rather than just smiling with a 'Thanks, Chloe' and then sticking them in a drawer somewhere in the house never to be looked at again. That would be a waste of money.

I browsed around, and finally picked out a sterling-silver diamond heart necklace, a box of Milk Tray, slippers, a personalised 'Mum' pen and a box set of My Family. I just knew Mum would love them. Diamante gold cuff links and Hugo Boss aftershave seemed like the perfect presents for Jason. I decided against chocolates for him, as I knew he had been watching his weight recently and going to the gym a lot. Mollie would hopefully be delighted with the Swarovski crystal earrings I picked. That was one thing about her: when she shopped, she spent most of the time staring in jewellery shop windows looking at earrings she could never afford.

I entered my card details, feeling satisfied with my purchases. Then I walked over to the window and looked out at the quiet street down below, thinking back on all the weeks that had passed. No one had been following us around, watching our every move. It had seemed to end all of a sudden, and the silence was more frightening than anything. That got me thinking: was this all leading up to something? Could they possibly have an ulterior motive? Maybe there was more to it than they were letting on. Should we be worried?

We had been tracked for months, people shadowing our footsteps, keeping eyes on us. They must have had an intention, surely? Day by day, week by week, they had made us suffer, trying to push us over the edge. We'd had no contact from Dave or the governor at the prison, so we didn't know exactly what had been happening inside. Not that we wanted to know right enough, but the fact that we had been getting hassled at home was bad enough.

I yawned, moving away from the window, and changed into my nightwear and slipped into bed. Tomorrow was another day.

I had just sat down at the table for our Sunday afternoon dinner when the door opened and Jason came limping into the living room with a walking stick.

'Jason, you hurt your leg!'

'Gosh, you have good eyesight, Chloe, I'll give you that,' he replied sarcastically.

I rolled my eyes. 'What have you done to yourself?'

'It was that stupid treadmill at the gym,' Mum replied, shaking her head. 'I told him to go easy, but Jason overdoes everything.'

He sighed at Mum, taking his place at the table and putting his stick next to his chair.

'I take it you've been to the hospital then?' I asked. That was a dumb question. Like, where else would he have got the stick?

'Yes. Unfortunately, I've got a torn ligament. The doctor said I have to take a few weeks off work. I phoned my boss to let him know. He wasn't impressed and didn't seemed that interested really. Like he had more things to worry about than me.'

'Huh!' Mum scoffed. 'Where's the employee morale? The incentive? The compassion and concern?'

'He's got a lot on his plate just now, Karen. I think his head was elsewhere.'

'But you're a member of his staff, Jason. He should at least make an effort to care. That doesn't say much about him. You won't be going back to work with a leg that you can barely walk on.'

'I've to go to my GP's tomorrow so they can sign me off work, but I'll see how I feel after two or three weeks. Hopefully, it'll be better by then. I need to get back to work, Karen. I've never taken time off before.'

'That leg is not for walking on,' Mum answered sharply.

I could tell Jason was trying to change the subject as he dug into his dinner. 'Oh, Karen, this chicken is delicious,' he declared, savouring his meal.

Mum gave him a slight scoff, shaking her head as she picked up her cutlery and began to eat. Debate over.

Half an hour later, the plates were emptied and lay in the kitchen sink. I was sitting in Dad's chair and Mum and Jason were snuggled together watching an episode of The Antiques Roadshow.

I turned to Mum. 'You know, it's been over a month since I've spoken to Mollie. Maybe I should call her. I've been thinking, with all that's been going on, we need a bit of joy and

Christmas cheer around here. Could we possibly set one more place at the table?' I asked, biting my lip.

'Of course you can! The more the merrier, especially on Christmas Day. That sounds lovely, Chloe.'

'Thanks, Mum.'

I walked out and was just about to head up the stairs when there was a knock at the door. I opened it, only to find a smiling Mollie on the step, standing there with her hood up and rainwater pouring down her jacket.

'Mollie!' I called, delighted to see her. Letting her in the door, I gave her a cuddle. 'We were just talking about you there. I was just about to call you.'

'Oh yeah? What's going on now? This house is always full of drama.'

I shook my head, knowing she was only joking. 'Do you want a drink? I have Irn Bru or fresh orange.'

'I'll take the orange, thanks.'

I nodded and pulled out the carton from the fridge. Taking the glass into the living room, I came straight out with what I had to ask.

'Now, as you are my best friend and it's been a really rough year for us, we've been discussing something. We want this Christmas to be a really special one, and I couldn't think of anyone better to spend it with than you. So, what do you say? Would you like to spend Christmas Day with us?'

She looked at me, her eyes wide in disbelief and her mouth open slightly. 'Are you serious? Of course! I would love nothing more. Oh Chloe, thank you!' She grinned like a Cheshire cat and came over to give me a bear hug, then spent the next few minutes thanking me tearfully.

As much as Christmas was about family, I had known Mollie all my life and I felt like she was part of mine. She just had to be here on that special day to celebrate with us. She asked me what present I wanted for Christmas, as she was going out with her family to do their shopping together.

'Ghost perfume,' I replied happily, not letting on that I'd already got hers.

'I'll have to check with Mum and Dad to make sure they're not going anywhere, but I'll let you know. I'm sure I heard them say something about going around to Aunt Elsie's for Christmas Day. To be honest, I could do with an excuse to get out of it.'

'Don't you like your aunt then?' I asked.

'Well, put it this way, you'd need a whole can of air freshener with you if you wanted to set foot inside her house.' She laughed.

I made a face of disgust and we both giggled away. Poor Aunt Elsie and her hyposmia.
We spent the rest of the evening having a right good laugh and playing a game of Scrabble. Jason won, and I patted him on the back and said, 'Well done.' With his bad leg, he needed a bit of happiness. Poor Jason.

CHAPTER 36

December approached quickly and all the windows in our street were covered in Christmas lights. Every home was brightly decorated – except one. The windows in this house were bare, and there was no wreath hanging on the door, no Christmas spirit.

I walked up the path and stopped, looking ahead of me. There were so many memories here that used to make me happy. Now there was nothing. No cheer, joy or laughter. It was going to be hard without Dad here to celebrate with us. At this time of the year, the gas fire would be on and we would sit around it with hot chocolates and sultana cake. We had to make sure the traditions would go on as normally as possible. I had picked up two cakes on the way home to give Mum a surprise when she got in from work. I knew that would make her happy.

I could remember one Christmas when I was about eight years old my dad took me up to the Barras. It was such a day of excitement as we headed out for my first ever time on the train to Glasgow. I stared out of the window, watching all the buildings slowly pass by, before we arrived at the large station. The mass of bodies rushing in and out of the carriages startled me. I held my dad's hand tightly, not wanting to get separated from him as I feared I would get lost. We walked through the centre, passing all the shops and big buildings, for what seemed like ages, before finally arriving at a large red entrance sign.

It was very busy that day. We walked past stall after stall with vendors trying to get customers to buy their stock, calling over the music playing loudly in the background.

'Any two for ten pounds! Come and get your t-shirts –

any two for ten pounds,' a vendor shouted.

'Here, mate, I'll sell you this CD player. Normally, it would be thirty pounds, but you can have it for a tenner,' another haggled.

I held Dad's hand tightly, clinging to him as he looked to see what was on offer. There were so many Christmas trees on sale, and people selling decorations, wrapping paper and gifts.

'Chloe, have a look around and see if there's anything you'd like.'

I looked up at him with a smile on my face, feeling happy that I was allowed to pick something of my own choice. I found a stall that sold children's animated videos and posters.

'Dad, look at all these!' I said to him excitedly, glancing around and tugging at his arm. 'Can I have one, please?'

'You certainly can, sweetheart.'

Something caught my eye and I picked it up, gasping. 'Look, Dad, it's The Lion King!' I called, amazed. There had been adverts on the TV for the movie and it looked really good. I just had to have it. I lifted the video up from the table and handed it to the vendor.

'Hi, mate. I'm selling the video, poster and CD for twenty pounds,' the vendor offered.

Dad looked down at me. 'Would you like that, Chloe?' he asked.

A large smile grew upon my face and I nodded fiercely. Dad put his hand in his pocket and gave the vendor the money. The vendor placed the items in a plastic bag and handed it to Dad, and then we walked around some more. I was so desperate to watch the video, I just wanted to go home right then. But we went to a snack bar to get a bag of chips first, before getting the train back.

As soon as Dad opened the front door to let me in, I ran to the video recorder in the living room, put the video in and pressed play on the remote control. Then I sat on the floor, glued to the screen.

That was one of the happiest times of my childhood. That memory would be with me forever and always make me smile – Dad and I up at the Glasgow Barras.

A little later, I was standing under the loft hatch with the ladders as Mum walked in the front door, back from work. This wasn't something I wanted to do on my own. I wanted it to be special. The Christmas tree and decorations were to come down and be placed in the back corner of the living room. It had always been Dad's job to bring down the seven-foot green tree every year. He would always be so happy that day, wearing his Christmas jumper and singing Christmas carols.

'I could go up if you'd rather, Mum. It's okay. I'll be careful.'

'No, sweetheart. I'll do it,' she said, gripping the ladders, and began her climb.

I held the ladders steady for her as she reached the top, unhooked the wooden door and lifted it into the big black hole up above. She pulled herself up into the loft and vanished from sight. I climbed up to the top step and passed the torch to her, and she switched the bright light on and flicked it around the space. Then, stepping around the beams carefully, watching where she was standing all the while, she searched for a big red box.

'Ah-ha!' she called, finding the tree and box of decorations.

She handed them to me and I took them down to the living room. Mum closed the hatch over on the ceiling and walked down to help me begin decorating.

I took the tape off the box, lifted the flaps and found the CD that we played every year at this point. I took the disk out and inserted it into the CD player, and we set up the tree listening to Jive Bunny sing Christmas songs. This time last year we had been dancing around the tree; the lights and baubles were up and Dad took my hand and twirled me under his arm and around. I laughed, feeling joyful. No one had ever made me as happy as my father had.

It was over an hour later that the tree and living room were fully decorated. We sat on the couch with a hot chocolate and slice of sultana cake, feeling satisfied with the work we had completed. The tree was lit with multi-coloured lights, as was the outside of the house. Mum had got Jason to come over with his ladder and put the lights up outside, as well as the decorations on the ceiling. Everything sparkled brightly and I sat there feeling emotional.

'Do you remember when I was little and Dad used to lift me up to the top of the tree so I could place the star on it?'

'Yeah, I remember that well. You loved doing that.'

'Still do.' I smiled. 'I know you wouldn't have it any other way.'

Mum turned to me suddenly and held me tight. 'You know your dad loved you so much, Chloe. He was so happy when you were born. You were his shining star.' She sniffed.

'Oh, don't, Mum, you'll set me off.' My eyes welled up and I couldn't hold back. After a moment we were both crying onto each other's shoulders.

'Dad wouldn't want to see us like this. He would want us to be happy. Especially tonight.'

'You're right.' She smiled, wiping away a tear. 'He would scold me for doing this. All your dad wanted was for us to be happy.'

'We can be, Mum. Even though Dad's gone and we miss him so much, we still need to carry on.'

So we did. We carried on with the traditions that we did

every year. We danced away to the music around the tree. Mum took Dad's place, twirling me around under her arm, and for that brief time, it felt like nothing had ever changed.

Later on, I walked out into the back garden, closing the door behind me, and looked up into the crisp starry sky. I just knew he was looking down on us. The door opened again and Mum came out.

'What are you doing out here, Chloe? It's a bit nippy.'

'I'm just gazing up at the stars. There're so many. It's a beautiful sky tonight.'

'It certainly is.' She gazed up.

'I have an idea. What do you think about naming a star after Dad?'

'I think that's a lovely idea,' she said. 'Your dad would be very happy with that. What star would you like to pick then?'

I looked around, trying to find the perfect one. The one that stood out the most.

'What about that one?' I pointed up at the sky. 'Next to Orion's Belt – see the big one there, shining brightly?'

'I see it! That looks perfect. Okay then, we'll name that after your father. That star will be named Jack.'

I looked up at it with a tear in my eye. 'Hi, Dad. I love you.'

She put her arm around me. 'And he loves you too.'

I leaned my head on her shoulder. Mum was right. Dad would be very happy and proud. From then on, every night when the stars were out, I would stand here and look up at them, and he would be in our hearts and up in the sky, twinkling away brightly.

My presents had come earlier than I expected them to. Someone chapped on the door just as Mum was in the kitchen washing the dishes, and I hurried to sign for my delivery. I took my boxes upstairs and quickly wrapped all the gifts, including an extra-special one. I had been looking through the photo album and found one of Mum, Dad and me together one Christmas. I'd bought a special frame for it which had 'family' inscribed at the bottom. Mum could sit it on top of the fireplace, a treasured possession.

I walked into the living room quickly, trying not to be noticed, but it was too late. She had already caught me with my arms full as she came out of the kitchen, drying her hands.

'What are you up to?' she quizzed.

'Oh, just putting the presents under the tree.' I smiled. We would celebrate together because we still had each other. We stood looking at the tree lights sparkling away. I felt a warmth spread through me as my excitement grew. I simply could not wait for the special day to arrive. I guessed it would be a lovely Christmas after all.

CHAPTER 37

I stretched my arms as I woke up and stared at the ceiling for a moment, before rolling out of bed and walking into the bathroom. As I came back out, a sudden gust of cold air made me shiver. I wrapped my arms around myself, looking down the stairs to find the front door was open. Odd, I thought. Maybe Mum was outside talking to one of the neighbours. I headed back into my room, pulled my housecoat from the back of the door and went to find her.

There was no one outside. The street was as quiet as ever. I turned around and saw the gate to the back garden was open – and Mum's slipper was on the path. I walked over and picked it up, wondering what it was doing out here. Something was most definitely wrong.

The other gate, which led out to the woods, was open as well. I walked over, looking around, and found her other slipper. This was beginning to get really weird.

I ran my hands over my face, feeling worried, and went back inside. I put the slippers in the living room and checked all the rooms, but she was nowhere to be seen. Everything was as we'd left it the night before – clean, tidy and organised. It was as if she hadn't even been here. Not a thing was out of place.

I went into her room and looked around. Her bed was unmade, the duvet pulled back, which was strange. Mum always made her bed every morning before she left. That was just part of her routine. Sometimes she was practically flawless.

I went over to her side of the bed and switched off her mobile charger, leaving her phone on the bedside table. Then I ran out of the room like a shot and down the stairs. After quickly putting on my trainers, I grabbed my mobile from the coffee table and headed out to look for her. I couldn't think straight. I didn't know what to do for the best, but I knew I had to find her. Closing the back garden gate behind me, I headed out into the woods to find my mum.

If I'd been thinking clearly, then I would have known better and called the police straight away and left them to find her and do the work themselves. But I didn't have the patience to sit around and wait for them to come and question me and then head out to do their search, while I stayed at home, pacing the floor, worried sick. My poor mum. I couldn't even begin to think about what she was going through right now. It was my duty as her daughter to go out there and find her and bring her back safely. That was, if we made it back at all.

The woods were quiet. I called her name out a couple of times, but there wasn't a sound. Fear ran through me and I would have rather been anywhere else but here. But there was simply no choice in the matter. I had to find out what was going on.

Being here brought back so many bad memories for me. My whole body trembled as I walked, turning around every few seconds for the slightest glimpse of anything at all. I called out again with everything I had, practically screaming her name, and wiped away tears from my cheeks as I powered through into the depths of the woods. I didn't know what route to take. I didn't know where I was going. I just continued to walk through the dead grass and broken branches.

Eventually, I started to feel defeated. With no trail to follow, I felt lost. My pace slowed and I groaned to myself as I looked down at the ground, watching my feet. I stopped as I caught sight of something to the right. I took another step towards a branch and pulled what looked like pink fluff from it. Holding it between my fingers, I rubbed my thumb over it. It took me a few seconds to realise what it was – fibres from Mum's housecoat. I was sure of it.

I had to start looking for hidden clues, anything at all. I just had to find something. This discovery gave me some hope that I was on the right track. Feeling determined, I persevered, checking for any trace of footprints or clues that Mum may possibly have left me. I was sure that I would come across something.

It wasn't long before I stopped again as I found the print of a bare foot. Bending down and running my fingers over it, I felt positive it was Mum's. I knew just then that I was close. I knew she was around here somewhere.

The more I walked along, the more of a trail she had left. My pulse began to race and my breathing quickened. Adrenaline ran through my body. I walked up a steep hill, holding on to a tree to keep from falling. A faint sound made me freeze. I stood still, listening for it again and wondering whether this could be a trick to lure me in and trap me. Was I being paranoid? My senses told me I was. No, there was a muffled cry, I was sure of it.

I ran, feeling more hopeful than ever, wanting to be where she was. Then I came to an abrupt halt. There was a figure crumpled at the foot of a tree. As I made my way over, I could make out a housecoat and a face. It was my mum.

I ran to her, crying out, giving it everything I had, almost tripping and falling, spreading my arms out to save myself, and I was beside her in an instant.

'Mum!' I cried.

She mumbled behind the gag that was lodged in her mouth, her eyes wide with terror. I carefully untied the dirty strip of cloth.

'Chloe!' she gasped as I pulled the gag off her and threw it to the side. 'Get out of here! You need to go!' Her voice was barely a croak.

'No, Mum, I'm not leaving you. Who did this? Tell me.'

She looked at me, terrified. Her skin was pale, her lips dry and chapped from the gag. 'You can't be anywhere near here. I need you to go, now! I don't want you to be part of this,' she rasped.

I moved over to the rope that secured her to the tree and tried with all my strength to loosen it and free her.

'Chloe, just leave me! Save yourself!' she cried.

I was too distracted trying to unfasten the rope. The knot was too tight and I couldn't get it to loosen. I cried out, panicking. The rope just wouldn't come undone. I tried and failed, almost losing all hope.

But by this time, it was too late.

'You should have stayed well clear, Chloe,' I heard a muffled voice say.

I jumped back, terrified, as I saw the figure standing beside me. A dark balaclava covered his face. My breathing shook.

'Who are you?' I managed to say in between cries. I held out a hand to Mum and she laid her head against it.

He lifted off his balaclava. I let out a massive gasp. Dave stood towering over us. His face was menacing and there was fiery rage in his eyes.

'How did you get out?'

He tilted his head to one side. 'You've got to know your way around a prison to know how things work.'

'But...why?' I cried out.

'Well, let's just say revenge is a dish best served cold.'

'You didn't have to do this, Dave. You didn't have to torture us. There was no need. We never did anything to you!'

'She took my brother!' he shouted in my face, pointing his finger towards Mum. 'He was all I had in this world and she took him!'

301

'She didn't take him!' I shouted back. 'He died of a heart attack! There was nothing any of us could have done! Don't you think we were all hurt by Dad's death? Most of all Mum? Don't you think I could hear her crying herself to sleep every night, wishing he was right beside her?'

He stepped back for a moment, looking as if he was thinking about something as he rocked back and forth on his heels. Then an evil look took over again.

I walked over and stood between him and Mum. He was so close I could feel his breath on my face.

'Move,' he growled.

'No,' I answered, standing my ground. I couldn't protect my dad from death, but I would do everything I could to protect Mum. I wasn't going to lose her too. I was a shaking, quivering mess, but I couldn't let Dave see that. I stood with my hands clenched into fists.

'Back off,' I growled through my teeth.

He just looked down, sniggering at me. I knew I was no match for him.

'Don't tempt me, Chloe. Stay out of my way,' he snarled.

'Never!'

He let out a deep breath and shook his head, looking disappointed. I really didn't know how far he would go, whether he would kill us. But I wasn't backing down.

'Last chance, Chloe.'

'Stay away from my mum,' I growled back at him. I was tensed up.

He sniggered one more time, before backing off for a moment and turning around. And then the worst thing happened.

He came at me in an instant, and I screamed and felt myself being flung out of the way. My body hit the cold, hard ground with a thud. He bent down in front of Mum and was back up in a second and walking away. I looked at Mum. Her eyes and mouth were wide open with terror. I clambered over to her.

'Mum, what did he do?'

She simply looked down to her stomach, and as I gently pulled her housecoat away, I gasped in shock at the blood pouring out. She had been stabbed in the abdomen.

'MUM!' I shouted, terrified, putting the housecoat over the cut to try to stop the bleeding. Tears fell as she simply looked up at me, her breathing quick and shallow.

'Chloe, go get help.'

I tried to put pressure on the cut, but there was too much blood. I simply couldn't leave her lying there. Her face was scrunched up with pain. I could tell she was trying to hide it from me.

It was at that moment that I remembered my mobile. I took it out of my housecoat pocket and tried to dial for an ambulance. There was no dial tone. No service. Holding the phone high up, I tried to get at least one bar up. Nothing I did made any difference.

'Come on!' I cried out, feeling helpless.

Crawling back down to Mum, I placed my hand on her cheek. 'Someone will find us. There's bound to be someone around. I'm not leaving you,' I sobbed.

I listened to her rapid breathing, desperately wanting to untie the rope and take her out of here. But I feared she wouldn't make it. After a few moments, she spoke to me.

'Chloe. I just wanted you to have the best life ever, sweetheart,' she whispered.

Tears ran down my face. I couldn't lose my mum. She was all I had. There was no chance I was letting her go. I held her tight as my body shook.

'Mum, please don't leave me like this. You can't go. We have a great life together. Look at all we've done. Look at all you've done for me. I love you, Mum. Please don't go,' I cried.

I held her in my arms, pleading with her not to fade away. I rubbed my face with the back of my hand, wiping away tears. I didn't care that my hands were covered in blood. I just wanted her to stay alive. That was all that mattered. She was all I needed. I sat on the ground holding her, feeling her heartbeat get slower and slower. I rubbed my hand over her hair and kissed her head. Tears fell into her hair and disappeared.

She coughed lightly. 'Chlo, you must do something for me.'

'What, Mum? Anything.'

'Promise me that you'll live the best life when I'm gone. Promise me, Chloe.'

I scrunched my face up as pain stabbed through my heart. Those words were too hard to hear. Letting her go was impossible. This was too heart-breaking to even comprehend. I gritted my teeth as my body trembled. How could I possibly carry on without her? She was my life and I loved her so much. She'd made me the person I had become and without her I would be no one. My soul would be gone.

She smiled up at me as she lifted her hand to my face. 'My beautiful girl.'

Her eyes closed and she lay still. I didn't want her to be in pain anymore. I watched her fade as every second she got closer to death. I held her tightly to me and kissed her head over and over.

'Mum,' I whispered.

'Yes.'

'I love you. I'm sorry I put you through some really difficult times. I'm sorry that I ever made you cry or hurt you or made you angry. I loved the life we shared together and I'm glad that you're my mum. Thank you for always being there for me when I needed you the most. I'll never forget you.'

'Oh, sweetheart,' she whispered through a shallow breath. 'I love you, Chl...'

I sat still and in shock. She had stopped breathing.

'Mum?' I called. 'MUM?'

I shook her gently. She was unresponsive.

'MUM!' I screeched. Tears filled my eyes as I shook her body.

I called her name over and over, wanting her to look me in the eye and give me a smile. I clung on to the housecoat she wore, tilted my head back and screamed. Mum was gone. What was I going to do now?

I lay there holding her and sobbed my heart out. This wasn't happening. It couldn't be. How would I cope without her? I sniffed, stroking her face. She was at peace now.

I lay against the tree. There was no feeling in my body. I couldn't move and I didn't want

to. There was no point. Without Mum there was nothing. I was an orphan.

Hours passed. The grey clouds continued to hover above me, growing darker, threatening rain.

A blackbird flew onto the tree high above me and began to squawk. I barely even heard it. I was in a dark place. The heat had left my body and I lay there frozen, barely blinking, staring at nothing. I didn't care anymore. Mum was gone and I wanted to go with her too. To see my dad. Like it always used to be. Just the three of us. The way I liked it. That was my family.

The bird squawked again and again. I blinked a couple of times and ever so slowly looked up. It moved its head from side to side, cawing away, and suddenly looked down at me and cawed once more. All I could do was stare.

I looked over at the lifeless body beside me. The colour had disappeared from her cheeks and her skin was ashen. Blood began to flow from her nostril, passing by her mouth

and down her chin, dropping onto her lap.
I tilted my head onto Mum's shoulders, closed my eyes and
fell asleep.

CHAPTER 38

I saw a bright light. I heard laughter. Ahead of me was a younger version of Mum, smiling and laughing away, her auburn hair glistening in the sun shining down on us. She gazed at me fondly and reached out, taking my hand.

We ran together around the back garden, laughing, having fun. We were barefoot on the warm grass. It was summertime. I was wearing the floral printed dress that she had bought me as a gift when I was nine years old.

She lifted me up onto the swing and pushed me. I giggled, enjoying the sensation of rocking back and forth. I loved that swing, with its baby-pink frame and plastic seat and pink ropes; there wasn't a day that went by when I wasn't on it. I would swing for hours in my own little world, feeling nothing but happiness. I was one of the luckiest children in the world.

Just before dinnertime, Dad came to the garden gate, arriving home from work. He wore his light-brown suit and had his briefcase in one hand; his jet-black hair was combed to one side. He opened the gate, looking straight ahead, smiled and called my name. I ran to him as he bent down to pick me up.

'Daddy,' I giggled.

I was delighted to see him come home to me. Throwing myself into his arms, I tucked my head under his chin and closed my eyes.

Mum came out of the back door with her apron on, smiling, and gave him a welcome home kiss. I grabbed Dad's hand and dragged him over to my swing, and he began to push me. Higher and higher I went, squealing with happiness and giggling away. I wished it could stay that way forever.

I woke with a gasp, coughing. My throat was sore and my mouth was parched; I licked my lips. I felt stiff and uncomfortable from sitting on the cold, hard ground. Looking around, I realised we were still in the woods. Daylight had gone and darkness had crawled upon us.

I squeezed my eyes shut, moaning as my head pounded and my body ached. Moving my arms, I tried to push myself off the ground to get help. I turned my head and saw Mum's body lying still, her housecoat covered in blood. Flies buzzed around. My stomach turned and I fell to my knees and vomited over and over. I started to hyperventilate.

I crawled away, trying to calm myself down, taking frequent deep breaths. Closing my eyes, I inhaled and breathed out steadily through my mouth. I opened my eyes and looked at the bare trees ahead of me. My hands shook. I needed to leave.

I turned and walked over to Mum and put my hand up to my mouth, trying not to be sick.

'I'm sorry, Mum. I love you.'

Moments later, I was staggering around, trying to get my balance back to normal. I felt dizzy from sitting for hours. I squeezed and rubbed my eyes, flinching at the sight of my hands, feeling queasy and emotional. Mum's blood looked like oil on my skin. I rubbed my hands on my housecoat, trying to get it off, but it didn't work. It was dried on.

Continuing with my deep breaths, I tried to find a way out, thinking back to the way I'd come. I found the hill I'd walked up and carefully descended it, and surprisingly I found the trail that led back home. It took me quite a while, and by the time I arrived back it was pitch black.

Still a shaking, quivering mess, I staggered through the garden to the front and out onto the street. I honestly didn't know how I had made it back without collapsing. It must have been the adrenaline that kept me going.

I was still in one piece, safe but traumatised. I took a left turn on the street, worried about the next thing I was facing. I had to break this awful news to Jason. He would be devastated. Crushed. I had never seen him upset before. To be honest, I was really scared too.

I stood outside Jason's front door deliberating about breaking the news to him. How could I possibly tell him the woman he had been spending so much time with for months had now gone? He wouldn't be able to take it. But I couldn't not tell him. Do the right thing, I said to myself as I took a deep breath. I felt a lump in my throat and I couldn't breathe.

I banged on the door with my fist over and over, hyperventilating. My legs were weak and shaky. I didn't know for how much longer I could stand. Sobbing, I waited for it to open.

'Jason!' I shouted through tears.

The door opened swiftly and I fell to my knees on the ground, crying out. Standing there with a t-shirt and boxers on was a bewildered-looking Jason.

'What the hell? Chloe, what's happened?' he asked.

I couldn't talk through the sobbing. He bent down and slowly helped me up, and the confusion on his face changed to shock.

'You're covered in blood! Whose blood is that, Chloe?' he asked, horrified.

I leaned on him as he took me through the hallway.

'I'm going to be sick,' I panted.

He rushed me up the stairs and into the toilet. I threw myself down onto the cold, hard, tiled floor. My knees ached as the pain shot up into my legs. I was continuously sick, my stomach heaving. Jason stood right behind me, holding my hair back from my face, and then he handed me a tissue to wipe my mouth.

Leaning back on my heels, exhausted, I finished and flushed the toilet. I sat back against the tiled wall and panted, closing my eyes. Now's the time, I thought. I had to tell him. My body trembled and I couldn't talk. He asked me repeatedly what was wrong and I still couldn't speak. I felt too stunned.

'Chloe, please tell me what's happened,' he said gently one more time.

I took a deep breath, and with all the courage I had left in me, I answered him.

'It's Mu-Mum,' I stuttered.

He stood up instantly and walked into his bedroom and was on the phone in a moment asking for the police and an ambulance. I still hadn't moved. I couldn't. It was all just too real and I didn't want this to be happening. All I could see was her lifeless body crumpled in front of me. The pain was too much to bear.

He was beside me again and he knelt down before me. 'Where's your mum, Chloe?' he asked gently.

'Woods,' I breathed.

Jason told the call handler everything that had happened since I came to his door, every single detail, with his eyes on me, looking serious and concerned. He stayed on the line while the call handler put the details into the computer and arranged to get paramedics and police out.

I put my hand on his arm. 'Jason. Mum's dead.'

Shock and horror filled his face as he stared at me, mouth wide open, phone still in his hand. Ever so slowly, he spoke into the receiver.

'The woman who's in the woods, Karen Stanson, her daughter's just told me she's dead,' he said, his voice lifeless.

Jason was stunned. He just sat, staring at the floor. I heard a voice on the other end and he looked at me.

'How did she die?' he asked with no feeling.

'She was murdered,' I said through my tears. I didn't actually think the pained look on his face could get any worse. He shook his head, moving away from me, and walked into the hallway, where he paced back and forth as he tried to take in the information. He stopped just outside the doorway and looked at me suddenly.

'Who murdered her?' His face was stone.

'Dave.' I couldn't breathe properly through the sobbing. My hands hadn't stopped shaking since I'd left her and my ribs ached. I just didn't want to carry on anymore.

Five minutes later, Jason had managed to take me down into the living room and I sat at the table watching out the window, waiting to see the flashing blue lights. I knew how this was going to work and I didn't know if I could go through with it.

Jason hadn't stopped crying since he'd got off the phone to the call handler. I could hear him in the kitchen, sobbing his heart out. I didn't know whether to go into him or not. It felt too uncomfortable to sit in one room while poor Jason was crying in the other, so I wiped my eyes and walked through to join him in the kitchen. He held an arm out to me and I walked into his embrace, and we both cried our hearts out. It was a devastatingly sad day for the both of us. We cried onto each other's shoulders, distraught about how badly we wanted her back.

The police turned up, and Jason let them in, rubbing the tears from his eyes. Two officers walked into the living room to question me, and I went over the day's events, explaining exactly what had happened from the moment I saw the front door open and the slippers on the path, to leaving Mum lying still tied to the tree. I felt awful about not being able to move her, but there had been no other choice in the matter.

I was still wearing my blood-stained housecoat as they questioned me. I shoved it off and handed it to the officers, and they placed it in an evidence bag. They wrote everything down on their notepads as I sat on the couch taking deep, shaky breaths.

'Take your time, love, there's no rush,' one of the officers said softly. 'Now, can you tell me about your uncle? Do you know what he was wearing? What he looked like?'

It was agonisingly painful to go through the day's events, but I had no choice. They had an escaped convict – now a murderer – on the loose who was a high risk to the public. I thought for a minute. Did I remember what he was wearing? I racked my brain, trying to think.

'I didn't really pay attention. There wasn't much time. I think maybe a dark jacket and blue trousers.' My voice was hoarse.

'Okay, that's fine. Do you remember anything distinctive about him? Was he any different to the last time you saw him?'

'He had a bald head. Completely shaved. That's about it.'

'And did he say anything to you or your mum? Was it anything out of the ordinary?'

'He told me I should have stayed well clear. And he blamed Mum for Dad's death. My dad died of a heart attack. Dave shouted at me. But I shouted back. And then – then he stabbed her!' I wailed.

Jason held me in his arms again as I sobbed my heart out. I couldn't take this pain. It was too much.

'I just want my mum back!' I cried out. The sobs were uncontrollable.

I ran up the stairs and threw myself over the toilet bowl and vomited violently. Out of everything that had happened, this day had been the worst one of my life. And

I didn't want to be living it. I wanted to be with my mum.

I came back down a short while later and the officers were gone. Jason was sitting on the couch, arms on his knees, staring ahead of him. His eyes glistened as he turned to me, wiping away tears. I walked over to him and he put an arm around my shoulders.

'Oh, Chloe.' He sniffed, wiping his nose with a tissue. 'I just can't believe this has happened. I only spoke to her last night on the phone. She sounded...happy. Peaceful. She was really looking forward to spending Christmas with us all. She wanted me to go shopping with her too. She said she had something special to get for you. Now we'll never know what it was. I'm so sorry, sweetheart.'

'Christmas!' I called out and began crying once again. I didn't want that day to come anymore. I wanted to spend it in my bed, sleeping right through till the New Year, and not have to go through any of it. I really couldn't have thought of anything more depressing.

'I miss her so much, Jason. I just want her back. I miss everything about her. It just doesn't seem real. Any of it. I just don't understand how it all happened. How did she end up out in the woods with him? That monster. I don't get it.'

'Well, the officer said there's going to be an investigation into how it all came about. They're heading out into the woods right now to look for her and find him.' He squeezed his eyes shut like he was trying to put that image out of his head.

'Why did he need to murder her, though? I mean, I know he's going through stuff because my dad died. But how could he possibly blame her? I don't understand it.'

I was really perplexed. It would never make sense to me that anyone could possibly be so nasty, vindictive and evil. He was simply a barbaric, cold-hearted murderer.

'Death and grief really can do a lot of terrible things to some people. I'm not for one second trying to make

313

excuses for him or what he did. I would never do that after what he's done to us all. But that man does seem to be having mental health problems. He's obviously not seeing clearly.'

'How can you be so calm at a time like this?' I asked him, astounded. I honestly thought Jason would be utterly shattered.

'I'm devastated, Chloe, of course I am. Don't get me wrong, I miss your mum terribly. All the time that we spent together has been so incredible. I've loved every minute of it. In fact, she meant that much to me that I'd bought us both a gift for Christmas. It was for summertime next year. I booked a surprise cruise. It would have been the holiday of her dreams.'

I looked at him in amazement. He really did think the world of my mum. He had stood by her in the worst possible times when she needed him the most. He was a true gentleman. And there I was thinking those were hard to come by these days.

'A cruise? That sounds wonderful! I know Mum would have been absolutely over the moon. And that just makes this all the more heart-breaking. You were starting to build a life together and now it's all come crashing down.'

He sat on the couch with his hands over his face, looking distraught. Why had the person we loved so much in the world been taken away from us? It just didn't make sense.

'Oh, Karen!' he wept. Just how could today have possibly gone so wrong?

My insides were racked with pain from crying for hours. I didn't think it would ever stop. Every time I thought of Mum, the tears would start all over again. I felt low, disorientated, dizzy and weak to the bone as I lay back against the couch and closed my eyes.

'I'm so tired. I just need to sleep for a bit.'

He rubbed his face and turned to me. 'You'll be needing it. You've had a tough day. We both have. You can sleep in the spare room.'

He gently helped me up from the couch and saw me up the stairs. I held on to the banister, doubting that I would feel good ever again. Wrapping the duvet over me, I lay on my side, exhausted. My eyes were half-closed as he sat at my side.

'Try to get some sleep,' he said softly, and he stood up and walked out of the room, closing the door behind him. I honestly didn't know how I was able to cry any more, but I did. It took me a while to fall asleep; a constant battle, twisting and turning for what felt like hours. Finally, feeling too exhausted, I managed to drift off – and that was when the nightmare began.

CHAPTER 39

It was dark. Really dark. The space I was in was almost suffocating, leaving me barely any room to move. An endless brick wall faced me, and all I could hear was my own breathing.

There was noise. All around. I turned my head to the left. And then to the right. I didn't know where I was, but it seemed like a sort of narrow corridor. A damp, echoing place that felt like hell. Around me there was a clanking sound like metal on metal. My teeth chattered. It was so cold. The clanking sounded again. I looked to the left, but I couldn't see a thing in the darkness. I tried to walk to the right, holding my hands out in front of me. I was scared of falling. Suddenly, my eyes widened in terror as someone came up behind me and stood too close, breathing down my neck. I slowly turned around and let out a high-pitched scream. Dave stood there, wielding a knife high above my head.

I ran.

I let out a loud scream as I sat upright, panting and soaked in sweat. It wasn't real, I realised. Closing my eyes, I ran my fingers through my hair, pulling it out of my face. I was in Jason's spare room – the room I had been in before, with the ever-so-comfy bed and hidden TV at the bottom. The blinds were open and sunlight was pouring in through the windows.

I held my head in my hands. That was one hell of a nightmare. I badly needed ibuprofen for my pounding head. Slowly, I slipped out of bed, and I was about to head out of the room when I stopped, hearing a noise coming from downstairs. It was the front door opening. I heard voices and footsteps walking into the hallway as the door was closed. There was a lot of talking and then silence. I guessed it was news about Mum.

The visitors didn't stay long. I heard them leaving again and the front door closing. The house was silent. I sat on the side of the bed and listened as Jason came up the stairs. He walked into the room. His face was distraught and his eyes were blotchy and glassy.

'Was that the police you were talking to? Have they found Mum?'

He sniffed, nodding slightly. 'Yeah, they found her. Tied to that tree.' He squeezed his eyes shut as he said the word 'tree'. 'They said they found a trail of footprints and it looked like there was a struggle out there.'

'A struggle? You mean she was forced out? Dragged? Why didn't they contact us to let us know he had escaped?'

'Well, the police said they tried to call the house phone several times, but the line was dead.'

'The house phone was working fine. The line must have been damaged somehow. So Mum must have been kidnapped then. Pulled out of the house. That was why the front door was open. So for the last few hours of her life she was terrified. But at least we got to see each other one last time,' I whispered, eyes welling up. 'Poor, poor Mum. She never deserved any of that.'

Jason sat down beside me. 'Chloe, love, the coroner has been out to inspect her and the doctor has signed the medical certificate. We need to collect it and register the death. The funeral also needs to be arranged.'

I shook my head. 'Funeral? I can't, Jason. It's too much! I can't deal with this. Losing her is bad enough, but arranging her funeral? That would send me over the edge!' I cried.

He took my hand in his. 'Hey, I'll be right there with you. I'll stand beside you every step of the way, Chloe. You're not alone. I'm going through this as well, you know.'

'Yeah, but she's MY mum, Jason. You haven't known her as long as I have. You don't have a clue what I'm going through!' I cried.

He looked at me as if I'd slapped him in the face. I knew I'd hurt him and I deeply regretted it in an instant. I pursed my lips, shaking my head. 'I'm sorry.'

He turned around and walked towards the door. 'Breakfast is on the table when you're ready,' he said, and left me to it, walking down the stairs.

Why was I lashing out at the one person I needed the most?

Five minutes later, I sat at the kitchen table, ready to apologise to him. I felt awful about speaking to Jason like that. I was ashamed of what I'd said; there was no truth in those words at all. My head was pretty messed up and it seemed I was just making things worse. For both of us.

'Jason, I can't begin to apologise enough for that outburst. What I said... none of it was true. We're both going through the same thing together. I'm so sorry.'

He nodded, giving a slight smile. 'It's understandable that you would lash out. But Chloe, we have to stick together and be here for each other. Do you understand that?'

'Yeah, of course. I just feel really messed up right now.'

'I know. But if we're honest with each other, we can get through it together, yeah?'

'You're right. I'll try from now on. It's just so hard. What I wouldn't give to have my mum here right now. I don't think I can cope.'

It would be a constant battle to get through each day. If Jason was right and if we worked as a team, maybe, just maybe, we would get through it. Right now, we had to start by looking after each other. One thing was badly needed.

'I really need a shower, but I don't have a change of clothes with me.'

He nodded in understanding. 'I'll go for you, don't worry. Just give me your keys and I'll head around when I've finished breakfast.'

'They're on the living room table. You'll find everything in my wardrobe. Jeans, socks, a t-shirt and my jacket. That'll do. I need to contact Mollie as well...'

He put his hand over mine. 'I'll call her and let her know the situation.'

I was really touched. Jason was too kind-hearted. I didn't know how he found the courage to stay strong. Being a doctor in a hospital, he'd have the training, stamina and perseverance. He was brave.

I surprised myself when I was able to eat some Weetabix. It was something at least.

Jason left, and was back twenty minutes later with my clothes and toiletries. I took my time in the shower, washing the worst day of my life from me. The hot water hit me and I closed my eyes, revelling in the spray. Today was going to be tough.

I stood at the front door with an emptiness inside me. My soul had been ripped out and I had nothing left. No matter how hard I tried, I would never be able to feel happy again. Staying strong was one thing I doubted I would be able to do.

Jason led me out to the car and into the passenger seat without saying a word. He started up the ignition, pulled out of the driveway and headed to town to deal with getting the funeral preparations started. He tried his best to speak to me in the car, tried to make me smile. But nothing worked. He parked the car and left me inside while he took care of things. He must have known I wasn't up to it.

It seemed like hours later when we arrived back at Jason's house after picking up the death certificate, going to the register office and arranging the funeral. I collapsed on the couch in a state of sadness and depression, and he put a blanket over me and switched the television on, trying to give me some comfort. Sky News was on and something oddly familiar showed up on the screen. I recognised it, but I didn't know how. I continued to watch before it dawned on me. They were filming at the spot where my mum was murdered. I look at Jason in shock.

'Is that the woods?' I asked him, my body starting to quiver.

'It looks like it. They'll be out hunting for him. Do you want me to turn it off?' he asked, holding up the remote

'No,' I answered quickly. 'I want to find out what's happening. He must have damaged the phone line right around the time he got to the house. I want to know how. He needs to be caught.'

Video of the investigators scouring the woods was on replay. The news ticker scrolled across the bottom of the screen: Murderer at large.

What terrified me was that he could come after me next. But he hadn't hurt me in the woods. Not physically. Emotionally, I was scarred beyond repair and it could take years to recover from what I had been through. Was he slowly planning his revenge, one by one? He'd had his chance to kill me and he really could have if he'd wanted to, but he hadn't. Now he was out there hiding, but where? How long could he keep running every day? Would he ever be caught? I put all my belief into hoping that he would. He just had to be.

The two people who used to be the centre of my world were now gone completely and I was never getting them back. Just how could I possibly move on from that? I used to have a loving home with people who meant more to me than anything in the world. That house was just a shell now and I didn't want to be near it.

Jason was kind enough to say I could stay with him until I felt well and strong enough to be on my own. But what I needed more than ever was to move away. I didn't want to become a burden.

Was I scared? Did it frighten me that Dave had murdered my mum and was on the loose? It terrified me to the core and sent chills down my spine. He would stop at nothing to get his revenge and I wondered whether he was planning to do something else.

I looked down at the floor. 'I don't know if I can keep this up any longer. I've got nothing left. I can't go on anymore. All this is just getting too much for me.'

'Hey,' Jason whispered, rushing over to me. He put a hand on my shoulder. 'You have plenty to live for. You still have college to finish and you have your job to go to. You also have me and Mollie, and there's a whole world of exploring out there for you. That, right there, is what you've got to live for. Chloe, your mum would be angry with you if she heard you speaking like that. She wouldn't want you to talk that way.'

He let out a deep breath, looking at me. 'Look, I know it's so hard right now. But the pain will get slightly easier to deal with as time goes by.'

I lifted my head and looked him in the eye. 'I don't see how.'

'Time heals all wounds. Look at your dad, for instance. You were in bits when he passed. But it's not so bad now. I know you still miss him, but it's nothing like how you used to feel.'

I nodded, knowing he was right. He was a medical professional and good at his job. But the agony that I felt right now would stay for a long time yet.

'Your mum was very proud of you. You know that, don't you. She really couldn't have spoken highly enough of you, Chloe.'

'I know. She said something to me just before she died.'

'Yeah? What was that?'

'She made me promise to have the best life ever. To live life to the full, enjoy it and be happy. But how can I, when she won't be here to enjoy it with me?'

He laughed slightly. 'That sounds just like your mum. She was devoted to you. With college and your new job, she always knew you were a smart girl.'

I smiled at him through my tears. That did sound like something Mum would say. She wouldn't want this for me, to see me sitting here, lifeless. She would be angry with me. I closed my eyes.

'I need sleep. I think I'll just go back up to bed again.'

I left him standing awkwardly in the living room and I headed up to bed and pulled the covers over me. Right now, I was completely lifeless and couldn't face anything.

As night approached, it was another disturbed sleep. I barely slept, waking up constantly with fear and paranoia. All I could see was his face as he threw himself towards Mum. I woke up at one point screaming, shouting out for Mum, only to find myself in complete and utter darkness, the sweat pouring from me. I threw my head back on the pillow and cried. I would never get a peaceful rest. Tossing and turning, I was fed up and exhausted. My bones ached and my eyes nipped.

The next morning wasn't any better. If anything, I awoke feeling worse than the day before, in a depressed state. I stayed in bed, not wanting to get out. Jason moved around downstairs, cooking away. The smell drifted up from the kitchen into the room. My stomach rumbled, but I couldn't eat. Food wasn't something I could face.

Shortly after, Jason came up with a mug of tea, a glass of water and a plate of toast on a tray and set it down on the bottom of the bed for me.

'How are you feeling this morning?' he asked, sitting on the side of the bed.

I just shrugged, not bothering to look up at him.

'Oh, Chloe.' He put his arms around me and held me tight. I cried ferociously into his shoulder and he let me stain his t-shirt with tears. I couldn't take the pain anymore and couldn't stop crying. It was all too much.

Letting me go, he took a small bottle from the tray and shook out a tablet into his hand.

'I got these for you early this morning. They're prescription sleeping tablets. It'll help you get through the night. I heard you screaming this morning. You want to talk about it?'

I just shook my head. It hurt too much to think. I took the tablet from his hand, picked up the glass of water and swallowed it quickly, then lay back down again. He knew I was in no fit state to talk. Leaving me be, he walked out of the room, closing the door behind him.

Drowsiness kicked in and I fell into a surprisingly peaceful sleep, away from the living hell that was my life.

I woke and waited a minute for my eyes to adjust to the darkness in the room. I got out of bed and slowly tiptoed down the stairs in the dark and poured myself a glass of water. Sitting on the couch, I flicked the TV on and pressed the mute button. Not much had changed on Sky News; they were still showing the same scenery.

I tried to picture Mum and how she used to be. The day we brought down the Christmas tree, dancing around it, singing along to Jive Bunny. That was a happy day. We were preparing for a lovely Christmas with Jason and Mollie – sitting around the table pulling crackers and laughing, telling jokes, eating our fill of Christmas dinner and generally enjoying that special day. But from now on Christmas would be a day I would never enjoy. Those memories made me cry. I would never get a day like that ever again.

I found it easier to lie in bed, hiding away from

everything around me. At one point, when I did get up, I found myself in the living room watching the street, busy with officers walking up and down for hours, wearing their high-visibility vests and speaking into their radios. There was a highly dangerous man on the loose and the public were being warned to stay in their homes. I watched as one officer walked up Jason's path and stood at the doorway, keeping guard, protecting Jason's home. At last. If only they had done that before now, my mum would have been here today.

Sky News began showing a video of the prison, and the news ticker scrolling by at the bottom of the screen read, Convict absconds from HMP Nostow. Helicopters hovered above the prison as the news reporter spoke.

'Police are warning the public to be on high alert. It is said that he went on a rampage after losing his brother to a heart attack. David Stanson, forty-one, is wanted in connection with the brutal murder of his sister-in-law, Karen Stanson. The forty-four-year-old mother tragically passed away after being stabbed.'

It was real now. The media had caught it. The whole of the UK, and the world, would be seeing this. I was truly ashamed to have him as my uncle. What would everyone think? How could I possibly face anyone who knew us now? I worried that people may think differently of me. I didn't want to have the same surname as Dave, let alone walk on the same ground as he did. He disgusted me to the core.

Jason came in with some chicken noodle soup and bread and set it on the table. He muted the TV.

'Chloe, come and eat something, please. You will make yourself ill if you don't. You need to keep up your strength.'

I looked over at the bowl. 'I don't know if I can keep it down.'

He stood beside me and put his hand on my back. 'There was nothing you could've done. You need to stop tormenting yourself. It would have been impossible for you to take him on. He was far more dangerous than any of us could have ever known. I just hope the police catch him soon. He needs to be put in a maximum-security unit and watched around the clock. He's far too dangerous to be let out on the streets.'

'I really don't know how much more of this I can take, Jason. I've lost my mum, and he's on the loose. It's just too much to deal with.'

I put my hands up to my face, feeling overwhelmed, and paced the floor anxiously as my emotions ran high.

'Chloe, please come and sit down. You're making me feel edgy.'

'I don't want to sit down!'

'Come and eat this soup. Like I said before, you'll end up ill.'

'So?! Can't feel much worse than I already do.'

I turned away from him, hands on the window ledge, looking out at the dramatic scene outside. I felt trapped, depressed and low, and I began to hate myself.

A car pulled up outside Jason's and I quickly opened the front door as Mollie attempted to walk up the pathway. The officer on duty stopped her at the gate and wouldn't let her past as she wasn't on his list.

'Please!' she begged. 'You've got to let me in – she's my best friend!'

'Mollie! I called. 'It's alright, you can let her through!'

The officer stepped aside and spoke into his walkie-talkie. She ran to me, flung her arms around me and burst into tears.

'Chloe,' she cried, 'I'm so sorry.'

I held her tightly, letting her cry onto me. We stood in the doorway, arms wrapped around each other, while the officer stood guard at the entrance, looking from side to side.

When we walked into the living room, Mollie said hello to Jason, wiping her eyes, and shook her head.

'I heard what happened on the news. I just can't believe she's gone, Chlo. It's utterly devastating. I just can't get my head around it.'

'I know, Mol. It's the same for us. My life has been ripped apart. Watching him kill her like that... It was like he was inhumane. Like he took pleasure in it.'

'You were there?' She gasped. 'I don't understand.'

I filled her in as she sat holding my hand, all the while listening and wiping away tears.

'I can't believe you had to go through all that. You must be traumatised.'

'I am. Every time I close my eyes I see it over and over. Jason's been there for me every step of the way. Been my shoulder to cry on when I needed him the most. And he's going through this as well. But we've stuck together.'

'I wish I could have been here sooner, but they wouldn't let me leave my own house. Can you believe that? The street is totally closed off. Dad and I had to explain the situation so they'd let us come around here. It was him who dropped me off. He's heading back home to Mum again.'

'This just doesn't feel real. Any of it. I just want to wake up from this nightmare and see Mum again. I've been crying non-stop. I feel exhausted.'

'You will be. Everyone's on high alert just now. No one's allowed to walk the streets. It's like a bomb is about to go off. That's how it feels. Can I ask, do you know when the funeral will be?'

'Yeah, it's next Wednesday at ten a.m. Crematorium, then back here for tea. Oh, Mol, I miss her so much.'

'I know you do.' She smiled sweetly, rubbing my arm.

'I miss her too. She was a wonderful woman. Mum sent a card round for you both. She has cards in stock for every occasion.'

She pulled it out of her coat and passed it to me. I opened the cream envelope and took out the sympathy card inside. It read:

Words can't express how you feel right now, dear

And it's alright sometimes to just shed a tear

For whenever you want to talk, day or night,

Your mum and dad are among the stars shining

bright.

Our deepest condolences at this sad time.

Thinking of you both.

June& Stan

I set the personalised card on top of the fireplace. Mum had now joined Dad in the stars.

As the days went by and Sky News continued to report on the story while the police searched high and low for the murderer at large, we wondered whether he would ever be caught. No one knew where he was and no one had come forward with any information.

The secular funeral went quietly. Police officers stood around the area, keeping a lookout, which made me feel on edge even more. I held Jason's hand every step of the way, finding it hard to keep from collapsing. Jason had written a eulogy and he gave it to the humanist, Grace, to read out. Grace was a warm character with short-brown bobbed hair and a round, smiley face. She spoke about Mum and her wonderful life, from when she was at college and met my dad, to her last days, spent getting ready for Christmas with her loved ones. Those memories made me smile, and I knew she had a lot of love spread around her. At the end of the cremation, 'One More Light' played in the background. I left in tears and headed out to the car.

Jason's house was full. A small table of sausage rolls, sandwiches and cakes sat in the corner. The staff from Sue and Win Lawyers came to pay their respects. They were kind and compassionate, sharing happy memories, telling us how she would be sadly missed at the office. She had worked there all her days and everyone knew her well. I was proud to stand there as her daughter, knowing that she had given me the best possible upbringing any mother could. It really had been a lovely service.

I began to feel a small change in me. Not a change towards happiness, but acceptance. I was now an orphan, with no mum or dad to live with, and apart from Jason and Mollie, I had no other family.

Just before Christmas arrived, I finally plucked up the courage to go around to my house, feeling scared and vulnerable. Jason had taken time off work, so he was at my side, giving me courage and praise for my willingness, and I knew from then on I would never be alone. I would have him there with me for however long I needed him.

We walked around the corner and reached my front gate. Jason lifted the police tape for me, and I ducked under it and walked up the path. I took my keys from my pocket, unlocked the door and walked in. Passing through the hallway into the living room, I saw that nothing had changed. Everything was as it had been the last day I was here. The morning my mother was murdered. As I looked at our Christmas tree, my eyes welled up again and I felt Jason's hand on my shoulder.

'Are you okay?' he asked.

I nodded with a lump in my throat, trying to be brave. The presents sat untouched exactly where they had been. I bent down and picked up the extra-special one, running my thumb over it as a tear dropped onto the wrapping paper. Mum would never get to open it. I sniffed, slowly tearing at the parcel to unravel the paper, and took the gift from its box. Mum, Dad and I smiled in the photo with Christmas hats on our heads.

I walked over and placed the special photo frame on top of the mantelpiece, next to Mum's gold pendulum clock, as a stranger stood outside the house, looking in and watching us, before climbing into a car and driving away.

ABOUT THE AUTHOR

J.L Kerr was born and raised in Renfrewshire Scotland and has worked in various jobs ranging from Volunteering and retail.

In 2015, J.L Kerr joined Johnstone writers group, which led to the creation of The Survivor. A story based on real life events that has happened in her life, mixed with fictional characters and stories. This is her first novel.

Printed in Great Britain
by Amazon

57701309R00188